The Lies We Tell

Meg Carter worked as a journalist for twenty years before turning her hand to fiction. Her features have appeared in many newspapers, magazines and online with contributions to titles including *You* magazine, *Independent*, *Guardian*, *Financial Times*, and *Radio Times*. She is on the advisory committee of Women in Journalism. Meg recently relocated from west London to Bath, where she now lives with her husband and teenage son. *The Lies We Tell* is her first novel.

Also by Meg Carter

The Lies We Tell
The Day She Can't Forget

THE LIES WE TELL

MEG CARTER

1© CANELO

First published in the United Kingdom in 2015 by Canelo

This edition published in the United Kingdom in 2021 by

Canelo
Unit 9, 5th Floor
Cargo Works, 1–2 Hatfields
London, SE1 9PG
United Kingdom

A CIP catalogue record for this book is available from the British Library.

Print ISBN 978 1 80032 093 2
Ebook ISBN 978 1 910859 01 8

Look for more great books at www.canelo.co

Printed and bound in Great Britain by Clays Ltd, Elcograf S.p.A.

6

For mum

Prologue

Surrey Hills, July 1989

Two girls walked ant-like towards the copse in search of shelter as the sun crept towards its highest point in the sky. Everything, from the parched footpath across the heath it had taken them three quarters of an hour to traverse to the scabbed earth beneath their plimsolls, shimmered like beaten silver in the pulsing heat. It was the hottest day of the year by far. A day dense with the drumming of insect battalions; its air tainted by an acrid tang like distant smoke. An intense heat that made the cotton of their sundresses suck their thighs.

'Come on Kat, this way,' urged Jude, the taller of the two and clearly the leader. Her full-bodied voice was self-assured. Confident her companion would follow as she always did, she pressed on without breaking her stride. Her steps were punctuated by frequent shakes of her head to toss loose the raven swathe of hair from the hot skin at the back of her neck. For both girls had quickly tired of tying back their hair school-style now they no longer had to.

With an anxious frown, the second girl paused and fumbled for a moment to disentangle damp fabric from pale skin flecked with the telltale blotches of nettle burn. It had taken longer than she hoped to retrace their tracks to the spot where they sunbathed the previous day and she felt light-headed and weary. Slipping the tin water bottle out of the side pocket of her rucksack, she hastily drained the last mouthful of body-warm fluid then straightened up to run a sticky palm through her bobbed, chestnut hair.

'Wait for me,' Kat called in the truculent whine of a heel-dragging child. But Jude was impervious. Single-minded, too, as she strode on towards the copse.

With a final rub to the back of her legs, Kat set off in her wake. What was Jude's problem? she wondered, miserably. For her so-called friend had blown hot and cold since before the exams. If Kat only knew what she'd done wrong she could make things better. But she hadn't the courage to ask Jude direct, not like that, for fear her friend would interpret this as a sign of weakness. So she'd decided to keep quiet. To smother the resentment now bloating her insides. Because she knew – and had done since their first meeting two years earlier – that if they fell out she, not Jude, would come off worst.

The copse was a welcome blemish on the heath's gnarled face, a kind of sanctuary. Yet the world inside was thick and sticky; the air beyond full-blown. Above the ragged branches now shading their heads, criss-crossed vapour trails looked like wire threads.

Kat rubbed her eyes with heat-swollen fingers. Ahead she would soon see the tiny clearing just beyond the clump of rhododendron where Jude was headed. But try as she might to catch up, she was forced to halt every few steps by limbs of bramble trailing across her way. Then, just before she could draw level, she was halted by an unexpected sound. A dull metallic click, undeniable though barely heard. The sound of a lighter. A Zippo perhaps like the one her brother, Andrew, used to have.

At one with the copse's dank stillness, blood pounding her skull, Kat's ears strained for further clues. Despite the heat she shivered. What was it they were told on their arrival at the outwards bound centre at Gallows Hill? To remain in pairs. Stick to the designated footpaths. Watch out for adders. Keep at hand their emergency whistles. What a joke it had all seemed at the time.

Yet since she and Jude first visited the copse earlier in the week, a vague sense of unease had dogged Kat like a distant

2

echo. Earlier, out on the wide expanse of open heath, she'd felt vulnerable; exposed. Then, once inside the copse, she'd been reluctant to follow Jude's lead and strip down to her pants to sunbathe – for fear of being seen.

Always the timid one, just like Jude was always leader. Though that was only part of the story, wasn't it? For aside from all the fuss that had been going on at home in recent weeks, there was how Jude's behaviour towards her had changed. Kat had grown sore from the poison tip of her friend's ill will. The way Jude looked at her sometimes through angry, slitty eyes. The things she said, quite unprovoked. Those barbed grenades, meticulously lobbed then swiftly defused by a jovial dig or encouraging smile.

Now, with urgent eyes, Kat scanned the barricade of foliage encircling her. Until, a beat later, she heard another sound. A muffled cough, low in timbre. Male. Someone else was in the copse. Close by, too. Unseen. A realisation that yanked Kat's world inside out, triggering her charge back towards the footpath.

Running fast, she barely felt the twigs and thorns tearing into her limbs; the ground, pitted with knotted roots and jagged stones, jarring her body. Or how the undergrowth was starting to thin. Not daring to look behind her for fear of slowing her pace, Kat headed towards the lunar light of the open heath. But as she hit the dusty path dumb panic was replaced by the searing pain of rational thought: Where was Jude?

Casting an urgent glance over her shoulder and seeing no one behind, Kat stopped.

The copse was still; the day silent, apart from the sound of her lungs rasping the soupy air. She slipped off the canvas rucksack Andrew had lent her. Let her fingertips skim pale skin beneath her arms where the webbing had chafed. What had possessed her to bring her sketch pad, watercolours tin and box of pencils? Still panting, she took four or five deep breaths then pinched the stitch ripping into her side.

'So. Here we are, then, thrown together by fate!' Tears of relief poked Kat's eyes as, straightening up, she saw Jude leaning against a nearby tree. Her arms were loosely folded. Her face was calm; her expression almost serene. A cream-coloured flower freshly picked from a nearby rhododendron nestled in her hair. 'Hey,' Jude continued in a languid drawl. 'What's got you all steamed up?'

'Where were you?' Kat gasped.

'In the clearing. I came looking for you when you didn't come.' A shard of something hard glinted in Jude's pale grey eyes. 'Why, what's the matter?'

'We have to leave. Now,' said Kat, reaching for her bag. 'Come on.'

'But we've only just got—'

'Now.'

Amused by the unfamiliar urgency in Kat's voice, Jude shrugged. 'OK. I'll just go and get my...' But her words were lost as she turned away and stepped back into the undergrowth.

'No. Wait!'

Yanking Andrew's rucksack back over her shoulders, Kat plunged into the bushes towards the spot where Jude had just been standing. Once inside the depths of foliage it was hard to ignore the tiny flies as white as ash that clung to the leaves; the fetid air that hung heavy with the smell of something rotten.

With mouth clamped shut, barely daring to breathe, Kat parted the branches and saw her companion adjusting the fastening of her bag. Slipping a strap over her sunburnt shoulder, Jude rose to her feet. But as she straightened up her body froze, her attention snagged by something in the tight-lipped bushes. A vague movement perhaps, or an unexpected noise. Shadow shifted in the leafy darkness as a man stepped into view.

Fearful of revealing herself, Kat struggled to stifle her cry. But neither figure before her seemed to have noticed as they stood just a couple of feet apart. Face to face, they waited for what felt like a lifetime until, without warning, the man lunged forwards and grabbed Jude by the neck. Deftly, he clamped his other arm around her waist.

One moment Jude was standing upright, mannequin-still, the next her slender frame was crumpling beneath his superior force. Cream flecks of petal tangled from her hair. The strap of her dress slipped loose off one shoulder. The stranger's face pressed against her ear as if poised to share some intimate confidence. A tense flinch signalled her mute acquiescence before he roughly tugged her back towards the bushes.

'Run, Jude! Run!' bellowed Kat, slapped back to her senses by the sudden brutality of it. But it was too late. One minute Jude was there, the next the foliage was closing around her like a final curtain.

Chapter 1

London, July 2013

She wakes with a jolt, her heart pounding, swallows hard then winces at the acid taste of her throat. Shouldn't she be used to this by now, the persistence of memory? Yet it's not surprise Katy feels, but a familiar downward tug on her spirits that comes this same time each summer, year after year, until the day passes and the shadow of it retreats between the cracks in her protective shell.

'Hey, are you OK?' Michael whispers softly in her ear.

Though his breath warms her face she keeps her eyes firmly shut; wills him to believe she's still sleeping. To leave her alone. Morning will come soon enough and then they can talk, but not now, she thinks as a bead of sweat trickles down one side of her cheek. The night is heavy – too close even for a sheet. But lying beside him naked on her back, she feels vulnerable. Exposed.

Resisting the urge to roll over, Katy listens to Michael's breath as he undresses. Feels the mattress dip as he lowers himself down beside her. Then he tries again, gently squeezing her shoulder this time. Getting no response, he runs his hand downwards and strokes her breast. His touch is light but determined and despite herself she feels the nipple harden. Strengthening her resolve, she lies still. Registers the smell of cigarette smoke in his hair. Wonders about the time. Well past midnight from the sporadic pulse of distant traffic through the open sash, she guesses. Where did he go after leaving the pub? Back in twenty minutes he texted, but that must have been at least an hour ago. As Katy rolls away and onto her side, Michael's disappointment is tangible.

'Then you won't mind if I take matters in hand, then,' he murmurs.

The mattress begins to shift rhythmically in time to the movement of his hand, like a tiny boat on a swelling tide. Sweat wells at the base of her hairline but Katy resists the urge to wipe it dry as his body stiffens and the rhythm grows more intense. Then, at last, a muffled gasp marks the breaking of the wave and he lies spent and still beside her until his breathing returns to normal and, at last, he falls asleep.

Shifting back onto her front Katy carefully positions her arms and legs so they aren't touching any other part of her body. Or his. Stifled by the dull weight of the city's night time heat, she marvels at the fact that little more than two months ago it was snowing. That this time last year, vast swathes of the country were being lashed by torrential rain. Further evidence of a displaced Gulf Stream, the papers said when they weren't bemoaning the latest austerity measures or the sickening situation in Syria.

Turning her head towards the bedside clock, Katy's eyes sift the grainy darkness. 2:07a.m. Wednesday July 3, the digits taunt like angry eyes. Can it really be that long ago? Over twenty years. More time has passed since that distant summer day than how old she was when she last saw Jude. She thinks about this for a moment then tries to erase it from her mind, but it's too late. Now she's wide awake and in the instant she knows it recalls, with a sinking heart, the big morning she has ahead at Janssen's, the design agency in Victoria where she's worked for the past six years.

Following a recent promotion her boss Sally-Anne, the company's UK managing director, has asked Katy to present the strategy behind a new corporate identity for a top five high street bank to Janssen's founder and four of his senior management team who are flying in from Amsterdam. The redesign is likely to be as controversial as it's so far been top secret when it goes live, thanks to the State bail-out that's kept the bank afloat since the 2008 crash. A reluctant public speaker, Katy has been dreading the presentation – though she knows the morning will provide an opportunity to shine, if she can master her nerves. For she loves her job and the meritocratic nature of the world she works in. A creative environment in which a self-starter like Sally-Anne can rise to the top propelled by street sense and stubborn determination rather than formal qualifications. Unlike banking, the dusty realm her father, Charles, had always hoped she'd follow into for a 'proper' career.

Katy stares at the dark mass of Michael's back. Is he already asleep? Then, as if on cue, the shape beside her emits a deep sigh, blindly rearranges itself then starts to snore with a soft rumble on the inward breath then a low whistle on the outward. It's a cartoonish sound that, despite the late hour and her eagerness to sleep, makes her want to laugh.

On the floor beside her bed is the pocket radio Katy keeps for restless nights like this. Reaching down with her hand, she pats the floor for a moment until she finds it, tucks in the tiny ear-pieces, then turns it on to hear a late night phone-in debating the risk climate change poses to indigenous insect species. Gently, Katy rests her fingertips on Michael's hip as the presenter bemoans an infestation of ants in his ground floor flat. Carefully, she adjusts her other arm, placing her right hand on the barely perceptible doming of her belly.

Closing her eyes, she finds herself back by the canal near where she once used to live. Picnicking with her brother, mum and dad. Lying on her front, head resting on her hands, watching soldier ants. A meticulous procession marching in time to the bitter beat of parents' arguing.

–

Michael is lying spreadeagled in the middle of the mattress as Katy wakes just before the alarm a few hours later. Careful not to disturb him, she disentangles herself from the knotted earphones, turns off the alarm then settles back onto the pillow to observe his slumbering form.

How she loves the early morning contradiction of his body. Its strength and vulnerability. The decisive jaw line and the baby softness of the skin. The soft tuft of armpit hair she yearns for yet dares not touch for fear of how grumpy he will be if she wakes him too soon. Her eyes pan down his body past the firm contour of his undulating chest, the nest of dark hair below, the rounded firmness of his thighs before settling on the symbol tattooed on the small, triangular piece of skin just beneath his right ankle. It is a cross, arms bent at right angles, with a tiny dot nestled within each quadrant.

He had it done long before they met on a night out in Sydney, or was it Hong Kong – he could never quite remember. *My mate's idea of a laugh, though I can't say I got the joke*, is all he'd said, dismissively. Then one day, with nothing better to do, Katy had searched on Google to discover it to be an ancient spiritual symbol still widely used throughout Asia. But when she mentioned this to Michael later he'd seemed indifferent. Reluctant to push him, she hadn't mentioned it again. Isn't everyone entitled to a little secret?

Restless, Katy slips out of bed. Stepping over the clothes from the night before which Michael has left scattered on the floor as usual, she picks up a discarded sarong and wraps it around herself before padding downstairs to the bathroom on the second floor to shower.

Standing at the mirror a few minutes later, damp-haired and flush-faced, she scrutinises the freckles that always come with summer for any sign of change before applying moisturiser then a dusting of bronzer. She turns her attention to her eyes. They are slate-blue, a colour quick to transmit whatever mood she is in: dull grey when tired, dark and leaden when angry, azure when all is well.

Carefully, she applies a light brush of mascara. Only then, as her fingers arrange her hair, is her gaze drawn to the ring she now wears on her left hand. A tiny silver band with a single diamond that had belonged to Michael's mother. Elegant but a bit tight – she shouldn't really wear it until she's had it adjusted, though she won't do this for another few weeks. Not until she's begun to feel a bit more like her old self. Which she would do any time now, everyone says. When the sickness starts to ease and the swelling in her joints subsides.

Katy frowns. For it is taking time for her to come to terms with the unplanned pregnancy. More time than it has taken Michael, to be sure.

Throughout her twenties – a restless decade during which Katy drifted from one dead-end job to the next, struggling to find her way after what happened and then her parents' separation and all those messed up exams – the idea of having a child had never entered her mind. As she entered her thirties, tentatively assembling foundations, the thought of fitting responsibility for someone else into her life just as things were finally starting to take on some kind of shape seemed laughable.

Following secretarial college, she acquired a business administration qualification. After years periodically scouring small ads for the next flatshare, she bought a small place in Balham using what her father left her for the deposit. Then came Janssens, where she not only met Michael but a champion in Sally-Anne – if she could earn the woman's respect. *You know how it is*, Katy would shrug if ever pressed. *I'm just not the maternal type.* Though she hopes she'll become so now, of course. And will, too, just as soon as Michael stops making a fuss.

Throwing open the window of the first floor kitchen, Katy leans out into the sunshine as she waits for the kettle to boil. The back of the upper maisonette overlooks the garden they share with the downstairs flat which has been empty for the past six weeks since its owner Phil, a TV producer and one of Michael's best friends, left to shoot a documentary about urban farming in Detroit.

Really, summer is the cruellest season, she thinks, gazing down onto the wilting plants. A shadow briefly stirs but she battles to resist it. Not now, she tells herself. For despite the date, today is just a day like any other. Katy refocuses on the dusty beds below. But as she starts to make a mental note to do some watering later, she is distracted by a noise. The low grinding of a key. A sound which appears to be coming from the French windows of the flat below. Which is impossible, of course, because the place is empty.

A hooded figure steps into full view on the patio below. A man – probably in his early twenties, she deduces – though his face is obscured by the hood of a white sleeveless top across the back of which is emblazoned the word Everlast. Although slight, his body is toned, she notes, her eyes drawn to the muscularity of his upper arms and, in particular, his left biceps around which a black ring of thorns has been tattooed. His feet are bare beneath the dusty hems of his black sweat pants and then, as he starts to fill a watering can with water, splashed with wet.

Strange behaviour for a burglar, she thinks, watching him water the nearest line of bedding plants, wondering who this stranger could be. A friend of Phil's, probably. Though she doesn't recall having seen anyone like him hanging around the place before.

Another noise from the neighbouring garden snags the attention of them both. The sound of chanting. It's the woman who lives in the downstairs flat next door. A lawyer, Katy recalls, though they have never spoken. She had rarely seen her at all, in fact, until just before last Christmas when the woman went on maternity leave and swapped sombre suits for T-shirts and lycra. Now, with the door open wide, she is standing on the sun terrace outside her back door dressed only in an oversized granddad shirt with arms outstretched as if in honour to the morning sun.

'Caught you!' Michael laughs, burying his face in her neck. As his free hand reaches to unfasten the towel still knotted around her, Katy halts it.

'Don't,' she hisses, gesturing towards the open window through which she can now see her neighbour performing some kind of yogic genuflection to the morning sun. Or perhaps it's t'ai chi. 'There's someone down there. Outside.' Her gaze shifts to Phil's garden but the hooded figure has gone leaving only a damp trail of footsteps which have already started to evaporate in the morning sun.

'Spoil sport,' Michael sighs. He shoots a quick glance up at the kitchen clock then turns back towards Katy. 'Come back to bed for a bit. It's still early.'

'Not today it isn't,' she smiles, relieved to have a real excuse. 'I've got to be in early for this morning's presentation.'

In the bedroom, Katy pulls out a selection of clothes. In the bathroom, Michael lines up the badger brush, razor, soap and balm on the glass shelf as the basin fills for his daily ritual. As she dresses Katy can see without looking each stroke of the blade as the silence is broken every half minute or so by a gentle splash of water and then, when it is done, the brisk slap of lotion on skin. Familiar sounds that until recently would reassure. A slice of male intimacy she has come to relish since moving in with Michael three years earlier. Though now it is merely a fleeting distraction.

For since she discovered she is pregnant something about the proximity of their living arrangements has begun to pall. He's crowding her – that's how it feels, at least. Michael. And his mother, Jean.

Katy grimaces at the thought of how her mum-in-law to be, widow of a Scottish Presbyterian minister, had taken it upon herself to place an announcement in the *Telegraph*. She'd done it within hours of her son confiding their recent decision to finally get hitched, with a small, informal ceremony scheduled to take place at a local west London church in just two months' time.

Though they'd both been annoyed Michael had said nothing, of course, for fear of upsetting her. Goodness knows what the woman would say if she knew the reason for their haste. Which reminds Katy of something.

'Ring me later about dinner tonight at Mum's, OK?' she calls, crouching down to retrieve a missing shoe from beneath the bed. 'I should be free by midday.'

Straightening up from the sink, Michael turns towards her as he pats his face dry. 'Ah. Yes. About that.' Carefully, he dabs his neck with the hand towel. 'Look, I don't think I'm going to be able to make it. I got a call yesterday from an old school friend who's a headhunter. They want to meet for dinner to discuss an executive creative role they're looking to fill. I'm really sorry, Katy. But we weren't going to tell either granny-in-waiting until after the scan, were we — not till we're sure everything's OK?'

Annoyed, Katy is about to object from the upstairs landing where she now stands then thinks better of it. How irritable she's become these days, she reasons. Though it is surely her rampaging hormones, that's all. And the oppressive heat — the hottest July in seven years. The time of year, too — always her least favourite. And then there's the date…

A new job will be good for both of them, she knows. Having missed out on promotion the previous Easter, the extra money will help cover the cost of the childcare they'll need when she's ready to return to work. Noticing yesterday's shorts and T-shirt which Michael has left on the floor where she now stands, to remind himself at some point to put them in the laundry bin, she smiles. Swiftly grabbing the bundle with her free hand, she deftly lobs the knot of clothes in his direction. It takes him by surprise, catching him on the shoulder before he has time to duck.

'I'll send your apologies,' she calls down, brightly. 'You can make it up to me later.'

'Sorry, I didn't quite get that.' Katy adjusts the mobile phone so the earpiece is a little further from her ear. Running up the steps towards the street level exit of St James's station is making her breath come in short, shallow gasps and beads of sweat have gathered at the back of her neck where hair meets skin.

'I said: you're late,' Sally-Anne booms.

'I know. There was a problem on the District & Circle, but I won't be long—'

'Where are you?'

'Just coming into reception,' Katy lies.

'Well you'd better be here in five – we need to have a final run through before the presentation which, I might add, is due to begin at half past.'

She bites her lip. Being on the receiving end of one of Sally-Anne's bad moods always makes Katy feel like a naughty schoolgirl. She might still make it though, just. 'OK. Better go – the signal's cracking...'

Slipping the mobile back into her bag she breaks into a run, only slowing her pace once she turns off the pavement into the darkened walkway leading to the offices within. Catching sight of her reflection in the chrome and black corridor that once was state-of-the-art office design, she straightens her blouse and smoothes her hair before casually walking past the receptionists who are already busy fielding calls. As soon as she's out of their sight, she darts up the stairs two at a time.

'Good of you to join us,' Sally-Anne declares, shooting Katy an ice-pick stare as she bursts through the door.

Katy re-sets her expression to businesslike. She's worked with Sally-Anne since first arriving at Janssens as a temp six years before – long enough to know better than to waste her time concocting gushing apologies or elaborate excuses. The woman is firm but fair if you play a straight bat, as her father used to say. A cricketing term the origin of which Katy could never fathom. Because it was Sally-Anne who secured her a full-time position and under whose guidance she has since steadily risen up the ranks to become acting head of client services while Miriam, the official holder of that title and her immediate boss, is on maternity leave.

Rising from her desk, Sally-Anne picks up her pad then reaches for her skinny cappuccino with an immaculately manicured hand. On her feet the woman still has on the yellow and red Masai Barefoot Technology trainers she wears to work in the vain hope of offsetting the stubborn thickening of her ankles. Otherwise she is dressed today in a fuchsia linen trouser suit with yawning buttons that tell their own story of the struggle to contain the woman's heavily-tanned chest. Around her neck, the paste choker modelled on the Bulgari necklace Keira Knightly wore on Oscar night almost obscures the blossoming of her second chin. Her flawless fingernails bear witness to how rarely she taps a keyboard nowadays.

'Just coming,' Katy calls out lightly. But now she feels on edge and the air con makes her shiver. Uneasy, like there's something important she's forgotten.

Reaching for the presentation notes which she has left in a box file to one side of her computer, she slips the papers into an A4 notepad and clasps it tightly. Though she has gone through her presentation piece so many times she almost knows it by heart, the prop is reassuring and the tension in her jaw line starts to subside. Until, as she starts moving away from her desk, her attention is drawn to a Post-It bearing a message in a childish scrawl.

'Some woman rang for you around nine,' calls Dawn as she begins to read. Sally-Anne's PA is rake-thin and blonde with a fixation with Marilyn Monroe that today has her dressed in a tightly-fitted satin blouse and black pencil skirt despite the heat. 'She was most specific about the spelling,' she presses on, helpfully. 'A Judith Davies, spelled with an i-e-s. Hey, are you OK?'

The room spins for a moment and a number of things happen at once. As Katy sinks down into her chair, the notes slip from her grasp. As she closes her eyes, a sudden wave of nausea makes her skin prickle cold with sweat. Judith Davies. The name for which she spent months scanning the obituaries section of her father's *Daily Telegraph*. The abbreviation of which still makes her spirit bolt.

Tranquilo, she hears. The echo of Michael's voice is calm and reassuring, though the bile licks the back of her throat. *Relax*.

A beat later, Dawn's arm is curling around her shoulders. With the stifling heat, the younger woman's pale skin has taken on a wild and feverish glow and her perfume, a smell like pear drops, is overpowering. Fearful she will retch, Katy tries to think of something else. Like birthday dinner at Mum's, later. Michael's job interview. The presentation she's about to give. Only when she opens her eyes does the other woman step back. When will this end? she wonders, bleakly. Another week or two, perhaps. Surely no more?

'Drink this,' Dawn offers, breaking the seal on a plastic bottle of mineral water.

Exhaling slowly, Katy offers up a watery smile as a familiar voice from somewhere close by mumbles her thanks. She drinks and the pressure inside her skull begins to ease allowing her brain the space to think. Not for the first time she wonders if Dawn knows. Some second sense, perhaps. Or, maybe, she can just smell the hormones. Then, as her head starts to clear, it hits her.

Jude. It has to be. For how many Judith Davieses can there be who'd want to speak to her – today of all days? What can she possibly want after so long?

Her body stiffens. Not against nausea this time but the tension building between the rational side of her brain which is racing with questions, and the rowdy gang of emotions jostling for position. Curiosity. Relief. Shame. And something else. An exquisite collision of excitement and fear which makes her almost toss the Post-It into the bin. As quickly as it came, the urge is gone and she slumps defeated against the back of her chair. For what would be the point?

What's it people say about what goes around, comes around? Because the two of them are bound and always have been by what happened out on the scalding heath that day. Inescapable, that's the word for this moment, she thinks, her gaze refocusing on the yellow square of paper. Fate.

An impatient tut-tutting sound draws Katy back to the moment. Looking up she sees Sally-Anne, her faced locked into an impatient frown, standing the opposite side of the office holding the door open. No time for this now, she thinks, stuffing Jude's message deep into her pocket as she stumbles to her feet. Gathering her notepad, pen and papers Katy cradles them in one hand then pauses, briefly, to take another gulp of water. Though the hotness has passed, her face feels cold and clammy.

Katy wipes her mouth on the back of her hand. Which is when she feels it. Still there after all this time. The stubborn knot of scar tissue from Jude's pen that lurks just beneath the skin two inches below her right wrist. Touching it with her left forefinger, pressing it lightly at first then harder, Katy digs in the fingernail then twists it, sharply. Increasing the pressure, she relishes the dull ache. Embraces the old war wound that makes her feel alive.

Glancing across the room towards where her boss is waiting, her face tightens with the effort it takes to pull herself together.

'Just coming, Sally-Anne,' she smiles.

Chapter 2

London, July 2013

Reaching across the table, Katy pours herself another cup of coffee from the silver pot. The conference room air con has quickly turned her skin to goose bumps and she needs warming. Her presentation is done – and went well, judging by Sally-Anne's body language. But the meeting is still only halfway through and now her attention is flagging.

Diverted by thoughts of what to buy for dinner with Mum, her mind starts to wander. To the list of wedding-related things they must get sorted in the coming week. And yesterday's letter from the doctor's surgery with the date for her twenty-week scan. Disparate strands drawn together by her subconscious to obscure the note still nestled in her pocket. Then the spell is broken by the fitful drumming of a fly against glass. It is dying, she can see, slowly, as it flails against the hermetically sealed window. Is it her, or has the dull hum of the cooling unit got louder?

Katy's gaze slips towards the glittering world outside and as her mind drifts she finds her thoughts dragged backwards to inescapable exams in stifling classrooms. Coconut oil-stained summer dresses. The smothering weight of heat and hate and fear that bloated the heath that day. One minute they'd been two, the next all she saw was the abandoned bag that lay in the middle of the clearing on its side, its mouth gaping into the dusty earth like a silent scream. Otherwise there was nothing, she thinks. Just silence. An eardrum-pounding silence that felt like it would never end.

She can still feel the fear, lodged like a lump of dough at the back of her throat; remember how, for what seemed a lifetime, she was unable to move. The uselessness of her, she recalls, grimly. A living, breathing thing petrified by the horror of an instant. And then, without any conscious decision to do so, she was in flight.

Running.

Back towards the slender ash trees on the outer fringes of the copse and the distant footpath beyond that gashed the ancient heathland's face. Conscious thought – even the mere acknowledgement of the desperation of her situation – eclipsed by pure sensation. Fossilised teeth of jagged stones beneath her soles. Concrete earth jarring her body with the whiplash jolt of a live cable. Branches slapping her face like flailing limbs. And then all this and more dissolving into a single, inescapable plateau of pain. All she was aware of was the blood pounding in her veins. The tightening of her chest. Her head like a clenched fist. Then the sudden white light from the open heath that seared her eyes.

Jumping over smaller obstacles, ignoring how her ankles twisted, she pressed on, until at last she glimpsed the footpath ahead. A few more strides and it was hers. Only then, once she was on the dusty track, could she allow her pace to slow and risk a quick backward glance. The rough ground now separating her from the dense foliage of the copse was open and empty. Inscrutable, she thought, taking in her surroundings. To her left, the dusty footpath stretched away for a few hundred yards then disappeared behind a wide clump of gorse. And to her right… the same. In one direction, in a quarter of a mile or so, the track would fork and the wider path would lead her back to the camp. But which?

Hungrily, she scanned the Punch Bowl's tree-lined rim for any recognisable landmark. But the ragged horizon encircling the ancient heath now seemed identical in all directions. It was like standing centre stage in a giant amphitheatre trapped before an unseen audience. Then, with a sinking heart, she remembered: Jude still had the map and compass in her back-pack. With no time to lose, she had to make a decision.

Raising her eyes as if in search of divine inspiration, she took a deep breath, crossed her fingers just in case, picked left, then ran. Battling now to blot out what had just happened. Jude's body, crumpling as she was dragged into the bushes. An image that re-played in a distorted loop again and again in her mind's eye. How long had it been, now? Five minutes, perhaps, maybe ten. A lot can happen in that time. Too much. But Jude will be all right, won't she? She'd put up a fight if she hadn't already managed to get away. She's strong, and the mouth on her – that alone will scare many a would-be attacker away.

At last, the flatness of the ground gave way to a gradual upward incline with taller shrubs and maturing trees. But she was so focused on her mission she did not notice. Nor did she remember that the camp was, in fact, down a gentle slope. The going was getting easier which had to be good, right? Running through the trees she even began to pick up speed. Not far to go, now. Nearly there – the memory of it now makes Katy's chest tighten.

But then, no more than a second later, she burst from the shade into bright light and complete disorientation. Because there was no evidence of the outbuildings of the camp or even the rough track down which they'd arrived from the station just a few days earlier. Somewhere close by, though, was a low rumble. With nowhere left to turn there seemed just one way to go. So she ran towards the noise. Cleared a low fence in a single bound and then a grassy verge to find – too late – her feet on tarmac.

A lorry thundered past, swerving to avoid her towards the central divide of the busy A-road that circumnavigated the Punch Bowl's rim. Someone close by let out a scream that was more like a howl. But before she could identify the voice as her own the sound was obliterated by the screech of pumping brakes of the car now heading straight towards her. All she could do was smell the burning tang of rubber. Until, at the last moment, blindly, instinctively, she spun around.

Darted back towards the low fence.

Clambered up onto it. Over it.

Jumped…

…into thin air—

'Katherine, are you OK?'

Opening her eyes, Katy sees Dirk, Janssens' boss of bosses, staring at her intently. With a quick nod, she reaches for the water jug. 'I'm fine, thanks,' she replies, though her throat is tight. 'My fault for skipping breakfast.'

'On which point,' Sally-Anne declares, checking her watch, 'where are those sandwiches?'

Seizing the moment, Katy puts down the glass she's just drained. 'Why don't I go and chase up Dawn?' she offers lightly, pushing back her chair.

Sally-Anne carefully puts the lid back on the unused fountain pen she's held throughout the meeting. 'Yes. And don't worry, we can finish off here without you.'

As the door of the conference room closes behind her, Katy sees Dawn emerge from the lift carrying sandwiches bought from Pret à Manger which have been unpacked and carefully arranged on a silver platter. An unmistakable aroma of tuna makes her stomach clench. Fish of any kind has made her nauseous since discovering she is pregnant. Food poisoning is the excuse she gave Dawn when the PA marvelled at how, suddenly, Katy's lunchtime favourite had fallen from favour.

Registering her distress and quickly decoding the cause, the younger woman mouths a single word – 'Sorry' – as, with barely a nod, Katy darts past her through an adjacent doorway to the stairwell that will lead her down towards the ground floor.

–

The concrete city radiates a grubby kind of heat as Katy hurries in the direction of St James's Park a few minutes later. Her breath is short; her face slick with sweat. Yet she registers neither, for though it has taken immense effort, like the rolling back of a stone, she's distracted by the decision she's just made. To make one quick call, just to make sure. Not from work or from her own mobile phone but somewhere anonymous and private. Untraceable.

She strides towards two red phone boxes that stand sentry to please the tourists halfway down Birdcage Walk. As she reaches the nearest she sees the equipment inside has been smashed. Next door, a foreign student wearing a brightly coloured backpack is shouting into the receiver in Spanish. Exasperated, Katy clicks her tongue but has no choice but wait, jiggling distractedly against the pane until the tourist slams down the receiver and pushes his way outside.

Tugging the handle, she tries not to gag at the fetid smell within as with clumsy fingers she reaches into her bag. Does an 0207 code still mean central London? she wonders, staring at Jude's number, punching it in. After the sixth digit, however, she falters. What the hell is she doing? A trickle of sweat dribbles into her left eye which she crossly brushes away. What will she say? Nothing. She'll say nothing, she reminds herself. For when Jude answers she can simply listen. Hear that voice. Confirm it really is her. Then once she knows she'll decide what to do.

With a drumming heart, the final buttons are pressed. Tightening her grip on the receiver, Katy waits. There's silence, just for a second or two, but long enough for her mind to conjure those last few desperate moments amidst the thrashing bushes. To stoke the guilt that it took years to eventually acknowledge, accept, then pack away; to rekindle the old fear. Then there is a distant click followed by a dull monotone. Though deflated, her heart skips with relief as she replaces the receiver. She leans against the glass.

At least I tried, she thinks as a blonde woman in her twenties knocks sharply on the door, demanding in broken English to know if she has finished. It's not my fault the number is dead. Or if Dawn took it down wrong.

Pushing her way outside, Katy gulps the petrol air like a drowning swimmer. Tightening her grip on her bag, she crosses the road and heads into the park where office workers swarm along the footpaths, their laminated security passes blinking in the midday sun. On every patch of grass people sit in panting clusters nibbling sandwiches, swigging from bottles, carefully forking salad from greasy plastic tubs.

In search of refuge, she heads towards the bridge across the lake where a loose cluster of tatty pelicans desperately mug for tourists in the hope of a stale crust or discarded banana skin. She chooses a path through the dappled shade of trees whose foliage has grown heady in the unseasonably warm weather that's yanked high summer forwards a good six weeks. The arid grass beneath her feet has already turned a mustard yellow and the once garish occupants of adjacent flower beds now stand limp, their heads hanging like condemned men.

Ahead is a noisy cluster of French school kids taking it in turns to capture themselves on their mobiles pulling faces beside the ungainly birds. Beyond them Katy spots an empty bench that sits in the sun's direct line of fire and heads towards it. Sitting down, she feels her pulse begin to calm. She shuts her eyes, surrendering to the narcotic effects of the sun, and recalls the days that followed that last afternoon with Jude.

Her stay in the County Hospital had lasted almost a week. For the first day or two she drifted in and out of consciousness due to concussion. She had a dislocated shoulder and broken wrist. A cut on her cheek which needed eleven stitches. Extensive bruising. Nevertheless, she'd spent the last few days begging to be allowed to go home. Pleading to be allowed to phone Jude. But her parents were united, for once, in their determination to play down whatever it was that had happened.

A fire on the heath caused no end of confusion, her father, Charles, gently revealed. Then, just as a search party was being readied, word came that Kat had been found by a passing motorist. There was no mention of anyone else on the heath

– which had struck Kat as strange because, with an awkward glance towards her father's travel bag on the floor beside her bed, his face was lightened, briefly, by an apologetic smile. The look of him made Kat's stomach clench. The dark rings pooled beneath each eye. His chin which, unbelievably, was rough and unshaven. How his pinstripe suit was all creased. Had she caused this?

A sudden sob from the other side of the hospital bed made Kat aware of her mum's presence. Diane Parker was seated on a low-sprung chair in front of the window, carefully folding then unfolding an embroidered handkerchief. *I'm sorry*, Mum mumbled. *It's just I thought we'd lost you, again...*

When Kat got home she found the world poised on the cusp of change. Andrew, preoccupied, packing the last bits and pieces for his round-the-world trip. Mum, tearful and upset at his imminent departure. Her father, grumpy and irritable because of both. And everything tainted with the lingering aftertaste of the incident on the heath which hadn't even made it into the local paper. The closest reference she could find was a short news item about an outbreak of fire on the heath that same day which had most likely been caused by a discarded match or cigarette.

'Mind if I join you?'

Squinting upwards into the solar glare, Katy can only just make out the figure standing before her. His face is in shadow and there is an umbra around his head which makes her think of a Renaissance painting of a fallen angel.

Before she has time to answer, he is moving towards the free end of the bench. A mid-height man in his early twenties whose face is obscured by a pair of aviator-style dark glasses and the shade cast by an outsized snapback hat bearing the oddly punctuated logo: Im The Truth. Khaki combat trousers sag ludicrously low beneath the waistband of his boxers. A long-sleeved check shirt, worn unbuttoned over a white T-shirt, is spattered with black which also flecks the toes of his Nike high tops.

Sitting down at the other end of the bench, the stranger rummages in the pocket of his trousers then extracts a pair of white ear phones which look comically tiny, Katy decides, given the size of his hands. Then without a word, he stretches out his legs, places a piece into each ear, leans back and shuts his eyes. After a minute or so he reaches out his arms along the back of the bench and starts to drum his fingers. She can hear the music's faint jangle and recognises the track. Something by the Red Hot Chili Peppers, Andrew's favourite.

The youth's left hand now rests uncomfortably close to Katy's shoulder, so she shifts along the bench and gazes across the lake towards the distant Mall and Green Park beyond. As she drifts back to the afternoon she got home from hospital and how gently Andrew had helped her from the car, she closes her eyes.

OK, Shrimp?

Andrew always used to call her that, and she'd loved it. But her smile faded as she noticed his bulging rucksack, meticulously packed, waiting expectantly by the front door. She hadn't realised her brother would be leaving for Sydney so soon.

Carefully, he'd led her into the sitting room. Guiding her towards the freshly plumped sofa beside which a lavish arrangement of freshly cut flowers sat on the coffee table. But she'd barely acknowledged his concern back then as, frustrated with the awkwardness of her cast and the infuriating feebleness of her still healing body, she sank back against the cushions. *What time are you off, then?* How hard she'd tried not to notice the way the adventure that lay before him made his eyes gleam. Then he reached down for a white plastic bag on the floor beside the armchair. Dad was running him to the airport at seven, he said, upending the bag's contents into her lap.

Here, I got you something.

It was a selection of cassettes – some bought, others homemade – including the Red Hot Chili Peppers album she'd meant to ask him to record. Touched by this unexpected act of kindness, Kat looked up and smiled. Then she remembered the Zippo she'd bought him to replace the one he lost which was still wrapped in its plastic bag in her bedroom drawer.

Later, Andrew said, encouraging her not to get up before shooting a conspiratorial glance over his shoulder to check their parents were out of earshot. *Listen*, he began, awkwardly touching her arm. *Everything will turn out OK, you know. You'll feel back to your old self soon. Sixth form will be fun, just you wait and see. And Mum and Dad, well, they'll soldier on the way they always do.*

A lump welled in Kat's throat as she wrestled with the urge to tell him not to go; to admit how she longed for him to stay or – even better – to take her with him. But although touched by the intimacy of this brief moment she knew the days of their old closeness had long gone. Much had changed since he'd moved into the sixth form, and her friendship with Jude. She dropped her voice.

I need to call her. I've been asking and asking but mum keeps changing the subject.

While Kat was being seen to, Jude had turned up at camp alone, one of the girls' classmates, Ruth, had revealed when she'd visited her in hospital during the days that followed. Then, as Kat was being taken to hospital, Siobhan had turned up, unannounced, to take her own daughter home. It was the last anyone had seen or heard of either of them. *I've got to know how she is. Something happened, you see...*

Her voice faltered, and the silence was suddenly filled by a deafening roar. Until at last her brother spoke.

Haven't they told you? She's gone – I heard mum say. Moved away. He laughed. A dry, humourless sound. *If you don't believe me, call.* Her brother gestured towards the garden. *Do it now – I'll keep them busy.*

She could barely breathe as she dialled Jude's number a few minutes later, waiting for the familiar pause before the connection was made. But the silence lasted longer than usual.

A lifetime. Until, eventually, there was a click and then a dull tone. Kat replaced the phone in the cradle and dialled again but the same thing happened. Then she tried a third time, just to be sure. But there was little doubt. The line was disconnected.

It was a week before Kat made it into town. Charles's mood had lightened considerably since temporarily moving back in with Diane after visiting his daughter in hospital. He had booked a last minute holiday to a small village in the mountains just inland from Estepona in southern Spain. A private villa with a pool – not that Kat would be able to swim with her arm still in plaster. Nevertheless, a last minute dash to Boots for holiday toiletries was an ideal subterfuge.

He dropped her a little later that morning at the bottom of Telegraph Hill, usually a ten minute walk from Jude's house. But today it took closer to twenty which made her hot and sticky. By the time she turned into Station Road her head was starting to ache. Turning back, however, wasn't an option, Kat thought grimly as she stepped onto Jude's street.

The red brick house looked no different from the dozen or so others that lined either side of the road in almost every respect. But something was missing. Neighbours' homes had their windows thrown open, cars crammed in narrow drive-ways, and sprinklers on full to resuscitate wilting plants. Yet with its curtain-less windows, its ragged drive and brittle lawn, the Davies' place seemed lost in time.

How could she? a voice inside her wailed. *Leave without even a word?*

Rubbing the tears from her eyes Kat saw Jude's face. Her eyes were closed to the domed sky as she floated in the pool with hair fanned outwards like a lioness's mane. The pale skin around her nipples was puckered by the water's icy touch. Then a middle-aged man appeared, pulled towards her by a small terrier on a lead. *Do you know when they'll be back?* she called out brightly.

But no, he didn't. Because they left before dawn a few days earlier, he told her, his scarlet face now slick with sweat. Next thing everybody knew there was a ruddy great 'For Sale' sign standing in the front garden. Which ticked him off, he told her, the lobster-pink belly overhanging his waistband glistening in the sun. Because Siobhan still owed him fifty quid. Gone back to the coast where they originally came from, was his best guess; she'd been talking about it a lot since coming into some money a while back.

Later, when Kat told her, her mum said with a tight laugh that she wasn't surprised. That from what she'd heard, Siobhan was just the sort to do a moonlit flit. *Unpaid bills, probably. Or man trouble, more likely.* Then Diane's voice had softened, unexpectedly, as she grudgingly conceded that either way with a mother like that it was hardly surprising. *Poor Jude*, she added with a shake of her head. *I mean really, that girl never stood a chance.*

The muffled sound of a ring tone makes Katy look up. The tune, a few bars of a rap track she doesn't recognise, grows louder. The youth, who is still tapping his fingers to the jangle in his ears, seems oblivious. Reaching towards him, she touches his forearm.

'Your phone,' she says. 'I said: your phone – it's ringing.'

'What?' Pulling out an ear piece, he finally hears the sound. 'Yeah?' he barks into the phone. '…No, I'm in London, but I'll come to you if it's worth my while… Sounds a bit steep, if the gear's OK I'd give you £300… Send me a picture. Right, the Hotmail address. But remember it's J Davies all one word, no capitals. And the Davies is spelled i-e-s, OK? Great. Later.'

Katy stares as the youth slides the phone back into his pocket, slowly and deliberately leans forward, clears his throat then spits a shiny gobbet of phlegm onto the patchy grass at the foot of an overflowing rubbish bin. Then he turns towards her, and as his eyes meet hers his lips crease into a sly smile. Unnerved, she looks away. A coincidence, that's all, Katy reassures herself. Loads of people would spell out Davies that way.

Nevertheless, she makes a show of checking her watch then rises to her feet. Now all she wants is to get away from him. The memory of it. And besides, it's time she was getting back.

'Time's up, is it?' Now he's asking her a question.

'Pardon?' She reaches for her bag.

'Your break?' he repeats. 'Time to get back. To work?'

'Yes. Something like that.'

'Me too,' he calls after her as she turns her back and walks away.

A nearby clock strikes one and, as if on cue, through the gates of the park pour crumpled refugees in cheap suits from nearby offices. They are desperate to make the most of their allotted time in the sun, yet all Katy craves now is to be back indoors. Briskly retracing her steps, she heads against the tide towards the exit facing Birdcage Walk. She stops briefly at an ice cream cart to buy a Pepsi Max from an elfin-haired girl in an army-coloured Royal Parks T-shirt whose plucked eyebrows give her face an expression of cartoonish surprise.

Only as she is paying does a figure a short distance behind her catch Katy's eye. It's the youth from the bench. Leaning against a tree. And he is looking her way. Determined not to make eye contact, she drops her gaze. Stuffing her purse back in her bag, she hurries on.

Heading back along Birdcage Walk, however, she risks a quick glance behind her and spots him again. Standing beneath a lamp post, running his tongue along the edge of a cigarette paper. Without warning he looks up, sharply. Their eyes meet. Is he following her, she wonders. Or is it just an overactive imagination? Perturbed, she darts away. Turning swiftly down a side alley, then left again into a single one-way street, she doubles back on herself.

Finally, at the Underground station, she slows her pace to cast a nonchalant glance over each shoulder. But by then the youth has gone.

Chapter 3

So here we are then. Thrown together by... well, you know the rest. Though when you think about it, I never really went away. Which is why, if you are wondering what made me choose to come back now, you're missing the point. Because the two of us are bound by what happened that day. What we did and what we didn't do. The choices we made. Inseparable, like past from present. I didn't choose to come back, you see, Kat... sorry, it's Katy now, isn't it? Events forced me to. Though it was, as we surely both must know, always inevitable.

Chapter 4

Guildford, September 1988

A brisk knock on her bedroom door woke Jude abruptly. It was the morning of her first day at her new school, St Mary's, and she had overslept. Quickly, she reached for the dressing gown that until recently she'd so rarely bothered to use, hugging the silky fabric tightly around her body as she waited for the familiar refrain.

'Room service!' he called, knocking again.

'Hang on,' she replied, climbing out of bed before he could come in. Hovering at the door to steal a quick glance in the mirror, she ran a hand through her tousled hair then turned the handle. A moment later she was face to face with Dave, her mother Siobhan's new boyfriend, standing on the landing wearing a matching dressing gown to her own though his barely reaches his knees. Determined not to notice how disconcertingly the kimono gaped at his waist. How he appeared not to be wearing anything underneath. Holding out what he'd just carried upstairs – a warm pile of freshly ironed clothes – he let slip a sly grin then held out his arms.

While Siobhan did most of the housework, Dave's occasional domestic responsibility since moving in was putting away the laundry. It was a job he appeared to take seriously – rotating each item of washed clothing in the airing cupboard before neatly folding, stacking then putting away T-shirts, trousers and the lace-trimmed pastel rainbow of Jude's pants and bras. *Someone should give him a job at Benetton*, her mother often joked.

But Jude didn't find the early weekday morning knock on her bedroom door funny. She hated the meticulously stacked pyramid of clothes crowned, without fail, with a carefully folded item of her own underwear.

Now, as the alcoholic tang of his aftershave teased her nostrils, the burning in her cheeks told her she'd begun to blush, and in that instant she hated him more than she had hated anyone, ever. For his unwelcome intrusion. For the time alone with her mum which he had stolen from her. And for the way his lurking presence threatened to undermine her own carefully assembled self-confidence. Self-consciously, she looked away – she doesn't need to see his face to know that her discomfort has been registered. Then, grasping the laundry towards her chest, she moved to shut the door.

'Wait a minute,' he said, taking one step forward and firmly placing his foot against the doorframe to stop her shutting him out. Glancing down, she registered his toes, which were long with nails like polished pebbles, and hairless skin which was girlishly smooth. The heat in her cheeks intensified. 'Mum says she's got to work the late shift this evening so she won't be here when you get home to cook tea but I will, OK?' Jude looked up sharply. The familiarity of Mum instead of your mum seemed indecent, somehow. Working every muscle in her face, she concocted a blank stare then nodded. 'Just wanted to let you know, that's all,' he concluded. Then, with a wide smile, he took a step back onto the landing leaving the door to swing to.

Back inside her room, she sank down onto the bed holding the laundry then, feeling that it was still warm, quickly put it to one side. As she reached for the bra and pants on the top she hesitated, wondering for a moment whether she dared put the clothes through the wash again. But no, she'd rather not give him the satisfaction. Besides, what would she say to her mum? Sorry, but I don't like your boyfriend touching my underwear. Please make him stop? That wouldn't work, though, because mum would just think she was trying to cause trouble.

Jude selected another set of underwear from the top drawer of her dressing table. Across the room, she noticed her new school uniform was hanging from the handle of her wardrobe door. The black A-line skirt, unfashionably cut to the knee. The green and white check blouse with its ghastly cardigan in a complementary, verdant hue. And on the floor, beside freshly blacked lace-up shoes, the hideous felt cloche hat, squatting on the floor like a malevolent toad. Her blazer was downstairs where her mum had spent the previous evening meticulously darning a hole in the right sleeve. *Beggars can't be choosers*, Siobhan Davies had said the night before, laughing at the look of horror on her daughter's face as she bit off the final thread on the last name tape she sewed on to every single piece of Jude's new school clothes.

The list of required paraphernalia Jude would need for St Mary's had run to almost two A4 pages. Yet Siobhan relished the challenge of how to exceed expectations on a shoestring by cleverly scouting for budget alternatives to the overpriced stock offered by Kinch's, the official uniform supplier on West Street. Miss Shackleton, the headmistress, had been pretty helpful, too, assuring them that St Mary's was a school that prided itself on supporting bright pupils from less well-off families. *Only we're nothing like beggars are we, Jude?* she had continued, pausing briefly to re-thread her needle. *We don't owe anyone anything, and don't you forget it. You got that scholarship fair and square. And, thank God, now you've got a real chance to make something of yourself.*

Jude scowled, though there was no one to see. She'd not wanted to leave her old secondary school in the sprawling south coast town where she grew up, let alone move to a place she'd barely heard of in the heart of the Surrey commuter belt. How she dreaded meeting the other girls who'd be in her new class, all of whom would surely live in double-fronted timbered piles down leafy lanes with a pony or two tucked away in the stable. What would they say when they spotted that much of her school uniform was second hand and find out that she lived in a modern house unfashionably close to the commercial hub of the town? St Mary's was an all girls school, too; she just knew it was going to be awful.

Yet Jude knew that following her mum's break up with Colin Dixon they'd had little choice but to move on. He had what Siobhan coyly referred to as a bit of a problem with drink. Or, to put it another way, he knew when to stop but more often than not did not care. Proof came late one night after an argument got out of hand and he almost broke Siobhan's jaw. The following morning they'd moved out of their rented flat and into a bed and breakfast in a small village on the seaside city's outskirts from where Siobhan began planning the new life they would soon begin in the Surrey town which had last been her home over a decade before.

Slowly, Jude started to dress. In the bathroom, she glared defiantly at the stranger in the mirror as she brushed her hair. Angrily tugging the mane back from her pale face into a tight ponytail, her grey eyes took on a vaguely oriental slant. Sitting on the edge of the bath, she pinched the cupid's bow of her upper lip between her forefinger and thumb for precisely three minutes before examining her handiwork in the mirror. It was a daily ritual she'd begun three months earlier as an angry insurance policy against inheriting the flaccid line of her mother's lips. And it was starting to work, she thought as she assessed with grim satisfaction how the shallow V of her own upper lip was finally taking on a sharper shape. A minor triumph, but victory nonetheless in the secret battle against becoming Siobhan.

Pulling a face, she tested the look of cool disdain she calculated would be appropriate for her first day at St Mary's. *You've got to speculate to accumulate*, Siobhan had explained when she took her daughter out of her first school, where she'd been happy, to send her to a better one in a neighbouring catchment. Which was how Jude had come to attend three schools before her eleventh birthday. And why she'd given up trying to fit in long ago. Why bother if you'd not be staying?

Yet she didn't hate her mum, not really. For she respected the way Siobhan single-handedly raised her after Jude's dad died in a traffic accident. How she'd worked hard, taking on a series of soul destroying day jobs then studying nights to train as a dental nurse – a stubborn, defiant approach to life Jude secretly knew she would emulate. It was the way Siobhan tried to live through Jude the life she could have had, had she not fallen pregnant that was intolerable. How cowed Jude felt by the dull weight of her ambitions. That's all.

'Don't you look the part!' Siobhan exclaimed as Jude walked into the kitchen a short while later. Pushing a strand of bleach-blonde hair from her eyes with the back of one hand, she gave the pan of fast-congealing scrambled eggs a quick stir with the other. 'Don't you think, Dave? Doesn't she look the part!' she repeated, re-tucking her top, a low-cut satin blouse of dazzling cerise, into the waistband of her black pencil skirt, smoothing the front panel.

Jude glared at her mum's boyfriend who was leaning against the worktop cradling a mug of tea, willing him not to speak.

'Yeah, you show 'em, girl!' As he raised his mug his lips curled into a teasing smile.

'You're a bright girl, Jude, and just as good as anyone else,' Siobhan cried, suddenly darting across the room to her daughter to put an arm round her shoulders. 'Remember,' she added, tapping her head. 'What's in here is what really counts.'

'Thanks, Mum,' Jude muttered, momentarily disarmed by such innocent desire for everything to be OK.

Clearing his throat, Dave reached for a piece of fresh toast now cooling in the toast rack. 'Hands off,' Siobhan scolded with an expert snap to the back of his hand with her tea towel. 'That's Jude's. You'll get yours later.'

Taking a seat at the table, Dave grabbed Siobhan around the waist then tugged her downwards onto his lap. 'I look forward to that,' he chuckled.

It was good to shut the front door behind her, Jude felt, as she stepped out onto Station Road to inhale the fresh September air. And despite the damp tarmac and the welling clouds above suggesting it would rain again later, her spirits stirred.

Turning left at the gate, she slowly walked along the street. Their street now, a world away from Hill Rise, the windswept crescent of Seventies semis Jude would always think of as home – a red brick tiara crowning the last hill between the South Downs from a brackish sea. The new place was close to the city centre, too – an unfashionable location where a cluster of once grand yet now decaying Victorian residences were being systematically demolished to make way for new development. No one wanted to live in town any more, it seemed, as anyone who could afford to had traded up to sprawling homes nestling in neighbouring villages.

Looping a finger through the hook of her blazer, Jude swung it over her shoulder and set off down the street. Stoical and determined, she covered the ten minute walk at a steady pace but as she caught her first glimpse of the imposing Victorian façade of St Mary's Upper School for Girls she couldn't help but note, with a sinking heart, how her old life on the coast had never felt so far away.

Chapter 5

'Where did you say Michael was this evening?' asks Diane Parker, neatly dissecting the last asparagus spear on her plate.

With her hair newly styled, freshly manicured nails, and the silk shirt she bought in the mid-season sales, Katy's mum looks radiant and younger than her sixty-six years. She seems buoyed, too, by an air of birthday self-indulgence and the sense of freedom the fifth floor flat in the stylish Parkview development overlooking Richmond Park still gives her six years after the unexpected windfall she received in Katy's dad's will.

Guilt money − that's what Andrew had called it when, having missed his father's funeral due to food poisoning, he'd come over from Washington a few weeks later with his new wife, Dee, to help Diane move in. Now, as Katy scans the room in which she sits, she can only smile at the memory of how worried they'd been that with its stripped floors and whitewashed walls the flat was unwelcoming. Dour, even.

There'll be plenty of time for shag pile and thermals when I'm in my dotage, Mum had chided. *For now I want to have some fun in my city pied-à-terre. Charles owes me that much, don't you think?*

It was the city bolt hole Diane had always dreamed of. An ideal base from which to pursue the cream of the capital's cultural pursuits. Evidence of these exploits is all around the room, from theatre posters of her favourite West End shows to shelves heaving with books and coffee table guides to latest art exhibitions. An African mask with beaten-bronze nose guard and demonic horns – a memento from a trip to Mali the previous year – hangs above a large sofa covered with a rainbow-coloured artisan quilt picked up for a song in Marrakech.

Can it really be just eighteen months since the woman had been rushed to hospital with a suspected heart attack, Katy wonders, taking another sip of soda. A development which had drawn Katy back into Mum's daily orbit.

Carer was a role she was unused to, but duty forced her to concur. Andrew was now living in the US and given the lack of any other close family members nearby, there really was no one else. Though short-lived, Diane's health scare was a timely reminder of the need for vigilance after being diagnosed with high blood pressure following Charles's death. Following this, the woman had carefully adjusted her daily routines to cultivate a healthier lifestyle which, bizarrely, had emboldened her to be more adventurous, not less.

Katy smiles. Yes, Mum has certainly done her best not to miss out on the swinging Sixties second time round. 'He's having dinner with another design company interested in hiring him. If he gets the job it would be a real step up,' she replies. 'Although I know he'd rather be here.'

'So tell me, how are things?' Diane dabs her buttery lips with her serviette. 'And I don't just mean with work, I mean with Michael. The two of you – is everything OK?'

How long has it taken, Katy wonders, her face tightening with the effort of resisting the urge to check her watch. Half an hour at most. Shifting position in her seat, she wills her body to relax; her mind not to rise to the bait. For theirs is not a relationship built on easy confidences. Mum has always been direct, a side to her personality sharpened by the bitterness of her separation from Charles.

Long-dreaded, the eventual split brought only temporary relief, her mother once confided. Like the misjudged lancing of a stubborn blister. For Diane, never quite managing to fall out of love with her husband, failed in her attempts while he was still alive to move on. The 'parting', as Diane would forever after call it – for Charles and she never quite got round to getting a divorce – diminished her, somehow.

Alone, Diane grew brittle, at times sharp-tongued. Judgemental. A lasting legacy of both parents' over-protectiveness and high expectations for their children when young, Katy reasoned, but of course it had all begun with Jude.

Jude.

The friend who, at the lowest point in her parents' marriage, was the one thing they stood united on. Or, rather, against. The friend they feared was a bad influence, someone who'd distract Katy from her studies and lead her astray. The only best friend Katy ever had, for she'd struggled to construct any close female friendships since. The one person to whom she is still inexplicably bound.

Stop it, Katy tells herself, brusquely. Don't let Jude in – not now. Tonight is about Mum. And this time is about me. I have a life now. A new life with Michael that's taken years to achieve and now my focus must be on what lies ahead. Because here and now is when the main act is about to start.

'Fine, thanks,' she hears herself reply.

What else is there to say? Even now – after the years she and Michael have been together, the time they've spent sharing the flat, the almost but not quite splitting up followed by the getting closer thereafter, and just a few weeks ago the twelve week scan… She is lucky and knows it, so is it any wonder she's wary of tempting fate? Fearful that her feelings for him are still too fragile a flower to expose to the piercing light of Diane's expectations.

Perhaps things will be different once everyone knows. *Better late than never, Shrimp*, she imagines Andrew will say.

Katy smiles. How proud she'll feel recounting to her mum how great Michael has been; how he offered to support her however she felt, whatever she wanted to do. How he'd even suggested they marry, which they will – soon. How, fingers crossed, everything has worked out OK. Because there's always a proviso; a but. For coming to terms with having a baby and now getting married is taking longer than she hoped. She cares about him enough now and soon, surely, she'll believe it, too.

Christ, how can she explain any of this to Mum?

'Good,' Diane declares, rising to her feet to clear the plates. 'No, no – you stay there, we can have a break before the main course, can't we? Pour us both another drink.'

Pulling the wine from the cooler, Katy refills Mum's glass then sits back and surveys the room. From the open French windows to her left drifts a heady mix of scents from the hanging baskets, pots and tubs that fill the narrow balcony beyond. The room feels fresh despite the evening's heat thanks to a light breeze blowing in from the park below. She closes her eyes.

Got your eye on filling Miriam's Louboutins, have you? Sally-Anne teased earlier, once she'd returned from the park after lunch. *I'll have to tell her to watch her back!* Katy had been busying herself sifting through the outstanding correspondence awaiting the return of Sally-Anne's second in command who was due back from six months' maternity leave the following week. Periodically setting members of her team against each other is one of Sally-Anne's favourite pastimes and, she seems to think, an effective way of keeping underlings on their toes. How will the woman react to another pregnant employee? Katy now wonders.

Opening her eyes, she gazes at the mantelpiece opposite, along which stands a battalion of postcards, pictures and photographs – some framed, others not. In the middle is one of Katy's favourites: a picture of Diane in her early twenties taken just after she first met Charles. With her long auburn hair carefully pinned back into an elegant chignon, the twenty-something version of Diane is wearing a satin cocktail dress. And her tiny, pinched-in waist and satin pumps are to die for.

The picture stands beside a bright orange piece of folded cardboard featuring Katy's twin nephews' hand prints which someone – the dutiful Dee, probably – has turned into a pair of butterflies with a few deft strokes of a felt tip pen. It was taken somewhere in Kensington by a friend of Charles's as they left some work function or other. Diane had been looking forward to it for weeks, then he was late picking her up. But in the end it hadn't really mattered, her mum would fondly recall, because when they got there it turned out to be the perfect evening. Katy sighs. If only the same could have been said of the years that followed.

'Here we are, then!' Diane declares, placing a platter of cold meats down on the table.

'Mum, I said I'd prepare the rest of it,' Katy objects.

'I know,' Diane laughs. 'But I couldn't resist!'

Grateful for the distraction, Katy retreats to the kitchen where she chops mint into the new potatoes before collecting cutlery and plates and loading the rest of the main course onto a tray. As she walks back into the sitting room she sees her mum has turned her chair away from the dining table to gaze out over the shadowed contours of the park below. The sun has only just set and along the gashed horizon the clouds bleed scarlet rays.

Putting down the tray, Katy leans across the table to light the candles.

'Ta-dah!' she says as the burning wicks flare in the thickening air with a defiant certainty she yearns to match. 'Happy birthday, Mum!'

–

Asleep a short while later, fitful and restless, Katy recalls how raised voices woke her early the day of the post-exam trip to Gallows Hill. Remembers, too, how she used to feel staring up at the fine cracks in the ceiling above her bed. Navigating their familiar contours, imagining a snowy mountain ridge or the delicate filigree of a parched river system viewed from space, had lulled her for as long as she could remember. Not that morning, though, as her father raged and Mum sobbed.

Eager to block out the sound of her parents' argument, she reached for her Walkman and a Talking Heads cassette – one of Andrew's current favourites. Maybe he would let her borrow the tape to take with her to summer camp, she mused over the opening bars of Burning Down the House. But Andrew had another week at home before setting off on his round-the-world trip and was bound to take it with him. Or, perhaps, she could get him to make her a copy. She would ask him at breakfast, she decided, picking up the small tub of Astral she kept by the bed. Slowly, she began to rub a gobbet of the oily cream into her cuticles.

The rough slam of her parents' bedroom door a few minutes later made Kat jump. Wiping her hands on the duvet cover, she took off the headphones. Her father's leaden footfalls as he descended the stairs were accompanied by the dull thud of an overnight bag being bounced downwards. After a moment, the front door clicked open then snapped shut. A minute later she heard a car engine roar and the angry cough of tyres on gravel as he sharply pulled away.

Another week, another business trip. Though it was unusual for him to set off on a Thursday morning.

Stifling a yawn, Kat rolled out of bed. The black holdall which Mum had lent her sat on the floor beneath the window. It was almost full with underwear neatly rolled, shorts and T-shirts carefully ironed. A sundress, freshly washed and pressed, waited on a hanger. Over the back of a chair hung her denim jacket also freshly laundered and, Kat registered with a sinking heart, with neat creases pressed into each arm. She glanced at her alarm clock. She was due at the train station at just after nine. She hoped her parents' argument wouldn't make her late.

Summer camp had been a last minute idea. The school trip was to be a post-O levels treat for the fifth years at St Mary's and more than half of her class had signed up to five days at an outward bound centre just over the border with Hampshire in an area known as the Devil's Punch Bowl. Yet Kat had been reluctant to go. Because of Jude.

Friends since Jude's abrupt arrival at the school six months earlier, they'd worked as allies during preparations for the mock O level exams a few months earlier – revising together after school, testing each other, providing mutual encouragement and support. They shared a precocious intelligence and a mutual desire for the freedoms they knew good grades would bring: St Mary's was that kind of school. And both had done well.

Since spring, however, something had changed. An advancing shadow had gradually darkened their friendship and now the final exams were over Kat felt unease not excitement at the prospect of five days in her friend's increasingly volatile company. Worse, Kat's parents had been arguing badly for weeks. Then there was Andrew's big trip: she so wanted to make the most of his last few days at home..

Foolishly, Katy had confided all this to a petulant Jude who used it to twist her arm. *It will be a trip to remember,* she'd cooed, wooing Kat into non-resistance before dealing her coup de grace. *And you know Andrew, he'll be so busy hanging out with his mates he won't even notice you're not there.*

Kat knelt down on the floor to finish packing her bag with her hairdryer and brushes, moisturiser and wash bag. Opening the bottom drawer of her desk, she carefully reached to the back and pulled out the lash-thickening mascara and cherry-tinted lip balm Jude had given her for her birthday and quickly poked both down and out of sight towards the bottom of the travel bag. Unlike Jude's mum, Diane Parker did not like her daughter wearing make-up.

But this was only the beginning of the world of differences that divided her mum from Siobhan, as Jude's mum liked everyone – including her own daughter and her friends – to address her. Tall and slender with blonde hair which, judging by the colour of her eyebrows, was bottle-enhanced, Siobhan Davies was not like other mums. She was younger, unmarried – though she had a boyfriend – and worked in a dental surgery. The tops she liked to wear were low-cut and fitted snugly into the triumphantly narrow waistbands of her skinny-fit jeans and pencil skirts. And she had a magpie penchant for gaudy colours and costume jewellery.

Visibly uncomfortable on the days she did make it to the school gate, Siobhan always seemed to be waiting for someone to cast some negative comment or put her down. Which, perhaps, explained why when collecting Jude on the days she came back to Katy's after school for tea, the woman announced her arrival only with a brief blast on the car horn as she waited outside for her daughter to gather her things. Her own home was red brick and far smaller than Charles and Diane's, though to Kat's mind the combined effect of magnolia bubble bath and stale nicotine give its interior an exotic allure.

It came as no surprise, then, that when the trip to Gallows Hill was first mentioned Kat's mum hadn't wanted her to go. For despite a perennial desire to give her daughter the opportunities she never enjoyed, Diane Parker still treated her youngest like a child. She openly admitted she was overprotective, even made jokes about it. It's how she'd been ever since a family picnic down by the canal one stifling summer afternoon a decade before when Kat almost drowned. Eventually Diane relented, of course, but not before squeezing from Kat repeated assurances that, yes, she would be careful and, no, she would not wander the heath alone.

Andrew, his head buried in a copy of *The Times*, had almost finished his breakfast when Kat entered the kitchen. He was wearing a crumpled T-shirt with yesterday's jeans. The hair on each side of his head was gelled flat while the top was artfully spiked. And by the look of it, Kat noted with wry amusement, he was failing miserably in a vain attempt to cultivate stubble. But though she greeted him brightly, the cassette request playing on her mind, he merely grunted.

Her brother had changed so much since going into sixth form, and now his A levels were over he couldn't wait to escape the stifling atmosphere and stale familiarity of home. At the local sixth form college, he quickly fell in with a new bunch of friends. He started a band, too, and frequently returned home after midnight smelling of beer and cigarettes. Yet in her brother's aloofness, constant conviction he alone was right and his increasingly short temper, Kat saw only a younger version of their father rather than the rebel Andrew so clearly yearned to be.

Taking a seat at the table Kat poured herself a mug of tea and stared at her brother who remained unmoving, his head bowed. How like dad he was becoming, she mused with a stab of satisfaction at how horrified Andrew would be at the merest suggestion. She almost grinned, but her mood quickly darkened as Diane wandered into the kitchen. Still dressed in her quilted dressing gown, the woman's eyes looked puffy and the skin on her throat was blotchy and red.

Kat reached for some toast. Though she was sorry for her mum she was angry, too – at the predictability of it all. Ever since she could remember the tension in her parents' marriage had been a smouldering backdrop to family life. Brief periods of calm were always cut short by some flare up or other and then, when tempers were at their shortest, work would call her dad away – on one occasion for six months. Life slipped into the gentle rhythms of relative normality during their father's absences for Kat and Andrew, but both could see that Diane found these periods of separation almost as hard to deal with as times when inter-marital hostilities were in full swing.

Secretly, Kat had always sided with her in any confrontation against her dad whose uneasy informality and frequent absences made him cold and aloof. Yet for years she'd craved Charles's attention and praise, convinced if she could somehow change – be better at school, better at swimming, a better person – everything could be made all right.

Andrew rose from the table and walked towards the door. *Have a good trip, Shrimp*, he called to Kat without turning his head as he left the room. Kat's eyes welled at the sudden realisation that when she got back from camp the following Tuesday there would be just one day left before he flew to Sydney, and that she wouldn't then see him again for almost a year. She remembered the goodbye present she'd bought still wrapped in its plastic and tucked away from view beneath T-shirts in an upstairs drawer. A new Zippo lighter to replace the one he lost; she would wrap it when she gets back.

They drove into town in silence. The only acknowledgement of what might or might not have happened between her parents before breakfast came when, waiting at a set of red lights just outside town, Diane reached out and gently patted her daughter's knee. *Everything will be all right*, she murmured, more to reassure herself than Kat. *Just you wait and see.*

As they turned into the station car park, Kat quickly located a group of her classmates standing outside the main entrance watching the drop off zone where one of their number, Ruth Creighton, was helping her dad tug an unfeasibly large, purple sports bag from the boot of his car. *Here we are at last!* Diane smiled, almost looking like her old self. *Have a wonderful time.* She handed Kat a small, knotted plastic bag containing six ten pence pieces and a folded slip of paper. *Don't forget to ring. Or the new number – I've written it down, just in case.*

The phone company had just changed their number and taken them ex-directory after a series of nuisance calls – the silent kind; there had been a dozen or so since Easter. Maybe Mum would relax a bit now.

Briefly, Kat kissed her mum then clambered out of the car. She walked round to the boot where her bag was stowed but then, as she reached for the handle, the car began to pull away. A moment later, Diane slammed on the brakes and stopped abruptly, forcing the driver of a Citroen attempting to back out of a parking space to her right, to screech to a halt with only a few inches to spare. *Darling, I am so, so sorry—* she began. A slight tremble shook her voice. *Don't worry, Mum*, Kat muttered, casting a defiant glare at the man who in between pounding his horn was shaking his fist in their direction. *We'll be back*, she added, almost apologetically. *Andrew, me… just you wait.*

Hurrying towards her friends, Kat resisted the urge to look back. Diane's distress was humiliating and she didn't need to look to know her classmates were staring. Whispering. Though a sudden laugh almost made her crack. Until she realised it was her mum. Regaining her composure, Kat readjusted the strap of the travel bag to stop it from cutting into her shoulder. Tried to ignore, too, the sense of the widening gulf between them. The sound of Mum's fingers drumming the roof of the car as she waited for her child to turn and wave.

–

The sound – like fingers tap-tapping a hard surface – wakes Katy at around two.

It's only the faint rattle of the fan's leftward sweep that's woken her. But by the time she's identified the cause Katy is too awake to resettle. She is alone in bed, naked, with a parched throat. Reaching for the glass on the bedside table she finds it empty. Clasping it in one hand, she climbs out of bed. In the bathroom she fills the glass then takes a few deep gulps. Only as she turns to retrace her steps back upstairs does she hesitate, puzzled by the barely perceptible shift in the depth of darkness.

The house is south-facing with taller houses with an extra storey overlooking it at the rear which means that at night, the main source of light comes from the two street lamps at the building's front. But now, as she looks down towards the sitting room, she can clearly see the difference. Fumbling for the cause, she wanders downstairs into the sitting room, then just before she reaches the window, snaps to attention. There's an unexpected sound outside like someone stamping on ice. Then the muted yet unmistakable crunch of breaking glass.

Hurrying towards the blind, Katy peeks through two of the wooden slats just in time to see someone throwing something at the street light opposite. Glass splinters again and the darkness deepens.

In the middle of the road where, until a few minutes earlier, two pools of light reassuringly interlocked, Katy can just make out three kids, their faces obscured by the darkness. What are they up to, she wonders. Abruptly, one turns her way then hesitates for a moment before breaking into a low run towards their house. A moment later he has disappeared from view behind the honeysuckle explosion of their front fence. She shifts position to get a clearer view but now the figure below, who must now be in their front garden, is hidden by the slope of the porch roof.

With a pounding heart, Katy turns her attention once more to the others who are still standing in the middle of the street where one is carefully removing a handful of something from a small bag slung across the other's back. Suddenly, they look up in her direction. Have they seen her? Quickly, she ducks out of view. But before she can check, a missile explodes with a dull crack against the glass by her side closely followed by two more.

Peering through the gap between the blind's edge and the window frame, Katy sees them, brazen and expectant. Why are they doing this, she wonders. What can they want?

Then the first figure is back in view. Skipping out through Michael's front gate. Darting along the pavement towards a nearby parked car. Springing onto the bonnet then stepping up onto the roof to stand triumphant for a moment, arms outstretched like the king of the castle, before jumping up then down making the metal buckle. Again, and then again. Only when, at last, the figure is back on solid ground does Katy realise the car is hers.

Torn between fear and anger, she cranes her neck to see what they will do next. But now the trio appear to be readying to leave. They are on their bikes, straddling the cross bars to exchange high fives outside the lawyer's house next door as a running figure breaks from the shadow and draws to a halt by their side. He is taller than the others – an adult, perhaps, on the return leg of a late night run. Though now they are talking in low voices and, for a split second, he wrestles something the size of a paperback from the front pocket of his hoodie and gives it to the nearest one. And then it is over. They are gone, pedalling furiously into the night, and the man, now alone, turns towards their house and walks towards it. Unlatches the front gate. Heads towards their front door.

Katy spins back from the window, bruising her back as she slams against the wall. Her hands clench into fists then un-ball, rapidly, as she braces herself for the sound of the doorbell. But it doesn't come. Instead she can just make out what sounds like the distant scrape of a key turning in the lock. Which is impossible, of course, she thinks as she slips down onto the floor and hugs her knees to her chest. She waits for any audible clue of the stranger's advance up the stairs towards her and Michael's flat but there is none. Just the masonry murmur of the downstairs flat's front door being pushed to.

Michael's voice suddenly echoes in Katy's head as she turns back to the window and stares down onto the dented roof of her car with its frosted latticework of cracked glass where once a windscreen had been. *Just like living in the bloody Wild West.*

It's what he said after a recent front page story in the *Evening Standard* about a drive-by shooting involving rival gangs in Shepherd's Bush. But that was a mile away, the expanse of a continent in London terms, and nothing like this has ever happened to them.

Slumped onto the sofa, she hugs a cushion to her chest. Weary and frightened, she is suddenly overwhelmed by despair. Where's Michael now? she wonders, miserably. Why isn't he here?

Katy reaches for the phone and dials his mobile number but the call goes straight to voicemail. As she hangs up without leaving a message the sudden and unexpected banshee wail of an emergency vehicle just a few streets away makes her flinch. Is it worth calling the police, she wonders, fleetingly, before dismissing the idea. For what would be the point? Those kids would be long gone by now and the downstairs flat is silent.

49

It must be Phil's friend – the one in the garden, earlier, watering the plants – who she's just seen entering the house, Katy reasons, slipping the phone back into its cradle. For whose presence and behaviour there is, surely, a perfectly logical and innocent explanation.

Even so, she takes Michael's camping torch – a heavy duty Maglite the size of a rolling pin – from the landing cupboard and carries it back upstairs to bed. The weight of its rugged, aluminium handle reassures Katy as she carefully positions the makeshift cosh within easy reach by her side upended on the floor. How bad is my car, she wonders. What did the stranger downstairs see? But to discover either she must wait. Only a few hours, she tells herself firmly. Until daylight. Everything will look better in the morning – it always does.

Closing her eyes, she crosses her fingers without thinking.

Chapter 6

London, July 2013

'Thought you might need a bit of a pick-me-up,' Michael says, setting the tray down at the end of the bed.

Sluggishly opening her eyes, Katy registers the tumbler of water on the bedside table, undrunk. The raw pain now pounding her left temple. Then the smell of toast. Her stomach clenches and she thinks she might be sick as, through narrowed eyes, she squints at the tray in his hands. He's brought her coffee, too; Alka Seltzer and an unopened strip of Nurofen. She reaches first for the tumbler with a sheepish smile then quickly checks the clock. For the first time in as long as she can remember, he has woken before the alarm.

'You're up early.' The sound of her voice is a husky rasp.

'I've got a breakfast presentation at half-eight.' He pours himself a mug of coffee which he drinks strong and black then lies down across the bed, staring at her intently. 'That's what I was working on last night when I got back, but I guess I must have fallen asleep. Then, after I came to sort you out – you were in quite a state when I found you downstairs – I thought it best to spend the rest of the night on the sofa bed in the office. You were dead to the world as soon as your head hit the pillow, you know. And snoring like a train.'

Popping two pills in her mouth with what stale water remains, she gulps them down then exhales, slowly. 'You were here? All the time?'

'Asleep. Downstairs. But what about you, it must have been quite a party.'

'Party?'

'At your mum's. I must admit I was quite surprised seeing you like that – I thought you'd forsworn alcohol, for the next few months at least.'

'I have. I mean, I wasn't drinking. It's just – I was upset. About... What happened to the car, have you seen? And you weren't here.' Katy shivers. 'Christ, I feel awful.'

Michel smiles. 'Yes, I've seen you look better.'

'How bad is it?'

'What, the car? Undriveable. It was down to some kids, apparently. A bunch of chancers – Phil's younger brother, Kevin, saw them. I bumped into him earlier, so you know. He's in between flats at the moment so will be staying downstairs for a week or two until he gets himself straight. He says when he gave them some cigarettes they happily went on their way. I'll call the insurance company later – see what they can do.'

Katy frowns. Given how dark it was last night with the street lights out of order, it's difficult to be sure quite what she saw. But the sudden memory of the hooded figure in the early morning sunshine watering the flowers makes the pressure pounding at her temples start to ease. 'And dinner, how did that go?' she sighs.

'Hard to call,' Michael answers with a noncommittal shrug. Stifling a yawn, he reaches down to scratch the soft skin on his ankle around his tattoo. Then, leaning across the mattress towards the electric fan that sits on the blanket box at the foot of the bed, he sets the button on the base to maximum rotate. 'It's going to be another scorcher, everyone's saying so. You'd be best off taking a duvet day. Get your head together then maybe find somewhere cool and shady to sit in the garden later. You owe it to yourself...' He lets slip a gentle smile. '...the both of you. I'll ring the insurance company when I get into work.'

'Oh God,' Katy groans, suddenly remembering. 'I've got to stand in for Sally-Anne at eleven at a meeting with a new client.' She slips a leg out of the bed and rests her foot on the stripped wooden floor to ground herself then, feeling queasy, sinks back against the pillow. What's wrong with me? she wonders. Because this is worse than just a hangover. Or the fallout from something she ate in last night's dinner. Without wanting to, she thinks of Jude. The stranger in the park. The youths last night on their street. Though the room is hot, she suddenly shivers. Her body is limp, her energy drained by a looming sense of dread. 'I can't go in,' she croaks.

'No, you can't,' he agrees, reaching into his pocket and pulling out her mobile phone. Scrolling up and down with his thumb for a moment, he scans the screen then sets the timer. 'Give it an hour then leave a message for Dawn just before nine – she's rarely in before quarter past.'

'OK,' Katy replies, taking the phone from him without thinking to ask why he'd had it. 'The alarm, right – in case I fall back asleep.'

Michael nods then stands up. 'Listen. I'd love to stay and chat but I really need to go. Don't worry, I'll call the garage about the car.' Bending down he kisses her, tenderly. 'Take it easy,' he adds as she closes her eyes. 'Tranquilo. Everything will be OK.'

–

Michael's parting words drift like flotsam in Katy's head over the next hour or so as, her mind ebbing and flowing between oblivion and distress, her body twists and turns in the building heat. But the more she tells herself everything will be all right the more it seems a shabby mantra. And the more something else, another voice from long ago, vies for dominance as memories stir in her pressure cooker mind.

It started with a conspiratorial whisper closely followed by gentle blowing in her ear, she recalls. *Shake a leg!* Though she had turned her head away, Kat could not so easily ignore the warm breath on her face. Or the pinch on her arm that followed. *Come on*, grinned a victorious Jude as her eyes cracked open. *Let's go for a swim!*

It was gone six on their first morning at Gallows Hill. After arriving the previous day, the girls had spent the afternoon on an orientation ramble across the Punch Bowl's southern sweep. A little later, seated outside the main building in the fading light, senses softened by a heady cocktail of baked heathland and barbecue smoke, Kat watched Jude flirt with Ben, the camp's young Australian cook. She seemed happier than she'd been in weeks. And as Kat lay back on the grass, gazing up at the first star to puncture a cloudless sky, she'd wished the day would never end.

Are you mad? Kat mumbled, feeling beneath her pillow for her watch. *Everyone's still sleeping. It's – what's the time – Christ!*

They stole out of the dormitory past the room where Mrs Willis, St Mary's' deputy head, and Miss Gordon were still snoring. Creeping along the corridor, a distant clatter from the kitchen signified the first preparations for breakfast. Then, as they padded barefoot into the outside world, Kat was struck by a sudden and unexpected acute awareness of every detail around her. As if the focus of her senses had been sharpened. The gentle freshness of the air as they slipped through the main glass doors in reception. The tantalising dampness beyond of the neatly manicured strip of lawn against her feet. The rubber tang of the plimsolls she held in her hand.

Like co-conspirators, Kat thought, suddenly elated. Partners in crime. It was the two of them against the world. And in that instant she felt closer to Jude than she'd done in months.

Duck – so we won't be seen from the kitchen, Jude instructed in a commanding whisper as she led the way, combat-style, in a crouched run beneath the windows of the centre's administrative office. *Wait a minute, how—* But Jude's only response was a conspiratorial tap to her nose. *Keep down*, she mouthed, with a bold wink. *Don't dawdle. Let's go!*

At the end of the wall the girls slipped on their shoes to make a break for it across the dusty car park separating the main building from the pool area. Less than a minute later they reached the poolside fence. Jude rattled the padlock. *Not to worry*, she grinned. *We can climb over.* To their left was a metal drum that once contained pool chemicals. Though empty, it looked robust enough to stand on. Jude pushed it into position then hopped on and pulled herself up and over the fence. Kat, emboldened by an intoxicating rush of excitement and fear, clambered up after her then hoisted herself over the top and slithered down onto the paving stones the other side. Jude was already crouched down at the water's edge gazing down through the slick surface into the still depths beneath.

Kat sat down by Jude's side and slipped her legs into the water. Cold needled her skin, yet the sensation was not wholly unpleasant. Slowly, she began swinging her feet left then right in a figure of eight, entranced by the tiny eddies the action formed. Taking a seat next to her, Jude began doing the same, and in the early morning stillness Kat imagined she could almost feel the re-plaiting of the fibres in the bond that once so closely bound them. Soul mates, that's how Jude had described it soon after they first met one day in the playground as they sat, side by side, compiling an unofficial audit of their lives so far. And Kat could only agree.

Jude had stood out from day one as different, of course. Everyone else in their class was locally born and bred; Jude was the outsider. Everyone else lived a short drive or train journey outside town; Jude lived a short walk from the school gates. Everyone enjoyed the reassuring predictability of being part of a nuclear family except for Jude, who lived alone with just her mum. Though as Kat would later confide, while Charles remained physically present emotionally he'd walked out on his family many years before – which made her and Jude not so different after all.

In Jude, Kat felt, she'd not only found someone like her who did not fit in but, better still, someone who didn't seem to care. She could still remember the first real test of their friendship when, just before that first Christmas, she was almost grounded by her parents. Rather than catch the usual bus home after school one Friday, she and Jude had gone into town Christmas shopping.

Unable to find a working pay phone to alert Diane to this last minute change of plan, she arrived home two hours late to find her parents about to call the police. They were livid, of course, threatening to go back to driving her to and from school if she couldn't prove herself to be more responsible. And they would have done, too, if Jude hadn't intervened. Sensing Kat was in trouble, she'd rung her house that evening – not to console her friend but to speak to Diane. Kat never discovered quite what was said but Jude, it seemed, had apologised profusely, blaming herself for losing track of time and urging Diane not to treat her too harshly. The unexpectedness of this intervention and its apparent charm seemed to soften Kat's parents' line, leaving Kat awed by her best friend's nerve and grateful for her protection. Which is how, over subsequent months as things got worse at home, she came to see their friendship as daily affirmation that in the end everything would be okay.

A flash of emerald green drew both girls' attention to the centre of the swimming pool. A dragonfly was drowsily skimming the water's oily surface trailing a line of tiny, ever-expanding rings in its wake. For a minute or two they watched the glittering insect in silence until, with a final swoop, it soared sunwards and out of sight. Jude turned to face Kat. *So here we are again, then!* she declared, staring at her companion for an instant before jumping to her feet and tugging her T-shirt up over her head. *What are you waiting for? Let's swim!*

Bending forward to unbutton her shorts, Jude let her clothes slide to the ground. Struggling not to register her surprise that her friend wore no underwear, Kat looked away. Then Jude stepped forwards, lining her feet up carefully on the paving stones that fringed the pool's edge. Standing tall, she looked up towards the sky with outstretched arms to embrace the day. Christ-like, Kat thought, though there was nothing devotional about Jude's nudity which seemed more like a defiant shout. *Geronimo!* Jude cried as she stretched up on her toes then executed a faultless dive into the glassy water leaving her friend alone in the balmy air.

Kat bit her lip, cursing herself for not bringing her swimming things. How she envied the sleek confidence of Jude's body – the fullness of her breasts, her rounded belly, her long legs. She felt the familiar resentment that her own – awkward and childishly thick-set by comparison with its clumsy limbs, oily skin and stubborn hair that never straightened, even with crimping irons – was conspiring against her. She sighed. Because she knew there was nothing else she could do. That of course she must follow Jude's lead: she always did.

Slipping off her dress, Kat unhooked the teen bra Mum had optimistically bought her the previous Christmas, and wriggled out of her M&S pants. Quickly, her self-consciousness outweighing the water's icy bite, she slithered in. As she dived down beneath the surface, her body tingled with pleasure at the water's icy suck and as her head broke the surface a few moments later she could not help but laugh at their recklessness. For it felt good to be alive as she breaststroked towards Jude who was now lying motionless on her back with eyes closed.

As she swam closer, Kat stared in awe at how the hair between her friend's legs glistened like a sea anemone in the early morning sun. How her breasts moved in the soft swell like jelly fish. The way the water's chill made Jude's breathing quick and shallow. The faint flicker every now and then of the lids of eyes. And yet as she lay there, in watery suspension, she looked as comfortable as if she were lying on a mattress. Her lips, slightly parted, imperceptibly twitched into a beatific smile. Relaxed, Jude could almost be mistaken for angelic.

Gently treading water, watching, something deep inside Kat stirred. A curious and unexpected realisation which at once both intrigued and horrified. For she was suddenly aware of an overwhelming sense of desire. A yearning for the sensation of the slippery skin puckering so invitingly towards the nipple's dark pebble. To feel the weight of Jude's smooth, milky breasts in the palm of her hand. *Want to touch?* Jude had opened her eyes and was now watching her, intently. Despite the cold, Kat's cheeks burned. *Sorry*, she mumbled.

For what — looking? There's no law against that, Jude laughed then stopped, abruptly. *Come on*, she added softly. Teasingly. *Don't be embarrassed. It could be fun.*

Confused by her friend's words and alarmed by her own feelings, Kat dipped down beneath the water and swam away, praying that when she re-emerged from her icy submersion the awfulness of what had just happened would have gone. Stroke after stroke, she swam beneath the water's sparkling surface, on then on. Only when Kat's lungs felt fit to burst did she finally surface, panting and flushed. With no idea in which direction she had gone, she was surprised to find herself close to the pool's far side.

Turning to see where Jude was, Kat felt a vague sense of disappointment to see she was now calmly swimming lengths, her bobbing head slick like a seal's in the strengthening sun. Kat knew she couldn't escape the reality of what had just happened, but decided to gamble. Taking a deep breath, she swam slowly but purposefully back towards her friend.

Let's go back to the copse we passed yesterday, Jude called brightly when Kat got close. As if nothing had happened. *They're organising a paper chase. We could skive off and when we get back later say we got lost. Let's take books and lie in the sun.*

Kat smiled with relief.

Come on, then, Jude urged with a sudden grin. *Let's get some breakfast.*

—

With her heart still racing, Katy wakes at nine. She is hunched on her side, her body tense, with her right arm clamped between her thighs and as she frees her hand she can feel her fingertips are wet. Grabbing the sheet from the floor where it has slipped, she covers herself quickly. Her face is hot with shame. Don't let Jude do this to you, she tells herself, fiercely. Don't let her in. Because it wasn't your fault. None of it was anything to do with you.

Suddenly she is sitting upright in bed. The phone in the sitting room is ringing. But though her head now feels clear and her hands no longer shake, she isn't quick enough and by the time she's pulled on the silk dressing gown Michael bought her in Thailand and made it downstairs, whoever it is has rung off leaving their message on the answer phone. Cursing softly, she pulls the phone from its cradle and stares at the screen which shows the last caller's number was withheld: a typical Sally-Anne trick. She decides to call her back quickly to prove she really is at home, poorly, but when she does there's no answer so she leaves a voicemail for Dawn. But before she can pick up her message, two sustained blasts from the front door bell make her drop the phone.

Katy hesitates, struggling to keep calm. Admonishing herself for being so jumpy. It's the postman, probably. A parcel delivery, perhaps. They usually come at this time. If she creeps downstairs she could use the front door peephole just door to be sure. Better sign for it now than have to go to the Parcelforce depot which is miles away in the shadow of Wormwood Scrubs. So softly, she creeps downstairs to the ground floor and slips into the hallway.

Through the whorled glass of the front door the dark outline of the figure beyond makes her chest tighten. With clenched fists she steps forward, oblivious to the whitening of her knuckles as she carefully approaches the door, then pauses. But she has miscalculated. Though she's not turned on the overhead light there is enough daylight coming from the door to the upstairs flat, which she has left open behind her, for the visitor to register her movement. Which is how, before she can even peer through the peephole, a youth's voice is cajoling her to open the front door.

'Just a minute of your time,' the stranger calls. 'That's all it would take to take to change a young girl's life.'

'I'm sorry?' Her voice is faint.

'Sixty seconds, that's all I ask.' Barely aware of what she is doing, Katy secures the chain then opens the front door a crack to see a pale youth with an earnest expression and damp grey eyes whose shoulder-length dark hair hangs lank in a thin ponytail. He is almost good-looking despite his pockmarked skin. Scars from an accident of some kind, perhaps, or maybe teenage acne. A charity T-shirt which hangs low below his black jeans – Action Against Abuse, reads the logo beneath a simple drawing of interlocked hands and a pyramid of three capital As. 'Do you support good causes?' he purrs, swiftly following through.

Katy frowns. 'I... well, of course I do.' She despises doorstep charity fundraisers even more than the ones who hunt in packs for direct debit mandates along the nearby high street. 'But I don't like being—'

'Good for you!' he declares. 'It's a dreadful thing isn't it, teen rape?'

Katy reaches out an arm to brace herself against the door-frame. 'Sorry?'

'Rape.' The chugger frowns, casually resting an unexpectedly large hand on the side of the front door. 'Of young teens below the age of sexual consent. Typically, by an older predatory male—'

The ground seems to shift and Katy finds herself gulping for air. 'No,' she gasps.

'Yes,' he corrects. 'And I'm afraid it is more common than many of us would like to think. Which is why none of us can afford to ignore the psychological trauma – the upset victims go through – and the need they have for intimate and sustained support. Which is where the charity I represent, Action Against Abuse—' at this he points with a nicotine-stained forefinger to the logo emblazoned across his chest '—a.k.a. Triple A comes in.'

'I'm sorry, but—'

'Triple A works with young teenage girls who've been the victims of—'

'I said, I'm sorry but—'

'—sexual assault, providing a place of support and refuge—'

'No!' Katy cries, finally reconnected to her senses. Shifting her grip, she grasps the side of the front door. Heaving it to, it crushes his hand against the frame. 'I'm sorry, but I don't pledge money like this, not to just anyone who comes knocking on my door. I just don't, OK?'

'Fuck you, bitch.' The youth's exclamation is so unexpected she wonders for a moment whether she has heard it right. Yet there is more as the shadow on her doorstep bends down and pushes open the letterbox. 'But judging by the state of your door I guess I'm not the first and won't be the last to tell you that, you selfish cunt.'

As the metal flap of the letterbox snaps to, the phlegm-shovelling sound of a deep throat clearing is swiftly followed by a sharp spit and then, some seconds later, the clatter of the front gate swinging to. Stunned, Katy sinks back against the wall but as her body makes contact her knees buckle and she slips down onto the floor. Has he gone, she wonders. Her heart is pounding and her breath now comes in short, sharp gasps. Or is he still out there, waiting to burst inside with further abuse?

Too frightened at first to crack the door open to check, she sits slumped on her haunches, waiting for the fear to subside, for her strength to gather so she can slowly pull herself upright to glimpse through the peephole into the world outside. When she does so at last, it looks no different to normal. She bites her lip. *Judging by the state of your door*, he said. But what did that mean? And then she remembered. The youths from the night before. What else had they done?

Taking a deep breath, Katy releases the catch. Peeping through the crack to make sure the coast is clear, she frees the chain then steps outside. The porch is empty and the narrow strip of front garden appears to be so, too. More confident, now, she steps onto the front path. The first thing she sees is a gobbet of phlegm that sits slug-like on the paving stone before her, glistening in the morning sun. The second is the scattering of broken egg shells and congealed yolk close by. Slowly turning around, she refocuses on the front door. Reads the letters. Translates the literal meaning of it.

Fuck You Bitch! is scrawled across the front door in red spray paint.

Stumbling backwards, Katy steps on something sharp. With a sob she looks down to see broken glass from the porch light which has been smashed. Stepping back onto the wooden door step, she reaches out to balance herself as she examines the pad of her bare foot. Carefully, she extracts a small shard of glass and rubs away the blood which is starting to well.

Who could have done this, she wonders, dully. The youths from last night, of course. First her car and then this, but why? Reaching out her hand she gives the first letter sprayed onto the door a tentative rub, but it won't even smudge. It will take more than a few minutes with some detergent and warm water, she thinks, tears welling in her eyes. It will need repainting. Card Room Green. That was the ridiculous name of the paint they'd used when it was redone just last year. From Farrow & Ball.

'Everything OK?'

It's the maternity leave lawyer from next door. Dressed in a pair of Sweaty Betty capris and a tight fitting vest, she has looped back her strawberry blonde hair into a thick plait. The only evidence of the slumbering occupant of the buggy she is pushing is the chubby foot that dangles from beneath a pink cotton sarong pegged across the front. Late for some coffee morning with the yummy mummies, probably, Katy thinks, noting how the woman has barely slowed her pace.

'All fine, thanks,' she calls to her neighbour with a plastic grin. 'Just some kids mucking about – you know what they're like.'

Unsure what else to say the other woman offers up a sympathetic grimace then quickens her pace, her mind already elsewhere. As is Katy's, too, as she tries to distract herself with the practicalities of the next things she'll need to do. Phone the insurance company about the car. Find someone to repaint the door. Get more paint. Noting her headache has returned, she quickly rubs the tears from her eyes then retreats inside. Upstairs once more, she gulps down two more Nurofen before heading into Michael's office.

It's not a room Katy uses much, or likes. L-shaped with a large airing cupboard built into the corner adjoining the bathroom, two of its walls are filled with floor to ceiling shelves which groan with books and files creating a hemmed in, claustrophobic feel. Any remaining wall space is crammed with Michael's photographs. Most date back to before he and Katy met; all feature the faces of strangers. Except one, on the window sill – a framed picture of a dour looking woman with scraped-back hair and a pale face. Her in-law in waiting, Jean.

How different they are, Katy ponders for a moment, both in nature and in temperament. For Michael's easy going approach to life was one of the first things that had attracted her to him. Along with his innate ability to empathise with others and a seemingly total lack of awareness of his looks. More like his father, then, though she would never know for sure. Because Michael's dad died during the first year of his A level studies, throwing his academic career into disarray and prompting a restless few years spent running with the party crowd in various Mediterranean resorts, Goa and Thailand. It's why Jean Ross eventually agreed to help put him through art school. Anything to have him back home.

Unable to find the insurance documents in any of the desk drawers, Katy turns on the computer. Gazing out of the window as the screen flickers into life, she watches a tall woman with short cropped hair hanging out washing in the garden directly behind theirs. At her feet, a small child wearing just a nappy sits playing with a cardboard box of pegs. Will this be her in a few years time, she wonders: a stay at home mum with a fractious toddler, the career that was starting to blossom on hold? Or will she be another yummy mummy, smug and secure in the knowledge her job remains open for her to return to? Comforted by the conviction that this is really what she wants?

Noticing how her hands have once more naturally migrated down to lightly rest on her belly, Katy quickly moves them back onto the desk's top, placing them palms down. The polished surface, which is solid and smooth, feels dependable and reassuring. As her attention drifts back to the illuminated screen before her she remembers the call she missed earlier, picks up the phone, presses the short code then raises the handset to her ear.

'Phone tennis! Don't you just love it?' a woman purrs. Not her boss. Someone else. 'So sorry to hear you're not well. Heavy night last night with mommy dearest, was it? Poor you. So, Kat. I just had this crazy idea. As you're having a bit of a duvet day, I thought to myself: why don't we do it? You know, get together? Meet up. Right here, right now. Well, some time later today, at least. What do you think? Are you feeling up to it?'

As the mobile slips from Katy's grasp, she scans the room – half-expecting to catch an unexpected observer, watching. Hurrying into the sitting room, she peers outside.

If she looks to the right she can see the street which looks the same as usual. Cars are parked nose to tail each side and, as usual for outside rush hour, the regular pulse of traffic is moving freely. To her left, a blue-rinsed retiree two houses down is watering her front garden. The elderly man who lives in the house opposite is trimming his privet hedge.

Everything seems normal. But if this is just an ordinary day how can Jude possibly know her home number? The same way she found out my number at work, Katy concludes, miserably. Though surely no one at work, not even Dawn, would be stupid enough to give out personal contact details without permission.

That voice, she thinks. A sugary purr with a West Country lilt. A shared joke, the origin of which she struggles to recall which she once laughingly described as 'a little bit Caramel Bunny'. The charm of which was only ever short-lived. For it was the voice Jude always used when she was after something. Like sunbathing in Coulters Copse.

Katy stares blankly at the screen, idly picking the cuticle around her thumb. Barely noticing the welling blood as her attention is drawn to the winking icon before her confirming receipt of new mail. Hours seems to pass until she can resist no more. Because even before she clicks on the Inbox and opens the message, she fears she's been out-manoeuvred. Knows it, too, as soon as she sees the message is from a Hotmail account in the name of JDavies. Spelled with an i-e-s, of course.

'Your place or mine?' reads the subject line.

Leaning back in the chair, Katy rubs the knotted scar tissue on her hand. There is, it seems, nowhere to hide. No place left to run. Whatever Jude wants she will get. Just like she has always done, as the old anger buried deep inside her gut starts to stir.

A beat later, puppet fingers dance across the keyboard as she clicks on the blank message then drafts her reply. 'Sure, let's meet,' she types. 'How about down by the river? Three o'clock by the bench outside the playground, opposite St Paul's boat club.' A busy stretch of the riverside footpath and neutral ground, Katy reasons. Better there than to invite Jude to the house. Wearied by the long-dreaded exchange, she reviews the message and then, before allowing herself a chance to give in to second thoughts, quickly presses Send.

Within a few minutes another blank email lands in the in box. Again, the message is in the subject line. 'It's a date,' it reads. 'TTFN'.

Cradling her head in her hands Katy lets her full weight rest on the desktop as, with eyes screwed tight shut, she tries to ignore the tightening of her throat. Her chest aches like it does after a long run. Her mouth is dust-dry. What's that relaxation technique the doctors at the County taught her? *My left hand is feeling heavy*, she thinks. *My arms and legs are heavy and warm…* But though she tries to remember the words are quickly crowded out.

Soft yet insistent, soaring then swooping, the echo of Jude's voice circles the inside of Katy's head like a bird of prey.

Chapter 7

Guildford, September 1988

'Everyone, give a warm welcome to Judith Davies who starts with us today fresh from secondary school in Portsmouth.' As Miss Willis beamed at the upturned faces of 4W the girls, as one, turned to stare. Most nodded or smiled, a few said hello. Then some smart Alice at the back intoned in a sing-song voice: 'Hey Jude'.

Biting her tongue, she smiled. 'Hi,' is all she can think of to say, but it was all that was required.

Miss Willis adjusted her glasses then, with an encouraging nod, indicated the empty seat which she should take next to a sulky-looking girl called Katherine Parker. The desk had been left vacant by a Gillian Scott-Warden, Miss Willis explained. Her father, some army bigwig, had recently been posted abroad and taken his family with him. As Jude put down her bag, her new neighbour offered her a watery smile then looked away. And so it was until mid-morning break when, with a clatter, the class rose to its feet.

It was raining outside and the girls had a half hour of free time which they could either spend in the classroom, the main hall or the library. Most rose and left the room but a handful, including Katherine, chose to stay. A tall girl with a shining helmet of bobbed hair and a beak-like nose sauntered over to where Jude was sitting then hovered by her side.

'So where were you before, then?' she barked. The voice was flat. Nasal.

Seated at her desk, Jude continued to flick through the latest edition of *NME* which she had lifted earlier from Dave's bag. Only when her interrogator showed no sign of leaving did she eventually reply. 'Just outside Portsmouth,' she said, without looking up.

'The Royal Naval School?' The girl responds, knowledgeably. 'I've a friend there, her name is—'

'No. The County.'

'The County?' The girl hesitated, clearly confused. 'Is that a new one?'

Jude looked up defensively, willing herself to remain calm. Aloof. 'Actually, I think it was built in the Sixties,' she said simply. 'I doubt you'd know it.'

'Ah, a comprehensive,' lisped a second girl. Dumpy and plain, her oily hair was tied back into a single wide plait, and when she opened her mouth Jude saw from the metalwork inside she was wearing a serious orthodontic brace. Noticing the direction of Jude's gaze, the girl quickly covered her mouth with her hand then rubbed her nose.

'Yes,' said Jude.

'That figures,' commented the girl with the beak.

'I beg your pardon,' Jude's voice was a delicate balance between sarcasm and politeness as she rose to her feet and looked down on the girl. 'But did you say something, Gonzo?'

'Um. No. Not really,' the girl muttered, taking a step back.

Jude turned to stare inquiringly at the girl with the lisp. 'Anything else I can help you with, Metal Mickey?' she asked, lightly. The girl's cheeks blushed scarlet as she struggled to find her voice, and failed. 'Now, where was I?' Jude sighed as if to herself, resuming her seat and finding her place on the page. Feet shuffle as the girls move away but she did not look up, leaving it a full minute before raising her eyes to find the room empty apart from Katherine who was now sitting at a desk near the door reading a book. Looking up, the girl glanced in Jude's direction.

'I'd watch out for Deb – sorry, Gonzo – if I were you,' Katherine smiled. 'She might look a bit geeky but she's a real cow. A lot of the girls hang out with her because they don't want to cross her. Ruth, on the other hand, just runs with the crowd.'

Jude's hackles softened, but only slightly. 'Is that right?'

'It is, yes.' Katherine snapped shut her book. 'And I should know,' the girl added. But rather than get up to leave, she twisted her body round to face her. 'It's a fix, isn't it?' she continues, nodding towards the open pages on the desk in front of Jude. The latest weekly chart showed Phil Collins was still number one with *A Groovy Kind of Love*. 'I mean, who buys this stuff, anyway?'

'I guess it depends on whether you judge decent music by whether or not it makes it into the pop charts,' Jude shot back, instantly regretting the sharpness in her voice when she saw Katherine's wounded expression. They are roughly the same height, she noticed for the first time, and share similar colouring, too, though her own hair is a couple of shades lighter. Her own weight, Jude quickly calculates, is probably six pounds lighter.

'Actually, I like Elvis Costello and REM,' Katherine replies. 'The Red Hot Chili Peppers, too. I was just trying to make conversation but if that's how you feel, well—'

'No. Wait,' Jude cut in, suddenly feeling foolish. This girl was only being friendly. Besides, if Deb and Ruth were typical of her new classmates she needed an ally.

Katherine waited for Jude to continue but their conversation was cut short by the sound of a bell and the return of their classmates. It wasn't until lunchtime that they had an opportunity to pick up where they left off in the dining hall.

Standing alone clutching her tray, Jude watched as Katherine carefully positioned herself beside her in the lunch queue. 'Not sitting with your friends, then?' she said, gesturing towards the dozen or so girls from their class sitting at the table nearest the door. They were talking vigorously amongst themselves as they ate, glancing in her direction every now and then.

'Apparently not,' Katherine replied, shuffling towards the food counter. 'Watching Deb Malton stuffing her face is not exactly good for the appetite.'

Taking a plate from the pile, Jude held it out towards the dinner lady, a plump woman with a ball of long, grey hair secured by a hairnet beneath a small white hat. The woman's cheeks, pink and flaccid, were the perfect complement to the unappetising slabs of cold meat pie she was dishing up. Outside the clouds had cleared and the rooftops glistened damply in the early autumn sun.

'Where do you live?' asked Katherine as they headed towards an empty table by the window a few minutes later.

'In town,' Jude answered vaguely, bracing herself for the follow-up but none came. Surprised, she pressed on. 'We've only been here since July. Mum fancied a change so decided we should move. She used to live here a while ago.'

'And what about your dad?'

'Who?'

'Did he come too?'

'He's dead.' As always, Jude relished the familiar and perverse pleasure that lay in the embarrassed silence that always follows this revelation.

'Oh. Sorry.' Katherine looked genuinely contrite, and once more Jude felt an unexpected stab of guilt.

'Don't be, I never knew him,' she replied, softening her tone. 'There was a car crash – it happened just after I was born.' She cleared her throat as she feels her eyes start to prick. Better to change the subject, and fast. 'And I suppose you live with Mummy and Daddy in a rose-clad cottage in some quaint village surrounded by rolling hills? Got your own pony, have you?'

'Actually, no.' It's Katherine's turn to sound snippy this time and Jude noted that she had clearly touched a nerve. 'We do live in the country, but I hate horses – not that it's any of your business. I don't see why I should have to apologise for my home or family to anyone.' Her eyes looked watery. 'Besides,' she added, looking away. 'Money can't buy happiness.'

'Perhaps not.' Jude spoke carefully, testing the ground. 'But it can help.'

'Does it? Really?' declared Kat, turning back to face Jude with narrowed eyes. 'Well that may be what you think, but I know different. My dad may put on the stiff upper lip, but I know for a fact he's as miserable as hell with Mum and for all her vain attempts to pretend nothing's wrong, Mum's got a broken heart.' She bit her lip, evidently regretting her sudden outburst.

Jude stared at her in genuine surprise. 'Sorry.'

'What for?'

'For being...' Jude thought for a moment, then leaned forward and grinned. 'Look, I'm only here because Mum applied for an academic scholarship, OK? We couldn't afford the fees. And I've been dreading everyone looking down their noses at me just because we can't afford to buy the poncy school uniform new, or because we live in a modern semi.'

'Well none of that bothers me,' Katherine replied, brusquely. 'I like people for who they are. Unlike many people here.' She waved towards the tables of girls now finishing their meals and starting to clear their plates. Some were the daughters of upwardly mobile professionals with jobs in London, others the offspring of local businessmen made good. All basked in the smug halo of parental affluence. 'Deb Malton, for one,' she added, tightly.

As Jude wondered what untold history the girl had with Gonzo, a self-conscious movement drew her gaze to the inside of Katherine's right arm where a latticework of faded pink scratch marks scarred the pale crease of skin. Eczema, Jude noted. 'Look,' she said conspiratorially, 'I'll keep your family life quiet if you don't tell anyone I'm on an assisted place. Is that a deal?'

Katherine looked anxious for a moment then, catching the glint in Jude's eye, nodded. Without a word, the pair then rose to their feet, scraped the debris from their plates into a large open-lidded bin before stacking the dirty utensils on a nearby trolley, then left the dining hall, arm in arm.

Chapter 8

London, July 2013

Worlds collide on the bleached paving stones of the Thames-side walkway where it narrows to become the riverside path as Katy hurries towards their meeting.

Pallid office workers with rolled up sleeves stand sipping ice-cold beers toe to toe with muscular workmen whose bronzed chests and dusty boots signal their imminent return to nearby building sites. Earnest mums compare notes over glasses of rosé as their limp wards doze in buggies huddled in the scant shade of a solitary tree. Students sprawl across the threadbare grass careless of their discarded bikes. There are dogs to negotiate, too: mongrel breeds that are overcooked and tetchy.

Arriving early at her destination, Katy takes up position on the far side of the seat taking care to avoid a splatter of murky white deposited by a passing pigeon. She has allowed herself a good half hour to get to the place she agreed with Jude – a solitary bench in the no man's land between two popular riverside pubs just before the path dog-legs behind an exclusive line of waterside mansions with plastered facades like wedding cakes. But nervous energy has made her walk so fast that she's reached the river at Hammersmith Bridge with ten minutes to spare.

The sun's glare has made the metal arm rest too hot to touch so she folds her hands in her lap, overheated and self-conscious in the outfit she's chosen to wear. 'The fine art of defensive dressing' Mum would call it when, as a child, Katy would spend what seemed like hours watching her carefully back brush then style her hair and make up her face before going out for the evening. Katy knew that the clothes she chose for her meeting with Jude could magnify or undermine her. So she is wearing plimsolls, a favourite pair of navy silk trousers and a white linen shirt, its sleeves loosely rolled, which she's left untucked to disguise her thickening waist.

Shifting position on the bench, Katy shoots a glance back the way she's just come. It is an ideal vantage point, she decides. There's a clear view of the footpath in either direction which will provide her with ample time to prepare for Jude's approach. But for now the path in either direction is empty. She relaxes, slightly.

In the tiny playground behind her, a small boy standing behind the turrets of a once brightly-painted wooden pirate ship sings to himself as he stares at the world through a toy telescope the wrong way around. The Polish woman seated next to his empty pushchair speaks loudly into a mobile phone while at her feet two pigeons perform a drunken sword dance around the broken neck of a beer bottle. Katy stands up and walks over to the river wall. The slate-grey bricks that line its top have been smoothed by the years and are warm to touch.

On the opposite side of the river, a line of trees marks the boundary of St Paul's school playing fields. She stares for a moment at four figures in lycra shorts and wellingtons on the shore below readying a rowing boat for launch from the muddy bank, their tanned arms glistening in the sun. Warmed by the simple innocence of this scene, her body slackens and her gaze dips downwards to the water's surface, brown and eddying.

The current at this particular point of the river runs deceptively fast and, though uninviting as she lowers her face to inhale the compelling cocktail of mud, diesel and salt she remembers how much she loves living by the river. How it almost feels like living by the sea. The light is different, somehow; the sense of powerlessness in the face of a superior force sharper. Just the previous week a thirteen-year-old boy had jumped into the water not far from here – whether as a reckless act of bravado, an act of desperation or to cool off from the sun, it's still not clear. He drowned, becoming merely another statistic – one of a hundred or so people to be smothered each year by the city's watery pulse – when his body, bloated and bruised, washed up three days later by Greenwich pier.

Resuming her position on the bench, Katy registers the footpath is still empty in either direction. Oblivious to the heat, she shivers as a memory of the day before she last saw Jude stirs.

–

It was later on in the day of their dawn swim that it happened. On the return walk to Gallows Hill from Coulters Copse. They'd been sunbathing. Then when it was time to leave, Jude, first to the clearing's edge, was irritated Kat was taking too long. So she had waited, but only long enough for Kat to reach her side before setting off once more at a brisker pace.

With her head now pounding, Kat stumbled along a few steps behind until the edge of the copse where shade gave way to solar glare and the track grew more overgrown. Dizzy, her pace slowed further as she tried to sidestep the thorny gorse tails lashing backwards in Jude's wake. And it was while waiting for the foliage to resettle that a backward glance towards the copse shook her to the core. Because there was a dark shape standing at its edge in a space she was sure had been empty just a minute before. A solitary figure, observing their retreat.

Just a gap in the foliage – an upright sliver of darkness between the trees, she'd reassured herself. Or the shaded trunk of a tree. Yet they'd walked just a little bit too far for her to be sure.

Spinning around, back towards Jude, Kat noticed with a jolt of panic that her friend was almost out of view. Checking the copse once more she could see the figure was still there, though now it appeared to be standing in partial sunlight. No longer a shadow. Definitely a person, watching. As she broke into a run to close the gap between them, Kat begged her friend to wait. But Jude wouldn't listen as she tried to tell her what she'd seen. *Quit whining,* she'd snapped, turning away. *Always whining, you tedious child.* As Kat's eyes welled, Jude moved on.

Ahead lay a dusty sea of heather and gorse punctuated by dazzling explosions of yellow. And as the distance between them widened Kat's gaze skimmed the Punch Bowl's tree-lined rim, its outline sharpened by the afternoon sun. Above her head against a blameless sky drifted two specks buoyed by an imperceptible zephyr. She watched for a moment, waiting in vain for the dive-bombing of some unknown earthbound prey. Looking back the copse, now empty, seemed a shimmering dream. Looking forward, Jude was gone.

Struggling to rearrange her cotton dress to tug free the damp fabric from her heat-swollen body, Kat's attention was drawn to a cloud of something swarming upwards a short distance ahead. Curious, she crept a few paces forwards – close enough to identify them as flying ants without stumbling into the fray.

Repelled and intrigued, she stared in awe at their swollen bodies. Their wings glistening slick like oil. The nuptial flight, Kat knew from books she'd read. The single day each summer when ordinary ants magically take to the skies on wings of gossamer specially grown for the occasion. Having mated in flight the young queens, once fertilised, bite off their own wings before resuming their normal pedestrian guise ready to start nests of their own – capable of laying eggs for up to fifteen years. The males, though, would be consigned to an earthly death soon after mating. *Proof there is such a thing as justice in this world,* Jude had said, which had made Kat laugh. But now she was awed by the magical brutality at her feet.

Silent and unmoving, she watched an ant scale the rubber toe cap of her plimsoll, stirring a distant memory of another long, hot summer's day and a pair of strawberry-patterned sandals. How hard she'd concentrated on the lining up of each shoe on that sun-baked afternoon years before – gently nudging one forward then the other, side by side, to face the grey slab of stone at the canal side's edge. A shake of her foot was all it took to toss the ant off her shoe and Kat watched with a curious sense of satisfaction as it darted in frantic circles before finding its bearings and scuttling away. A bit like her friendship with Jude.

For there were times when she knew Jude was toying with her – a truth that made her face burn with shame. Because theirs wasn't a friendship, was it? She was welcome in Jude's orbit only on Jude's terms for as long as she served a useful purpose. A thought that made Kat loathe herself more than she hated Jude and despise how overawed she'd been by her so-called best friend; intimidated, too. Sometimes, even, a little bit scared. Though her friendship with Jude wasn't just one way, was it? Hadn't Jude given her the confidence she needed to carry on? Wouldn't being without her be like losing a limb? Jude did care, and Kat needed Jude – for now, at least.

It was getting late but blocking Kat's way was the swarm. With dense clumps of gorse either side of the footpath, she had no choice but to run through it. So taking a deep breath and covering her mouth and nose with her hand she counted – three, two, one – then charged full pelt into the ants' midst with eyes screwed shut, stopping only once she was a good ten paces the other side. One or two ants clung to her arms and the skirt of her sun dress but she was otherwise unscathed.

With a shake of her head, she brushed herself down before completing the rest of her walk back to Gallows Hill fuelled by a curious sense of triumph.

–

'Bench, wall, bench – got ants in our pants, have we?'

The voice is familiar yet different, weathered by the passing years. The laugh a dry, humourless sound. Both make Katy spin round on the bench with a start to see a slim woman dressed in a dark silk skirt and scarlet, sleeveless top. Freckles betray the coarsening texture of Jude's suntanned skin. Her hair, once long and jet-black, is lightly flecked with grey and cropped short. Her mouth is carefully painted the same colour as her top and toe nails. But when she takes off her sunglasses, a pair of oversized ovals that dwarf her face, the familiar stare is piercing like sunshine on wet slate.

How long she's dreaded this moment, Katy thinks. And yet she is flushed by a fleeting stab of smugness. For though they are the same age a stranger observing she and Jude would surely put them at least five years apart, if not more – in Katy's favour. The moment of triumph quickly evaporates, however, as she registers the other woman's gaze deftly frisk her own body. The barely perceptible shift in Jude's expression. Yet it is enough to produce in Katy, even twenty years on, that familiar feeling of discomfort as she feels as unsophisticated and gauche as the child she was when they first met.

Without thinking, she raises her hand then brushes with her lips the barely perceptible knot of scar tissue.

'I thought we agreed the bench at three,' Jude observes coolly as she sits down in the position Katy has just vacated. Then she pats the empty space to her left hand side with an immaculately manicured hand, as if she owns the space.

'We did!' Katy lets slip a nervous laugh. Jude looks OK, doesn't she? Whatever happened... she was – is – OK.

'Well I've been waiting a quarter of an hour and when you did finally come you acted all antsy. And yes,' Jude adds before Katy can ask. 'I've been watching you, Kat Parker.'

Katy's throat tightens. 'It's only just three now, so I don't know what you're talking about.' She hopes she sounds calm despite the volcanic forces now stirring deep inside. 'Look.' Holding out her watch, Katy notices that the second hand is still. As if her world stopped at one minute to three.

'No matter,' Jude cries with a magnanimous wave of a mani-cured hand. Square-tipped nails the colour of burnt rose petals glisten in the afternoon sun. 'Come on. Sit down. Take the weight off your feet!'

Katy does as she is told, inwardly cursing her decision to concede her position on the bench. Where she now has to sit, the sun shines straight into her eyes. In her rush to leave the flat she forgot her sunglasses, too, so now she's no choice but to use her hand for shade.

Jude sits in silence for a few minutes gazing out across the river. Katy stares ahead trying not to look at her but finds the temptation impossible to resist.

Pretending to follow the path of a river cruiser, she turns her head just far enough towards Jude to scrutinise her profile. Before she can help herself, however, her eyes are mapping the rounded contours of her companion's breasts. The absence of any formal support beneath the spaghetti straps of Jude's top. The unmistakable outline of the nipples rubbing against silk. Observations that make Katy's pulse race and she hates herself for it. Despises the sudden, unwanted memory of the creamy softness her friend's skin once had. The soft, floral smell of her hair. The smooth firmness of her lips.

Unbearably hot all of a sudden, Katy scoops her hair from her face, shakes her head then lets it fall loose once more. Clearing her throat, she stares down at the ground where the battalion of ants is working to transport a discarded crust of bread to a destination unknown. A beat later, the other woman turns towards Katy with a wry smile.

'So here we are then,' Jude declares, stretching out her legs to slip off her sandals and brown her feet in the sun. 'Thrown together by fate!'

Perched stiffly on the edge of the bench with legs crossed, Katy's face pricks with sweat. Why am I here? What does she want from me? They are sitting side by side looking straight ahead towards the river, but as time opens up like a giant fissure between them her breath starts to quicken. Stay calm, she tells herself, forcefully. Don't be the first to break. But then, at last, before she can stop herself the stand-off is over. 'Well then. Jude. So. What do you want?'

'That's not very friendly, is it, when you've not seen someone for – oh, what must it be…?' Jude pauses, as if struggling with the maths before turning back towards Katy. 'Feels like a lifetime, right? Look, I just wanted to get back in touch, OK? So come on, you first. What have you been up to?'

'Oh, you know…' Katy mumbles. Struggling to find the right words feels like speaking a foreign a language.

'Well you seem to have done all right for yourself.' There's a hint of sarcasm in Jude's voice. With another broad sweep of her hand she gestures towards the iced facades of the five-storey houses nearby, then sweeps her hand towards the distant floodlights of Craven Cottage just visible at the point where the river bends out of site to the east. 'Fulham's a pleasant part of the world to be in, I'd imagine. If you can afford it.'

Fulham? But this is Hammersmith, Katy thinks. Chiswick, almost. How can Jude know where she lives? 'Well, yes. Although I share with a friend.' Oh for Christ's sake, girl, Katy silently chides. Why are you making excuses? What's wrong with admitting to Jude that yes, by many people's standards I am doing OK?

'And your boyfriend – is he… nice?' Jude reaches into her tan shoulder bag and pulls out a packet of cigarettes. 'Come on, now, don't be coy. As I said: I've been watching you, Kat Parker.' Katy struggles for breath for a moment as she tries to suppress a sudden and overwhelming desire to cry out as if in pain. What the hell can Jude know about her and Michael? How can she know what he looks like? 'Because it's obvious,' Jude presses on, seemingly oblivious to Katy's distress. 'You look so loved up. And who can blame you – he's certainly a looker, your man, isn't he? But enough of love. Tell me more. About you and the rest of your life. Like those dreams you always had to go to art school and become a graphic artist. How did that one turn out?'

Sweat snakes down the left side of Katy's face, momentarily criss-crossing the telltale scar beneath her left eye. But she doesn't dare wipe it away. Because even something like that could be seen as a sign of weakness. Be strong, she tells herself. She's doing this on purpose, just like she always did. To control my feelings. But I am older and wiser now, the voice inside her urges as she forces herself to regulate her breath. So no, I won't give in. Though I must respond. I can't leave the gaping void between us unfilled.

'You found out my work number so you must know what I do,' she blurts. Too petulant, she silently curses. Childish.

'Now, now. Don't get tetchy,' Jude chuckles. 'I'm genuinely interested. So come on, tell me. Are you a designer?'

'Kind of.' Too late, the words are out.

'Sorry?'

'I'm in design,' Katy corrects herself, quickly wiping the dampness from her face with the back of her hand. 'Design management,' she adds, needlessly.

Jude snorts. 'You don't sound too sure—'

'So go on: thrill me,' Katy snaps, angry before she can control it. 'How's the acting – that's what you always wanted to do, wasn't it? And were more than well enough qualified for, too. Been on *The Bill*, yet? Or is am' dram' more your level?'

Despite the harshness of these words, Jude laughs. 'Come on. I'm not having a go, honest. It's just ironic, isn't it. How things turn out? Me?' She lights a cigarette then inhales, deeply. 'I'm a bookkeeper. Come on Kat, why the sad face? It suits me fine. I'd have been hopeless at learning lines. Anyway, I needed something I could train for part-time when James was small.'

'Sorry?'

Jude hesitates, savouring the moment. 'My boy!' she exclaims.

Katy wonders what she can mean. An affectionate name for her lover, perhaps. 'Sorry?'

'Well, not so little now. Never doubt it when anyone tells you to savour every moment. How nowadays they grow up so fast. He's in his mid-twenties!'

'Oh.' Words seem hard to find as Katy's sluggish brain fumbles with the logistics.

'So,' Jude continues breezily. 'Not yet married, but soon to be?' She points at the third finger on Katy's left hand.

'No. You?' Katy quickly bats back, preoccupied by the maths of it as desperate thoughts career around her head. Mid-twenties. Which meant... no, it couldn't be. Because that would mean she'd had a baby some time during the months following the last time they'd seen each other. But she'd have known Jude was expecting a baby, wouldn't she?

'Briefly. But things didn't work out. He was jealous of James. When Steve and I met, James was ten, you see. They never took to each other and Steve grew jealous. Kept telling me lies about things James had done, or said. Like having two kids, really. That said, I suppose it always was going to be tough.' Jude locks gazes with Katy then narrows her eyes. 'What with James's dad never being on the scene.'

'He wasn't?' Katy responds on automatic pilot, her voice a whisper. No Jude, no. It wasn't... You weren't... Because it would have come out if you had been. There would have been newspaper reports. Police. Christ, how her head now aches.

'No.' Jude's expression taunts Katy, accusingly.

'So, um. Where was your boy born?'

Jude shoots Katy an arch smile. 'You mean when, right?'

Katy's stomach lurches at the unspoken question that now hangs above her head like a sword she dares not grasp. She tried to help, honestly she did. Tried to stop it. But she was only a child. What else could she do?

'I got pregnant,' Jude continues, slowly, 'around the last time I saw you. Just before we... moved away.'

Katy looks away for a moment and across the river without taking in the view, blinking her eyes wildly against the piercing light that skitters off the river's surface. Then she stares down at her lap, noticing for the first time how carefully each of them seem to have positioned themselves. As if to minimise the chance of direct physical contact, or even the unwitting exchange of a stray fibre.

Like two islands, she thinks, scrutinising a whisker of cotton that's begun to unravel from the hem of her shirt. That's what we are. Though both of us are inextricably joined beneath the surface. Because of what happened.

Was that why Jude hadn't wanted to speak to her after the incident? Why she and her mum had moved away? It was hideous. Overwhelming. And, in a curious way, reassuring. For she feared the worst during those long and lonely months that followed and now she knows she'd been right. It was true. But what to say? Sorry couldn't start to cover it. Katy's head spins for a moment. 'I think I need something to drink. No… water, I mean,' she rasps as, with a laugh, Jude's gaze darts towards the nearest pub. Standing up, she sways slightly, cursing her decision to skip breakfast. When am I going to stop feeling like this, the voice inside her wails. 'I'm sorry, I'm not feeling well. It's the… heat.'

Jude slips on her sandals and rises to her feet. 'I ought to be getting on, too,' she declares, checking her watch. 'Things to do. People to see. But listen, there's still so much to catch up on, don't you think? We really must do this again.' Reaching out she grasps Katy's arm, her painted nails digging firmly into the skin. Then, a beat later, she is swooping towards Katy to kiss her.

They embrace, and the mechanical convention of it is momentarily distracting as Katy finds herself craving for an instant a long-forgotten cocktail of high street cosmetics and cheap shampoo. But, instead, a heady blast of Chanel No 5 assaults her as cheek brushes cheek and Jude lets slip her parting words. Imparted in barely a whisper as the woman's lips skim Katy's ear.

'Because we've unfinished business, you and I,' she murmurs in barely a whisper as her lips brush Katy's ear. 'Because I know what you did. Because you owe me.' With that Jude turns to leave. Shrugs her bag higher onto her shoulder. Starts walking away – down the Thames path, Chiswick-bound. The opposite direction from which Katy has come.

Only then, as Katy struggles to digest the meaning of it all, does she glimpse the implication of what's just happened. What can she mean by *unfinished business*, she wonders, still reeling from the intensity of their encounter. Still torn by the mix of emotions she feels observing Jude's retreat. Registering the care with which Jude holds herself; the meticulous swing of her hips. As, with a hammer blow, her face starts to burn with shame. For what happened that day was down to her. She is the one to blame. Always the weaker of the two. The follower. The one who ran away.

With a start, Katy tugs free the mobile phone now ringing in her pocket and presses it to her ear.

'Katy?' The sound of Michael's voice feels like salvation. 'How are you doing?'

'Fine,' she lies, quickening her pace as she hurries back towards the line of pubs, the bridge and the main road beyond that will lead her back home. 'I'm down by the river. Just popped out for some fresh air. But my headache's coming back, so I'm on my way back to have a lie down.'

'Take it easy,' he soothes. 'Go back to bed if you need to, or chill in the bath. I'll see you in a bit, OK? Won't be late, I promise.'

The afternoon drinkers who throng the river walkway in even greater numbers now, are faceless obstacles to be sidestepped, overtaken, and pushed by as she retraces her steps. Desperate to be back indoors she strides on, oblivious to irritation or complaint; her head churning. Because at least she knows now, for sure, that something bad happened to Jude. That if she hadn't done it, it would have been her. And she feels vindicated. It was rotten luck she'd not got help in time, that's all. Fate made her take the wrong path.

Then Katy frowns, struggling as she always does to recall the precise sequence of events. Angry at the ragged holes in her memory. Guilty, as always, at the fleeting thought that what happened was some kind of payback for how mean Jude had been. The not knowing, she decides, turning into her street: it's the not knowing what happened that's been the real burden.

It takes a moment or two to open the front door of the flat some fifteen minutes later, as someone has pushed the post and a copy of a West London free sheet beneath it. Bending down to pick up both, Katy catches sight of the paper's front page. Schoolgirl Raped, the headline blares. A coincidence, that's all, she reasons, grimly. Nevertheless, it fells her like a punch to the solar plexus. As she slips downwards onto the bottom stair beside the open doorway, her head slumps against the wall. Burying her head in her arms, Katy rocks her body to and fro, hugging her knees tight as the child inside her starts to howl and tears come hot and thick and fast. Until she is stilled by a familiar voice.

'I'm sorry... is this a bad time? Only I realised we didn't swap numbers, did we? So I thought that seeing as you'd already decided to have a duvet day and it turns out they don't need me in work this afternoon, well, perhaps we could reminisce some more. Only maybe this isn't a good time—'

Words that spill from a mouth pressed against the front door's letterbox which is wedged open by a taloned hand. Then Jude's face peers in. 'Oh dear, Kat, is everything OK?'

Chapter 9

The perfect life — that's what I saw when I first saw you again. Because you've done all right for yourself, haven't you? What with your job that's going somewhere. Your house in a fashionable part of town. Your boyfriend who loves you. A baby on the way — I could tell, even on that first meeting. Did I mention how much I would have loved a little girl? A right to right a wrong, isn't that what they say? But I wasn't so lucky. Never have been. So can't you really blame me for wanting to make you unlucky, too? I saw the cracks in your facade, you see. How convincingly you'd lied, not just to the world but to yourself. And I saw the truth: that however much you'd been punishing yourself for all those years, it wasn't enough.

Chapter 10

London, July 2013

The letterbox closes and for a moment Katy's spirits stir with the sudden hope that her unexpected visitor will take the hint and leave.

Yet when she looks up Jude's outline is clearly visible through the whorled glass of the front door, stubborn and expectant. Unsure what else to do, Katy raises her hand towards the intercom on the wall above her head. Because Jude's seen her, crying, and it's pointless to hide or pretend everything is OK. So she presses the button that releases the catch on the front door.

'Come on up,' she calls out, turning her face away as the door opens so Jude will not see at close range her tear-streaked face. Quickly, she risks a surreptitious face wipe on her sleeve. How has she found out where she lives? Was it the same way she tracked her down at work and found out her personal email address, or did she simply follow her? 'Go on in,' she adds, hesitating on the first floor landing as Jude draws level then waving towards sitting room door. 'I won't be a minute.'

Locked inside the bathroom Katy quickly scrubs her face. She is as eager to wash away the tears, recrimination and self-doubt as to leave Jude the least amount of time to scrutinise her surroundings. To unpick the fabric of her and Michael's domestic life. Pry into private things. Yet she is desperate, too, to regain control of herself and that means putting on fresh clothes and a light dusting of make-up; combing her hair.

Cornered, that's how Katy feels. Vulnerable and exposed. For there is no alternative, she knows. No place to hide, she thinks, angrily. Because whatever Jude wants she'll get.

The intruder sits in Michael's leather armchair, idly flicking through an edition of *Professional Photographer* when Katy steps back into the sitting room a few minutes later. The seat is low-slung and her dress has ridden up to reveal a tanned expanse of thigh. A scene that's anything but threatening, Katy reassures herself. In fact indoors the outfit Jude is wearing makes her look businesslike – elegant, almost – and enviably slim. Her relaxed demeanour, meanwhile, almost makes her presence here, in their home, seem like the most natural thing in the world.

Though, of course, it is anything but. Jude being here, uninvited and unannounced, is a deliberate act of violation.

'An eclectic mix,' Jude declares, approvingly, with a wave towards the collection of CDs that fill the shelves of the alcove to her side. 'He's got good taste, that man of yours.'

'How do you know they're all Michael's?' The sound of her voice – more defensive than she intends – makes Katy wince. Snap out of it, she tells herself, digging a finger nail into the dry cuticle of her thumb. Doesn't she have the upper hand? She is in her own home, after all. Well, Michael's. But Jude is right: just one shelf belongs to her, a mixture of compilations, mainly, as she pretty much lost interest in music after secretarial college.

Jude looks up. 'Just a feeling. And judging by the look on your face I'm right.' She takes *Now That's What I Call Music* compilation off the bottom shelf and turns it over to scan the track list. 'God, we used to love this stuff, didn't we?' she exclaims. 'Go on, put this one on. I've not heard it in years.'

Without a word, Katy presses a button on the laptop open on the coffee table by the fireplace, finds the appropriate album on the screen and presses play. As the music begins to play from four free-standing speakers carefully positioned in each corner of the room, she sees her hands are shaking. 'Fancy a drink?'

Pressing together her palms, Jude's lips curl into a beatific smile as Madonna starts to sing the first line of 'Like A Prayer'.

A song that instantly transports Katy back to rainy afternoons in her old bedroom at home when she and Jude would lie on the floor, playing tapes and reading magazines. 'Sure. Why not? And while you get it I'll make use of the facilities, if I may,' Jude replies, rising to her feet and heading towards the bathroom Katy has just vacated before her host can reply let alone direct her to the guest toilet downstairs.

Katy makes a spritzer for Jude and a fizzy water and lime for herself, both in matching wine glasses, then takes a seat on the sofa opposite where the other woman has been sitting to await her return. 'Love the view from upstairs – a real selling point,' Jude gushes as a few minutes later she sinks back down into the armchair, crosses her legs and begins to tap her foot in time to the music. 'As and when Michael and you decide to sell.'

Katy tightens her grip on the glass. 'Sorry?'

'Well you're going to need more room soon enough, surely – what with a little one on the way?'

'How the—'

'Oh my goodness, I'm so sorry,' Jude interrupts, her expression now one of furrowed concern. 'I saw the Pregnacare vitamins on the windowsill upstairs and just assumed... well... I'm so sorry. Of course the first trimester is always tricky.'

'As it happens you are right, I am expecting,' Katy answers, softly. Words that seem strange to hear coming from her own mouth, but not unpleasant. 'It's just we've not told many people. Yet.'

Jude smiles. 'Which is totally understandable, of course,' she declares. 'Considering the challenges of being an older first time mum. Waiting to go public until after the secondary scan rules out any potential problems – Down's and the like – am I right?'

Anger ignites in Katy's veins yet somehow she manages to keep her face set in a rictus grin. For this is textbook Jude, isn't it? Still determined, as she always was, to say the unspeakable. Provoke. She is fishing for information, that's all. Ammunition to use against her, somehow. But no, she thinks, I will not rise.

'What are you hoping for? A girl, I expect. I'd have loved more after James, of course. Girls especially, given the handful he turned out to be. And I deserved a break, didn't I? But it was not to be. Though I got pregnant again both were ectopic. Unexplained infertility, they called it. As a mum already I was luckier than most, my GP told me, the insensitive prick.'

'And your baby's dad?' Katy enquires politely, knowing as soon as the words are spoken that this is an inappropriate thing to say. But she is determined not to let Jude walk all over her as she once used to. Intimate, playful and conspiratorial one day; distant, spiteful and manipulative the next. Bullying by any other name, though Katy can now see how willing a participant she'd been in the delusion that she was stronger, more confident and resilient in the warmth of Jude's reflected glow. 'Wasn't he able to—'

'Even if I'd known who he was I'd never have asked him – for anything,' Jude snaps, riled for an instant before the tension in her subsides.

But there's something about her response, her evasiveness or maybe the speed of her denial, that leaves Katy unconvinced. This is a lie, she notes, and not the first. Clearing her throat, she re-crosses her legs. 'Right then,' she says, eager to change the conversation's direction. 'So. What exactly is it that you want?'

Jude laughs – a brittle sound. 'Well that's not very friendly, is it?'

'How did you know my address?' Katy snaps. That hurt tone is simply infuriating – she must work hard not to show it; to convince Jude she's not got to her, not really. That this is simply another attempt to intimidate. But this time she knows for sure from the shard of amusement in Jude's expression that her failure at small talk is making her anxiety and discomfort all the more obvious. Nevertheless, she can't give up now. 'Did you follow me?'

'Why, not intentionally!' Jude exclaims. The lightness in her voice is like a playground promise. 'I parked in this road, you see. I suppose you could call it… a lucky coincidence.' Katy shoots Jude a wary glance but says nothing, fearful of loosening the precarious grip she has on her emotions. Besides, if she says less maybe Jude will reveal more. 'Oh all right then, haven't you heard of Google? I was intrigued, that's all.' Jude reaches across to pick up a framed photograph Andrew had taken of the twins aged around three, each dressed in matching sun suits and hats with faces smothered in ice cream. Her face tightens. 'What a handsome pair!'

Katy's hands clench. How dare this uninvited guest, this intruder, pick through the minutiae of her life like this? It is too much. Enough. 'I'm sorry, but you'll have to go,' she declares, carefully, putting down her glass then rising to her feet. Though her voice is calm her mind is skittish so struggles to back up this instruction with any credible reason. 'My boyfriend will be coming from work soon. We've got people coming round—'

'I don't think so,' says Jude, taking a slow sip from her glass before continuing. 'Because Michael doesn't usually get back until half six or seven, does he?' She makes a show of checking her watch. 'And that won't be for, well, another four or five hours.'

So Jude really has been watching her. It's the only way she can know about her and Michael's movements, Katy thinks, almost sobbing in despair. Why can't she just leave, now. For good. Just leave me alone. Yet maybe the only way to make this happen is let her come to say what she's come to say.

'So it looks like it's just you and me. Home alone,' Jude smiles, draining the rest of her drink then raising her glass. 'Oh, and I'd kill for another one of these, if there's one going.'

Leaving her own drink unfinished, Katy goes into the kitchen to prepare two more. By the time she returns Jude, who is still holding the picture of the twins, is smoking a cigarette.

'Oh you don't mind, do you?' The voice is cold with not even a hint of regret as she leans forward and casually flicks ash into the carved Indian candlestick Diane bought Katy the previous Christmas. Without a word, Katy reaches out to take the picture which she replaces on the mantelpiece.

'So tell me about your man.' Jude points towards a framed photograph of the two of them looking out to sea. Michael's friend, Spike, took the picture when they visited the house near the coast he and his girlfriend were renovating for a long weekend the previous January. 'He looks like quite a tasty catch.'

'We met at work,' says Katy, taking another sip of her drink. Though she doesn't have to tell Jude anything about her personal life, she finds she can't resist. As if she is trying to prove a point, though to whom she's not quite sure. 'He's a photographer. We've been together five years.'

'And is it l-o-v-e?' Jude looks her straight in the eye as she slowly runs her forefinger around the rim of her glass.

As she answers Katy notices how she hesitates, just for an instant. 'As good as.'

'Hardly a resounding yes.' Jude chuckles, gazing thoughtfully at her wine which is, as yet, untouched. 'So what's the problem?'

'Why does there have to be a problem?' Katy snaps. 'And even if there is, which there isn't, it wouldn't be any of your business.' Angrily, she feels her cheeks flush. She hates herself for so readily taking the bait.

'Oh dear. I didn't mean to touch a nerve,' Jude smiles, leaning forwards. 'So let's cut to the chase. As you put it so eloquently earlier: what do I want?'

Bracing herself, Katy stares longingly at the cigarette butt still gently smouldering in the impromptu ashtray. She does not smoke, certainly not now she is pregnant, though she did for a number of years after leaving school. Now Jude holds out the packet and waves it at Katy. Then she flips open the lid to make it easier, revealing a silver lighter nestled inside.

'No, I don't,' she mutters with a shake of her head.

'Not now.' Jude nods. Her tone makes it seem part statement, part question.

'Not for a long time, actually,' Katy corrects.

'Well what I wanted was a chance to talk,' Jude continues, reasonably. 'To catch up. To clear the air.'

Katy hesitates, distracted by a fleeting image of a younger face, one side of its mouth foamed with spittle. Its cheeks freckled with dirt. Eyes dulled by pleading. She knows the intensity of this picture comes from imagination, not memory. That it's the fantasy fulfilment of a waking dream she had, for years. The one in which she, not Jude, was victim. In which she fought back rather than ran away.

Stop it, Katy thinks, willing her hands to stop shaking. Don't think of this. Not now.

'I'm not sure what you mean.'

'Oh I think you do, Kat,' says Jude. 'About the first thing, at least. Why you did what you did—'

'That's not fair—' Katy objects. At last, she thinks, a chance to explain. But though she's both feared and longed for this moment, her struggle to find the right words is hampered by sudden and unexpected echoes.

Stop it! Someone had yelled. A girl's voice.

'—I tried, I really did—'

'You fucked up, that's what you did. Big time.'

'No, I only wanted to help,' Katy mumbles. The room has darkened, like a cloud has obscured the sun, though beyond the sitting room window the world still seems sharp and clear. Then that voice, again. Less muffled, this time. Outraged. Accusing. *You frigid lezzer*, it taunts. *What the fuck have you done?* She raises a hand to her face to touch her cheek. The faint scar there, barely visible when she is wearing make-up, always seems whiter when she's been out in the sun. 'But then I got lost. Then there was an accident. I ended up in hospital.'

'Don't expect any sympathy from me,' Jude snaps. 'I'm not the one who ran away.'

Katy braces herself against a sudden wave of panic that makes the room start to spin. Then she is reeling as, as fast as it has come, the sensation is gone. Not nausea this time but something less distinct. A sense of the world somehow slipping slightly out of kilter. A vague and intangible feeling of fear. She is cold suddenly, though her face is damp with sweat. 'That's not fair,' she mumbles. Because it's not, is it? Because Jude is as much to blame.

'Is that really all you can say?'

'Yes. I really am sorry, and what happened was awful...' Katy replies, trying not to think of Jude's earlier reference to her son. Wearily rubbing her eyes, she struggles to ignore the shadows now looming in her peripheral vision just beyond reach. Suddenly, she finds herself engulfed by the sensation that she's forgotten something really important. 'But—'

'It's not your pity I want. I want you to understand that the things people like you, your brother, your thoughtless shit of a dad do, ruin other people's lives. How all of you in your own way took away the things that mattered, the people who could have made a real difference.' Jude seems distracted for a moment but whether by rage or regret it's hard to tell. 'Or if you want to put it another way: you owe me.'

'What? I don't understand—' Katy shoots an anxious glance towards the latest studio shot taken of Andrew, Dee and the kids which stands on the bookshelf behind the TV.

Following her gaze, Jude's jaw clenches. 'Ah, the sainted brother. His fragrant wife and their precious little darlings. My, what a picture of happy families that simple portrait paints.'

Katy glares at Jude, unable to speak. She isn't about to challenge the trite summation of her brother's life. To dismantle the snide suggestion that he has fallen on his feet. To counter the dig that he has it all with an account of how he and Dee had tried so hard for so long to have children. It had taken four rounds of IVF before she'd eventually conceived the twins and then she'd almost died for loss of blood during their complicated birth.

Despite the distance that still separates Katy from her brother – a distance that was far more than just geographical – she suddenly feels fiercely protective of him. 'And your point is?' she retorts, coolly.

'Don't play the innocent with me,' Jude snaps, rising from her chair. She takes three paces towards Katy and stands over her blocking any chance of escape. The closeness of her, the heat of her physical presence, makes Katy squirm like a worm on a pin. 'You all knew what your dad was like, everyone did. What was it your dear old mum so coyly called him? A bit of a ladies' man. And she should know, right? As she happily swept his dirty secrets under the carpet. Flashed her cash to make it go away. So I suppose the joke was on us, then, really. Wouldn't you say?'

Katy slides down the sofa, desperate to be on a level footing with Jude. 'I'm really sorry,' she says, carefully. 'But I don't know what—'

As she speaks, however, a vague realisation begins to take shape. The unstoppable, upwards force of a dark shape slowly emerging from fathomless waters. Her brain screams with the effort of trying to put the pieces together as the thing continues its slow yet irresistible ascent. Her dad. What did he ever do to Jude? They had barely spoken, to her knowledge. In fact he had taken an instant dislike to her, even urging Katy on one occasion to break off the friendship. As if she could forget.

Yet what if it wasn't something he had done to Jude but to someone else? Katy stumbles to her feet. 'Tell me what you mean.'

But as Jude opens her mouth to speak the expectant silence is shattered by the sound of the phone. Desperate for her answer, Katy does not move so the pair stand, two statues barely breathing, listening to the phone's insistent ring. One... Two... Three... Katy counts, willing time to accelerate as the answer phone would only click on after three more. And then it comes. A stranger's voice, urgent and briskly efficient.

'It's Nurse Richards calling from the West Middlesex Hospital for Katherine Parker. Your mother, Mrs Diane Parker, has just been brought in with cracked ribs and concussion following an incident on Richmond High Street. She's stable but asking for you. Could you please call us as soon as possible—'

'No,' Katy cries out, diving towards the phone. 'Hi, it's me. Katherine. Sorry, I was just upstairs. Is she OK?'

Gently, the nurse tells Katy to find a pencil and paper to take down a few details then helpfully advises her just what bits and pieces she can bring to make her mum more comfortable. A calm and soothing voice carefully honed to make upsetting news palatable and a bad situation almost bearable, she thinks, so totally immersed in her fear for her mum that she totally forgets Jude's presence for the rest of the phone call.

Replacing the phone in its cradle, Katy stares dumbly at the piece of paper in her hand. Then, a moment later, the urgency of the situation numbs her fear and shock. Quickly, she scans the room for her bag then frisks it briskly for her car keys. Only as she clutches them in her hand does she remember the youths from the night before and the attack on her car. How can she drive with a shattered windscreen?

Frantically, she fumbles for her mobile then scrolls up and down the address book in search of a number of the local cab firm. With the phone wedged between her left shoulder and ear, she listens to the call dial then connect as she checks her purse for money. But the nearest cab company has no drivers available for an immediate pick up. 'Damn it,' she mutters, hanging up and scanning the room once more for the Yellow Pages. And then, at last, she sees Jude standing silently in the doorway, watching.

'Oh dear, is there a problem with your car? How unfortunate. Why don't I drive you to the hospital?' Jude's voice is even, her face serene.

Looking up, Katy sees Jude has already picked up her bag and is holding her car keys. As if Jude being in the flat isn't bad enough, she thinks. The thought of willingly incarcerating herself within an even smaller, more closely confined space with this unwelcome intruder makes her want to scream. But she has no choice – not if she wants to get there quickly. It is the obvious solution. 'If you're sure—'

'Of course,' Jude answers, brightly. 'You need to be there, by her side.'

Reluctantly, Katy nods. 'OK,' she murmurs. 'Thanks.'

–

Katy slaps the smeared glass with the palm of her hands, impatient to get inside. But her efforts only seem to make the revolving door turn more slowly as shuffling forwards, quadrant by quadrant, she waits for a gap to open just wide enough for her to wedge her shoulder then pushes her way through. Only once she is within the hospital's reception area does she hesitate to orientate herself before hurrying towards a large desk laden with box files and computer screens.

Behind the counters sits the gatekeeper – a grey-haired woman whose unnaturally deep sun tan makes her face look like an X-ray. As she hurriedly provides her details, Katy leans over the counter in an attempt to scan her mum's admission details which are displayed on the woman's computer screen. As soon as the gatekeeper notices, however, she tilts the monitor away. 'Go to the back of the building and take the left-hand lift on the right to the fourth floor,' the woman instructs, lifting a phone by her side to call upstairs to tell them Katy is on her way. 'Ask for Maynard Ward.'

A young man holding a baby carrier with the price tag still attached is rooting in his trouser pockets for spare change while the woman at his side cradles a newborn baby. A grey-faced man in too-short pyjamas is shuffling towards the main door wheeling a walking frame. An elderly woman clutching a balled tissue in her hand sits stony-faced on a bench outside the ladies loo. But these figures and more are barely-glimpsed ghosts, a mere trick of the light played by her peripheral vision, as Katy urgently makes her way towards the ground floor lift that will take her to the fourth floor.

'Room for two more,' the hospital porter calls as the metal doors slide open. He is stationed behind an elderly man in a wheelchair attached to a drip.

Though it's the third lift to pass through the ground floor station while she has been waiting, it's the first with enough room for Katy to squeeze in and it's only as she does that she becomes aware of Jude's presence; how she is still there, like a stubborn shadow. Yet in the adrenaline rush that propels her towards mum's bedside, Katy doesn't think to send her away.

Exiting the lift on the fourth floor, she falters, nonplussed by identical corridors stretching away in four directions into a muted world in which sharp edges have been rounded, sounds dulled and every available surface is pale blue. But then a porter suddenly appears and she is directed to the ward through the last door on the left where she finds her mum lying like a broken bird in the bed by the window.

From a distance, Diane's skin looks whiter than the sheet on which she is stretched. Only as Katy draws closer does she see the explosion of colour across the far side of her face. The bruising is also visible around the neck and across one shoulder. But it is the alien tube puncturing the translucent skin on the back of her hand that makes Katy want to cry. 'Mum?' she whispers, hardly daring to speak for fear of hurting her further.

A nurse appears at her side as if from nowhere and gives Katy an encouraging smile as Diane, despite her obvious discomfort, slowly turns her head. 'Don't worry,' the patient croaks. 'Everyone keeps telling me that it looks worse than it really is.'

'What happened, Mum?' Katy cries, hurrying towards the bed. There is no chair to sit on so she perches gingerly on the bedside. Though desperate not to stare at those terrible bruises, she finds herself unable to resist.

'I was coming out of Smiths when this boy stopped to ask me the time. But when I looked down at my watch he hit me in the face and grabbed my bag. The next thing I knew I was on the ground. Then a taxi driver helped me into the back of his cab and rang the police. He was ever so kind. Then someone brought me some tea while we waited for an ambulance. And I ended up here. Such a lot of fuss.'

Katy puts her hand on her mum's arm and gives it a gentle squeeze. She tries in vain to ignore the telltale signs of ageing her mother usually so deftly conceals beneath her favourite cosmetics. The budding liver spots. The filigree of broken veins beneath the skin's translucent surface. The inward pull of the slate-grey eyes.

'Did you get a good look at him?'

'It's all a bit hazy.' Diane coughs, weakly. 'But I'd say he was in his late teens or early twenties. With dark hair.'

'She's been very brave,' the nurse soothes. 'And extremely lucky. You wouldn't believe how often this sort of thing happens in broad daylight nowadays, and your mother was extremely fortunate to get away without any broken bones.'

'It just wasn't my time to go, I suppose,' Diane sighs, suddenly noticing Jude, who throughout this exchange has been standing back, hovering near the doorway. 'My goodness, Estelle, how lovely to see you! But what on earth are you doing here?'

Bewildered, Katy scans the otherwise empty ward then finally looks behind her, back towards the door. She stares at Jude with a sense of confusion which only deepens as her friend begins to speak.

'I was visiting a distant relation down the corridor, and I was just leaving when I recognised you and thought I'd pop in to see if you are OK. I do hope you don't mind.'

The voice is calm. Controlled. Which makes the lie all the more plausible, Katy notes as she struggles to speak. As her mind races to catch up with unfolding events she stares dumbfounded by the audacious figure now commanding the room's attention. The woman hijacking the moment to divert her away from her mum, the person who really needs her. What bizarre game is this? Mum, it seems, has some passing acquaintance with this stranger who has exploded back into her own life with her carefully assembled armoury of half-revelations, veiled threats and innuendo. And for her sake, Katy thinks, she can't afford to let this go.

'That's good of you,' Diane replies before her daughter can respond. 'Isn't it, Katy? Estelle works at the theatre in Richmond – you know the one where Joyce and I've taken groups to see various shows?' She coughs again, but this time can't stop. Katy quickly fills a glass with water from a jug on the cabinet beside her bed and holds the drink to her lips. 'Estelle, I'm sorry,' her mum says eventually. 'This is my daughter, Katy.'

'Ah, so you're the famous Katherine Parker!' says Jude, stepping forward and holding out her hand. 'Diane's told me so much about you. Nice to meet you.'

Katy stares at Jude's hand in disbelief. Although enraged by Jude's lies she is more stunned by her nerve. Teetering on the brink of losing self-control, torn between anguish at what has happened to her mum and rage, she slowly replaces the glass on the table and turns toward Diane.

'Mum.' Her carefully modulated tone is a triumph of self-restraint. 'I'm desperate for a cup of tea, can I get you anything?' Katy turns towards the nurse with questioning eyes; the other woman nods. 'You need to take it easy, rest a little before the doctor comes. I'll just pop downstairs. Won't be long.'

'Tea would be lovely,' murmurs Diane, closing her eyes.

Katy kisses her mum gently on the forehead then walks towards the door, forcing Jude out into the empty corridor. As the door swings to behind them her hand closes around Jude's upper arm and she briskly marches her a few paces along the corridor before firmly pressing her against the wall. 'What are you doing?' she hisses through clenched teeth. 'And who the fuck is Estelle?'

Jude pushes Katy's arm away and straightens her dress. 'Calm down dear, for God's sake,' she says in a low voice with a quick glance up and down the corridor. 'Don't go making a scene.'

'Like the one you just did?'

'Yes, well. There's a perfectly reasonable explanation—'

'I thought you said you were a bookkeeper,' Katy snaps, suddenly aware of the rapid clenching and unclenching of her fists. Itching to hit something.

'Let's get a coffee, we can talk downstairs—'

'No. If you've got something to tell me then you can tell me straight. Right here, right now.' Katy notices a flicker of uncertainty flash across her opponent's face and it stokes her confidence.

Jude glares at her a moment before answering and when she starts to speak the peevish note in her voice suggests she feels she has been back-footed. 'I am a bookkeeper…' she objects '…although it's been hard to find work these past few years, so I've done all sorts. Telesales. Estate agent-ing. The job at the theatre.'

'How nice for you.'

Ignoring the interruption, Jude presses on. 'I met your mum, although I didn't know she was your mum, quite early on. She was always very nice.'

'And Estelle?'

'My middle name. I've used it on and off for years. I started using it again a few months ago because coming to London seemed, well, like a fresh start.' Jude's eyes are wandering, Katy notices, as if she's reluctant to look her directly in the face. 'Look, I didn't know she was your mum, honestly. But you and I, we still need to talk—'

'No. At least not now, and certainly not here,' Katy cries in exasperation. She cannot be doing all this now. Making sure her mum is OK and getting her home safely is all that mattered, and to do that she must make Jude leave. 'Go away,' she says suddenly, giving Jude a firm push towards the lift. And then another. 'Now. Go.'

Jude does not resist. Instead, she tightens her grip on the bag slung over her shoulder and turns to leave. But before she does she fires just one, final passing shot. 'You pretended not to know what I was talking about earlier, but you don't fool me,' she says, coldly. 'And if you really are that stupid, do one thing for me, OK? Ask your precious mum about your darling brother and your dear, departed dad. When she is feeling up to it, of course.'

Too angry to translate her words and too eager to see her gone, Katy strides back towards the lift where she waits to watch Jude leave. To the left of the lift shaft is a balcony on which she now leans, staring down into an open void as tall as the building. On the ground floor directly below is the reception area, the main entrance and the car park beyond. Peering down, she waits for Jude to cross her line of sight heading towards the main doors which she does a few minutes later.

Adjusting her position, Katy watches the other woman push her way through the revolving door then stop on the pavement outside where, a beat later, a car pulls up that looks just like the one Jude just used to drive them to the hospital. Leaning across the front seat, the driver opens the passenger door. Jude climbs inside then, before she has fastened her seatbelt, the car is pulling away and out of view.

Too preoccupied with thoughts of cancelling bank cards, changing locks on doors and getting hold of Michael, however, Katy gives none of this a second thought.

—

The air in Maynard Ward hangs still, its muffled silence punctuated only by a sharp PVC squeak every now and then as she shifts position in the chair. The shirt she's wearing is damp against the wipe-down covering. The backs of her legs are slick with sweat. Through the window, a concrete mountain range of slate peaks and tarmac ravines spreads eastwards towards Westminster. Above it, a passenger plane locked in a holding position hangs disconcertingly low in the vaporous sky.

Yet Katy registers none of this. *How long have I been sitting here?* is all she can wonder, dully. *Waiting for Mum to come round.*

They had taken Diane down to theatre some time around four to right a dislocated shoulder – a procedure Katy had been relieved to hear they would not try on a woman her age without a general anaesthetic. Now, however, as she sits by Mum's side listening to the shallow rattle of her breath, Katy's not so sure. She knows it won't be long before the figure beside her stirs. Before the inanimate face with its sunken sockets and taut skin will come back to life. Yet there is something about it, the way its muscles twitch every now and then, how they flicker like a broken TV, that fills her with unease.

It's not the thought of how much worse it might have been; how she might have lost her. It's the realisation of how, with the passing of time, roles are starting to reverse. The fragility of her, Katy thinks. How can she not have noticed until now how much her mother has started to age? Yet not so long ago the woman now lying before her was the stronger one, safeguarding her from danger. Providing her with refuge, protection, commitment – each part of an unspoken pact sealed with the sugary kiss of chocolate biscuit cake and home-made lemonade. None of the implications of which Katy has had to consider before.

Of course Diane was knocked sideways by Charles's death, despite having been separated for all that time. But she had rallied. Positively bounced back after the knee-jerk shock. Embraced life to the extent that, in recent years, all who knew her had remarked on her renewed energy and vigour. Now, though, all Katy can feel is an overwhelming urge to touch her mum, hold her, protect her. Never to let her go. To make things right so that nothing can hurt her again. A bit like how Diane must have felt by her bedside, in the County, all those years ago.

Those early hours that she had lain there in hospital, she thinks. Floating somewhere between oblivion and conscious thought, she'd heard her. Her mother. Weeping. Begging her, her daughter, to be better.

Because we almost lost you, Mum had said.

That same refrain, first heard down by the canal side then, again, a decade later after what happened with Jude. Was that why Mum had been as she was, Katy wonders. So eager to repackage, to re-edit, to re-present events so as to minimise potential hurt; to smooth away the corners and edges of life? Just like the way they tried so hard for so long to conceal from her and Andrew the extent of the cracks in the foundation of their relationship.

Like they'd hated so much her friendship with Jude.

Jude.

Diane always said she was a bad influence; that she would lead Katy astray. Though in reality, of course, what she'd turned out to be was a bully. It's ironic, really, Katy now thinks, rubbing her eyes, how at the end Diane seemed so determined to keep them apart. As if she hoped that through sheer determination and force of will she could ensure the two girls had no further contact, ever. If Diane had only known, knew now, goodness, what would she say?

Don't play the innocent with me, says a voice. *A bit of a ladies' man*. It's Jude. The memory of what she said earlier that afternoon makes Katy shudder. *Cash to make it go away.*

Why has she tracked me down? a voice inside Katy's head now cries. Because she's a born troublemaker, that's why — just like mum always used to say. And if I don't rise to her bait, if she doesn't respond to any further advances, Jude will lose interest and go away. Folding her arms, Katy's left hand brushes against her belly. I, meanwhile, must look after myself and the tiny life that's now unfurling inside.

No regrets?

Michael had asked her when she'd told him. And each had worked hard at persuading the other that there were none. Though she'd never wanted to start a family, not really. The one she had already had seemed trouble enough. All those years she'd spent drifting, trying to find her way. She'd had boyfriends, but none she could ever imagine staying with once the first flush began to fade. Certainly no one who made her want to settle down. No one for whom it seemed worth letting down her guard.

Oh, the pressure to let people in that she'd resisted. All the questions, too. Like the prying she'd endured in the specialist unit at the County during those difficult first few months when Diane had been so worried that her morose state, her pendulous mood swings, might be a lingering after-effect of concussion. If only I could turn back the clock, Katy thinks. To do things differently. To appease whatever greater power it is that needs appeasing. Anything to make sure that everything will be OK.

The sudden sound of raised voices from the nurses' station at the far end of the ward draws Katy back to the present. With a quick glance at her mum, whose expression and position in the bed beside her remain unchanged, she pulls herself upright and cranes her neck to see what's going on, to see in the distance a male nurse of rugby-playing dimensions frogmarch a wiry figure in jeans and T-shirt towards the main door.

A short, sharp pulse against her thigh distracts Katy from the scene and she extracts the mobile phone from her hip pocket. A text from Sally-Anne. Rather than read its contents, however, her gaze is drawn to the icon at the bottom of the screen that shows she now has four missed calls and at least one new voicemail message. Michael. She should have called him, of course, but what with everything that had been going on it quite slipped her mind.

With a final glance at her mum, Katy rises to her feet and makes her way across the ward. She will buy a coffee, sit in the walled garden by the cafe for a few minutes to get some fresh air and make the call. As she draws level with the nurses' station, however, she stops in surprise.

On the chair behind the counter stands a floral tribute. An explosion of foliage tethered by a black, satin bow. A curious concoction, more like a wreath than a bouquet. Slim-sheathed Longi lilies nestle against foxglove. Strands of devil's ivy entwine with lilies of the valley and lotus seed heads. A single peacock's feather dyed jet-black reminds her of an Edwardian hearse. Only then does she register the sticky stamens and the leaf sap's sour reek.

Overwhelmed by the smell, sickly-sweet and just beyond full-blown, Katy grips the counter's edge to steady herself. The moment passes quickly, however, and as her head starts to clear, she sees the rectangular card carefully secured between the nettles and ivy. Its lettering carefully hand-printed, again in black.

'With heartfelt condolences,' the message reads. 'Mrs Diane Parker. R.I.P.'

Chapter 11

Guildford, November 1988

It was a brackish Tuesday afternoon in late November when Jude first met Diane Parker. Kat had invited her to tea and though excited, she was a little bit intimidated by the prospect of a visit to the Parkers' home. 'Mum, this is Jude. She lives with her mum in one of the houses on Station Road,' Kat gushed as the pair tumbled through the front door, damp-haired and flush-cheeked from the run home from the bus stop.

'Pleased to meet you, Judith. Do come in,' the woman replied, holding out a hand to shake which Jude ignored. For there was something in her eye, a barely concealed look of disdain, most likely triggered by the name of her road, that made Jude bristle as her eyes quickly registered the floral print shirt the older woman was wearing – Laura Ashley, she rightly guessed – and the denim slacks with their designer label.

'Actually it's Jude, Mrs Parker,' she answered coolly, tossing her school bag after Kat's onto the floor beneath the coat pegs then tearing off her raincoat. 'I can't stand the name Judith, but it's a burden I must carry. A bit like Katherine, I suppose—' she flashed a conspiratorial grin at her friend '—and her preference for Kat.'

'Kat?' The smile congealed on Diane's face as her eyes dipped briefly to the floor where Jude now realised a small puddle was starting to form beneath her dripping coat. Then the woman turned towards her daughter. 'Who calls you Kat?'

'Why everyone, of course – everyone at school, at least,' Jude laughed before the other girl could speak.

'Yes, everyone,' Katy echoed, reaching for Jude's coat then hanging it along with her own on one of the pegs behind the front door. 'Come on, come and see my room,' she added, tugging Jude by the sleeve.

'She's not always like that,' she apologised in a whisper as she pushed ajar her bedroom door. 'But Dad's been away a lot recently – they've been going through a bit of a bad patch. So come on, what music shall we play?'

Jude stood in the middle of Kat's bedroom floor marvelling at the collection of records and home-made cassettes piled along the narrow floor to ceiling shelves to the right of the bay window. Bending down to browse the records' cardboard spines, she quickly selected albums by The Pretenders, Lou Reed and David Bowie and tugged them free. 'Well these will do, for a start.'

Crouching down, Kat pulled out a wicker basket from under the bed. Inside, beneath a single, neatly-folded blanket, were a selection of glossy women's magazines, film periodicals and out-of-date *Smash Hits*. 'A combination of my own and Andrew's cast-offs,' she grinned. 'A bit like the music, really, but between us we do all right.'

'So is he going to be around later?' Jude asked, lightly. She was yet to meet Kat's brother but was already intrigued after all that her friend had told her about him. They were close, it seemed, and though not as close as they used to be it was clear that Kat idolised him.

'No.' Kat frowned. 'He's got football training tonight which is a shame as I'd have liked you to meet him.'

Jude smiled. 'Don't worry, I'm sure I will.'

The pair spent an hour or so playing music and browsing magazines until Diane called them down for tea. As they entered the kitchen and Jude saw Diane already seated at the table nursing a cup of tea, her spirits dipped at the realisation that Kat's mother was clearly intent on joining in their conversation. Taking a seat opposite Diane, she examined the contents of her plate with satisfaction. Shepherd's pie was one of her favourites.

'Help yourself to peas and corn,' Diane gushed. 'I hope you like it. I should have checked with Kat but decided it would be a good choice because everybody likes shepherd's pie, don't they?'

'Actually, I try to avoid red meat.' The words were out before Jude could start to think where they had come from, or why. It's just there was something about Kat's mum, a vague sense of superiority in her look and tone, that made the child within Jude want to thumb her nose and back-foot her, somehow. Diane's face tightened as she gathered her thoughts but before she could speak Jude had leaped back in. 'But don't worry,' she added, guiltily. 'It doesn't upset me, or anything.'

'Good,' Diane replied. And for the first time Jude wondered if she had misread the woman's expression.

All of a sudden she looked smaller, somehow. Deflated. Probably as a result of that bad patch with her husband, Charles, that Kat's been talking about, Jude thought. What was he like, she wondered. Kat so rarely talked about him, but from what she has said he sounded distant and aloof. He worked in finance, she remembered. Travelled, too – a lot. She wondered if he and Diane's marriage had ever been truly happy.

'So, um, Jude. How are you finding St Mary's?'

'It's OK, Mrs Parker,' Jude replied, grateful now for the chance of conversation. 'I mean, it's smaller than my last school which is nice. It's a bit strange not having any boys, though.'

Kat stifled a giggle and the pair exchanged a cryptic look which Diane clearly registered but tried to ignore before pressing on. 'Where was your last school, then?'

'On the south coast. Portsmouth. It was a bit of a dump. So when Mum decided she wanted to move here I thought let's hope it's a change for the better. Then I got into St Mary's and, well, here I am.'

'And is it?' asked Diane, pouring herself a second cup of tea.

'Is it what?'

'A change for the better.'

'Don't know yet,' Jude replied, helping herself to more peas without asking. She glanced towards Kat. 'Time will tell.'

Once they finished eating but before being excused, Jude rose from the table. She needed the toilet, and the woman's pained expression as she politely gave directions, made her almost wet her pants. Stifling a smile, Jude retraced her steps back upstairs to find the bathroom. From the kitchen below came the sound of Kat clearing away the plates; her mum stacking the dishwasher.

The bathroom was straight ahead of where she was now standing, but her attention was snagged by an open door to its right. Unsure quite why, Jude stepped into this open doorway and peeped inside. She expected to find Kat's parents' bedroom, but the space she found herself staring at appeared to be used by just one person.

Scanning the interior she could find no evidence of Charles's presence, even his existence, just female accessories. A patch-work quilt across the double bed in shades of pink and pastel blue. An army of perfumes and cosmetics arranged along the top of the chest of drawers. A pile of Georgette Heyer novels on the bedside table. A mahogany dressing table stands by the window and on its top arcs an assortment of framed pictures of children including a recent studio portrait of a stiff-lipped Kat and a boy with dark, messy hair and an easy grin who looks a couple of years older. The older brother, she noted, and good-looking, too. But where, she wondered, did Kat's father sleep?

Retracing her steps back along the landing, Jude passed a closed door on her right and hesitated. A beat later she had given into the devil inside as her hand turned the porcelain doorknob and she peeped inside.

It was a small room, smaller than Kat's, and the air hung heavy with an unfamiliar tang. There was a single bed, a large oak wardrobe and an antique chest of drawers. A row of men's shoes stretched along the floor beneath the window. Through the half-open cupboard door she could see neatly hung suits and shirts. Along the window sill stood a row of pictures – mainly of children, but also Diane standing next to a tall, dark-haired man with a severe hair cut and military stance. He looked at least ten years older than Kat's mum, and in a number of the more recent-looking pictures he was wearing a distant expression. On the bed were spread a selection of official looking papers.

Intrigued, Jude crept towards the bed to take a closer look at the papers. Beneath a notepad and some business letters was a buff folder containing a legal-looking document concerning someone's divorce.

'Can I help you?' As Jude span around she was struck by the sharpness of Mrs Parker's voice. Unsure where to look, she felt as if her cheeks would burst into flames any minute. 'I said…' The woman took two steps towards her. 'Can I help you?'

'Sorry Mrs P,' Jude replied in a voice as light as she could muster. 'The door was open and I couldn't resist a look inside.' How pathetic was that? But she felt tongue-tied and foolish under the spotlight of the woman's angry glare.

'I thought the door was locked,' Diane replied, casting a glance towards the papers on the bed. Turning her head towards the door, her eyes narrowed as she stared at the inside of the lock. 'Where's the key?'

'Um, there wasn't one,' Jude stuttered. 'Honestly. OK, the door was shut but it swung open easily enough. I didn't force it or anything.'

'Oh.' Diane appeared unconvinced. 'But even if that is the case that's still no excuse for you to be snooping around other people's bedrooms.'

'No,' agreed Jude, firmly. 'I know. It isn't. Sorry.'

'Well then,' Kat's mum added more lightly, seemingly disarmed by her opponent's honesty. A crimson flush now encircled the skin around her neck, like poison ivy. 'In that case we'll say no more about it, then. On one condition, that is—'

Jude looked up. 'I'll keep your little secret if you keep mine.' Gesturing briefly towards the papers on the bed, Diane let slip a deep sigh. 'Nothing's decided yet — neither Katherine nor Andrew have the faintest idea, and until we've sorted everything out I'd like it to stay that way.'

Baffled for a moment, Jude stared at the bed then the penny dropped. 'Oh, right,' she said. 'Of course.'

Standing to one side, Diane held the door open to let her pass by.

An awkward first meeting, Jude concluded later that evening. But then, a week later, when she and Kat wandered down into town one Friday evening after school to do some Christmas shopping she found it had an unexpected side effect. For as she waved Kat goodbye at the bus station some time after six Jude could tell from her friend's anxious look that she knew she'd be in trouble when she got home for being out late.

Retracing her steps back up the high street to her own house at the top of town, Jude had an idea. She would take the blame and call Diane herself when she got home to tell her so. If the woman sounded like she might punish Kat in some way, well, didn't she now just have the ideal trump card to play?

Chapter 12

London, July 2013

Katy sits at a round metal table beneath the scant leaves of a sickly chestnut tree. To her left, two female patients dressed in cotton dressing gowns and flip-flops are talking in low voices. No one occupies the table to her right, though a pigeon is standing on the table top brazenly picking at a half-eaten sand-wich.

Dully, she stares at the fat white china mug of coffee she's just bought from the hospital cafe which looks more like tea than cappuccino as she replays in her mind the scene she witnessed just a few minutes earlier. How one of the nurses who'd been periodically monitoring her mother's blood pressure had darted back behind the counter, grabbed the tribute from the chair and stuffed it beneath the desk beside it and out of view, then cursed as she quickly recoiled. The way she'd scrutinised her left hand, its thumb welling with blood from a deep puncture wound inflicted by something buried deep within the wreath. An antique hat pin inserted, upended, within the stems and leaves. When at last the woman turned back to face her there were tears of pain in her eyes.

So sorry, the nurse had cried, grabbing a handful of tissue from a large cardboard box on the counter top. With her thumb encased she squeezed it firmly, holding upright the injured hand. *You shouldn't have seen that. Some idiot from the flower delivery people. Goodness knows how security let him in.*

A mix up, clearly, echoes Katy's response as she tries to reassure herself once more. *No one's fault. Not to worry. Clearly, a mistake.*

Exhaling slowly, she struggles to order her thoughts. Tries not to think anymore about the funereal wreath. Forces herself instead to focus on trying to remember what she needs to do. Reaching into her bag, she pulls out her mobile. Of the four calls she's missed three are from Michael while the other is from a number she does not recognise. Sliding her finger down the screen, she calls up her voice messages and listens to his voice. It's angry at first but in the second message his tone is different. Urgent. Worried.

'Where are you?' he said. 'Call me as soon as you get this, if only just to let me know you're OK. I'm still at work but have the mobile with me, switched on. Call me back, OK?'

Ashamed, Katy puts down the phone. How could she not have thought to call him? But so much has been happening, how could he blame her for not having time?

She rubs her eyes, thinking back to the first time she saw him. The charcoal linen jacket he'd worn over a white T-shirt and faded jeans. The tiny silver ring in his ear. A tall man approaching his late thirties with thick hair the colour of burnt sand, high flat cheekbones and dark eyes. And then, as he shook himself free of a bulky camera bag and what looked like a portfolio, that broad grin. *Can you point me in the direction of the creative department?* The first words he had spoken to her. Asked with a dip of his gaze to the reams of A4 she was clutching against her chest – part of that month's stationery order.

Tongue-tied by how attractive she found him, Katy had simply beckoned him to follow her through a set of double doors leading to a large, open-plan office. *I'm Michael Ross, the new boy*, he added, putting down his bag. *Pleased to meet you…*

He'd recently returned to England heavily in debt following an extended round-the-world trip, he explained later over a beer or three at The Old Star. Emboldened by the tangible spark between them, Katy interrogated him about his past career, where he went to college, where he grew up. As a kid, he'd lived for a while with his mother and three brothers in a small town on the east coast of Scotland but thanks to his dad, an army major, was then sent away to school. Later, despite starting an MA in photography at the Royal College of Art, he switched to commercial art and design. Desperate for paying work, he would pursue his artistic ambitions later.

So Kate Adie, he concluded. *How about you?*

Katy's left hand fluttered against the side of her face, her fingers skimming the skin above her left cheek bone where the cotton thread of a fine scar was visible only to the tutored eye. It felt good under the spotlight of his attention, yet though flattered by his interest, she felt self-conscious. There was something about the way he looked at her, his apparently genuine desire not just to chat her up but find out who she was. She hesitated, wondering what to answer. She was usually good at keeping people at arms length, adept at steering clear of awkward questions. But not tonight. Beneath Michael's steady gaze it felt like there was nowhere left to hide. A thought which made her pulse race.

Nothing special, she mumbled awkwardly, looping a stray wisp of hair behind her ear; forcing her face into a sardonic smile. *Born and bred in the suburbs, seduced by the bright lights of the big city.*

But then he'd teased her by calling her a liar. As if he knew the truth. How long before she moved to London, when she had her sights set so firmly on art school, she'd yearned for how she knew the city would make her feel. Energised. Vibrant. Alive. How once she'd arrived her hopes had been so swiftly diluted by the harsh reality of it all. Failing her exams. Dropping out of sixth form. Being nudged by her parents towards secretarial college to gain a practical skill she could always fall back on. How quickly she'd come to value the ease with which you can lose yourself in the city. To be cauterised by the hustle and bustle of it all, dislocated from the natural rhythms of life.

I'll winkle it out of you, Kat, I'm good at that.

Confused, she'd tried to calm her nerves with a large mouthful of wine. But this only served to make things worse.

Of course he'd only meant it playfully, yet her tone was waspish when she answered back. *Not Kat, Katy!* Because only one person had ever called her that. Then seeing his look of surprise she'd tried to explain. *I just hate the name, OK? Cat from* East-enders, *Cat Deeley — such a cliché. Besides, it's what everyone used to call me at school.*

It was a damp June that summer, Wimbledon would prove to be yet another a wash out, and it had only just stopped raining later that same evening as they skirted the edge of St James's Park then headed across Parliament Square and down towards Victoria Embankment. They stopped beneath the trees and stood, side by side, staring across the river's oily surface towards the now stationary Millennium Wheel. At the foot of the South Bank's river wall, bald patches of grey mud that emerged each low tide glistened in the light of a gibbous moon.

Not much of a beach, is it? he murmured.

Beggars can't be choosers, I suppose, Katy sighed before pressing on without thinking. *Though I don't really like summer.*

Because she couldn't remember a time when it had been different. As a child, it would loom at the end of each school year like a playground bully. While classmates chattered excitedly about plans for the weeks of freedom that lay ahead, all she could think was that it was eight weeks too long. Then, after that last summer with Jude, came summers of constructed jollity while her parents were still living together. They were divided by summers when they were not, dancing on eggshells as mum careered between breathless optimism and frequent tears. And frantic summers vigorously shuttling between estranged grandparents in north Devon and Kent as if somehow this would make thing right.

Even into her early thirties, summer remained a time associated with a vague, nostalgic yearning for life before things started to go wrong.

Dark eyes watched her for a moment then he looked away. *Everyone has their reasons,* he murmured, softly. And she had loved him for that.

It was approaching midnight and the damp air was like warm breath on their skin. They were standing close, but not near enough for any part of their bodies to touch. After a minute or two, without saying a word, he leaned towards Katy as if to whisper something in her ear. Her body tingled as his chin rubbed against the soft skin of her neck, her pulse quickening in anticipation as she waited for him to speak. Then his hand was on her cheek, gently but firmly turning her face towards his. And before she could think of any reason to resist, they kissed.

They caught a black cab back to her flat in Bayswater because it was closer than his. Neither spoke as they rattled along empty streets that glistened in the street lamps' orange glow. It was only when the taxi pulled away that Katy finally found her voice as she fumbled for her key. *You know*, she began. *I don't normally do this.* Opening her hand, he took her key.

Standing back, he let her enter first before stepping inside and softly closing the door behind them. Before placing an arm around her waist and firmly tugging her towards him. Her body trembled as he ran his hands through her hair and the warmth of his breath made the night's edges melt into one. He kissed her hard, working his way inside her blouse with one hand while the other slipped around her waist, blindly searching for the fastening of her skirt. She reached behind to give him a hand, covering his hands with her own to release the fastening with ease. As the skirt slipped towards the ground she kicked it to one side making it fly up into the air. Which made them laugh.

Leaning into him, she kissed him lightly before putting her mouth to his ear to give his lobe a playful bite. As he unhooked her bra she reached down to unbuckle his belt. *Tranquilo*, he whispered as he began unbuttoning her blouse. *Relax.*

Katy checks her watch. It's after seven – he's working late. Did he mention that earlier? She can't recall. That morning, the tray he brought her in bed, the writing on the door, her meeting with Jude, all of this, everything, seems to have taken place a lifetime ago. Of course he is right, she should have called. To let him know why she wasn't at home. Not to worry, that she was OK. She will put things right, now. So she dials his mobile and he answers after just one ring.

'Christ, Katy, at last! Is everything OK'?

'Kind of, I'm at the hospital—' she begins, reassured by the sound of him even if his voice sound tight.

'Katy, are you all right? I mean the baby, is everything—' Words tumble in a rush now, like a dam has burst.

'No, no. Not that. It's fine. I mean, it's not me. I'm all right but Mum—'

'Thank God,' he declared. 'I thought you meant—'

'I know, I'm sorry. But no, it's not that. Mum – she was attacked earlier. Mugged, in the street. She's unconscious. Well, she was conscious earlier, but they had to give her a general anaesthetic to reposition her arm.' Katy rubs her eyes, over-whelmed by tiredness.

'That's terrible. And you, are you OK?'

'I'm fine, Michael,' she sighs. 'Honestly. Just upset, OK? It's terrible seeing her, you know, like this—'

'I know,' he soothes.

'—and knowing there's nothing I can do.'

'There's nothing you can do – she's in the right place.'

'I know.'

'Where are you?'

She looks around her. Stares at the pigeon which has almost devoured what's left of the sandwich. Notices the puddle of white it has let slip on the neighbouring table. Feels the contents of her own stomach curdle. 'In the hospital cafe.'

'No, I mean which hospital. Great Western?'

'Yes.'

'If I leave now I can be there in half an hour—'

'No, no Michael. Please, you don't have to.'

'I can pick you up. Drive you home. You must be exhausted—'

'No. I think I'd better stay. They said I can—'

'Katy. There's nothing more you can do. She's in the best place. You need to look after yourself, take care of you. Let me drive you home. We can get a takeaway for dinner. That way you can be sure of getting a good night's sleep. Really, Katy, I do think it's the best—'

'Listen to me, Michael. I feel I should stay – be here, you know, when she wakes up? You're right, I'm sure, but I'll be fine here, honest. As you say, we're in the best place. Besides, it will give you a chance to finish off whatever you're up to without having to dash off then, tomorrow, when I'm back, we can do everything you've just said, OK? Which reminds me, could you call Sally-Anne for me in the morning – tell her what's happened and why I won't be in?'

'Katy—' Now there's an edge of steel in his tone, and an impatient insistence that she is wrong and he is right which she has heard before. Tightening her grip on her mobile, she braces for what will come next. 'Please don't do this again?'

'Sorry?'

'You know what I'm talking about. I mean, don't push me away.'

'But that's not what I'm doing, honestly. I just need you to understand—'

'Remember what I said before – about letting me in. Seriously Katy, don't shut me out. This is a big deal for me, really, if any of this is going to work it's got to be because we are together, you and me. Being open and honest with each other. No hiding, no secrets, no running away...'

'Of course I remember what you said before,' she replies, a bit too quickly.

How could she forget?

The argument had been sparked by such a trivial thing. A light-hearted after dinner conversation at his friend Spike's one evening when the group around the table had began a round robin confessional with each obliged to offer up a guilty secret. But when the spotlight fell on her she'd felt so awkward and tongue-tied she hastily excused herself and retreated to an upstairs bathroom where Michael had found her, a good half hour later, red-faced and damp-eyed.

He'd had the decency not to quiz her until they got home. Then, when he did as they were getting into bed, he'd reacted with hurt and anger at her unwillingness to explain. *Like unpeeling an onion*, he'd said. A gradual process of mutual exposure, mutual acceptance. A building of intimacy and trust as two people get closer. *Without that, what the hell's the point of any relationship?*

They'd split the morning after and separated for almost four months – a period during which she'd had ample time to analyse her inaction. Her inability to talk to him about things that really mattered. To confide. But how could she do any of this if she wasn't able to come to terms with what had happened herself? If she wasn't able to remember exactly what occurred when, when she tried to save her friend but only ended up making things worse?

She hated herself for what she'd done and, if he knew the truth, so would he.

Soon after, Michael moved to New York to work out of Janssens' US office on a three-month project for a major new client. It was a relief not to see him at work, of course. But as the days became weeks Katy felt worse, not better. Though they'd not been living together at the time of their split, she had been spending more time at his place than her own – a rented studio flat in the end of the North End Road. Now, left to her own devices, she began to appreciate for the first time the extent of how much she missed him.

What a fool she'd been for not letting Michael all the way in. Yet alone, Katy convinced herself she'd left it too late to make things better. Besides, in a way she felt maybe she didn't deserve him – not really. That in the greater scheme of things, the loss of him was some kind of payback. A rebalancing, or getting even. Until, coming out of the tube station on her way to work one morning, she'd seen a familiar figure queuing to exit via the ticket barrier a short distance ahead. He was back.

Before she could panic about how she looked or what to say, how he was or with whom he'd been, she was weaving in and out of the commuters ahead. Darting a few steps to the right then to the left. Desperate to close the gulf between them. *Michael,* she'd called out impetuously. Breathlessly.

Turning towards her his expression was wary for a moment until, sensing the mix of awkwardness and hope behind the boldness of her greeting, his features softened. And then he grinned. There'd been no one else while he was away, he told her later. Just plenty of work and, in between, time to take stock. He was sorry if he'd pushed her too hard, but she should know the hurt the distance she'd maintained between them had caused.

At first, Michael confided, he'd suspected her of seeing someone else. It had happened to him before. He revealed that the reason for leaving his last job and joining Janssens was his need for a fresh start after discovering his last serious girlfriend, Megan, had had an on-off affair with one of his work colleagues for most of the time she and Michael had been going out.

Believe me, I understand how once you've been hurt how difficult it can be to let people in, he told her. *But Katy, really, we've nothing without trust.*

He thought that she, too, had been let down by someone in her past. And in a way this was true, wasn't it? So as they got back together, she vowed she would tell him the whole of it – eventually. Everything. Just not yet.

'Of course, I remember, clearly,' Katy adds, more softly now. 'I remember how much I hurt you before. I remember how I promised to work harder to let you in. And I did, didn't I? Things have been good these past few months. I know neither of us expected a baby, but that's going to be good, too. Is good already, or at least will be once this bloody morning sickness has passed—'

She laughs, briefly. Trying to lighten the moment.

'—please, don't mix up what's happening now with what happened six months ago. Everything's OK, really. Except Mum's in hospital and for now I need to be with her by her side. I'll be back tomorrow, OK? I'll see you then. And until then, I'll be thinking of you, all right?'

He sighs. 'Of course.'

'Thank you, Michael.'

'And Katy?'

'Yes?'

'I love you.'

'Me too.'

'Keep me posted, then.'

'I will.'

'On the mobile. Because I'll be out later... with an old school friend.'

'Another one?'

'What?'

'Old school friend. Wasn't the headhunter...?'

'An estate agent. I just thought it might make sense to consider our options – you know, because soon we might be in need of a bit more space?'

Leaning back in her chair, Katy shuts her eyes. Surely she should feel relief at the success of this deflection. Yet all she feels is hollow. Why is it so hard to let him in? she wonders. If it wasn't for the baby now growing inside her would they still be together, trying as hard as they are now to make all this work? How she wishes she could be sure. Just like she wishes she knew how she really feels about becoming a mother. Can anyone really know it's going to be right for them when they find out they're pregnant for the very first time?

Or maybe's it's never right. Perhaps that only comes with time, when you're left with no choice. Is that why when pressed so many people, even women who know what they want, admit that there's never a perfect time to be a parent.

'You finished with this, love?'

A hand reaches in front of Katy across the table towards the cup she has left untouched, the contents of which are now cold. Looking up, Katy finds herself staring into the face of a pale-faced girl wearing a brown chequered tabard. Her bottle-black hair has been carefully peeled back, secured with grips then confined beneath a hair net. A quick nod, then Katy gazes back down. Should she call him back? she wonders. Try to explain some more? Now she finds herself regretting the prospect of not seeing him for another twelve or maybe eighteen hours. Maybe it would help to have him by her side. To confide. But tell him what, exactly. How much?

Katy slips the phone back into her bag. No, she knows what she must do and she needs time, too, to get things straight in her head. This business with Jude. How, despite using a different name, she appears to have built the beginnings of some kind of relationship with her mum. She shudders. Much as she wants to, she can't wish Jude away. And now, she sees, she'll need to see her again if she's going to understand what's going on. Looping the bag over her shoulder, Katy rises to her feet then retraces her steps back to the ward somewhere upstairs in the building above, in which her mum would soon be coming to.

–

Diane lies in the bed with eyes closed, her chest gently undulating beneath the pale cotton sheet. She is wearing a hospital gown and there is a plastic tube taped to the back of her right hand. Asleep. Though as Katy watches, her face twitches. Though only a barely perceptible movement, it is a welcome indication of her upward drift towards consciousness. How frail she looks and old, too, Katy thinks, her eyes welling at the contrast with the image of her mum's younger self captured in the photo of her wearing that cocktail dress.

Ten years her senior, Charles had just returned to England after three years working in Geneva at the head office of the insurance firm he worked for, when they had first met on the central concourse at Marylebone Station. Diane had just been taken on as a secretary at Baxters, a firm of educational book publishers based just off the Edgware Road. New to the city and still living at home, she commuted daily to and from London from the leafy countryside near Thame. He'd been running late, as usual, having just missed his train. As she rushed from the platform she'd bumped into him – quite literally – as she hurried towards the main exit. Her bag went flying; he picked it up, then conscientiously dusted it down before handing it back.

It was a silly, inconsequential shred of gallantry that seemed so proper, somehow, at the tail end of a decade that had grown so disrespectfully louche. Charles Parker, it seemed, was the perfect gentleman. Over the weeks that followed, they exchanged a few polite smiles without her realising that to do so he must have switched to a later train. With no time after work to fraternise with colleagues in London and no single friends to socialise with left at home, Diane was easily flattered by his attentions. Then, the week before Easter, he invited her out on a date.

They went to a West End cinema to see a new film, *What's Up Doc?* Afterwards, he paid for a taxi to get her back to the station just in time to catch the last train home. She'd not had the heart to admit she hated Barbra Streisand – a secret dislike she endured for years despite the numerous records he bought her over countless Christmases – but it had been a pleasant evening, nonetheless. Soon afterwards, she moved into a flat in St John's Wood with an older woman, recently widowed, who Charles knew through work. He became a frequent visitor, often dropping in unexpectedly for dinner, until late one evening he missed his train and stayed the night. Two months later she found herself pregnant.

The first few years weren't easy. After a low-key registry office wedding and a hasty relocation to an up and coming town nestled in Surrey's leafy commuter belt, Diane gave birth to Andrew and then, two years later, a daughter, Katy. It could have been the perfect happy ending. But, instead, Charles made little effort to conceal from his wife how much he resented the broken nights of sleep. How infuriated he was by the constant noise and disarray that bedevilled their home. Or how deeply he despised the way motherhood was changing his wife. Always tired and listless, often distracted, Diane survived in the hope that when the children got older things would change – meticulously overlooking the creeping coldness of his touch.

So went the story Katy concocted from memory and imagination. For she'd never understood the breakdown of her parents' marriage nor the reason why, after its deterioration seemed irreversible, they stayed together so long. For the children's sake, perhaps. Some old-fashioned sense of duty. Whatever the explanation, neither of her parents commented on it then or after. For the past was not a language the Parker family spoke.

Where did it all go wrong, Mum, Katy wonders. Between you and dad; between you and me?

'Love?'

Opening her eyes, Katy quickly narrows them against the unfamiliar shards of light that cut through the white plastic blinds still drawn at the window. Stiffly, she shifts position. Slowly, she turns her head towards the bed where her mother now lies propped up against a mound of pillows. 'Mum?' she whispers. 'Is everything OK?'

'You've not been there all night, have you?' Diane's voice is a croak.

Katy nods, briefly, then shrugs away her mother's concern. 'Actually, it wasn't that uncomfortable,' she lies.

'You always were a hopeless fibber,' her mother chides as she road-tests a cautious smile. 'When you were little I could always tell – there was an expression you had, nothing obvious, just a subtle look... That and the fact that when you were doing it you could never meet my eye.'

Katy, who without thinking has dropped her gaze to the floor, looks up quickly. 'All right, Mum, you've got me: it was an awful night!' She smiles. 'But really, it doesn't matter. How are you?' She leans forward to pour water from a jug which stands on a narrow chest of drawers beside the bed into a plastic cup and passes it to Diane.

'Thanks, love,' Mum replies, slowly bringing the plastic to her lips. 'My throat feels parched.' She takes a sip then winces.

'Still sore?' asks Katy. When will the nurse come with more painkillers, she wonders. Diane nods. 'I'll call someone.' She reaches towards a small control panel attached to a white cable knotted around the metal framed bed head. At the touch of her finger, a red button on the plastic box lights up. Sitting back in her seat, she struggles to stifle a yawn.

'You were sleeping, though, weren't you?' Diane looks guilty. 'I'm sorry I woke you. Only you were mumbling to yourself. Something about the dew.'

Katy looks away towards the window. She is unaware she's been dreaming of anything at all let alone talking in her sleep. She's not done that in years, and the sudden memory of it makes her ashamed. It was only in her late twenties that the recurrent hate dreams – a series of imagined heated confrontations with Jude – had finally stopped.

Often, the two of them would be having stand-up arguments in public places; always they involved Katy finally confronting Jude with how she really felt about their so-called friendship. In the early years she'd often woken before dawn, feverish and tense, convinced it had been she who'd been dragged into the bushes, not Jude. That it was she who'd stood her ground, not run away. Confronted him. Defended her friend. It would certainly have been easier to live with. Rather that, surely, than this feeling of uselessness that had permeated into even the finest crevices of her being and lodged there still, waiting to split her apart.

'How are you feeling this morning, Mrs Parker?'

A nurse has approached unnoticed and now stands at the end of Diane's bed adjusting the curtain that separates her area from the next bed along. In her hand she holds a small paper cup. 'I thought you might need something for the pain.' As Diane nods, weakly, she moves towards the head of the bed and holds out the cup. 'Ah, good, you've got some water,' she adds, smoothing down the sheet. 'A doctor will check in on you shortly then, once he's given you the all clear, there'll be toast and tea.'

Diane swallows and, with her tubed hand, hands back the paper cup. Then, when the nurse has gone, she turns back to Katy. Raising her free hand towards the damaged side of her face, she stops just short of touching her face. 'So go on, tell me the worst,' she murmurs. 'How bad does it look?'

Katy stares at the swollen skin which is ripening towards the colour and sheen of a full-blown aubergine. The eye on that side is puffy and wet. Bruising is now also starting to show around one side of her neck. 'Well the doctor said it would look worse before it started to look better,' she begins. 'And I'm afraid to say he was right.'

'Ah.' Diane closes her eyes. 'But nothing broken.'

'No,' smiles Katy. 'So with a bit of luck you'll be home soon. Unless you'd rather come back to ours...' Her voice trails away at the thought of Michael. He wouldn't mind, would he? Which reminds her, she must try ringing again – catch him before he leaves for work. He said to try any time. 'Mum, if you're OK for a few minutes I think I'd better call him.'

'Send him my love,' Diane murmurs as Katy walks out of the door.

Although early, a long line of hospital staff and bath-robed patients are already queuing for cappuccinos and croissants by the time Katy reaches the ground floor. Breakfast, however, is the last thing on her mind as she quickly counts another two messages on her answerphone. The first isn't from Michael, however, but a friend of her mother's – Joyce Patterson, the retired school teacher who lives in the flat opposite at Parkview.

Poor old Joyce. She and Diane had been due to go to the theatre the night before to see a Noel Coward revival but, instead, she'd driven over to the hospital with a bunch of flowers and an overnight bag of bits and bobs to make her friend feel more comfortable. Now, though, the woman's usually calm voice is upset and agitated as she relates hearing someone moving around Diane's flat when she got back home late last evening. At first she thought it might be Katy collecting some more things for Diane but, when she'd knocked on the door and called out her name, no one had replied. Perturbed, she quickly retreated into her own flat, secured the bolt and chain and dialled 999. But by the time a policeman arrived the intruder was long gone.

'Call me as soon as you get this message,' the woman implores. Katy leans back against the wall to let a heavily pregnant woman shuffle by. 'The locks will have to be changed, of course. But it's not just that. You'd better come over. Because whoever it was, they've been through… everything.'

Chapter 13

What else would you have had me do, Kat – curl up in a corner and die? There were times it was tempting, of course. No, not to die but slip from view and reinvent myself as someone else. A nicer, better, cleaner person. An Estelle. But I was trapped, you see, by the stuff life threw at me. Have you ever felt what it's like to have everything you ever believed about yourself turn out to be a lie? That's my story, Kat. But shit happens and all you can do is respond. You can't blame a person for simply dealing with other people's mess as best they can. It makes you stronger. Because you've got to be strong if you're going to get by.

Chapter 14

'I said: a Bacardi and coke, a half of Merrydown and two bottles of Becks, OK?' Jude shouted against the dizzying roar from the Christmas revellers now packing the saloon bar.

Removing his glasses, the barman pinched the skin on the bridge of his nose with bloated fingers red and raw from years spent wiping down tables and rinsing out glasses. 'And I said: we don't serve alcohol to anyone like you who's under age,' he shouted back, articulating each word carefully as if talking to a halfwit or small child. 'If you want me to sell you a drink, prove you're over eighteen.'

'Miserable old git,' Jude spat back, stuffing her five-pound note back into her jeans pocket before heading back towards the table where the others were sitting. Drawing close she could see Charlotte, who was perched precariously on Bob's lap sharing his cigarette, let out a piercing laugh as Graeme dropped what was left of an ice cube from the bottom of Jude's empty glass down the front of her blouse.

'Wanker!' the girl declared, brightly, with a toss of long, bottle-blonde hair that had been so vigorously back-brushed and lacquered that the only thing that shifted position was a festive hair band made of tinsel.

With a stupid grin, Graeme stretched his arm across the wall of glasses between them – a movement which brought Jude to a halt three tables away where she stood, unseen by the others so far, wondering what he would do next. She knew it was a trivial test of his loyalty. But it was also a measure, of sorts, of their fledgling relationship.

As his hand touched the front of Charlotte's blouse, the girl adjusted her position to lean towards him. However it wasn't this that caught Jude's attention but the brief exchange of glances between Graeme and Bob – a knowing look that seemed to suggest unspoken agreement between them that whatever belonged to one could, by rights, be shared. A beat later and Jude's boyfriend was slipping his hand down Charlotte's top to extract what was left of the ice. There wasn't much, and when he pulled out his hand his fingers are dripping. Then, holding her gaze, he brought his hand to his mouth and slowly licked his fingers. Leaning towards him conspiratorially, Charlotte whispered something in his ear then all three of them laughed.

The spell broken, Jude stepped to one side and out of view behind a pinball machine. What did she expect, she wondered, crossly. The three of them, sixth-formers two years older than her who attend the local technical college, always hung out together. Might even have had a bit of a threesome going on, according to some reports, though the subject had not even been hinted at over the three months she and Graeme had been going out.

They'd met in the same pub in September just after the start of Jude's second year at St Mary's. Siobhan had finally agreed that now she was in the fifth year she could go unaccompanied to the weekly youth club at the Christian Fellowship meeting rooms opposite the multistorey car park at the bottom of town. But it hadn't taken long for Jude to tire of the awkward assembly of teenagers who loved nothing better than an hour shuffling with heads bowed to the sound of Seventies B-sides that crackled from a second-hand tape deck.

Just a dozen paces from the Christian Fellowship meeting rooms, The Three Pigs on Maiden Lane with its dank carpets, sticky table tops and nicotine walls was another world. It was peopled, too, by an alien race of off-duty squaddies from the army training camp ten miles out of town, blunt-faced youth opportunity scheme conscripts and sharp-faced shop girls – the last place she would ever have expected to bump into anyone she knew from school let alone Dave and Siobhan which, of course, had been its appeal. And it was here, the first Friday night Jude ventured inside, alone, that she'd run into the students from the local tech.

Graeme Willis was the youngest son of St Mary's deputy headmistress. A tall, dark-haired athlete with wiry chest hair sprouting at the neckline of his skintight cotton T-shirt, he wanted to join the army like his older brother, Shaun, who'd fought in the Falklands. Mrs Willis, however, was determined Graeme should keep his options open so had persuaded him to defer his decision until he'd got some technical qualifications. That way he'd have something to fall back on, she'd said. Which was how Jude came to lose her virginity to Graeme on the newly-laid, faux terracotta lino on her deputy headmistress's kitchen floor.

Though not the best, the sex was sharpened by the looming shadow of parental disapproval. For in a way it seemed that each was the other's forbidden fruit. When she made it home just in time by her official ten o'clock curfew, dishevelled and not a little sore, Jude was elated – by a heady sense of pride and relief that at last, the initiation was over. Graeme, however, was an arms length kind of boyfriend. Though it was clear when they were alone how much he fancied her, whenever they went anywhere or did anything with his college contemporaries, he seemed offhand. All too often conversation revolved around their shared experiences, frustrations, jokes – almost as if Jude wasn't there. At times like this she'd cheer herself by thinking of her classmates, still fettered by over-anxious parents to evenings at home eating TV dinners in front of Cagney & Lacey.

Yet Jude felt torn and grew restless and frustrated with Graeme, with Siobhan, with Kat. During her early weeks at St

Mary's she'd been drawn to the pale-faced loner and intrigued, too, by how different from their classmates her new friend appeared to be. Like many of the girls, Kat had been to St Mary's since she was seven yet while she had friends, she'd been one of the few not to participate in the obligatory pairing off that seemed so naturally to occur as the girls prepared to move up from junior to senior school. Alienated from the general flow of things, Kat seemed reluctant to compromise in order to fit in. And Jude respected her for that. She was grateful, too, for the licence her friendship with Kat had granted her to be accepted by her new classmates and, eventually, elevated to the status of someone other girls wanted to be 'in' with. But it did not take long before their shortcomings and limitations tipped the balance to make an increasingly cocksure, sharp-tongued and frustrated Jude someone the other girls went out of their way 'not to cross'.

It was an evolution in herself that Jude could see Kat enjoyed being part of, and she got pleasure from that. Until Kat's inability to evolve at the same pace left her straggling behind like a dawdling child and the more Kat dawdled, the more Jude's resentment grew. It wasn't Kat's fault Diane and Charles were stricter than Siobhan, of course, but that wasn't the point. The more time they spent together, the more something in Kat's make-up began to grate. For as long as Jude could remember she had kicked against the machine, resentful of situations others created for her. Her mum's poor taste in men. Her dad's prema- ture death. In contrast, Kat appeared to believe that in the increasingly fractious breakdown of her own parents' marriage she was somehow complicit. It was a fundamental weakness Jude came to despise as their flowering friendship flatlined towards little more than a marriage of convenience.

'Shit!' someone behind her exclaimed as beer spilled down her left arm. Crossly spinning around, more than ready for a confrontation, Jude found herself caught off guard. 'Hey, I'm really sorry,' the voice continued as she turned to face him and then, as their eyes meet, they both laughed. 'Wow, Jude, I didn't recognise you!' Andrew said, dropping his eyes to skim the cleavage exposed by her low-cut top before he could stop himself. 'Um… you look great.'

'As do you,' Jude retorted, making a show of shaking her beer-soaked sleeve.

'Let me get you something,' Andrew offered, taking a gulp from his glass. 'I think I owe you that much, at least. What will it be?'

'A pint of Merrydown would be good.' The others could sing for their drinks for all she cared; they probably hadn't even noticed she'd been delayed.

Leaning back against the pinball machine, Jude watched Kat's brother retrace his steps towards the bar, lean forwards and shout the order at the barman. The jeans he was wearing, faded and frayed, were tight across his crotch leaving little to the imagination. The silver studded black leather belt he wore matched his battered biker's jacket.

Jude grinned. She had always liked the look of Andrew although until that evening had only met him briefly a couple times. Since starting at college the autumn she began at St Mary's, he seemed to have spent as much time as he could playing on various sports teams or studying after hours in the college library. Well, that's what he had told Kat's parents and, judging by how frequently they commented on his busy academic schedule being the reason for his absence from the dinner table when Jude went to Kat's house after school for tea, they believed him, too. Now, up close for the first time, Jude noted with approval the pouch of tobacco tucked into his back pocket. His scuffed DMs. The ease with which he handled himself.

Andrew passed her cider then took another sip of his beer. 'Here on your own?'

'No.' Jude waved casually over her shoulder towards where Graeme and the other two were sitting. 'Just hanging out with a few friends.'

Shooting a glance towards the distant table, Andrew chuckled. 'Graeme Willis.' He nodded. 'Someone told me he'd been seeing a girl in Kat's class. So, is that you?'

'Was,' Jude declared, impetuously. 'I just dumped him, actually.'

'Good for you,' Andrew smiled, raising his glass in toast to her wisdom. 'He's a prick!'

Jude sniffed. 'I know.'

As a couple sitting to their left rose to leave Andrew darted towards the empty table before anyone else could sit down. Turning back towards Jude, he patted the seat next to him. 'Join me,' he called, and there was something about the way he said it that Jude found impossible to resist.

'So—' she began with mock solemnity as she shifted position in her seat. 'Do you come here often?'

'Actually it's my first time,' he smiled. 'We've got a gig in the room upstairs tomorrow night. I only stopped by to bring some equipment over. I wasn't planning to stay.'

Jude took a gulp from her glass. 'We?'

'My band. I play bass.'

'What sort of music?'

'Indie rock. We all listen to loads of weird west coast American stuff. Although I like loads of different music. Stuff that's different, you know – retro. Bolan. Morrison. Velvet Underground. Not chart crap.'

'Sounds great.'

He shot Jude a glance as if unsure whether she is being serious.

'Seriously,' she added, relishing the thought that she'd backfooted him, albeit briefly. 'It does. I love all that kind of stuff.'

Andrew drained his glass. 'Well I've a demo tape upstairs you could borrow... if you're really interested.'

Finishing her drink, too, Jude rose to her feet. 'Well let's go and get it.'

While Andrew got the key to the upstairs room from the barman, Jude slipped up the stairs to wait for him on first floor landing. A moment later they were standing in the open doorway, peering into the room's darkened interior, willing their eyes to adjust to the gloom. In the far corner she could just make out an assortment of dark boxes and what looked like a collapsible keyboard beside a half-decorated Christmas tree.

Andrew strode towards the box and crouched down. 'Turn on the light, will you?' he called without turning round. 'Only I can't see what I'm looking for.'

Softly she shut the door behind them, firmly pushing it to. Slipping off her shoes, she padded across the room and crouched down beside him. 'I can't seem to find the switch,' she shrugged. 'Here, I'm good in the dark, let me...' Side by side in the grainy darkness Jude felt the warmth radiating from his body. The denim jacket he wore had a burnt, earthy smell. The sound of his breathing was measured, slow.

'It'll turn up,' Andrew murmured.

Pausing his search, he turned towards her. Despite the pounding she now felt in her chest, Jude's body felt chill. Like something stunned by an electric charge. Then, a moment later, his arm was around her. Tugging her towards him. One hand cupping her face while the other slipped around her waist, gently feeling its way between the fabric upwards towards the lacy edging of her front-opening bra.

'I'm good in the dark, too,' he murmured as their mouths met.

Chapter 15

Richmond, July 2013

Joyce Patterson, a stout woman in her late fifties as wide as she is tall with close-cropped silver hair, is standing in the open doorway of her flat, waiting, as Katy steps from the lift on Parkview's fourth floor. On his knees to her side, in the open doorway of Diane's flat, a locksmith dressed in a navy jumpsuit is packing away his tools.

'At last!' the woman exclaims, though it's barely turned nine. 'We've got to get this sorted before your mum gets home.'

'Good as new,' the locksmith declares, rising to his feet to hand Joyce the new set of keys. 'All done. And as requested I've fitted a Banham, too.'

Katy fixes her mother's friend with a questioning stare, but Joyce won't yet meet her gaze. 'It's so kind of you to come out at such short notice,' the older woman says briskly. 'I'm sure we all really appreciate it. Now Katherine, you go straight in while I accompany our gallant knight to the lift.'

As the locksmith chuckles, Katy steps inside to see an unexpected figure standing in the open kitchen doorway.

'Andrew! Why didn't you tell me—'

Katy exclaims hurrying towards him then halting, abruptly, as she registers her brother's frown.

'Why didn't you tell me?' he demands.

'I'm sorry?' she falters, processing the dishevelled state of him. His dull eyes. Five o'clock shadow. Crumpled business suit and skew-whiff tie. Andrew looks like someone who's just stumbled off an overnight flight. Which of course he has, he tells her curtly, having cancelled the direct Dubai to Washington red-eye ticket his work had booked him to break the journey in London to see Diane.

How close they used to be in the years before that round-the-world trip during his gap year, she thinks, miserably. A journey during which he drifted between continents before arriving in New York and hiring a car to drive from east coast to west. It was the highlight of his trip, he would later declare in his newly honed mid-Atlantic twang. Because in the latter stages of this epic drive when he pitched up in the southern part of the San Francisco Bay area, he met Dee. The thought of her sister-in-law makes Katy's expression tighten, as it always does. For she was the reason he'd not come back.

Though he'd returned to take up his place at university in Durham, as soon as he graduated he secured a lowly job not far from her family home at a small but ambitious US computing firm which, by the end of the decade, was flying high. He rose rapidly through the ranks, they married, and by the mid-Nineties his business card proudly boasted Vice President status. And in embossed print. Andrew now visits the UK infrequently but remains close to Diane. Which is typical. Because he's always been his mother's favourite. Even Jude once remarked upon it. When did it all go wrong between us, Katy wonders? During those long years she'd wasted; all that time spent running away.

'I only rang last night on the off chance, from the airport while I was waiting for my flight. Which is when Joyce told me mum was in hospital. For God's sake, Katy. Couldn't you have let me know yourself?'

Her cheeks burn. He has a point. Though there was hardly time even to call Michael. And even if she had thought of it she only had Andrew and Dee's home number on her mobile which would have been of little use as everyone would surely have been out at school or work. How was she to know he was travelling in Europe and the Middle East on business?

'Sorry,' she stutters. 'I didn't have your cell number on my mobile—'

'Is she OK?' he interrupts, dismissing her excuse with a wave of his hand.

Katy's stomach tightens. Why does he make her feel like this, she wonders, miserably. Ever the guilty schoolgirl. Even though she's now almost forty. A soon-to-be mother, too. How was it that as children they'd got on so much better? Had been friends, almost. Or maybe that was just a rose-tinted reversioning of the truth of it; a deceit she'd nurtured to obscure darker shadows.

'Mum's doing OK,' she replies, determined not to rise to it. He may think of her as his silly little sister; a passive victim of fate who's let herself drift, aimlessly, for half a lifetime. But she knows better.

True, instead of matching his academic qualifications and glittering career she lost her footing and ran away. But she is stronger than he thinks. And has to be, too – especially now. For the tiny life now unfurling inside her. For Michael. And for Diane. Katy tears a sheet from the notepad by the phone, writes out the name and directions to Maynard Ward then hands the slip of paper to her brother who tucks it into his inside jacket pocket with a nod. She offers up a tentative smile.

'She'll be thrilled to see you, I'm sure.'

'Are you OK?' he asks, turning away to retrieve the executive business case left propped against the side of the fridge. It is obvious she has just caught him as he is about to leave. 'You're looking a bit tired. Everything OK with that photographer, Martin—'

'Michael,' she interrupts, with little inclination to correct her brother any further. 'And yes, thanks for asking, everything's fine.'

'Good. Well, I suppose, I'd better get going,' he says with a weary smile, his right arm twitching for a moment as if he might be about to shake her hand. 'I'll be in London with Dee and the kids in mid-October so let's all get together then.' A sudden pulse from his smart phone announces the arrival of the taxi he has ordered as it pulls into the car park four floors below. 'Look after yourself.'

'You too,' Katy calls, stepping back to let him by. She sinks back against the wall as soon as he has gone. And as she listens to his brief farewell to Joyce, she is aware for the first time how much her body aches. Her back is knotted. Her feet and ankles feel swollen. But she must keep going for mum.

'So what's all this about, Joyce?' Katy demands as soon as the other woman steps back inside.

Taking care to first secure the front door catch, Joyce holds up her hand for Katy to wait for the dull clank from the lift that marks the locksmith's descent. Only when the sound fades does her hand fall to her side, but her expression remains strained. 'Sorry,' she replies. 'You can never be too careful.'

'Why all the cloak and dagger stuff, Joyce? What's going on?'

'Walls have ears,' the woman replies in a low voice. A retired chemistry teacher, Joyce is a voracious reader of crime fiction with a keen interest in amateur dramatics. 'Not literally, of course. But when someone's stolen your keys then used them to poke around your home... Well, you just never know. Come on, I'll show you what I mean.' She leads the way towards Diane's bedroom then, as Katy steps inside, hovers just outside the door. 'I mean, look.'

Katy surveys the state of the room.

Every drawer in her mother's antique cabinet yawns wide open with assorted contents poking out like scolding tongues. The bed, which would have been neatly made the previous morning by her mother's cleaner, Luda, is stripped back exposing the mattress. The shelves lining one side of the room stand empty, each book having been pulled out then stacked on its side on the floor beneath the window. Overall the effect is methodical, not random.

'Almost as if whoever it was wanted to make some kind of point,' she murmurs. 'I mean, it's not what you expect a burglary to look like, is it?'

'Quite,' says Joyce. 'Which is just what the police said. Look, I didn't want to worry you any more than necessary but I thought you needed to know. And besides, what with Monty – well, I thought it best for you to come and see for yourself when we knew what's happening with your mum. You know, to decide what to tell her.'

'Monty?'

A sudden shiver makes Katy think of what her mum used to say when she was small. Something about a feeling she got sometimes, like someone just walked over your grave. She runs a hand through her hair. It's damp and clumpy. What must she look like? Turning away, she walks past Joyce into the kitchen where every cabinet door has been left wide open. Beneath the sink where her mum keeps Monty's food, travel box and other cat-related paraphernalia, the main shelf is bare.

'He's gone.'

Katy spins round to stare at Joyce, who's now standing with her back to the kitchen window with legs apart and arms crossed. 'What do you mean?'

'Whoever did this took him with them. In his travelling box. I spent quite a while going over everything last night when the police were here. I thought maybe he'd just got let out by mistake. But it seems to be the only thing that was taken.'

'But why?'

'Baffling, isn't it?' Joyce says, distractedly fiddling with the silver hoop in her left ear. 'Unless this is the mark of the true cat burglar.' She lets out a humourless chuckle that stops as instantly as it began. 'Come on, there's something else you need to see.'

Too tired to make sense of what's unfolding, Katy shuffles into the front room where Joyce stands on the hearthside rug gesturing towards the mantelpiece. For a moment, she struggles to see what point the woman is trying to make. Then her frayed nerves finally begin to make connections.

The narrow ledge running the entire length of the chimney breast is crammed, as usual, with its snapshots and mementoes. But wait, Katy thinks, something is different.

Carefully, she scans the shelf from left to right registering with growing unease how meticulously someone has gone through the arrangement, turning each picture round to face the wall. Then, as her gaze reaches the centre where a framed photo of herself taken at Andrew and Dee's wedding usually sits, she stops and stares. The picture is flat on its face and as she slowly reaches forwards to stand it upright she sees the picture slipped out leaving the frame is empty.

As Katy turns it over her hand is stilled by a biro scribble across her own face so heavy it has torn the paper. 'Oh,' she exclaims, sinking down onto the nearest chair as the photograph slips to the floor. The next thing she is aware of is Joyce who hands her a glass of water before bending down to retrieve the picture. As she straightens up, the other woman scans the defaced image then quickly crumples it into a ball.

'Go on, drink it,' the woman urges. 'While I get rid of this – I'm sure your mother has the negative somewhere.'

'So someone broke in, trashed the place, left their mark,' Katy murmurs, wearily. 'Kids high on drink, or drugs, or both, I'd guess.'

'Right, yes,' says Joyce, uncertainly. 'Only they don't seem to have broken in.'

Katy looks up. 'What do you mean?'

'It seems they had a key. Though it won't work now the locks are changed, of course. Anyway, I'll ask Luda to come and do an extra clean ahead of your mum's return. I just thought you should see how it is, you know? The police said they'd be in touch.'

Joyce lets herself out a short while later leaving Katy to scan her mother's bedroom and bathroom for anything she might take back to the hospital to make her stay more comfortable. There's little Diane's neighbour hasn't already thought of, though. And having been advised by the doctor earlier that Diane should stay in hospital under observation at least another twenty-four hours, she decides instead to make a start on tidying the mess.

Doing something, anything, is better than waiting. Thinking. Worrying about what might happen next.

Katy works methodically, neatly returning contents to drawers, dusting down surfaces, replacing books, stripping then remaking the bed. Both kitchen and bathroom are scrubbed clean and what's left in the fridge is binned, just in case.

It's almost twelve by the time she's done and as she sits down on the sofa cradling a mug of tea she stares once more at the empty frame that stands on the coffee table before her. The defaced cardboard is now in the bin and if she puts another photo inside perhaps her mum won't notice. It will need to be a picture of her, though, she thinks, searching the mantelpiece for likely candidates. But which one?

Her gaze settles briefly on the old Polaroid of herself, blonde-haired and stern-faced in her favourite sundress, taken during the summer of '76. Long hot months during which the world had seemed to hold its breath, she recalls. A time when one parched day blurred into the next and even a trip to the playground became a brutal trek that turned once skipping small children into limping shadows. Queuing for water at the standpipes which stood sentry on every street corner. Air that scorched your throat when the breeze blew in from the nearby tinderbox heath.

Though the print has faded, she can still see the colour of that dress. Aegean blue, though you'd not know it by looking at the picture now. And she can still remember, too, how wearing it made her feel. The heart-burst pride she'd had earlier that same day opening the shoebox and gingerly parting the pink tissue paper to reveal the brand new sandals. The smell of the leather strawberries sewn so carefully onto the strap beside each buckle.

Still holding the photograph, she closes her eyes. The shoes were green and red, she recalls. Colours that still make her think of freedom. And deceit.

The picnic was Mum's idea. An afternoon in the Water Meadows which, that long hot summer of '76, were anything but. But what had started out as an idle distraction quickly soured. Tall, slim and self-conscious in his freshly pressed shorts, her dad strode ahead with the picnic basket and striped golfing umbrella. Stooped and sweating, mum buckled beneath the dull weight of a plastic cool box as she trailed behind.

Charles chose a spot between a tatty cluster of chestnut trees, beneath which a number of other families had already set up camp, and the abandoned lock-keeper's cottage. Eager to keep his distance from their neighbours, as always, she thinks. Then he stood watching in silence as mum spread the tartan rug then struggled to wedge the umbrella upright. Waiting until she was done before taking a seat on the blanket's furthest corner and carefully unfolding a copy of *The Times*. *I'll unpack all the food then, too, shall I?* Mum muttered, crossly. But no one bothered to answer.

Seated on a nearby tree stump, Andrew was using the rolled up comic in his hand as a telescope. But Katherine paid him little heed as she stood beside him transfixed by something on the ground a few feet away. Close to her feet were the biggest ants she'd ever seen with wings that glistened in the solar glare. The way they moved, how they shone, provoked in her an overwhelming need to step forward and crush all stragglers beneath her sandal as, somewhere behind her, her parents argued while mum slammed the contents of the cool bag onto a tartan picnic blanket.

With hands clasped behind her back, Katherine solemnly kicked dust clouds from the parched earth towards the ants. Trying, and failing, to ignore her parents' voices. Until, uneasy and ignored, she turned towards the canal.

It took until she was just a couple of feet from the bank for the crunchy sound her sandals' soles made on the granite shards to dull the human hum. For the sun that beat onto her arms and the back of her neck to make her head feel light and her skin prickle. Staring down at the leather strawberries on her feet, she carefully moved her left foot forwards then lined up her right foot alongside, a short step away from the edge. Leaning her body forward, she looked down.

Beneath her, about a foot below its normal level, lurked water gently slap-slapping against the canal's sides. Inky black, glistening, fathomless water which seemed to suck in rather than reflect back the afternoon's piercing brightness. Even her dress looked drab as she gazed down into the eyes of her solemn-faced, watery self. Mesmerised by explosions of light that came from the oily surface and sparkles like glittering jewels, she started to sway in time to its slight movement. Losing herself in the rhythm of the murky depths, unable to look away.

Yearning for the elation that would come when the surface once more burst into life.

Ebb and flow. Ebb and flow. Until it came, as if from nowhere.

The irresistible urge.

To jump.

It took only a single step into nothing to fly. Just for a split second, floating in silence. Until, with a thunderous splash, water closed over the young aviator's head and its alien coldness bit deep, jolting her body with its electric shock.

Her ears pounded. Her body floated for a moment as if in space quite capable, if she so chose, of turning a complete somersault or performing a pirouette. She opened her eyes in surprise at the chill now sucking her limbs. The baubles of light from above that exploded into a magical halo. The gelatinous pond weed gently soothing her sunburnt legs. The belief she could breathe underwater was thrilling and with head tilted back and mouth wide open, she began to laugh.

Then, just as her ears started to pound and her head felt fit to explode, an arm reached around her and a hand gently cupped her chin. Her heart leaped at the thought – the most natural thing in the world – of a water nymph, gently guiding her upwards, back towards the light. But as the waters broke and she saw sunlight as if for the first time, Katherine was aware only of anxious faces and another sudden and overwhelming urge. To cry.

Someone had found the frayed canal-side lifebuoy ring. Her saviour – neither angel nor mermaid but a boy with a sunburnt nose – dragged her towards the slippery, slate-coloured bricks of the canal's side. Arms reached down and she was hoisted upwards – flying again – then deposited back onto dry land. Her dress was soaked. She'd lost a sandal. Strangers' faces loomed then someone wrapped a towel around her and gently steered her back towards the picnic blanket.

How could you not have seen, Charles? You should have been watching. Though Mum was cross, the stifled sob she hiccupped every now and then made Katherine want to laugh. Dad reached to pat her dry then, practical as ever, offered her a chocolate biscuit. *Don't you understand how close we came to losing her, Charles? It only takes a second for a small child to slip and fall.*

Wrapped in a towel, Katherine sat beneath the shade of the umbrella while Mum stood by its side talking to grown-ups. Carefully, she peeled back the foil from the Wagon Wheel she was still holding. The chocolate was melty, her fingers sticky, and the biscuit inside was warm and soft. As she nibbled around the outside, rotating it carefully until the rounded edge had disappeared, she stared at Mum's toenails. Cherry Red. She'd helped mum paint them just that morning. But now the nail of one of her big toes was broken and the varnish was all chipped. Her father would be pleased, she'd noted. Because earlier he'd said the colour was too bright. Like a kind of tart.

Charles? Say something, for goodness sake! her mum pressed on now the crowd of rescuers had dispersed. *I said, it only takes a second—*

Screwing up her eyes, Katherine battled to cling onto the elation she'd felt just a few minutes earlier. But it was impossible.

Like trying to climb back inside a dream. So instead she started to cry again. Long, convulsive sobs that made her body shudder. *Please stop shouting*, she mumbled, gathering her breath to make her voice louder as she rocks her body to and fro. *Because it wasn't Daddy's fault, not really. Just because he wasn't watching when I fell.*

—

Why did I say that? Katy now wonders, reaching for the empty frame. But as always, the answer hovers just beyond her reach. She glances down. The Polaroid she is still holding is the only loose picture amongst her mum's prized collection. Too small, she knows, but it will have to do.

As she releases the catch on the frame's back, a slip of newspaper browned by age slips onto her lap. The cutting is dated the summer she sat her O levels, the last time she saw Jude. But her attention is drawn by a handwritten message written across the Polaroid's reverse. 'To err is only human,' reads the writing. Her father's hand. 'Forgive and be mine.' Katy's face burns with the shame. But before she can process the reason why, a sudden sound from the hallway behind her makes her body stiffen. A low, metallic grating noise like someone is trying to open the front door though as she turns towards it she sees the door remains firmly closed.

Quickly, she slips the picture and cutting into the frame. But as she replaces it on the mantelpiece, she hears something else. A hand pushing against the letterbox. From where she stands, she can see a copy of the local paper fills the basket on the door's inside which Diane uses to collect the post. No one peering through the flap would be able to see a thing other than the morning's headlines. Even so, she curses herself for not being more careful. Why the hell didn't she secure the chain?

Slowly rising to her feet, Katy slips across the room and steps out into the hall. Though the grinding noise has stopped, she still senses someone is standing outside the front door, just a step or two away. Softly, she inches forward, determined to secure the door. Until at last she is close enough and makes a swift decision to reach up to slip the bolt which is quieter than the chain. Then she brings her face in line with the fish-eye peephole to peer outside.

The landing, usually in semi-darkness, is fully lit thanks to a movement sensor. Even so, she is a beat too late to see more than the rear view of the departing figure. A dark-haired woman in a black sleeveless dress clutching a red leather shoulder bag. Though she can't see the visitor's face, something about the way she holds herself, the swing of her hips, is familiar. What the hell would Jude be doing here?

Rubbing the sweat from her face with a sticky palm, Katy hears the familiar echo as the lift descends from the floors above. And in that instant she knows what she must do. Because she's got to be sure. And if it is indeed Jude, she must determine why. She grabs her bag which she left on the hall table and the keys to her mum's car which sit in the glass bowl by its side.

With her face pressed to the door, Katy's ears strain for the sounds of the lift doors opening then closing. Then as soon as it is done she releases the catch and peers out into the empty landing. Quickly pulling the door to behind her, Katy hurries towards the stairwell which runs parallel to the lift shaft. The lift is a slow one, and if she is quick she might still get a glimpse of the visitor in the building's foyer. So she runs as fast as she can down the stairs, gripping the handrail for fear of falling. Damn this heat, she curses. For her body feels leaden, her ankles swollen.

Halfway down, the sound of a raised voice, a woman's, makes Katy briefly pause. It comes from the third floor landing only a few feet from where she now stands. Jude, for Katy is now in no doubt that it is she, is arguing with a man about some furniture he is eager to squeeze into the lift. Seizing the advantage, Katy starts to run again, taking two stairs at a time for fear Jude might abandon the lift in favour of the stairwell. Bursting out into the ground floor foyer, the first thing Katy sees is a department store delivery van parked by the main entrance. The second is her mum's car which is in one of the first residents' parking bays by its side.

Waving the fob of the car keys clasped in her hand, she unlocks the car as she hurries out into the car park then quickly slips inside. Crouched in the driving seat a moment later, peering over the steering wheel, she watches Jude emerge, pause for a moment as she squints into the afternoon glare, then turn to her right. Reassured that she has not been seen, Katy straightens up in her seat as Jude heads towards a silver hatchback parked in the far corner. Only then does it dawn on her that she has a decision to make, and fast.

Jude doesn't know she's here. She hasn't seen her. Nor does she know she's in her mother's car. How easily she could follow her, Katy thinks. Find out where she is going. Get an idea, perhaps, of what she might do next. The prospect is terrifying. What if Jude sees her? But somehow Katy feels she no longer has a choice. Things have gone too far. Diane is hurt. Her flat's been burgled and now Jude has come to her door. Tried to open it, even – though God only knows how she might have come by a key.

Katy frowns. Surely mum wouldn't have been so stupid as to give one to her new friend, 'Estelle'? For Jude can't have had anything to do with the mugging, given that at the time it happened she was with her in Michael's flat. Although her being there at that time was perfect timing, wasn't it? And not only had Katy provided Jude with an alibi, Jude being there when the hospital rang meant she was ideally positioned to offer Katy a lift to the hospital. All of which is ridiculous, of course. But then again, maybe it's not ridiculous, she decides, securing her seat belt as the engine turns over; as the old anger that her one-time friend has always stoked inside her is rekindled. Because with Jude, you never know.

It takes just twenty minutes to reach Jude's destination. Mandela Way. A treeless avenue in an unfashionable no man's land not quite close enough to Sheen to merit its own micro-brand of any big name supermarkets. No Underground station is within easy walking distance, either, making the rents more affordable, Katy guesses. Which is why the area appears to have become the neighbourhood of choice for students attending colleges across south-west London. Migrant workers, too. And anyone else on a tight budget. It is a part of the city's south-western reaches which Katy has never visited – not even used as a shortcut – despite how close it is to the locus of her mum's world. Though she has heard of it, of course. First heard of it, in fact, when she was at school – from Andrew.

We're called Sheen, he'd said, confiding over breakfast one morning during the first term of his Lower Sixth that he and his new best mate, Rizla, had formed a rock band and its name. *After the place Bolan died when his girlfriend wrapped him and the Mini she was driving round the trunk of a sycamore tree.* No such hazards in this street, though, Katy now wryly observes, pulling into a space four cars down from where Jude has just parked. Sliding down in her seat, she watches the other woman cross to the far side of the road then walk past three houses before stopping outside number twenty-two.

Jude's is a tall four-storey, double-fronted Victorian building which, like most in the street, has long ago been subdivided into an assortment of flats. But this one, unlike its neighbours, appears to be hosting some kind of party. For from the open windows of the top two floors pumps the leaden bass of dance music. A gaggle of young men and women in their late teens and early twenties drink from beer cans and a communal bottle of vodka as they sun themselves in the building's overgrown front garden. Students, Katy concludes, as she watches Jude hesitate, awkwardly, for a moment to extract her keys from her bag before marching past them without a word.

Rather than the main front door, Jude heads instead to the far side of the building where Katy can just make out a handrail suggesting a set of steps leading down – to a basement flat, perhaps. And as her quarry disappears from view, the main front door opens and a dozen or so more partygoers spill out onto the main steps. The front of the building seems a living, breathing thing as a handful of people, beers still in hand, begin to dance.

Her pulse now charging with fear of discovery, Katy waits for a few minutes then slowly climbs out of the car. Uncertain as yet quite what she intends to do, she makes her way towards the house in front of which three young women now sit cross-legged on the pavement passing a bottle of tequila between them. Someone has turned up the music and she can now hear the sound of more people talking and laughing from the rear of the building – the back garden, perhaps.

'Looking for someone?' A tall youth dressed only in flip-flops and a pair of denim cut-offs whose dark skin gleams electric blue in the midday sun has appeared by her side. He is holding a joint. As she struggles to find the right answer, he nods. 'The uptight lady from downstairs, right? Not that I mean anything by that – about you, I mean. Because you look... OK,' he drawls, punctuating an appreciative glance towards her swelling belly with a broad grin. 'She'll be out back,' he adds with a wave of his hand. 'Just go on round.'

Katy slips through the crowd towards the side return by the building's far wall. Unnoticed by any of the student gathering, she is grateful for the casual clothes she's wearing and their dishevelled state from cleaning her mum's flat. There is a narrow alley that leads to the building's rear. The passageway is empty and, eager to buy time to think, she slips into its shade. What is she doing, she wonders, grimly. Will there be enough people in the back garden for her to mingle, unnoticed? But before she can decide she is distracted by the sound of voices, one of which is Jude's, and they are coming from somewhere close by.

Spinning around on her heels, Katy braces herself against the wall half-expecting to see Jude standing beside her. But in either direction she can see the alley is still empty. Which is when she notices a line of three windows that run along the wall to her right. Each is only a foot or so in height and at knee level if you're standing outside. But through the iron security bars that encase each, it is possible to look down onto the lower level of the interior of the basement flat that lies within.

Crouching down beside the first window, Katy peers through the open slats of a wooden blind into a white tiled bathroom. Above the bath hangs a London 2012 shower curtain. A selection of hand washing is draped across the towel rail.

Inching towards the next window, she sees this one is open. The voices from within – Jude's and a man's – are louder now, though, and she guesses, rightly, as she peeps down inside – the kitchen below is empty. On the drainer is balanced a tower of yesterday's washing up. On a shelf above the cooker stands a black and white photograph in a cheap plastic frame of a man who bears a passing resemblance to James Dean. The image, which appears to have been torn up then clumsily stuck back together with Sellotape, has an unusual brown patina.

'And your conclusion is?' the man demands.

Jude laughs. 'How well she's worn.'

'Sorry?'

'Kat.'

'Ah,' he chuckles. 'I thought you meant the coffin dodger.'

'About that—' Katy hears the clink of glass. 'I'm not going to pretend we ever got on. But, for Christ's sake, you were only supposed to—'

'I know, I know,' he laughs. 'Blow the bloody doors off! But listen, how the fuck was I to know what would happen. The stupid bitch just wouldn't let go.'

Jude exhales, slowly, as if gathering enough strength to retain control. 'Why did you do it?'

'Sorry?'

'Your hair, it's just it makes me—'

'It was too hot, that's all,' he snaps. 'Not that it's any of your business.'

'And your hand – how did you hurt it?'

Something slams onto a hard surface. A beer bottle, perhaps. 'Get off my case, or you'll regret it. I'd say it did the trick, though.'

'Sorry?'

'Nothing.'

'What?'

'Fuck, woman, are you deaf or something? I said: nothing.'

'Listen,' she soothes, her voice suddenly dropping. 'Let's just take things one step at a time, OK? There's no need for you to charge in all guns blazing—'

'Forgive me for not being more patient, but I've not got much time, you know,' he snaps. 'They've given me to the end of the month to find another five thousand then, if I don't clear the balance in another four weeks, the boys pay me a personal visit – get me? So excuse me if I'm a little on edge. And by the way, don't tell me she's not loaded – I've seen her place.'

'Stop it!' Jude gasps as Katy hears what sounds like some kind of scuffle.

'You stop it,' he counters, roughly. 'Because I've had it up to here with your lies. You wouldn't tell Nan who he was, even when she begged you in her dying days. You've spent a lifetime lying to me. And now you think you can tell me what to do? Well you can't. Not any more, OK?'

Katy's hands clench at the sudden and unmistakable sound of a rough slap as Jude cries out.

'You should go to the gym,' the woman rasps when at last she can speak again. 'You know you always feel better after a good workout.'

'And you?' the man counters, his voice now calm. 'You should look to yourself.'

Footsteps on the stone floor below make Katy flatten herself against the wall. Someone has entered the kitchen – she wonders if it is Jude's boyfriend – and now the steps are approaching the sink above which she stands. Carefully adjusting her position so she can peer down unobserved, Katy can just make out the top of Jude's head as she leans forward to splash her face with cold water from the running tap. She can see, too, the white enamel now pebble-dashed with red.

Unable to move for fear that the merest flicker in Jude's peripheral vision will alert her to her presence, Katy holds her breath, praying the alleyway in which she crouches remains empty. Jude straightens up and dabs her face on a tea towel. Then she moves towards the fridge from which she extracts a bottle of white wine. Taking a tumbler from the draining board, she pours herself a large measure then gulps a generous mouthful. She is facing away from Katy now, but estimating her line of vision, she seems to be staring towards the black and white framed picture.

'Here's to you, Dad,' she mutters, wearily, raising her glass in a silent toast.

Katy's phone vibrates inside her pocket. Though the mobile is on mute, the chance Jude might look up makes Katy step back from the window. Briskly, she retraces her steps towards the front of the house and beyond that the safety of her mum's car but, by then, Michael has hung up.

Chapter 16

Guildford, December 1988

Jude shrugged off her dressing gown and stared at herself in the mirror. It was a daily challenge she had set herself since just after starting at St Mary's. To out-face the rapid changes happening to her body; to learn to love the shape she would become. Cupping a breast in each hand, she marvelled at their silky smoothness. Analysing her skin in the morning light, she registered with satisfaction its milky glow.

Turning sideways to the mirror, she scrutinised her near-flat belly which, as always, looked a little too round. Jude frowned. She was careful about what she ate – a lesson learned early from Siobhan who'd spent a lifetime dieting. Reaching forward for the tub of Nivea standing on the chest of drawers next to the tape deck, she applied the soft cream to her body in gentle sweeps with the careful precision of a soldier oiling a weapon. And as she did so, she thought of Andrew.

They'd been seeing each other almost four months as often as they could without arousing suspicion. For while outwardly both appeared to be buckling down to the final weeks of revision leading up to their mock O and A level exams, each also found themselves deliciously preoccupied with the welcome distraction of their relationship.

How easily Siobhan had been impressed by the number of revision sessions Jude scheduled after school at her friend's house! She'd have been less so had she realised how few had actually taken place. Diane, meanwhile, was monitoring her son's absences from the dinner table while he stayed late in the college library with mounting anticipation. Everyone was counting on Andrew to get four straight A grades, it seemed, even Kat. Kat! What would she say if she knew, Jude wondered, flashing a sly smile at her reflection at the thought of this. The secret felt like a kind of badge of honour, which was why she'd no intention of letting on. At least not yet.

Dressing quickly, Jude hurried down to the kitchen where she found Siobhan cutting a grapefruit in half. Without a word she extracted a bowl and spoon from the washed crockery piled onto the drainer then placed both on the table beside a half-consumed package of Special K. 'Where's the skimmed milk, Mum?' she demanded as she peered into the fridge.

'There's only gold top left,' Siobhan replied, surveying the kitchen room table with a frown. 'Is that all you're having? Honestly, Jude, you really need a better breakfast than that if you're going to last the day.'

'You know I'm never hungry at breakfast time,' Jude muttered, sulkily pushing the cardboard husks of air round her bowl with the tip of her spoon.

Placing the flesh pink slices of freshly cut grapefruit in a bowl, Siobhan set it on the table then sat down to eat. Today was a Red Day during which she would only eat food that was red-coloured or reddish, which in its broadest sense could cover most things that weren't green – her latest diet fad. 'I'm working late tonight,' she added, wincing at the acidity of her first mouthful.

Siobhan worked at the dental surgery on River Street where she got her first job, as a receptionist, almost sixteen years earlier. Ever since leaving Surrey for the south coast the year before Jude was born, Siobhan had dreamed of training to be a dental nurse – an ambition it took her five long years of night school to achieve. After qualifying, she got her first job at a practice just outside Portsmouth. Then, when things turned sour with Colin, she got back in touch with the River Street surgery to see if they had any vacancies. And she'd been lucky. Not only had her old boss provided her with the lifeline she needed to start afresh, it was also at the surgery that she had met Dave.

'Home alone with the mother's boyfriend,' Jude muttered, without looking up. 'Great.'

Siobhan shot Jude a hard stare which her daughter ignored. Jude knew her mum worried that she didn't like Dave, but she was determined not to give Siobhan the satisfaction of her confidence. Besides, what would she say? Sometimes, like when he brought the laundry to her room on a Monday morning, she hated him with all her being but, at other times, she supposed he could be OK.

The man was an idiot – almost as stupid as Siobhan who had excitedly confided after just a fortnight that, at last, she might have found 'the one'. A hot shot, the woman seemed to think. Just because he worked as a mechanic in a local BMW garage. As if that made a shred of difference because, at the end of the day, wasn't he just another toe rag working under a dingy railway arch? No, to Jude, Dave was just another unwelcome house guest seduced by a forced laugh and a brassy smile. Though, she had to admit, her mum was right: with his ear stud, motorbike and obligatory leathers, he did indeed bear a passing resemblance for David Essex.

'Come on, love, eat up and get a move on,' said Siobhan, glancing up at the kitchen clock as she poured herself a glass of filtered water. 'I want a shower.'

'Actually I've a free period first thing so they said we can use it for revision at home if we like. I don't have to be in until half ten.'

Back in her room Jude stared miserably at the pile of text-books spread out on the floor beneath her desk. With a sigh, she sat on the chair and bent down to pick up a Letts revision guide to Biology. But as she tried to read, the rhythmic drone of a vacuum cleaner softened the focus of her attention. The words on the page began to dance, and Jude's mind started to wander.

What minor misdemeanour was Dave seeking to amend? He'd picked her up from hockey practice the previous day, too. Because it's raining, he'd said with a self-conscious grin, although now Jude was not so sure. She'd seen him pull into the car park at the far end of the playing fields a good twenty minutes earlier than is strictly necessary, which gave him ample time to observe at leisure the pink-cheeked girls running around in their muddy box-pleated PE skirts. The brazenness of it had made Jude smile. Not now, though, as a crash from downstairs made Jude flinch, her daydreaming abruptly halted by the brief silent interlude that followed before Dave began fumbling in the cupboard beneath the stairs for a dustpan and brush.

'Everything alright?' Siobhan called out from behind the bathroom door.

'Yes, fine,' he shouted.

Poking her head around the sitting room door a minute later, the first thing Jude saw was the framed photo that has been the centre point of her mum's mantelpiece arrangements for as long as she can remember, smashed on the floor amidst a pool of brackish water.

Lying on its side on the tiled hearth, broken into jagged chunks, was a cut-glass vase that until a few minutes earlier contained a fading bunch of carnations – another hastily-bought guilt purchase from the petrol station at the end of their street. Dave was on his hands and knees dabbing at the rug with a clump of kitchen towel. But it wasn't to his side that Jude rushed but the fireplace where she dropped to her knees and carefully picked up the precious photo which was now sodden and flecked with green plant sap.

'Get us some more kitchen towel, then,' Dave muttered crossly but to deaf ears, his eyes darting towards the hall. 'Come on, help me here. Your mum will be down in a minute.'

But Jude was transfixed. She had cut her finger on some broken glass, and a tiny spot of blood veined the creases of the ruined picture. She stared, her gaze fixed on the rosy blemish colouring the handsome face of the young man sitting astride his Norton shortly before the fatal collision with a speeding car. The only surviving photograph there was of her dad. She opened her mouth to say something but instead, without any warning, emitted a single, heartfelt sob.

Dave's anger evaporated, instantly, leaving him awkward and contrite. 'I just knocked it with my elbow when I was vacuum cleaning. But it was about time – the water needed changing—'

Jude, however, couldn't have cared less about the stupid vase. 'What have you done?'

'It was an accident,' he shrugged. 'If it's important we could always get another print done. I'm sure your mum will have the neg somewhere...'

'If it's important?' Jude hissed. As she stared at the sodden paper in her hand she wondered, desperately, if she could salvage it by pressing it between some blotting paper and a couple of books. 'Of course it's important.'

'But your mum was only saying the other day the mantelpiece was getting too cluttered and it was about time she chucked it in the bin.'

'She can't have. She'd never have said that,' Jude countered, fiercely. 'He may be some old ex to her, but he was my dad.'

Dave laughed. 'You're having me on! Your mum told me about your dad... he's still alive.'

Jude shot him a disbelieving look, challenging him to take back his words. 'You're lying.'

'No, I'm not.' Dave rose to his feet. 'And if you ask me, you and your mum need to talk,' he called over his shoulder as he disappeared into the kitchen.

Still clutching the photo, Jude charged back upstairs into her room and slammed the door. Sitting on the floor amidst her revision notes, time stopped as she grappled with the enormity of what Dave had said. Her dad was dead – had been since she was a baby. End of story. Only now it wasn't, or so Dave claimed. Which was ridiculous, of course. But what if... What if he wasn't lying? What if this was just the beginning? The possibility that her mum had been deceiving her had never crossed Jude's mind before. Why would it?

The chance he was still alive made her angrier than she had ever been. Why had her mum told her he was dead if he wasn't? If he was alive, why had he never been in touch? And who was the man on the bike? Overwhelmed by a sudden surge of emotion that just as quickly left her high and dry, washed up, empty, she realised it was as if something integral to her very being had been ripped from her body. Her mind felt blank, her memory defiled. Then there was a tentative knock on her bedroom door.

'Jude?' Siobhan waited for an answer then, after a moment or two, gently tested the handle and the catch softly clicked open. 'Jude?' she called again. 'Dave just told me what happened. Can I come in?' Silence. Siobhan poked her head around the door, paused for a moment, then stepped into the room. Though dressed in her work things, her hair was still wet. Cautiously, she walked towards the bed. 'You needed someone to believe in,' she said softly. Apologetically.

Jude scowls. 'You lied.'

'No, when you saw the photo years ago you asked if that was him. I didn't tell you you were wrong: that's different,' Siobhan counters, firmly.

'No it's not.'

'So you would have liked me to tell you aged six that your real dad was a married man with a family of his own who'd made it abundantly clear he didn't want anything to do with you and certainly nothing more to do with me, ever again, would you? You deserved better than that.' Siobhan's look of surprise suggested that she knew she had said too much but couldn't stop herself.

'I deserved the truth.' Meeting her mother's gaze for the first time, Jude challenged her to look away. It did not take her long to win. 'So who is he?'

'Who's who?'

'The man. In the photo. Who is he?'

Guilt clouded Siobhan's face. 'I don't know.'

'What?'

'It was a photo I picked up… already framed… at a second-hand sale.'

Jude's heart felt fit to burst. She wanted to scream and shout, yet somehow she knew that making a scene would make it easier for her mum to deal with the situation. No, she would not let her off the hook so easily. 'How… convenient,' she said, tightly.

Tentatively, Siobhan took a seat at the foot of Jude bed. As she sat in silence for a few minutes, Jude read from the anguish now etched on her mother's face the inner struggle to decide just what to say next. Eventually, Siobhan reached out to touch Jude's leg. As if stung by something poisonous, her daughter sharply moved it away. 'Sometimes, you know, the truth hurts too much – especially when you're just a child. I always planned to tell you one day.'

'Did you, Mother? Really? Just when, exactly? My sixteenth birthday? Eighteenth? Or twenty-first? Just when would have been the right time?' Fury rocked Jude's core as she decided she had never hated anyone so much as she did her mum at that precise moment, and that she was unlikely to despise anyone as much ever again.

'I can't… Jude, I really can't say. It's not fair.'

'Not fair on who, exactly? Him? Does he deserve fair? Fairer than me? I don't think so. Not how he's behaved. We're the ones who've been wronged, here. He abandoned us: you and me. And you – you just don't seem to care.'

'Of course I care, Jude.' Siobhan's voice was icy. 'You have no right to tell me what I think or feel. I've lived with his rejection for almost sixteen years – at least you've spent fifteen in ignorant bliss.'

'Bliss? How can never knowing my dad, being brought up by a selfish cow with a string of greasy lovers be ignorant bliss. It's anything but. Face it, Mum, none of this would have happened if you hadn't been such a slut.'

Her mother's slap was as sharp as it was unexpected which made Jude's cheek throb and tears, finally, prick in her eyes. 'Don't you ever – ever – talk to me like that again.' Siobhan's voice was low and hollow. Menacing. 'It wasn't like that. He never told me he was married, let alone that she was pregnant, so how was I to know? I was young, Jude, and he was – well – persuasive. He bought me nice things. Told me he'd look after me. Then when I fell pregnant he dropped me like a stone.' She paused before continuing, eager for some sort of response from Jude who was doing her best to stare stony-faced into the middle distance.

'I only saw him once after that, about a month before you were born. I was walking past his house – he used to live at the top of town, along Pilgrim's View. And that was when I saw them: his wife, a pretty woman, standing in the doorway, waving, as he left for work. She was holding a little baby. There was a tricycle on the front lawn. He saw me and offered me money to go away. £2,000. Enough to start again. More than enough, he said, to fulfil his obligations. Nanny P and I left for the south coast a week later.'

'More fool you.'

'Do you know something, Jude?' Siobhan snapped, rising to her feet. 'You really are a cold-hearted little cow.' And with that she strode towards the bedroom door. Flung it open. Disappeared from view. Then, a few seconds later, from her bedroom the far side of the landing came the sound of a hairdryer's angry roar.

If I am you made me so, seethed Jude, as she lay back on the bed and stared up at the ceiling. She closed her eyes, and as her breathing calmed she realised she felt oddly dislocated from the situation, almost as if she'd just observed her mum arguing with someone else. So her real dad was still alive. In the light of that, her mum's apparently random decision to move back to Surrey now made sense. Did they move her so she could see him? If so, why, if their last meeting really had been as bad as her mum just described. Besides, wouldn't he and his family have moved on long ago? Perhaps it was pure coincidence, then. Unless Siobhan was lying, the woman was good at that.

Rolling over onto her side, something crumpled beneath Jude's thigh. Glancing down she saw it was the spoiled photograph of the stranger who, for years, she'd believed was her dad. 'Why did you do it, Mum,' she murmured. 'Why did you lie?'

Tugging free the picture Jude stared at it for a moment, bade it goodbye, then carefully folded it in half and tore along the crease. Then she repeated this action once, twice, three times. Again and then again she folded and tore until the confetti of false memories filled her lap. Cupping her hands, she gathered up the fragments then threw them into the air, upwards, with all her force, scattering the false truth Siobhan had concocted across the bedroom floor.

–

'Here you are!' Kat cried. 'I've been looking for you all over!'

Jude felt her cheeks flush with anger as the two sixth-formers she had just been talking to broke off their conversation mid-sentence to monitor Kat's approach with expressions of undisguised contempt.

'Hiya,' Kat smiled at Jude's companions. 'Hope I didn't interrupt anything!'

The two senior girls exchanged a withering glance, then smiled. 'Not at all,' said the taller of the pair, a girl known as Jinx. 'The grown-ups have finished talking.'

Jude turned round with a mixture of pride and satisfaction to register Kat's mortification, pleased by how naturally the older girls had counted her as one of their own. 'Just a minute—' The brusque wave of her hand caused Kat to stop a few paces away from where the other girls stood. 'It's OK,' she said in a low voice, turning to Jinx. 'I won't say a word... so long as I can come to the party on Saturday, too.'

'What do you think, Alex?'

Her companion nodded. 'I think it will be a laugh,' she said, her voice dropped conspiratorially. 'But don't forget your entry pass.'

'That's OK,' Jude grinned. 'My mum's boyfriend has a limit-less supply of booze and cigarettes.'

'Gav is simply going to love you!' Jinx, declared, patting Jude on the arm before the pair moved away.

As the two older girls headed back across the playground towards the sixth form block. Jude smiled. Saturday night was quiz night at The Fox & Hound which meant her mum and Dave would be out all evening. Gav Morton's parties were legendary, and this one should be a classic as his parents were out of town. She turned towards Kat. 'Did you want something?' she sighed.

'I just... wondered where you were, what you were up to,' Kat answered, awkwardly.

'Well I'm going to Gav Morton's party on Saturday night, for one thing.' Jude declared, crossing her arms triumphantly. 'What do you think of that?'

'Great.'

Jude frowned. 'Well you could try to look a little impressed. But then again, it's not really your sort of thing, is it? Parties, I mean.'

'That's not fair—'

'Parties,' Jude repeated, despite herself. 'Booze. Boys. Sex. It's not really your fault you're a late developer, is it, though? Just look at your mum and dad. At the end of the day it all comes down to genes.' A bubble of laughter welled up from some place deep inside at the sudden memory of Kat holding out her virgin denims for Jude's approval. What would Kat have said, Jude wondered, if she had told her Diane had bought her the wrong sort? Cried, probably, then taken them back to the shop, unworn. The wimp.

'That's not fair,' Kat retorted, crossly.

'No, you're right,' Jude admitted, surprised by a sudden feeling of remorse. 'But it is true, isn't it? Now don't get upset, but I've been thinking this for some time. You need to sort yourself out. Start acting your age. I know things have been difficult at home recently—'

Kat's eyes glistened, but with tears of anger this time. 'Don't bring my parents into it,' she cried.

'OK.' Jude raised her hands as if surrendering in defeat. 'But when you've got a lot going on at home sometimes it's easy to lose sight of the bigger picture.' She patted the other girl's arm. 'You could make so much more of yourself, Kat,' she added, silkily. 'Clothes. Make-up. Just the way you carry yourself. I only want to help. If even you can't be bothered with yourself, how can you expect any of the boys out there to ever be bothered with you?'

Kat looked away. The sound of shouts and laughter as a mob of younger girls charged across the playground faded to a distant hum. 'It's not easy,' she said at last. 'Dad's moved out for a while, Mum's always sad, and now Andrew's getting into trouble at college. I'm just trying to keep my head down.'

'And quite right too,' Jude said, softly. 'The bastard,' she added, softly.

'Who?'

'Your dad. Like all men. Bastards. I mean if he wasn't playing away from home—'

Kat rubbed her face on the back of her sleeve. 'Who said he's been doing that?'

'Well he must be, mustn't he? Why else would he move out?'

'He hasn't,' Kat scowled. 'They're just having a break from each other to sort things out.'

Jude sighed. She almost felt sorry for her friend. Because that's not what Andrew had said. The thought of Charles's son, however, now made her frown. He'd been away for the past three days on some kind of college field trip and she was desperate to see him. 'Sort what things out?'

'Things. I don't know. But he's not having an affair, if that's what you mean.'

'Of course not,' Jude soothed. 'But how can you be so sure?'

'It's not the only reason couples quarrel.'

'No, but it's one of the main ones.'

'Well it's not that, OK? Besides, we're all going to France together for Easter – Mum, Dad, Andrew and me. Mum told me last night. Why would we be doing that if he was having some affair?'

'Lucky you,' Jude said, dryly. Given how bad Kat claimed her parents' marriage to be, it was ridiculous how desperately they all tried to play happy families when it suited. She wondered briefly about her own dad – whether Siobhan and his marriage would have turned out similar if he had lived and they had married. Infidelity was, surely, an inevitability because how could anyone stay together with the same person for year after year after year?

'It's not Dad's fault,' Kat repeated. 'Or Mum's. It's just that sometimes relationships don't work out as you expect them to, that's all. Besides, all marriages have their ups and downs. Mum said so.'

'You're right.'

Turning towards the main school building, Jude glanced at her watch. The bell would soon ring for afternoon classes. Glancing back towards her friend she concocted up a smile. What was she doing, needling Kat like that, she wondered. Why did she so often annoy her so? But not any more. The cloud had lifted, and her mind was racing ahead. It would be unfortunate to fall out just now, not least because of what Kat might tell Andrew.

'I said, you're right,' Jude repeated. 'It's no one's fault. Sorry. Look, I didn't mean to upset you. Let's not argue. But I meant what I said about making more of yourself. After all isn't it every young woman's right to be beautiful and have fun?' She chuckled, conspiratorially. 'I could bring some stuff over to yours. Tomorrow night? We could tell your mum we'd be helping each other with revision. It will be our little secret.'

'That would be nice,' said Kat, fixing Jude with a hard stare. Then, as the bell rang for afternoon lessons, her pale face broke into a tentative smile. 'I like secrets!'

Chapter 17

London, July 2013

Diane is sitting up in bed eating scrambled eggs on toast when Katy arrives back at the hospital with Joyce seated by her side knitting what looks like it will be a black and white Sarah Lund jumper. Though still reeling from her visit to Jude's and baffled by the meaning of what she has overheard, Katy is determined to say nothing about the break-in.

'You look much better, Mum,' she says, leaning forward to kiss her good cheek. The skin feels cool to touch.

'It's a strange old system, this,' her mother smiles, dabbing her lips on a paper napkin. 'The last person in the bed appears to have ordered this for lunch, but at breakfast I got a cheese and tomato sandwich.'

Katy nods. 'So what's the latest on when you can go home?'

'Tomorrow afternoon.' Diane frowns. 'I keep telling them how much better I'd be after a proper night's sleep in my own bed, but no one seems to listen.'

'They're just doing their job, you know,' says Joyce, pulling a large paper bag of grapes from her shopping bag and placing it on the wheeled table that straddles the bed. 'It's traditional, don't you know. They're washed, by the way. And seedless, too – so help yourselves while I go and get us all a cup of tea.'

'Actually, I'd prefer a cappuccino if you're going down to the cafe,' Diane calls as the woman is already striding towards the door.

Katy grins. 'And you'd better make mine a double espresso.'

Diane sinks back against the pillows then pats the bed beside her. 'Come and sit – you look like you need it. Before you get too comfortable, though, would you pass me my overnight bag. I think the nurse put it in the bottom drawer.'

'OK, but while I do I'd like to ask you a question about your friend,' Katy begins as she leans forward, hoping her voice sounds casual. 'You know, Estelle?'

'A lovely girl,' Diane enthuses. 'Works at the theatre box office. And also in the cafe, and sometimes as an usherette. Always ready to help, and really helpful when it comes to block-booking tickets for the theatre club – she always makes sure we get the best seats!'

Bent double, now, Katy opens the bedside cabinet. 'Known her long, have you?' she asks, lightly.

'Only a few months, why?'

'Oh, no reason. I just wondered, that's all.'

Katy reaches into the cupboard. Inside is a clear plastic bag holding what's left from the contents of her mum's handbag. Her purse – now empty of cash. Two matching silver combs with diamante trim. A half-used strip of throat lozenges. A gold-coloured compact of pressed face powder. A miniature notepad bound tight by a twice-looped rubber band. No house keys, of course. She hands the bag to her mum.

'The bank says you should have your new cards in a couple of days,' she observes. 'At least you didn't have too much cash on you.'

'No, just a couple of fives and a few coppers. It's lucky it didn't happen half an hour earlier before I'd gone to the bank. I had close to £250 in tens and twenties which I'd collected to buy tickets for the next theatre club trip. No, no—' she quickly adds as Katy opens her mouth to speak. 'Don't tell me, I know.'

'Seriously Mum. You shouldn't carry large amounts of money around. It's why banks invented debit cards.'

'Anyway,' her mother counters. 'Tell me about the flat. Is Monty OK? I hope someone's thought to feed him.'

Katy hesitates, uncertain now is the best time to tell her mum about the break in; eager to divert the conversation before Joyce's return.

'Don't worry, everything's fine,' she says. But the ease with which she lies, even though she knows she has to, to protect her mum, makes her think of what she said down by the canal that day about her father not watching her when she slipped and fell. A sudden through which makes her want to bury her head in shame. Though it wasn't her fault, was it? Her parents' marriage.

'Although I'm afraid to say one of your pictures got spoiled when Joyce and I were tidying,' she presses on, eager to open a door on the past – perhaps, in some way, by making some kind of amends. 'The one of me at Andrew's wedding? I spilled something on it and I'm afraid it's ruined. The frame's still OK, though, and I'm sure Dee will have filed away the negatives somewhere so we can always get another copy. But listen,' she pauses, bracing herself before diving in. 'I was looking at that old Polaroid, you know the one of me the day we had that picnic down by the canal?'

Diane's face softens into a private smile. She nods.

'Well there was something written on the back I'd never noticed before...' Awkwardly, Katy clears her throat. 'I wondered if you could tell me about it.'

For a moment, the makeshift bridge between them sags heavy with the weight of expectation. Katy's eyes dart nervously towards the window. Well she's done it now, knocked on the door. Her spirits stir, kindled by the possibility of the moment. All she needs now is for her mum to let her in; to open up to her, if only a crack. Then, after what feels like an eternity, Katy turns back towards the bed to find Diane is smiling.

'It was something your father gave me a long time after the event.' She speaks softly. 'He blamed himself, you know, for you almost drowning – though he never admitted it at the time. Then, many years later, when other things were done and said and it seemed the only thing we could do for all our sakes was separate, he gave me that picture. Even after everything that had happened – it touched me.' She sniffs, and Katy waits for her to cry but no tears come though her smile fades. 'It made me think of the man he could have been.'

But Mum's wrong, Katy knows. Which is why she now has to speak. 'I jumped, you know,' she blurts. How can words that sound so simple feel so awkward to speak, she wonders, as somewhere deep inside her head a secret part of her begins to unclench. 'I jumped,' she repeats. Because contrary to subsequent Parker family mythology, she was instigator not passive victim. It was she who'd done the bad thing. 'Into the canal. It wasn't anyone's fault. You shouldn't have blamed him. Dad, I mean. It was me. I wanted to feel what it was like to fly...'

'I know.'

Katy looks up in amazement as her mum chuckles.

'Don't look so surprised,' Diane exclaims. 'I was watching you, waiting for you to turn away. Only you didn't. It was quite clear to me what you were thinking – we're more similar than you'd probably care to admit, you and me. Besides, the expression on your face said it all. Only your father had become so distant and disengaged by that point.' She sighs. 'So I suppose it suited me to shift the blame.'

Fearful of compromising the moment, Katy holds her breath. But she knows she must press on if she is to push open that door a little further ahead of Joyce's return. 'What did he do?' she begins. 'To make you so unhappy. Why didn't things between the two of you work?'

The excursion beyond neutral ground into territory clearly staked out over many years by her mother as strictly private makes Katy's pulse race as she tries to read Diane's expression. Embarrassment, maybe. Sadness, and something else. Relief? Emboldened by the suspicion that perhaps, even all these years later, like her, Diane might also see that long hot afternoon down by the canal as some sort of emotional touchstone, Katy leaps once more into thin air.

'He must have been a difficult man to live with,' she murmurs softly, willing her mum to latch onto the bait. 'And to love.' As if she didn't know.

'He was,' Diane sighs. 'When we first met he was so authoritative, and rather dashing. Once we were married, however, it was a different matter. I suppose he grew restless and bored.'

Katy seizes her chance. 'Is that why he went away so much?'

'One reason.'

'There were others?' Katy whispers, tentatively feeling her way; eager not to ask too much, too soon.

'Other reasons, yes,' Diane replies simply. 'He was unfaithful.'

I know, Katy wants to say. Somehow I've always known. Even when I was small and wasn't able to understand. Instead she waits for her mum to carry on, but Diane is lost in thought.

'I thought he might have been,' says Katy eventually, eager to say anything to bridge this gaping void. 'It's just something Andrew said once.'

'That wasn't for him to tell,' Diane snaps, then softens her tone. 'Yes. I suspected there were other women, of course, but didn't know for sure for years. And when I did… well, by then it was too late.'

'Too late?' echoes Katy, unsure how best to redirect the spotlight onto the early years of their marriage. The time when her dad's affairs began. The time, perhaps, when he might have met Siobhan.

'Too late for us to save the marriage. I used to think the secret of a lasting relationship was compromise, at least that's what your gran always told me. But there's only so far you can go when only one person is doing all the taking and that person isn't you.'

Katy stares at her mum, her heart racing at the closing of the gulf separating her from the knowledge she so craves. Yet she can think of no subtle way to coax Diane to answer her questions without upsetting the fragile calm. She hesitates as she thinks once more of the faded Polaroid and the long years following that hot afternoon when she had almost come to believe what others told her had happened – that she had slipped and fallen – despite the fact she knew this to be untrue.

No, the time has come to stop running. To stop running away from the truth. There really is no other way. Jude's revelations, Diane's attack and now the break-in at the flat have left her reeling. But while Katy feels bloodied by something deep within, the long-lost knowledge she was instigator not victim, her mum's acknowledgement that she jumped not fell persuades her she's not yet beaten.

'Do you remember Jude Davies?' she asks abruptly.

There is a pause before Diane replies. 'I do,' she says, her pale lips now pursed into a defensive Maginot line. 'Your best friend for a while, wasn't she?'

For a moment, Katy is unsure whether her mum is being ironic. 'Well,' she continues, treading carefully. 'I'd not heard from her in twenty years then, a week or two ago and quite out of the blue, she got back in touch. We met up. And she mentioned something about Dad.' Is it her imagination or has the temperature in the room cooled? Glancing down, Katy sees her bare arms dimpled with goose bumps.

'And what exactly did she mention?' Diane asks coldly. 'As if I need to ask. She always was a little stirrer. Like mother, like daughter, I always used to say. But then with a mother like that Jude never really stood a chance. Siobhan Davies was a tart. She flirted with everyone, especially the married men – positively relished the challenge. Although some married men were less resistant to her charms than others.'

Though shocked by the bitterness in her mum's voice, Katy presses on. 'Dad, you mean.' A statement of fact, not a question.

Diane gives her daughter a hard stare.

'Yes, your father,' she eventually agrees. 'It happened before you were born. She used to live in town then moved away. I didn't know about it until many years later – until long after Jude started at St Mary's. That was the final straw, I can tell you. When you and Jude became friends and then she started seeing Andrew I was convinced Siobhan had somehow put her up to it all to get her own back for the way your father treated her.'

All thought of probing her mum further on the timing of what Katy is now convinced must have been her dad's affair with Siobhan instantly evaporates. Andrew and Jude? How could she? And how could she, Katy, Jude's best friend and Andrew's sister, not have known? Jude and Andrew. Katy swallows and almost coughs as her tongue, dry and sticky, brushes the back of her throat.

'Are you telling me Jude and Andrew went out?' she says.

'Why of course, though only for a few weeks. Until your dad persuaded him to break it off, which was something, I suppose. Goodness, Katy – don't you remember it was you who told us, after all. And thank goodness you did, though you weren't to know why. So tell me – what did Jude want?'

But this is ridiculous, Katy thinks, willing herself to remember more clearly. I didn't. Couldn't have. Because I didn't know. It was only...

Then she feels the stirring of that old anger once again and, buried deep inside it, grasps the knowledge that what her mum is saying is true. The resentment she'd felt at how Jude was treating her. The hurt that came with how distracted she'd become. The risk that she might turn her attentions to someone else. The fear on seeing Jude and Andrew together in town one afternoon, sheepish and discreet. But surely they'd only bumped into each other by chance?

The facts hadn't mattered, not back then. For the coincidence of it was enough ammunition for Katy to concoct the lie then share it with her father to fuel his dislike of Jude. It had seemed the perfect way of getting back at both of them. Paying back Andrew for going away and Jude for... well, being Jude.

'Katy?' Diane repeats. 'What did Jude want?'

Though the swift shift of tack seems an obvious attempt to change the subject back to what her mum sees as safer, present ground, Katy grabs it. Perhaps Jude was lying. Or worse, maybe mum doesn't know and, if that's true, it's time to stop: Katy has to be sure before delivering that heavy blow.

'Why has she got back in touch?' Diane repeated, more insistently this time. In fact, Katy realised with surprise, despite her battered face and bruised body she now seems angry. 'What does she want? I can't imagine Jude doing anything without some ulterior motive or other.'

'She had a baby. A boy. A few months after moving away. He's over twenty now.'

'Like mother like daughter – what did I tell you?'

Ignoring her mum's look of triumph, Katy presses on. 'Mum, what did you really hear about why Jude and Siobhan moved away?'

Diane's attention latches onto a cotton thread dangling from the right-hand cuff of her top with which she starts to fiddle. The spirit has suddenly gone out of her. 'Well I only know what that dumpy girl in your year, the one with the brace – Ruth something, she became a doctor – told me when she came to visit you in hospital. You were late coming back that afternoon. There was a fire on the heath. People were sent out to look for you. But before that woman in the car found you, Jude came back, alone, feeling ill—'

Her mother frowns as, with a sharp tug, she snaps off the dangling cotton then carefully smoothes out the puckered fabric along the hem of her sleeve. Then she sniffs, disdainfully. 'Siobhan picked her up and took her home,' she continues. 'Then they moved away. A few months later, someone I knew who used to work with Siobhan told me they'd moved back to Portsmouth where Jude had had a baby. Apparently, they left town just before she got big enough to show.'

When would that have been, Katy wonders, thinking of Miriam from work. Four or five months, perhaps. Which would mean she got pregnant... some time in the spring. March, not June. A surge of relief courses through her.

'Why didn't you tell me before?'

Diane sighs. 'Tell you, but how could I? It took you months to get over the accident. You were so down for so long, not yourself at all. And we were all so relieved that they had gone. I didn't want to upset you. Besides, I didn't find out myself — you know, about the baby, until some time later.' She reaches towards the water on the table before her. The ice has melted. Brushing away a tiny fly on the beaker's rim, she takes a sip.

'Upset me?' Katy cries, tears of relief now burning her eyes at the possibility that Jude could have been pregnant before that dreadful afternoon. 'How could that have upset me?'

'Well, it's upsetting you now, isn't it?' her mum replies gently, reaching out to squeeze Katy's hand. 'And it's more than twenty years after the event. Really, where is Joyce with that coffee, you look all washed out! Katy? What's the matter, you look awful. Tell me, please.'

'Sorry Mum... It's just... I feel so... responsible. I thought it was all my f-fault.'

Diane clicks her tongue in frustration. 'What, Jude getting pregnant? Don't be so ridiculous. How? Honestly, sometimes you really can be such a silly girl. From what I heard she was in a relationship with a friend of her mum's.'

There is silence once more as Katy trawls her memories for anything useful that might back this up. She knew that her friend had had a string of boyfriends: an array of fifth- and sixth-formers from a neighbouring boys school, and a scattering of students from the local tech. She knew, too, that Jude had slept with a number of these — an open secret she had rarely tried to conceal; a valued currency when it came to dealings with her classmates. But an older man... surely she would have known if her friend had been going out with someone that much older?

Then again, Jude had grown increasingly distant and evasive over the weeks running up to her disappearance. So secretive that Katy had found it difficult to know when she was telling the truth. Like the time at camp when she challenged her about sneaking off grounds out onto the heath at the heart of the Devil's Punch Bowl, alone. Because there was someone else, wasn't there? Out on the heath that day. A figure she'd seen in the distance. Katy stares thoughtfully at the blunt-head lump on her left hand.

Budge up, Jude had commanded that last evening, pushing herself into the seat next to hers in the lecture theatre after tea. She'd not seen Jude since the quarrel out on the heath earlier. And as she stared at her, Kat noticed the top of her friend's I Ran The World T-shirt was puckered as if snagged by thorns. *Where have you been?* she whispered. But the other girl's face gave nothing away until, a moment later, Katy's hand was pulsing around a searing shaft of pain.

Distracted, she hadn't noticed the other girl's arm move. The blue biro clutched in its fist that thrust downwards into the soft skin on the upper side of her own hand. The force of it prompted a gasp of pain she struggled to suppress as she turned towards Ruth Creighton, the girl seated on her other side. But Ruth was so enraptured by the evening's speaker, a balding botanist from the local university, she noticed nothing. How can something so small hurt so much, she wondered, staring at the tiny circle of red around the puncture that marked the wound's heart.

With her right hand clamped firmly around her left, she slowly raised her head. Forcing herself to focus on the speaker. Willing herself not to cry as her friend's mouth loomed towards her ear.

I was here all the time, Jude hissed. *So shut it, OK?*

Had she arranged to meet someone that day, out on the heath. That would explain her behaviour. But who? Not the stranger they encountered, though. Her attacker. The man who… Briefly, the familiar scene plays out in Katy's mind. Jude crouched on the ground, fastening her bag. Watching her rise then stiffen, distracted by an unexpected sound. The man emerging from the bushes to grab Jude, abruptly. Pushing her down onto the ground. Straddling her, roughly. Forcing himself... But no, that's not right, is it? For Jude was dragged in the bushes and that's what made me run. In fear that he would come for me, too. For what could I do, a sixteen-year-old girl, brandishing a big stick. Far better to fetch help.

Katy's head is pounding, now. She rubs her eyes. For yet again she struggles to recall the precise chronology of events; the order of what happened when. Once more, it feels as if there's a blockage in her head that's obscuring her view. Countering her efforts to distinguish between what she saw before and after; confusing what was imagined and what was real. She remembers the weight of something heavy swung from her right hand. Hears Jude's voice again, too. *You frigid lezzer.* But why can't she remember when Jude said that?

'Listen, I know how much she hurt you, and also how worried you were about her moving away so abruptly. But it really had nothing to do with you, you know. And looking back on it, having been brought up by a mother like that with no known father, you have to feel sorry for her,' Diane repeats, firmly. 'Although I'll never forgive her for leaving you like that; out on the heath and all alone.'

Katy feels her cheeks burn. How can her mum say that, she wonders, when she'd been the one who ran away?

A low rumble in the middle distance makes them both look up as Joyce backs cautiously through the swing door by the nurse's station then strides towards them balancing three coffees and a packet of Hobnobs. A hot wind has begun to blow through the open window and the sky has darkened.

'Goodness me,' Joyce exclaims, as the blinds start to shiver and shake. 'Let's hope that's just a storm coming,' she smiles. 'Not the end of the world.'

–

The apparent lifting of the unofficial, self-imposed Parker moratorium on excavating the past leaves Katy giddy and light-headed as she makes her way back home from the hospital. The family has tiptoed around one another for so long that avoidance and evasion is their default position. Now, though, the thought of the arm's length nature of her relationship with Diane – her inability to confide in her mum about what happened, Michael, anything – that came about because of this fills Katy with regret.

Exiting the tube at Barons Court a memory stirs of when her mum and Michael first met one Sunday brunch-time over eggs benedict. The tight-lipped awkwardness of it had been reinforced by the setting. The soporific murmur of polite voices emanating from the tables around them in an overpriced brasserie. The obsequious nodding of the Covent Garden waiters. The starchy snobbishness of the place. All of this now makes her wince.

Was it any wonder that the official introduction once she and Michael had become serious had ended up being as joyless as any job interview? Diane said she feared they were rushing things, of course. But when the two of them were alone together in the ladies and Katy gently asked her whether living together for a while might have strengthened her own relationship with Charles, her mother's tart response was as good as a mind-your-own-business as any she had had.

Michael hardly seems the settling down type, she'd said.

It would have made Katy cross if she hadn't been about to move into Michael's flat. News she had also been planning to share but would now hold back until another day. The depth of what she felt for him back then was thrilling, she thinks as she turns off the main road and onto Linden Gardens. An adventure, like a new continent to explore. But she is quickly distracted by a distant figure walking from the front door to the gate of their house, exiting through their front gate, and now hurrying out onto the street.

The woman has come for their place, no doubt about it. And she looks familiar, too, even though Katy is still nine or ten houses away. Her build. The raven hair. The confidence of her as she moves in her emerald-coloured suit with its closely tailored skirt riding high above the knee. Looks just like…

Quickening her step, Katy hurries after Jude, for it is surely she, who is now striding away from her towards the far end of their street clutching to her chest what looks like a bunch of papers. What is she doing here, she wonders, irritably. Casting only a casual glance towards their house as she hurries by, Katy registers the open upstairs window. It looks like Michael is in. Did Jude come back looking for her? And if they did, did she and Michael speak? The gap between them is narrowing, but the woman ahead has stopped and now she's climbing into the passenger seat of a car. Katy breaks into a run but as she does a stitch tears into her side.

No, she decides, abruptly coming to a halt. She'll not catch her now. And as she pinches her side, she is proven right as the car pulls away.

Turning back towards their house, Katy sees another figure – Michael this time, stepping through the same front gate and onto the street. He is dressed in running gear and must already have in his headphones because when she shouts to him to wait he does not seem to hear. Instead, after a couple of hamstring stretches, he turns away then breaks into a run, back along their street towards the main road from which she's just come.

Damp-faced now from the heat, any energy Katy had a few minutes earlier has seeped away like spilled water. She is light-headed, too, and desperate to sit down. So she retraces her steps slowly, taking care not to rush herself dizzy, until she draws level with the front gate. Reaching out with a shaking hand to free the latch she hesitates at the sound of a vehicle rapidly approaching from somewhere behind then coming to an abrupt halt. Through its open window comes the walkie talkie crackle of urgent voices. Only as she turns to stare does she see the flashing light.

'Where is he?' a female paramedic demands, clambering out from the passenger door. Dressed in Day-glo yellow and hospital green, her waist-length plait of jet-black hair accentuates the paleness of her determined, blunt-chinned face.

'I'm sorry?' Katy mumbles.

The other woman frowns. 'We got a call out to this address. One of your neighbours reported a man lying in your front garden with blood coming from his head. They said he'd been attacked. D'you know anything about this?'

Confused, all Katy can do is shake her head.

'Do you live here?' the paramedic presses on. Impatiently, she points with her thumb towards the damaged front door then casts a glance up at the upstairs windows Michael's left open. Katy nods. 'Know anything about this?'

'No, I've only just—' Katy turns away from the paramedic to scan the front garden for any sign of anything untoward that might have taken place. But as her eyes skim the dusty ground at their feet she sees only a few dried leaves and a rogue empty crisp packet sitting amongst the gently expiring pot plants. Not even any remnants of the broken egg shells. Certainly no sign of any blood. 'Are you sure they said this address?'

The paramedic frowns. 'Calls are recorded as well as logged, now, you know, and I've already double-checked. The caller was a young male who said he lived in the house opposite. He described the victim as—' she checks a piece of paper she's holding in her hand '—male, tall with dark-blond hair, resident at number thirty-two. Said he wasn't moving and looked in a bad way. But as you can see, when we came we found nothing.'

She must mean Michael, thinks Katy with a jolt of panic. But that's ridiculous, she's just seen him leave. Glancing towards the curtained windows of the house opposite, she visualises the owners – a middle-aged couple with two teenage sons. She knows the family only by sight, but she supposes it is possible. A prank of some kind, perhaps. But then she recalls watching the family load up their car with bags to go on holiday the previous week and now, of course, by the look of the house they must still be away.

Following Katy's gaze, the paramedic clicks her tongue. 'You wouldn't believe how much time and money is wasted by false emergency call-outs,' she complains. 'Not to mention the risk to life. Wasted trips like this mean we're not on call for people in real need of help.' She refolds the piece of paper and puts it into her back pocket then stares hard at Katy for a moment. 'Tony?' she shouts to the ambulance's driver who's still seated at the wheel. 'We'd better get back to work.'

Katy watches as the ambulance pulls away and the street resettles. Every now and then a passing car slows to navigate the sleeping policeman outside the house three doors down. From somewhere close by comes the sound of an electric lawnmower. The tang of barbecue smoke. The normality of this is soothing.

Upstairs she finds a note from Michael propped against the TV screen. 'Gone for a run,' it reads, 'back… whenever'. Resisting the temptation to analyse the tone of this, she opens the fridge and extracts a can of Pepsi from behind dishes containing two tuna steaks gently soaking up a marinade of ginger, garlic and coriander and a freshly prepared salad. She glances up. It's almost six. How soon will he return?

Katy takes a seat in the kitchen, usually the coolest room in the house at this time of the day. There is a newspaper on the counter which she idly flicks through, though takes in little. Turning on the radio, a fractious debate on the drive-time phone-in jangles her nerves. She opens the fridge door again and peers inside. But the fish smell makes her want to gag. And besides, she isn't hungry.

Instead, she runs herself a bath. But before she is done she hears a loud rapping on the inside front door. Assuming Michael has forgotten his key, she clambers out of the bath and wraps a towel around her. Only as she stands on the bottom stair, staring at the door that separates Michael's flat from the communal hallway beyond does she think to call out.

'Hello?'

'Katy, is that you?'

Her pulse quickens. This is a stranger's voice, not Michael's. Tightening her grip on the damp towel around her, she struggles for a moment with what best to say and when she finally speaks, her mouth is dry.

'Who's asking?'

'It's Kev, from the flat downstairs – Phil's brother?'

The tentative, upward inflection which punctuates every couple of words of this brief explanation feels reassuring. 'Kevin,' she exclaims. 'Sorry, I'm just having a bath. Is it urgent, or can it wait?'

'Actually, it is pretty urgent,' he ruefully replies. 'I'm running late for my shift at The Boatman where I work the bar, and there'll be all hell to pay if I don't get going. Only there's a problem with the French windows which don't seem to lock properly. I just wonder if I go round into the garden at the back to give them a good push from outside if you can turn the key from inside – I've left it in the door.'

'The French windows, right. Well, OK, I guess so,' she replies, glancing up at the wet foot prints she's left on the stairs. 'Hang on while I get my keys. I'll only be a minute.'

Katy emerges from the flat a couple of minutes later tousle-haired in shorts, a T-shirt and flip-flops to find the communal hallway empty. Softly pulling shut the door to Michael's flat behind her, she pockets her door key then slips down the short flight of stairs leading to Phil's front door which, as Kevin said, has been left ajar.

About to step into Phil's flat Katy hesitates, flushed by the awkward memory of the last time she'd been inside. It was New Year the year before and the night had culminated in a furious argument with Michael. The party had gone on late and some time around three, with Michael enmeshed in an intense discussion with a picture editor from the *Telegraph*, Katy made her excuses to leave. Unlike the others, she'd been working that day and now all she craved was sleep.

It was in the hallway that it happened, just a drunken fumble – what Mum would have called 'a fleeting pass'. But though unlooked for, it was not entirely unwelcome. For Katy had always liked their downstairs neighbour, a no-nonsense straight talker from Durham whose easy charm and quick wit won him a steady stream of female companions, despite his irrational fear of what he called 'the C word': commitment. This had given Phil's attentions that evening added piquancy. Which was how, as they pecked cheeks goodbye in the open doorway, their bodies momentarily slipped into something more intimate.

Suddenly his hands were cupping her breasts beneath her shirt while hers slid below his waistband as, open-mouthed, their faces locked. And in that instant she saw herself in a different place leading a different life, without Michael. Which took her by surprise. They'd been living together a couple of years by that point, and despite that one brief period apart following that dreadful evening at Spike's, life together had been going well. With hindsight, a little too well, she now observes, thinking of the pressure he'd put her under around that particular time to commit.

For Michael had begun talking about marriage, albeit in general terms, a good few months before she felt comfortable with the idea that perhaps she would soon be approaching the same point. She loved Michael, yes. But could she see herself spending the rest of her life with him? She wasn't sure, not hand on heart; not yet, at least. Which made the momentary appeal of a more carefree existence so seductive. She did not want an affair. Yet nor did she want to close the door too soon on that as a hypothetical possibility.

Her body had shuddered beneath Phil's touch, she now guiltily recalls, and worse was his look of triumph as he registered it. Until, a beat later, it was over, their bubble pierced by Michael's presence in the open doorway. By Phil's guffaw, too, as he pulled away. It was drunken and therefore totally and utterly meaningless, they had both reassured him, separately, over the days that followed. Though Michael took a good deal longer to forgive her for the indiscretion than he did his friend.

Taking a deep breath, Katy steps inside to make her way towards the open-plan kitchen-diner at the flat's rear where French windows lead into the walled garden beyond.

A large overnight bag sits open-mouthed on the kitchen counter, its knotted contents – assorted T-shirts, socks and boxers – lie scattered across the wood block work top and on the floor. She pauses, her nostrils pricked by the fetid airlessness of the place; the sickly smell from the relics of half-eaten takeaways slammed carelessly into the kitchen bin. Registers, too, the oily ring on the nearest cushion of the pastel sofa from a days-old pizza carton which sits forgotten on the floor.

Kevin's got one hell of a clearing up job before his brother gets back, she decides.

Quickening her pace, Katy approaches the French windows which, as predicted, are open. Widening the crack, she steps outside. Standing tall, she opens her lungs to the world beyond with its baked air tinged with barbecue smoke and hot rubber. She glances towards the back gate separating the garden from the narrow alleyway parallel to the road which runs the entire length of the terrace. It is still padlocked from the inside, she notices. This is strange given Kevin said he'd go round the back to help secure the French windows from outside. How had he planned to get in?

The slam of a door from somewhere close by brings Katy back to her senses. With no clear route out of the garden, her heart races with the sudden thought that she is trapped. Is Kevin still in the flat behind her, waiting? Is this some kind of joke, though this feels anything but funny. Why didn't Phil tell Michael his younger brother was coming to stay? Assuming Kevin really is his brother – after all, they only have his say-so. But that's just ridiculous. Who else can he be? With no alternative but to retrace her steps, her body braces as she turns to go back inside.

A moment later she is pulling to the French windows behind her and feels another stab of panic as she realises just how easy it is to secure them. Trying to dismiss the thought that this was nothing more than a clumsy ruse to get her out of her own flat, Katy's ears strain for any sign of movement from upstairs. But there is none. So she hurries back towards the front door which, she sees with a jolt of relief, is still open – just as she left it. Stumbling out into the communal hallway, she slams the door behind her. It's just too bad if Kevin's locked out, she reasons. If he gets stuck he can always borrow Michael's spare.

'What were you doing?'

A figure is looking down at her from the short flight of stairs before her which lead to the open doorway to their flat, flush-faced and shining with sweat. He must have just got in for he is dressed in his running things and still wears the earphones connected to his smartphone which he is holding in his hand.

'Michael!' she exclaims, but as her face softens his tightens into a frown. 'It was Kevin, he—'

His eyes narrow. 'You were downstairs, with Kevin?'

Despite herself, Kat's cheeks burn. He can't be jealous, surely. But then again, why is she behaving like a naughty child caught red-handed with pockets filled with goodies filched from the biscuit tin? 'No,' she offers, drawing level with him outside the top flat's door. 'He asked me to help – there's a problem with the downstairs French window. I just—'

'Hold the explanation,' he pleads, his raised hand stopping her abruptly in her tracks. 'I've got to get some water.'

'You just missed me, you know,' she gushes, following him up the stairs. 'When you went for your run – I was only a few houses along, but coming from the other way.'

'Mmm,' he gasps, taking deep gulps from a pint glass hastily filled with tap water. 'I didn't see you, sorry. You should have called… to let me know you were on your way.'

And you – you could have waited, she thinks, though doesn't say it. For there is something far more important Katy needs to know. What Jude was doing here, leaving the house, just a few minutes ago. 'I saw a woman – leaving the house… just before you did.' She forces a laugh. It was Jude. Definitely Jude, but why? She hopes it sounds casual. 'Anything I should know?'

With a shake of his head, Michael drains the remnants of his drink.

'Well I've been thinking for a while it might be worth considering our options – you know, for as and when we need more space.' He drops his gaze as he slips off a trainer, but Katy wonders if there might be another reason why he now seems reluctant to meet her eye. 'The three of us? It seemed, well, a good idea to get someone round. You know, to take a look. I wanted to discuss it with you, properly, when I had all the facts. So I thought I'd ring the lot I found this place through, but then an old school friend—'

'Move you, you mean.'

It is a statement, not a question. For she has suspected something like this has been playing on his mind. But Katy's not thinking about the fact that given how many times she expressed her reluctance to move before the baby is bigger, he must surely know how much talking to estate agents behind her back would upset her. She is wondering why he's lying. About another old school friend popping out of the woodwork when, for years, he'd said his former classmates were so dreadful he'd severed all links. About the fact that this so-called school friend, a woman, had visited when she was out. And that this woman was Jude.

'She looked – professional,' Katy adds.

'Did she? Well, they have to don't they, I guess – to get the best clients?' He runs a forefinger around the neck of his running shirt which, despite the hi-tech breathable fabric it's made of, is damply clumped against his skin. 'All I've requested is an initial valuation, just a rough guide so we can have a sensible discussion about our options. Sorry, Katy, I didn't mean to do it behind your back.'

Do what? she wonders. Connive with a woman who, having tracked me down after all these years of not being in touch, clearly wants to do me and my family harm? Why's he not telling; what's he holding back? Unless she's mistaken, of course. After all, she only saw her from halfway down the street. But before she can ask any more Michael is walking towards her, up the stairs, eager to undress and shower.

'Give me a minute,' he calls, his voice now fighting with the sound of the water he is emptying from her bath. 'I just need a quick shower. Then you can tell me the latest about what's happening with your mum.'

Katy makes her way upstairs to their bedroom, slips off her shoes and lies down on the bed. Staring up at the pale glass of the cylindrical lampshade that hangs from the ceiling above, her eyes circumnavigating its circular rim, her anger subsides. And as her body unclenches she notes the aches and strains in her legs, her back, her neck as the muscles unfurl. She mustn't fight it, she realises. The way her body has started to change. The need to look after it. To protect them both from whatever else may be going on outside.

Without even noticing, her hands have come to rest lightly on her belly and it is as they settle, her fingers lightly interlaced, that she feels it. A butterfly tremble from the cavity beneath. Like a finger giving a light flick, but from the inside. A sensation so unexpected she is baffled for a moment by its cause and then, more anxiously, wonders what it might mean. Could all that's been happening over the past few days have unsettled the baby? Might more than usual physical exertion, especially in this heat, be damaging?

Gingerly, she rolls onto her side and reaches for the pregnancy guide that sits on the floor by the bed and flicks through its pages.

It is, of course, around the time she should start feeling it move – though she needs to re-read the relevant section to prove it. It's normal. She mustn't worry. He or she will be OK. It is the first time she's allowed herself to think of it in this way. True, the baby became more tangible for her following the twelve week scan. But the knowledge they'd need another ultrasound a month and a half on to check for abnormalities due to her age has squashed any temptation to start thinking about the tiny foetus eventually becoming an actual person.

He or she? she ponders. Diane had one of each; Michael's mother, Jean, had three – all boys. Which is why Michael has already let slip his excitement at the prospect of a little girl.

Yet Katy's not so sure. She's hardly excelled at her first mother–daughter relationship, has she? Then there's school. How cruel girls can be. The shadow cast by her own experiences make small boys' thump-and-forget tendency almost appealing. Besides she knows Michael has no preference, not really. With two nephews already it's clear he'll be a great dad, she thinks, stroking her tummy. A baby boy will cement things between the two of them. Repair the past. She must take care of herself; of them. This must be her priority from now.

'You look comfortable.' Michael is standing in the open doorway, a bath towel knotted around his waist. 'Stay where you are,' he adds, his expression softening. 'I'll make us something to eat and you can tell me all about it. Get an early night. Assuming you're still up for it, we've lunch in the diary at Spike's place in the country tomorrow.'

'Tomorrow?' Katy frowns, fumbling for the appropriate context. That would be Saturday. The weekend. And today? Friday. Spike, one of Michael's oldest friends, has just turned fifty and is hosting a weekend house party at the place in the country, near the south coast, that he bought a while ago to do up. 'But mum——' she begins.

'I know,' he interrupts, raising his finger to his lips. 'Don't say any more. Just think about it. I've explained the situation to him and it's OK if we just go for lunch and if you don't even feel up to that that's fine, too, if you don't mind me going alone. I won't stay over, though – I promise I'll be back be early evening.'

Katy sighs, wearied by the need to make a decision. Unsure what would be best, she simply nods as she slips back against the pillows.

It would be nice to get out of London, she admits. A change of scene would help take her mind off things. But only if she can be confident Diane really is OK. Joyce will be more than happy to collect her, of course, then she and Michael can stop by to see her back at Parkview on the drive home. Besides, given the lingering memory of Jude's visit the prospect of spending much of the day in the flat on her own now fills her with dread.

'We're out of milk, I'll be back in five!' Michael calls from the front door as Katy is patting herself dry a half hour later.

Slipping into a loose T-shirt and a pair of pants, she wanders downstairs and into the sitting room where she stands at the window for a minute, monitoring his progress along the street towards the corner shop before he disappears from view. Though the window is flung wide open, the air inside smells acrid. A staining odour that seems to stick to everything which it takes her a moment to recognise. Cigarettes.

Turning her back on the world outside, Katy scans the room from her vantage point by the window. From where she is standing she can see on the floor between the side of Michael's leather armchair and the wall the makeshift ashtray Jude used yesterday. The butts inside, their filters stained a blood red by Jude's lipstick. But on the coffee table beside the TV which stands in the opposite corner she sees something else.

It's one of the scallop shells she brought back from the weekend she and Michael spent in that sail loft in Whitstable. She used them as tea light holders and when empty they stood in a row along the upstairs bathroom window. Only this one has served another purpose. Stepping towards the coffee table, she picks up the shell. It contains a single butt. The same brand as in the other ashtray. But the filter of this one is stained by lipstick a different colour. Coral pink. Arguably a better match if you're wearing an outfit of emerald green.

It is Jude's, she knows with a plummeting heart. But why come to the house, again, while Katy was out?

Chapter 18

Guildford, February 1989

As soon as Jude saw the pale but determined look on Siobhan's face she knew something was up.

A wary aloofness had marked their relationship in the weeks since their argument over the picture of her so-called dad, yet in an instant Jude instinctively knew now was not the time to try to score points. 'What's the matter, Mum?' she asked, putting her school bag down on the kitchen table beside a box of official looking letters and bills.

'The surgery...' Siobhan did not look up as she spoke in a low, controlled monotone. 'They've let me go.'

'Oh,' said Jude, unsure what else to say. Staring at the pile of papers she noticed numbers on a bank statement underlined in red.

Following her daughter's gaze, Siobhan hastily placed a cardboard folder on the top of the pile. 'Sit down,' she said, patting the seat beside her. 'We need to talk.'

For the first time in months, Jude mutely did as she is told. A ball of panic nudges the back of her throat.

'Right,' her mum began, crisply, picking up a sheet of paper littered with hastily calculated sums. 'I'll have to get another job, of course, and – thank goodness – the school fees are covered by the scholarship, but in the short term things will be tough.' Jude said nothing. 'So there will be some changes. We're going to have to tighten our belts to keep up the mortgage repayments. Cut back on any extras. I may even have to sell the car, if we really want to stay.'

'What about Dave?'

Siobhan looked blank. Dave had gone away for the week with a bunch of biker friends to watch the TT Races on the Isle of Man. 'Of course Dave will help, too,' she replied. 'And when he gets back he's promised to help me work through all our finances—'

How generous, thought Jude, recalling all those times when Siobhan had complained about his reluctance to restock the fridge or make any other contribution to the gas and electricity bills. 'He could start paying rent,' she suggested.

Her mum's face darkened. 'Rent?'

'It's about time he started to contribute – you know, financially.'

'When I need your advice I'll ask for it,' snapped Siobhan. Sitting back in her chair, she pinched the bridge of her nose between forefinger and thumb. For a moment Jude thought she might cry, but she was wrong. 'I had Yvonne from the surgery on the phone a little earlier, the interfering cow,' her mum continued. 'Some woman she knows who's about to have a baby needs a home help. The bloody cheek. As if I'd take on any old thing. I didn't work so hard for so long to iron other people's underwear. But then Yvonne's always looked down on me, the patronising bitch.'

Jude hesitated. 'Perhaps she has a point—'

Siobhan looked up sharply. 'I beg your pardon?'

'I mean, you are going to have to get something to tide us over until you find another proper job, aren't you?' Jude stopped, realising she'd gone too far, but it was too late to disengage, so without pausing for breath she carried on anyway. 'Not that you should do something like that. I just meant—'

'I know exactly what you just meant,' Siobhan cried, rising to her feet. 'Well don't you worry your pretty little head about it. Mummy will sort it out. Haven't you got some homework to do?'

Jude stepped back to let her mum push past her then watched in silence as Siobhan opened a bottle of wine, found a glass then left the room to make her way upstairs where she would steep her wounded pride in a long, hot bath. Jude waited for a few minutes then slipped into the kitchen and took a can of Dave's lager from the fridge. Back in her room, she threw herself down onto the bed and closed her eyes, ignoring the homework she'd yet to complete. *If we really want to stay.* The doubt in her mum's words was unsettling. For despite her reluctance to leave the south coast, Jude had come to like her new life.

She'd done well in her mocks and her teachers were predicting six As and three Bs. If she achieved these grades or above she would have the chance of a scholarship into the sixth form at Clark's, a boys school on the outskirts of town. Otherwise there was the tech or staying on at St Mary's. Whatever she chooses to do, though, one thing was for sure. She needed three good A levels, including English, to get a place at the London University college she had in mind for her English and drama degree.

Some time later, having spent at least an hour on her bed reading the latest Armistead Maupin, Jude slipped downstairs to make a sandwich. The sitting room door was shut, the ground floor was in darkness, yet from behind the closed door she could hear her mother's voice. Intrigued, Jude hesitated, hovering on the bottom stair.

'…I know Nan, but we can't come back,' she heard her mum say. 'Jude's settled at school and we like our life here. I'll find another proper job, and until I do I can take on some other work… Of course he's said he can help, but that's not a long-term solution…' There was a long pause followed by a sharp intake of breath. 'Absolutely not. He gives me what he gives me and that's that – I am not going cap in hand to beg for more… Look, it's an arrangement that works and I want it to stay that way…'

At least it sounded as if Dave was paying his way, Jude thought as she crept into the kitchen to make a snack. She was glad, too, that her mum seemed reluctant to accept Nanny P's apparent suggestion that they move back to Portsmouth. After weeks spent in opposite corners, it seemed she and Siobhan now stood united – on this issue, at least. Then, at around eleven, her mum came back upstairs.

'How's it going?' Siobhan called, briefly popping her head around Jude's bedroom door.

'Oh, you know...' her daughter sighed. 'You?'

'Fine,' her mum said brightly, but her eyes looked dull. 'Keep up the good work.'

A little later, Jude heard her mother talking on the phone again. To Dave, probably. Turning back to her book, she realised her brain had disengaged from the written words at least half a page earlier, if not more. It was late, almost midnight, and she really should turn in. But as she made her way along the landing towards the bathroom to brush her teeth, something about her mum's tone – an urgent whisper punctuated by an occasional sob – lured her back downstairs.

'...I said it's not enough.' Siobhan's voice was an urgent whisper. 'Not now I've lost my job. Which is another thing. You can't drop it off at the surgery anymore, you'll have to deliver it here... I don't know how, that's not my problem. Just get it to me, all right? ... Of course I haven't told Jude. When I say we've got a deal we've got a deal. And we have got a deal, Charlie, haven't we? ... Well that's alright then...'

Now seated on the bottom stair, Jude's body tensed. Even if she wanted to, she knew she couldn't move – as if the bones in her legs had become rubber, or the connectors linking her feet to her brain were severed. So silently she listened at the sitting room door, her hopes fluttering moth-like. Until she heard the dull click of the phone being replaced. A sound like rustling paper followed by a cough. Then the unmistakable sound of tears.

Softly, Jude pushed open the sitting room door to see Siobhan sitting hunched on the sofa, her face in her hands, slowly rocking to and fro. The scene was unsettling, and Jude held back as her mind raced. The right thing to do would be to rush to her mum's side and give her a hug. Yet she cringed at the woman's lack of self-control. Her vulnerability and despair. For an instant she contemplated a retreat from the room, unseen, but then it was too late. Siobhan was turning towards her having sensed her presence.

'What is it, Jude?' her mum asked, weakly.

'Nothing. I just wondered if you were... OK.'

Siobhan sat up. Her face was red and blotchy. 'Oh, I'll survive,' she murmured, softly, as she unfolded then refolded the situations vacant section of the local paper which was still on her lap. 'I always do.'

'I heard the phone. How's Dave?'

'What? Oh, fine – he'll be back tomorrow night,' Clearly flustered, Siobhan reached for a half glass of wine on the floor by her feet. Having drained the contents in a single gulp, she replaced the glass and as she did so Jude noticed her hand was shaking. The bottle, now empty, stood by the phone, reminded Jude to dispose of the beer can she left upstairs before her mum could find it.

'Look, um, I just wanted to say... sorry.' The words were out before Jude had even thought what to say. But she'd struck lucky. Contrition was always a winning hand to play.

'Sorry?' Siobhan looked confused. Perhaps it was the wine.

'I know how hard you've worked,' Jude gushed. 'And I didn't mean to suggest... Look, I'll help any way I can, all right? And when Dave gets back I know you'll feel a whole lot better.'

'Yes, I will,' her mum sighed. 'He said to say hi, by the way.'

Liar, Jude thought as she undressed for bed a few minutes later. As she angrily sifted her memories for any previous mention of someone called Charlie. Lying in bed, she reached for her Walkman and pressed play. But as soon as the music started to play, she ripped out the cassette and flung it across the room.

Her sleep was fitful that night – disturbed by her mother's lie, troubled by the thought of moving away, excited by the looming exams which would bring her eventual liberation one step closer. Then she was woken just after six the next morning by the dull click as someone pushed open the front gate and then, a minute later, pulled it to again.

Unable to go back to sleep, she tossed and turned for a while then conceded defeat, climbed out of bed and padded downstairs to get herself some juice. Only as her foot touched the bottom step on her return journey, however, did she see it – a cream-coloured envelope lying on the mat at the foot of the front door.

It was expensive paper – ridged, like corduroy. The handwriting on the front was written in ink and addressed to Miss Davies. But no one called her mum Miss, ever. Despite this, Jude somehow knew the envelope could not be intended for her. Yet as she thoughtfully turned it over in her hands she found herself seduced by its dull weight and unknown contents. The mystery of it. Besides, she could always say she'd made a genuine mistake, couldn't she?

Slowly, very slowly and after a furtive glance up the stairs behind her, Jude slipped her forefinger beneath the flap and gently edged it around the V, then eased open the seal without a tear in case she needed to stick it back down.

The slim bundle of £20 notes inside was wrapped in a piece of notepaper which, like the envelope, was textured and bore a watermark. There must have been at least twenty notes, Jude marvelled, fanning them out like cards in her hand. But why? An accompanying slip of paper had dropped to the floor. Hungrily, she grabbed it and read the brief message: 'You keep your side of the bargain, I'll keep mine'.

Bargain, what bargain? Jude wondered, puzzled. Then she remembered her mum's words on the phone the night before. Something about a deal being a deal, and not telling her about something. Somehow Jude knew this anonymous note must be from the Charlie her mum had been speaking to. But Charlie who? He clearly knew Siobhan had a daughter, but Siobhan had never mentioned knowing anyone of that name. There was only one Charlie Jude could think of. Or rather, Charles.

Laughter bubbled in her mouth. The possibility that her mum and Mr Parker could possibly have some sort of a deal was simply ludicrous.

Jude looked up. From where she was sitting, she could see through the sitting room door across the room to the mantelpiece and the gap where the photograph of her so-called dad had once stood. Her mouth was dry, her throat felt tight. No, absolutely not. She made some quick calculations. Kat was four months older than her, which meant he would have been with her mum when his own wife had been pregnant... Then she remembered something. Didn't Siobhan mention something about seeing her father one last time just before Jude was born outside his house on Pilgrim's View, and that they had an older child?

Jude wondered, briefly, if the child had been a boy. An older brother. Andrew. But the idea was stupid. Ridiculous.

Carefully, she rewrapped the notes then slid them back into the envelope. The seal was still shiny with glue. But as she stuck out her tongue to lick it she hesitated. In her hands seemed to be a clue about her real father's identity. Now, surely, she had a chance to discover the truth. A truth no one in their right mind – Siobhan especially – could deny she had a right to know. So instead of sealing the flap Jude tucked it inside itself and slipped the envelope into her dressing gown pocket before softly making her way back upstairs.

–

It was raining when they got off the bus at the end of Kat's road. Tugging their school coats over their heads, they ran as one along the sodden lane. Ignoring the school bags pummelling their thighs, the mud splattered by their pounding legs, they dashed towards the open five bar gate and the gravel driveway beyond that led to the front door of Kat's house.

Jude no longer felt awed by the place's grand scale. Familiarity had shaped her conclusion that its mock Tudor timbering was artifice rather than awesome; that the building's wisteria-hung façade was twee, if picturesque. Today, though, other matters were playing out in her mind as Kat, who unlike Jude did not yet have her own front door key to let herself in and out whenever she so chose, rang the doorbell. Then, a beat later, Mrs Parker was hastily stepping to one side in the open doorway as the girls tumbled inside.

'Goodness, you're both soaked!' Kat's mum exclaimed as they shrugged off their coats and shook their hair.

'Hello Mrs P,' Jude grinned, spinning around on her heels with a flourish to hang her sodden coat on a free hook behind the front door.

'Nice to see you, Judith,' Mrs Parker responded, coolly. 'And let me take these,' she added, reaching for their coats. 'They'll dry quicker in the kitchen.'

With barely a backward glance, the girls tore upstairs with their bags. Inside Kat's bedroom, a large airy room with two sash windows overlooking the back garden and, beyond, spring fields like damp corduroy, the girls spread out their books on the floor – camouflage designed to convince the casual observer they were working. Then they pulled out the pile of magazines stowed beneath the bed.

As Kat searched for a suitable cassette to play, Jude rose to her feet. 'Just going for a wee,' she called out innocently. As she moved towards the door, Kat finetuned the volume on the stereo then leaned back against the bed flicking through last month's *Honey*.

Once inside the bathroom Jude lowered the toilet and sat down. She tore off some loo paper, balled the tissue in her hand then blew her nose. Exhaling, slowly, she tried to focus her thoughts but found herself distracted by Mr Parker's dressing gown which hung from the back of the bathroom door. It was ankle length, a rather grand navy and gold striped affair, in some kind of satiny fabric.

Having never met the man in person, she struggled to visualise him in it, though knew instinctively the garment would only ever be worn over pyjamas, never his naked body, Dave-style. Having spent hours chewing over the possible identity of her real dad, Jude's mind had grown attuned to every father-related nuance. In recent days, for example, she'd logged without fail even the merest mention of a Charlie or Charles living or working some place in town.

So she'd noticed for the first time the name of the milkman printed at the top of his weekly bill: Bill Charles. The landlord of The Salutation, Siobhan and Dave's favourite pub on the high street, was a Charles Clifford. And Charlie was the name Ruth Creighton had chosen to give her new pony.

Yet Jude was no closer to discovering the truth behind the note still carefully folded in her pocket. Just where to begin? Perhaps she was approaching this the wrong way round. Maybe a good place to start would be by ruling out the Charleses Charlie couldn't be.

Lobbing the damp tissue into the wicker waste basket beneath the sink, Jude rose to her feet and crept across the room. Softly, she opened the bathroom door. The landing was silent. Mr Parker was away on one of his so-called business trips. Andrew wasn't due back until after dinner. And from the distant clatter from downstairs, Mrs Parker was otherwise distracted by preparations for tea.

Crossing the threshold, Jude headed across the landing. But before she'd taken more than a couple of paces her body froze, every muscle tensed at the shrill sound of the trim phone now buzzing crossly on the side table in the hallway immediately below. Barely daring to breathe, she screwed shut her eyes, willing Kat not to come out onto the landing from behind the closed bedroom door just to her left; praying for Diane's hasty return to the kitchen.

At last, Kat's mother answered the phone then, after a moment's silence, slammed it back down onto its cradle with an audible crack before hurrying back to her tea preparations.

With no time to lose, Jude crept past Diane's room with barely a glance, as having explored this room on a previous visit, she knew she would not find what she was looking for there. Passing the spare room, she kept on going until she reached the end of the corridor where there were two doors, both closed. Impulsively, Jude turned to her left and twisted the nearest handle. Without a sound, the door swung open.

Peeking inside, Jude saw a room the near mirror image of Kat's but with walls hung with rock posters and shelves cluttered with old books and football memorabilia. It was the first time she'd seen Andrew's bedroom and being there, poised in the doorway, staring at the intimate footprint of his childhood, made her feel at once both excited and confused.

Up until that point their relationship had been conducted outside the confines of their respective homes on spare beds at student parties, the back seat of his second-hand Ford Escort, and on the bathroom floor of 'Jinx' Jones's parents' recently refurbished granny flat — twice. Now, staring into his room uninvited, Jude couldn't help but think the reality of who he was and where he'd come from diminished him somehow and yet, at the same time, her entire being craved his touch.

Stepping back onto the landing, Jude closed the door. Turning quickly to her right, she twisted the other door handle and briskly stepped inside to stare, in awe, and for the first time, at Mr Parker's study.

An entire wall was hung with shelves on which were crammed a closely packed line of books with crimson spines embossed with gold. An entire level below had been dedicated to neatly boxed collections of financial and business journals while the bottom shelf bulged with dusty photo albums, bulging A4 lever arch files and metal boxes of slides.

She turned towards the desk, an antique construction with a faded green leather top on which a large blotter, a carved wooden letter rack, and Newton's cradle seemed to have been meticulously positioned as if awaiting closer inspection by investigators shortly to arrive at a crime scene. Her gaze fixed on the central drawer which, a moment later, she had opened and was peering into. But it only contained a selection of stationery. Next, she tried the top drawer to her left but it was crammed with photographs. On her third attempt, however, she found what she was looking for: a stack of plastic folders containing a variety of personal correspondence.

Carefully, Jude pulled free the uppermost folder, opened it and peered at its contents. The top sheet was a letter, typed and signed with Charles's signature. Pulling out the note from her pocket, her heart starts to thresh like a hooked fish as she compared the two bits of paper. But his name on the printed letter was signed with such a flourish it was hard to be sure.

Hadn't she always known the very idea of it was simply ludicrous? Even so, she knew she must be certain. So she quickly rifled the folder scanning more sheets until she found another letter, this time written entirely in Mr Parker's hand. Once more she compared the sheet against the note to her mum.

Sinking down onto Charles's office chair, Jude stared again at the pieces of paper. For this time there was no doubt. Even the ink he'd used, a distinctive winter sea blue, looked the same.

You keep your side of the bargain, I'll keep mine.

So his side was paying her mum money, and her mum's? To keep quiet, about her. Jude. Charles's illegitimate daughter. It was the only explanation, she knew as anger churned her insides, poking fingers of something molten through her veins.

Conscious of an overwhelming desire to dash the contents of the drawer, the desk, the entire room, even, onto the floor, Jude resisted the urge to break, to smash and to destroy something – anything, it didn't matter what, so long as it was his. Or Diane's. Or Kat's. Though her entire being felt ablaze with hatred and resentment.

How dare he pay her mum to keep quiet so he and his family can enjoy all of this? How dare her mum lie to her; play such a sick joke! For what else could explain her mother's reason for moving back to Surrey then sending her to the very school where Charles sent his legitimate daughter? Kat. Katy. Katherine Parker. Sister. The word stuck in the back of Jude's throat like a stubborn lump of sick.

A brass carriage clock standing sentry on the window sill struck five with a plummy chime. Registering the papers roughly spread across the desktop, Jude hastily pushed them back into folder then returned it to its drawer. Stuffing the note back into her pocket, she sleepwalked back towards the door. In the bathroom once more, she flushed the toilet then washed her hands; splashed her face with cold water; checked herself in the mirror. How could she look the same when her world had just been wrenched inside out? Well, she could play their game, too, she decided, grimly.

The shock had gone now, replaced by a curious scooped out feeling. She felt numb. But beneath this, deep down within her very core, it was as if some sort of chemical reaction had started to take place. Gazing into the mirror, she roadtested a smile. It almost looked genuine. An unexpected feeling of satisfaction washed over her as she realises she feels invulnerable, somehow. Empowered. It was almost as if she could feel the thick, protective skin that had started to grow around her heart as Jude slipped back into Kat's bedroom.

Briefly, she hovered in the doorway looking down at her friend. The girl was facing away from her, lying on her front on the floor reading a copy of *Over 21*. With ankles crossed, her left foot was gently tapping in time to the Madonna track that was playing, 'Like A Prayer'. Frizzy hair, still damp from the afternoon rain, veiled Kat's insipid little face leaving the pale skin at the nape of her neck exposed. How would it feel to enclose that puny neck with her bare hands, Jude wondered. To squeeze with all her might until...

'You took your time,' she said, without glancing round.

'Oh you know how it is.' Jude delivered her words with a strangled laugh. 'How time flies when you're having fun.'

Chapter 19

West Sussex, July 2013

Katy and Michael leave London before breakfast on Saturday morning. They drive in his car south down the A3 towards Portsmouth, first along abandoned city streets and then down empty country roads. Neither has slept well and both woke early, alert and restless. But a shrouded sky makes the world feel drowsy and the hazy sun makes the landscape pulse with a sickly glow.

Spike's place is an old rectory he bought the year before in a village near Fareham which he and his long-term on-off partner, Crystal, have since been renovating. The last time Katy saw the place it had no roof. As the pair enter the final stages of decoration, however, the house party is as much a celebration of their project's impending completion as it is a marker of Spike's half century.

Michael's revised plan is that they just go for lunch. Katy will head back in his car at around four to rendezvous with Joyce. Meanwhile he will get a lift back later with Peter and Jen – mutual friends from Shepherds Bush who, thanks to fractious five-year-old twins, have also decided not to stay over. Michael has been pretty good about it all, really, given that Spike is his oldest friend. Yet as they drive in silence, the radio's easy banter cannot quite mask the awkwardness between them.

They stop for breakfast in a village just outside Petersfield at a small boulangerie on a tiny high street with a single table in the window. Katy orders a latte which is served not in a cup but in a bowl. To make it easier for dipping in pastries, the owner, an Englishwoman recently returned home after a decade in Paris, helpfully advises. The way she stumbles over the occasional English word as if her head's just too crowded with French vernacular to recall her mother tongue unites the two of them, briefly, with an eye roll and a conspiratorial grin.

'You know it's good to see you smile again,' Michael murmurs, once the woman has resumed her position behind the till. 'Perhaps we should have a weekend away, just the two of us,' he offers, tentatively. 'Once everything has settled down?'

Though his intentions are clearly sound, the tone of his delivery suggests he feels like someone tiptoeing barefooted around broken glass, Katie thinks. Which makes her tetchy and defensive. What's he driving at, she wonders, grimly. Is he suggesting she's not been paying him enough attention or, worse, that she's grown aloof? But that's simply not true and so unfair. For what else can he expect considering everything she currently has on her plate?

'When mum's got the all clear. And all's right with the scan,' she shrugs. 'Once things start to feel back on track again. Yes, it would be nice. Sure.'

Michael nods. He does not need to speak for Katy to gauge his disappointment in her apparent lack of enthusiasm. And for a moment she feels an aching pulse of regret at the realisation that not only can he never understand how she is feeling, she can never tell him the real reasons why. In part because she can't articulate it because its true cause is rooted so deep down inside her she can no longer tell. Will she lose him, she wonders. For good, this time?

A telltale vibration from Katy's pocket signals an incoming text. Worried it's to do with her mum, she quickly tugs free her phone to find a new message from Sally-Anne.

'Miriam's just given three months' notice,' it reads. 'Bad news for me but good for you. Be in by eight Monday a.m. to discuss implications.'

So her boss's number two has decided not to return after her maternity leave. It's what Katy had secretly hoped for until falling pregnant herself. Just a few weeks ahead of when she is due to break her own news to Sally-Anne, the timing could not be worse.

'Look forward to it!' she texts back, unsure how else to respond.

Undecided, too, how best to proceed. To tell now, or not to tell until later once her promotion is secured? Being honest up front is the only option if she wants to come out of whatever happens next with a shred of professional credibility. But what if something comes to light as a result of the scan? Speak too soon and, at worst, she might lose everything.

Shooting a quick glance at Michael, Katy wonders if she should tell him. But he seems distracted and, besides, she knows what his preference would be.

Stopping work altogether just isn't an option for her, though – not given how long it's taken her to come this far. Nor would she like to move out of the city, either, as he has also suggested. Because it's impossible for her to contemplate leaving it all behind her. Turning her back on the cauterising effect of the hustle and bustle of it all. The bright lights that so neatly obscure the shadow of the past.

Katy gazes out of the window. Biting her lip, she wills herself not to show the resentment she now feels at Sally-Anne inadvertently forcing her hand. Or the upset she still feels that Michael has still said nothing about entertaining Jude. Can she trust him, really? she wonders. Because if he has nothing to hide then why keep this secret? What has Jude told him; could she be somehow trying to steal him away?

Of course she has no proof of this, though. And she is fearful of challenging him without grounds after what happened before.

A while back, around the time things first started getting serious and she had her wobble about commitment and confidences, he accused her of being unfaithful. Could she risk doing this back to him with no evidence now she was expecting his child? She is desperate to ask him about his meeting Jude. But if she is mistaken she'll lose him for sure this time and she's not sure how well she'd cope. Alone, except for her mum. She must just hope, pray if needs be, that he will stick by her until Jude moves on.

Katy's thoughts return to the hospital. The doctors have recommended Mum stay in until Monday or Tuesday, just in case. Which means she is safe – for now, at least. Because not only was she attacked, the mugger 'broke into' her flat with her stolen key. Defaced a picture of Katy, too. Which makes it personal. And Jude is somehow involved, she is sure of it – even if she wonders, now, if maybe the woman she saw leaving their house the afternoon before was someone else. Without proof, who would believe her; how can she know?

Why Jude is doing this and what she can possibly hope to achieve is baffling. Yet despite this Katy senses that if she is to protect the people she cares for she must find the answers to both. But how? Confronting Jude now, armed only with gut feel and looming dread, is unthinkable, for she will twist things around to her advantage just like she has always done.

No, Katy decides, she must outsmart Jude and to do that she needs to find out more. About what happened to her – since that summer day and before. If only she could speak to someone who was around back them. Like Jude's mum, Siobhan. Though the woman played only a background role in her recollections of the months leading up to that long, hot summer she always struck Katy as approachable. And considering some of the things Jude used to say about her, Siobhan had few delusions about her own daughter's behaviour.

At last they are pulling off the B road onto the single track Bullfinch Lane which leads to their final destination. A few minutes later, a collection of classic motorbikes including Spike's prized Norton Commando, come into view by an ancient garden wall and Michael's mood lifts. As the engine stills, the murmur of their friends' voices drifts from the garden close by. But they have arrived empty-handed. So Katy suggests he goes straight in and make her excuses while she drives to nearby shops to buy the wine and flowers they didn't have time to arrange the day before.

'Go on,' she says, leaning across him to open the front passenger door. 'I won't be long. There's a Sainsbury's a few miles further along the way we've just come – I remember it from last time.'

Michael waits only long enough to blow her a kiss as she starts to reverse. By the time she's turned around the car, he's disappeared through the garden gate beside the kitchen extension. She listens for a moment as the voices swell into a crescendo of excitement, laughter and backslapping. Not to worry, she thinks, glancing at the dashboard clock. The round trip to the shop should take, at most, half an hour.

The cracked clay earth on either side of the road is thick with hornbeam as she begins the five mile drive to the junction she recalls from her first visit. Then, as the road starts to rise, woodland gives way to elevated downland to her left and to her right, irregular fields of maize bounded by roughly clotted tracks.

Sun has all but burned through the early morning haze, now. The sky gleams a metallic blue. And, for the first time in what feels like weeks, Katy realises she is hungry. Not like she has felt recently, when her body was weak and her blood sugar levels in need of boosting. This is different. What she feels now is more fundamental. A sensation that's not needy but elemental and muscular. Like something's sharpened her appetite; not just for food, but for life.

Winding down the window, the wind musses Katy's hair as she shakes the tension from her head and shoulders. And as it does she knows it will be all right: settling down with Michael, having their baby, moving forward together, as a family. She can do it. They are strong enough, together. She will be the mother she never had. The best bits of Diane and something else. Someone to talk to and confide in, who will really listen. Unafraid to admit her weaknesses. Comfortable to recount lessons from the past.

Until this point she's worried that Michael wants this baby more than she does. For sure he's seemed less tentative than she. But maybe he just covers it up better. She lets slip a private grin. Either way, she knows the time has come to show her commitment. Telling Diane, together, as soon as she's had the scan in two weeks' time, is when the new beginning she's been so wary of can truly start.

Two miles more and Katy arrives in a sprawling village where, on a crossroads in the middle, stands a petrol station and a Sainsbury's Local. Pulling into the rough lot by the mini-market's side, she parks in an empty spot facing the road. Turning off the engine, she notices someone has tried to call her while she was driving. But her spirits dip when she sees the caller was Andrew. He's left her a message, too. Complaining she's not yet called him this morning, she guesses. Though his time it must be, what, seven a.m.? He must only have just touched down. Annoyed, she slips the phone back into her bag. She will listen to it later.

As she releases the seat belt, Katy notices a road sign opposite to Cow Vale. The place, just five miles away, sounds familiar though for a moment or so she can't think why. And then she hears it. That voice, again. Jude. How she'd mentioned the name the day they first met. Cow Vale was where she and Siobhan used to live. The village to which their neighbour said they'd returned. Where Siobhan would surely still be. Infuriated by the lingering thought of Andrew's criticism, Katy glances at her watch. It's only just gone ten, she thinks. There's plenty of time.

Time for what? a voice inside her challenges. Just go inside, pick up the stuff you need and head back to Spike's. Remember why you've come and make the most of it. Lunch with friends.

In a lovely garden. Out of the city, away from the events of the past few days, before mum's discharge from hospital. Calm before the storm. But instead, Katy reaches for her phone. Scrutinises the flickering bars in the top left-hand corner, wondering if there's enough coverage. Presses on the screen to activate the web browser.

Will Jude's mum remember her? Probably not, but Katy still has a clear mental picture of her. A tall, slim woman with blonde hair which, judging by the colour of her eyebrows, was dyed and a penchant for dark red lipstick. A look Diane called brassy. Yet Siobhan was a striking woman – still is, probably – what with those high cheek bones. Lips that though lacking in the definition Jude so craved were, nevertheless, wide and full. Grey-blue eyes which spelled anger as surely as a gathering sky.

It was a week or two into Jude's first term at St Mary's that Katy first became aware of her, leaning against the school fence a little way away from the gate. There had been something about the woman that made her hard to ignore and in her white T-shirt, leather skirt and flat gold pumps she looked more like someone's big sister than a fourth-former's mum. And Katy had always rather envied Jude that.

Now she stares at the screen, determined to prove them all wrong. For she is anything but the passive victim. No, she will not take this lying down. Siobhan will prove what Jude said about her own parents' marriage is a lie. And knowing what her daughter is like, the woman might even be persuaded to help Katy by persuading her to drop it once she has confided in her what Jude has done.

Without Siobhan's present home address she must think laterally, she decides, tapping into the search box the few fragments that she knows. Wondering if it will be enough as the search engine does its work. Sifting. Filtering. Making connections. But reference after reference to Siobhan Davieses provide no clues. There is Siobhan Davies the dancer. The postgraduate student in Loughborough. The deputy chair of Whitney

Women's Institute. She thinks about what Jude said about her mum being ill and adds the word hospital. Again, nothing. Then hospices. There are two nearby – one is twenty miles away on the other side of Portsmouth, the other is just two miles from Cow Vale. And something about this feels right.

A wave of hunger makes Katy's stomach lurch. She needs to eat with an unexpected sense of urgency. The realisation distracts her for a moment. She is intrigued if unsettled, too, by the thought that the tiny life unfurling inside her is demanding of her already. No longer nauseous, though, she notes triumphantly. Perhaps, at last, that phase of her pregnancy has passed.

Inside the shop there's little to tempt her amongst the neatly stacked microwave-able pasties, stale buns and sausage rolls. So she forces herself to select a cheese sandwich and an overpriced bottle of orange juice so highly concentrated she knows it will make her wince.

On a low shelf beneath the magazine rack she spots stacks of newspapers yet to be untied. Behind the till, the assistant is listlessly cleaning her fingernails with the cap from a biro. She is a pale-faced girl with a dull brown rope of hair that reaches to her waist. Katy waves to attract her attention then waits as the girl slowly makes her way towards the magazine display. Pulling a box cutter from the front pocket of her nylon trousers, she bends down to release the tightly bound piles of newsprint.

As she waits, Katy's gaze ranges across adjacent shelves of jumbo puzzle books and cheap wax crayons until she spots a small selection of local guide books. Quickly, she selects one which includes a pull out map and places it on top of the copy of the local paper which the assistant is now holding out towards her like a peace offering. A few minutes later, she is back in the car examining the web of cul-de-sacs and crescents as she eats the sandwich.

It doesn't take long to locate the hospice. Strange to think how close she is, she thinks, after spending so many years running away. The possibility of discovering something even more awful than she fears fills her with dread. It's not too late to turn back, is it? Because no one knows she's here. There would be no shame in changing her mind.

But then she thinks of her mum. How her old school friend has tracked her down, inveigled her way into her life, lied to her. How she must have somehow been involved in her attack. She wouldn't put it past Jude to have sent those flowers at the hospital. Trashed her car, even. How can she know Mum will be safe when she gets home from hospital if she stands by and does nothing?

Katy shudders, the elation she felt a few minutes earlier now matched by something else. Fear, because that's how Jude had always made her feel. Frightened. But now the time has come to stand her ground, hasn't it? The past, though long gone is still part of her present. Like something lodged deep inside her. A weight she must carry every day. But perhaps by finally confronting it she can leave behind the creeping shadow of her guilt, once and for all.

Tossing the empty bottle and sandwich packaging onto the newspapers on the back seat, Katy leans forward, puts the key in the ignition and turns the key. To move on with the rest of my life with Michael and my baby, she thinks, this has to be done.

—

With its historic coaching inn Cow Vale once prospered as a suitable place for travellers to change horses, according to the guide book. But it's hard to imagine now, Katy, thinks, as the place looks just like any other area of south coast semi-urban sprawl. Its outskirts are punctuated by cul-de-sacs of bunga-lows and red brick crescents of cost efficient, Seventies-built family homes. Its centre is a cluster of drab cottages served by a terraced row of shops, all but one of which still serves its original purpose.

On the road leading northwards out of the centre stands St Olave's. She pulls into the verge opposite a pair of large, iron gates and gazes upwards at the painted sign. Behind it she can see an arc of gravel that leads up to a large, double-fronted Victorian house. Meticulous gardens stretch either side of the drive with beds planted with military precision and lawns trimmed to a consistent pile. As if the staff, unable to control the messier aspects of life and death within, have instead beaten the tiny patch of nature within their control into perfect submission.

To the left of the gate is a small wooden door built into the wall and beside it an entry phone. Staring at the buzzer, Katy plays out the words she has decided to use. She is an old friend of the family recently back in the country after years abroad who has heard Siobhan is ill and has come to pay her respects. That's the easy bit. What happens next she would have to play by ear. Suddenly a loud voice erupts from the tiny box on the wall before her, as if from nowhere.

'Can I help you?'

Katy stares up at the house with its façade set into a fixed grin by its gleaming paintwork; the window boxes defiantly bursting with life. The knowledge that someone is up there, watching, back-foots her. But the sudden thought of Andrew's message, the way he talked to her at Diane's the day before, spurs her on. 'Um, yes. Sorry. Well. I've come to see Mrs Davies – Siobhan Davies.'

'Ah.' There is a pause. 'Well you had better come in.' Then a click as the door is released.

Up the drive by the front door steps, a woman appears from the building's left and beckons Katy to follow through a side entrance. Slightly built with grey cropped hair, she is dressed in a tailored white shirt and a knee length floral print skirt. With an encouraging smile, the woman leads Katy inside then through a flagstone hall into a small sitting room crammed with ill-matched sofas and armchairs which remind her of a dentist's waiting room.

The building's interior is library quiet for a moment, as if the world within has been suspended in time. Until the illusion is quickly shattered by the pre-lunch clatter of a distant kitchen.

Katy takes a seat on a large leather armchair next to a pair of French windows which are slightly ajar. Inching forwards on her seat, she watches with a racing heart as the woman carefully positions herself in the chair opposite. Aware she is staring, Katy busies herself with trying to decipher the titles along the spines of the bound volumes in a nearby bookcase. There is a pause that seems to last minutes then, when at last she looks up, she notices how the woman's face has rearranged itself. Her expression now is one of compassion and regret.

'Would you like something to drink?' the woman offers.

'No. Thanks,' Katy quickly replies, eager to get the scene underway.

All she needs is a few minutes to pay her respects to Jude's mum; time enough to slip a few gentle enquiries into their small talk. About what happened to Jude. About everyone knowing what her own dad was like. About how Jude is now, and what's driving her apparent desire to take down Katy and all she cares for.

As the woman leans forward, their knees almost touch. 'You say you've come about Mrs Davies...' Her eyebrows steeple and her hands clasp together, as if in prayer.

'Yes, that's right. Siobhan Davies. I believe she is a resident here?' But as soon as the words are out Katy can see, as if a veil has been lifted. She is too late.

'I'm extremely sorry to have to tell you that Mrs Davies recently passed away.' The woman speaks gently. 'I thought her daughter, Judith, said all family and friends had been told.'

Unexpected tears cloud Katy's eyes. She is too late. The one link she had with their shared past other than her own mum is dead and there's no one else left she can ask. Except Jude. The disappointment of it is crushing. But there is other family, the woman has suggested. Family, like Jude's son, she never knew about. Perhaps there is still a way...

'Oh, I'm sure they were,' she gushes, surprised at the ease with which the lie now gathers momentum. 'Actually, I'm an old friend of the family – I've been abroad. I knew she was ill, but I didn't know she had died.'

Katy feels her face flush. What is she doing here, meddling with other people's lives and deaths?

'I'm so very sorry,' the woman replies, reaching out to place a warm hand on Katy's. 'But I can tell you where she is buried if you would like to pay your respects. Or, of course, you could drop by the house on Hill Rise – I believe some of the family still live there. Would you like something to drink, some coffee or tea, perhaps, while I get the details?'

Katy rises to her feet abruptly, her head feels engulfed by a sudden rush of heavy, pulsing heat. 'Thank you,' she blurts, trying not to register the other woman's surprise. All she wants now is to be back outside. 'But I really should be going.'

The room, cool with the sweet smell of recently-mown grass just a few minutes earlier, now feels oppressive; its dark wood-work, thick carpet and overloaded bookcases intimidating. Katy swallows. Her tongue is sticky; her mouth paper dry. It's like the air is being sucked out of this space, she thinks. To create a vacuum in which her pounding head will surely explode. Oblivious to the trickle of sweat, her flaming cheeks, she shakes the woman's hand with ham-fisted enthusiasm then blindly stumbles towards the door.

Back in the car, she quickly starts the engine and pulls away. But as soon as the house is out of view she pulls in once more and buries her face in her hands and chastises herself for being so stupid. She sits like this, hunched forward, gently rocking, for a few minutes as she struggles to decide what to do. But before she can come to any conclusion, she is tugged back to the awfulness of what she's just done by the ringing of her phone. Her bag is in the footwell of the passenger seat and as she fumbles for the phone its contents spill onto the floor.

The call is from a number she doesn't know which makes her hesitate. Will it be Jude? A beat later she has answered and her heart is soaring as she recognises Joyce's voice. But her relief is short-lived. The voice is anxious. Urgent.

'Katy, is that you?'

'Yes, yes, it's me. Is Mum OK?' A tourniquet of panic tightens Katy's throat.

'Your mother's fine,' Joyce soothes. 'But I need to talk to you about something that I didn't want her to hear.'

Deafened by relief, Katy doesn't notice the edge to the other woman's voice. 'Thank goodness,' she laughs easily.

'Katy, there was a picture of your mum…'

'Yes?'

'…in her bedroom – I only noticed the frame was empty once you'd gone…'

'Oh.' Katy checks her watch, wondering if she's yet been missed. What is Joyce driving at?

'Some time last night… someone brought it back—'

'Oh?' Katy struggles to grasp the implications of this.

'—torn up. Pushed all the pieces through the letterbox. I found them on the doormat this morning. At first I thought it was a strange kind of junk mail, but then when I pieced together what it was – the picture, Katherine, it was defaced. Whoever did it used red ink.'

Each clings to the end of the line like climbers left dangling, Kathy thinks, as a taste of blood wells in her mouth. Casting a quick glance into the rear-view mirror she sees she's bitten her lip.

'They'd written the F-word,' Joyce concludes in a low voice. 'F-you, bitch, it said. Have you any idea what any of this could mean?'

Katy tells Joyce to throw away the envelope and discard its contents then thanks her for keeping an eye on things. Reassures her she'll be there in an hour or two. Urges her not to worry. Just kids messing about, she says. A sick prank, that's all. Best not say anything about this to Diane. Unconvinced but marginally brighter, Joyce finally says goodbye.

Despite the sandwich she ate earlier, Katy feels light-headed. Overwhelmed by the strangeness of it, every sense seems numb. This cannot be happening, she thinks. And yet of course she is wrong. And now, worse, she knows for sure her mum is in danger. That when she comes out of hospital in a couple of days she will be vulnerable to further attack. Exposed. No time to pussyfoot around playing detective, she decides. She must confront Jude before things go any further. Not by text or phone, in person.

Directing her gaze towards the bus stop a short distance ahead on the opposite side of the road, she stares at three bare-chested teenage boys in baggy board shorts who are standing beneath it, laughing and chatting. They look no different to the youths who regularly patrol the streets of her own neighbourhood by bike, although their London cousins always seem to dress in hooded tops regardless of the heat, or time of day or night.

As she watches, a single deck bus draws up and the three-some disappear inside. The driver pulls away, slowly advancing towards her, but despite this it isn't until it is almost drawing level that Katy notices the destination written on the front. Hill Rise. Her hands shake as she once more unfolds the map and scans the squares straddling Cow Vale in search of the street where the woman in the hospice mentioned Siobhan had lived. It does not take long to find the L-shaped road that stretches northwards beyond the coaching inn. She stares at the phone still in her lap then picks it up and dials Directory of Enquiries.

'I'm looking for the number of an S Davies, that's Davies spelled with an i-e-s, on Hill Rise, Cow Vale.' Her voice is brisk. Urgent.

'What number Hill Rise?' asks the operator, an officious-sounding woman with an unidentifiable regional accent.

'Oh dear,' Katy bluffs, desperately. 'I can't quite remember.'

'Well I can't give you a number without the correct address,' the woman retorts.

'Listen, it's very important,' Katy begs. 'I just need to check my friend's still there. If you can't give me the number can you at least tell me if she is still listed? Please. It's a matter of... of life and death.' She bites her lip again, considering this final piece of dramatic embellishment.

The operator hesitates, then there is a pause before she comes back on the line. 'Look, I can't give you the number or the address,' she says. 'But your friend's still listed, OK?'

Jiggling her car keys in one hand, Katy traces the route on the map she needs to take with the other. Then she executes a brisk U-turn to follow in the bus's wake.

Chapter 20

It's a curious word, isn't it? Mum. Everyone has one — or had one, at least. I am one; you soon will be. A by-word for protection. Reassurance. Dependability. The one pillar in your life who you can trust. Well that's the theory. But now's the time to get real. Think about the facts, Kat. Because none of us — you, especially — can promise any of that, let alone deliver. All of us are fucked up by and as parents. The fairytale is screwed. Once upon a time there was Siobhan. Then there was your dad. Andrew. Then you. And what a mess you all whipped up, the lot of you. So I set out to serve you all right… and only ended up making things worse. But that wasn't my fault. How was I to know what he'd do? What either of us might be capable of?

Chapter 21

Guildford, February 1989

The house was cloaked in a damp mist, its upstairs windows slick with condensation, when Jude arrived home from school on the first Friday following spring half-term.

Siobhan was drowning her sorrows in the bath once more and, judging by the building's silence, its darkened kitchen, the empty coat hook behind the front door, Dave was out. Slipping off her shoes, Jude crept upstairs. A light was visible through the cracks of the bathroom door and she could just make out the gentle slap of water on porcelain as the occupier shifted position, but she was reluctant to alert Siobhan too soon to her return.

It was two days since she had identified Charles's handwriting on the note to her mum and she had spent that forty-eight hours in a state of suspended emotion. Stunned by the enormity of Siobhan's lie, she felt numb. Unable to decide how to respond, she did nothing. Life since had been negotiated on automatic pilot. Now, finally, she'd made it to the end of the week and all she craved was the release she would find in his arms.

Yet how could she seek that now? With Andrew.

The knowledge that through Charles they were connected was both thrilling and dreadful. She wanted him inside her, blotting out the dreadfulness of the world around them. But wasn't the fact that, despite everything, she still wanted this unnatural? Illegal? All of which left her feeling muddled and confused. A freak. He had no idea, of course, and she wasn't about to tell him. For no one else had even a clue that she knew. And besides, wasn't it obvious Charles wanted it to stay that way?

Jude checked her watch. They'd arranged to meet later that evening at The Bridge. It was a low rent kind of place but their preferred rendezvous now so many of Andrew's college friends hung out at The Three Pigs. Then, after a drink or two they would go back to the bedsit a mate of his had given them the key for while he was away for the weekend. Should she still go anyway? It wasn't right and yet the molten intensity of her desire to be with him, her need for physical contact, made her want to sob.

Once inside her room she closed the door softly, placed her schoolbag in front of it then sank down onto the bed. She knew she had to be with Andrew, whatever the consequences. Just like she knew she had to return the envelope, too, if she was to avoid arousing Siobhan's suspicions.

Against the wall opposite, to the left of her desk, stood a large bookshelf that almost touched the ceiling. Quickly, she manoeuvred a chair in front of this, stepped onto the seat then reached up towards the dusty top shelf. Feeling her way with her fingertips, her hand soon found what it was searching for.

The old anthology of Hans Christian Anderson fairy tales that until that morning had been forgotten for years fell open easily and she removed the envelope nestled within. Tugging the handwritten note from her pocket, she slipped it back inside the envelope before carefully sticking it down – not perfect, but it would do. Then she crept back downstairs and carefully positioned the envelope by the front door, partially obscured by the mat. A sudden dull knocking from the house's pipe work signalled her mum's bath time was over.

Softly opening the front door, she slammed it shut. Then, shrugging off her coat, she retraced her steps upstairs and paused outside the bathroom door.

'Mum?'

'Won't be a minute.' Siobhan's voice was slurred.

Leaning back against the wall, Jude drummed her fingers on the wooden door frame. A minute later the door opened and Siobhan stepped out, securing her kimono with a defensive hug. The damp towel tightly knotted around her head had tautened the slackening skin around her eyes giving her a cartoonish look of surprise. It was hard to imagine her mum with Charles. He was a man who'd always struck Jude as dully predictable and overly formal. What he could have possibly seen in her mum?

Swallowing hard, Jude struggled to beat back the resentful swell of emotion the thought triggered. Gazing behind her mum, she saw the steamed-up wine bottle and glass standing on the porcelain beside the taps. Both looked empty.

'Is there any hot water left? I'd like a shower before going.'

'Out?' Siobhan rubbed her eyes which, Jude now noticed, were puffy and bloodshot. She checked her wrist but wasn't wearing a watch. She seemed confused. 'Where?'

'The youth club. It is Friday night—' Jude waved a dismissive hand towards the wine bottle '—in case you hadn't noticed.'

Though she frowned, Siobhan refused to take the bait. 'Well make it quick,' she said. 'I need to talk to you about something first.'

Jude turned the shower onto its strongest setting and stepped inside. Adjusting the temperature to as hot as she could bear, she washed her hair. Vigorously massaged her scalp. Stoically ignored how the water needled her skin. Relished its rough touch, almost wanting it to hurt more. She craved sensation – pain, even – anything that might make her feel alive again. Dislocated from conscious thought, she reached for the nailbrush and moved it in controlled sweeps across her body. Her skin began to throb. Shampoo stung her eyes. But at last, she was starting to feel clean.

'What did you want to talk about?' she asked a short while later as she walked downstairs and into the kitchen, her gaze fixed on the fridge. Siobhan, who was leaning over the kitchen counter by the window, had her back towards her and her shoulders visibly flinched at the sound of her daughter's voice. Slamming down the phone, she spun around.

'Jude!' she exclaimed, raising a shaking hand to her mouth. 'I thought you were upstairs.'

'You said you wanted a word,' her daughter retorted, reaching into the fridge to extract a packet of sausage rolls. They were a supermarket variety – the meat looked grey, the pastry underbaked – but they'd line her stomach for the evening ahead. 'So go on, what's so important?'

Siobhan took a seat at the kitchen table then straightened the cloth with awkward fingers. 'I need to ask you if you are taking precautions.'

Jude was silent. This she had not expected.

'Precautions?'

'Yes. A little bird tells me you've been hanging out at The Three Pigs on Maiden Lane.' Looking up at last, Siobhan narrowed her eyes as she stared accusingly at Jude.

A bubble of laughter welled in Jude's throat which she fought hard to push back down. How dare she? Of all people! She rolled her eyes.

'You know you have,' Siobhan said sharply, then unexpectedly she softened her tone. 'Look, I've not forgotten what it's like being fifteen. But you've got to watch out for yourself.' She laughed briefly, a tinny sound. 'Or you never know you might end up like me.'

'God forbid.'

'That was a joke, Jude. But I hope you know what I mean,' Siobhan muttered, her tired face knotting into a scowl.

Jude stared at her mum, hating her for putting her on the spot. What business was it of hers what she got up to? How dare she demand an answer? 'Of course I'm taking precautions,' she sneered. 'Which is more than some people my age. Because you can never be too careful, can you, Mother. Especially if you're doing it with a married man. Like Charles Parker.'

What colour there had been in Siobhan's face paled to laundry grey. 'What?'

Too angry to think straight and too late to grab back the words, Jude pressed on. 'I said when you're doing it with a married man like Charles Parker. It was him, wasn't it? My dad?' Defeated, her mother buried her face in her hands as Jude walked over to the kitchen table to take up position by her side. 'So I'll take that as a yes, then.' Siobhan said nothing. 'But I have one other question. Quite a simple one, actually. Why?'

Her mum was crying now and her body shook with silent, heaving sobs. 'Why... what?' she said, eventually.

'Why come back here? Why send me to St Mary's – not just any school, but the school his own daughter went to in not just any year, but the same year as me?' Jude's voice was an angry shout against the emotional whirlwind roaring in her ears, loosening what remaining grip she had left on self-control.

'That's enough,' Siobhan cried, springing to her feet. A command, not a request. 'I came back here in good faith, convinced he and his family had moved on long ago. He was always very ambitious, you know. Always gave the impression that this town wasn't big enough for him. It seemed a good thing to do, for both of us. There was a good job for me here and for you, well, a great school. How was I to know he sent his daughter there? Charles was the last thing on my mind.'

'Is that so?' Jude sneered. Walking towards the door that led into the hall. Pausing in the open doorway. Pointing to the envelope clearly visible sticking out from beneath the mat by the front door. 'So what's that, then?'

With a cry of relief that sounded more like a wild animal in pain, Siobhan lunged forwards. Dropping to her knees on the mat, she hungrily pawed at the envelope before remembering herself then stuffed it deep into her dressing gown pocket. Slowly, she rose to her feet and turned around. 'It's just—' she began.

'No need to lie, Mum. I know what it's just. I opened it earlier, saw the money, read the note. And worked it out.'

'No,' Siobhan cried. 'You don't understand.'

'Oh but I do,' Jude shouted. 'It's from him, isn't it?' Siobhan hesitated for a moment then nodded. 'To keep things quiet?'

'No, it's not like that,' her mother pleaded, sinking down onto the bottom stair. 'I bumped into him quite by chance soon after we arrived and was as horrified as he was. The money was for you, Jude. He felt guilty, I suppose.'

Jude strode into the hallway then stopped to stare down at her mother's bent head. 'For me?' In spite herself she felt a jolt of excitement. How much could it be? She made some quick mental calculations. If this had been going on for, say, eighteen months on the basis of that morning's payment it could be at least a thousand, if not more. 'Well where is it, then. The money?'

'Some of it is in a high interest account for when you're older.'

'Some?'

Siobhan coughed, still unable to look up and meet her daughter's gaze. 'What's left after the extras we've had to buy for school,' she mumbled.

The excitement Jude felt just a moment before was gone, replaced by a taste at the back her mouth like metal. So that would be most of it gone, then. On all those little extras. How stupid of her not to wonder where her mum had got the money from. 'How very... convenient,' she said at last, through clenched teeth. Siobhan said nothing. As if sapped of all strength, her body slumped against the wall. Bored all of a sudden, Jude glanced at her watch. It was almost half past seven.

Siobhan flinched but said nothing as her daughter stepped onto the stair on which she sat.

Without slowing her pace, Jude retraced her steps back upstairs to her room to discard the clothes she usually wore to the youth club in favour of a black pencil skirt and a skintight, stripy top. From her make-up bag she applied a thick mask of make-up with angry relish. A firm rim of liner then three coats of mascara accentuated her almond-shaped eyes. Then, using a fresh stick of lipstick – pillar box red – she traced the cut-glass line of her lips and the twin peaks of her cupid's bow.

'I'll be off then,' she said to Siobhan, who hadn't moved from the bottom stair. Grabbing her stonewashed denim jacket from the peg by the door, she hesitated only briefly to cast a final approving glance in the mirror before freeing the catch, her mind now full with just one thought: seeing Andrew. 'Enjoy your evening, Mum. Oh, and don't bother waiting up.'

–

'Fancy a drink, gorgeous?'

His breath was stale and his voice slurred, but when Jude looked up she was immediately struck by the piercing blue of his eyes. She had seen him in The Bridge on previous Friday nights. Usually he sat in the snug on the far side of the public bar. Sometimes he spent the evening alone cradling a beer, at other times joking loudly with a friends. As soon as she had walked in tonight, however, she'd noticed him pacing the floor with an intangible, pent up energy that made her think of a caged lion.

'Fuck off.' Jude took a carefully calculated step back in an attempt to impale his foot with her stiletto, but the heel glanced off the reinforced toecaps of his Doc Martin boots. As she struggled to regain her balance and clutched onto the silver-capped rim of the bar the barmaid, Cherry, shot her an anxious glance.

'I said: do you fancy a drink?' he repeated, accompanying his request this time with a clumsy attempt to put his arm round her shoulder.

'And I said: fuck off.' She took another sip from her glass. Where was Andrew, she wondered, crossly. How dare he be so late?

'What did you say? Hey bitch—' the man added more menacingly when Jude didn't look up '—don't fucking ignore me.' He gave her shoulder a sharp push and the force of the impact knocked her off her stool. Scared now, Jude glanced around the bar in search of a friendly face. At the other end of the bar Cherry had her back towards her as she shared a joke with a couple of squaddies. Should she call out, she wondered. But before she could decide, her tormentor was at it again.

'Fancy some more, do you?' he muttered, and as he lunged towards her once more Jude braced herself for the inevitable impact. But then she heard another voice. Low, forceful and strangely familiar.

'Stop it, Mikey.'

Looking up, her heart leaped as she saw it was Dave. Realised his arms were firmly pinioning those of her would-be attacker. Leaning closer towards Mikey, who Jude now realised was not much older than she was, he whispered something in his ear that made his face melt into a leery smile as he turned back towards Jude.

'Sorry, darling,' he grinned, punctuating the apology with a hearty belch.

'Mikey was just going outside to get a breath of fresh air, weren't you, Mikey?' Dave said lightly before frogmarching him out of the pub. 'You OK?' he added a few minutes later when he was back, standing by Jude's side.

'Sure,' she smiled nervously, uncertain what Dave would say about her being here.

'So. What's a nice girl like you doing in a place like this?' He smiled then, before she had a chance to say anything, quickly added: 'No. Don't answer that. D'you fancy a drink?'

'Vodka and tonic, please,' she dared, braced for his refusal. Unlike the bar's regulars, he knew her real age. But he didn't say a word. Instead, he ordered the drink and a pint of Guinness for himself and beckoned Jude to take a seat by his side. Which made her smile at the thought of how annoyed Andrew would be when he saw her sitting with someone else when he arrived. But sod it! That would serve him right for being late. So she perched beside Dave and they sat and drank until the awkward silence was broken by another stranger's voice.

'So this is where you've got to!'

The woman's face was thin with a blood-red slash of a smile and a halo of unfeasibly black, back-brushed hair. What struck Jude most, though, was the suspicion in her pale grey eyes as she looked from Jude to Dave then back again to Jude. But no introductions were needed, it seemed, as Dave coolly turned towards the woman and lightly patted her on the bottom. 'Not tonight, OK, Jeanette? I've got something to see to.'

'So I can see,' she quipped, dryly, before teetering away.

Jude looked back at Dave with an inquiring look but said nothing. He took another sip of his drink, wiped the froth from his top lip on the back of his hand, then lightly tapped the side of his nose with his finger. 'Ask no questions and I'll tell no lies,' he said softly. She raised her glass in a silent toast in agreement, then smiled.

The pair talked until last orders, although no reference was made to what had just happened. Or home. Or even his trip to the Isle of Man. And especially not Siobhan. Instead, Dave pretended they'd only just met and asked her all the questions strangers encountering one another for the first time in a pub the wrong side of town might ask and Jude was more than happy to play along. Only when Cherry and the bar manager started emptying ash trays, upturning bar stools and stacking them onto tables was the illusion shattered as they were forced to leave. He helped her into her jacket and led her out onto the street.

Outside the wind was icy, late snow was forecast for the weekend, and she started to shiver. She should have worn a proper coat but as the bedsit where Andrew and she had planned to stay was close by she'd not planned on walking far. As he zipped up his leather jacket, Dave pulled a pair of gloves and a scarf from his pocket and handed them to her. At first they walked side by side, but after a few minutes Dave slipped his arm round her shoulders and began gently guiding her step.

She could feel the warmth of his body through the thin padded fabric of her jacket but now, with all thoughts of Andrew long gone, she didn't think of turning away.

'So this is what you get up to when your mum's back is turned,' he said, stopping suddenly.

They were outside Debenhams near the bottom of the high street. As he stared through the darkened windows where an explosion of gaudy, cut-price spring sale offers punctuated the interior's gloom Jude gazed at their reflection – huddled together, side by side, almost a couple – and experienced a mixture of guilt and excitement. With the spell broken, Jude braced herself as she chose her words carefully. 'One could say the same about you,' she answered, defensively.

'One could,' he replied, gently turning her face towards him. 'But your mum's no fool, Jude. She knows how the land lies. We have what you might call a… flexible relationship. And she likes it that way.'

'She does?' Jude frowned. She wasn't sure whether she believed him, but with the touch of his hand and his breath now warming her face she realised she didn't care.

'She does,' he whispered, conspiratorially. Her body relaxed into his and her pulse quickened in expectation, but then a beat later Dave had straightened up and stepped away. 'Let me walk you to your front door,' he offered, feigning an aristocratic kind of voice before bowing low and offering her his arm to take. 'Who knows what sort of ruffians are out and about at such a late hour.'

Confused, aroused and disappointed in equal measure, Jude slipped her arm through his then walked on in silence until they reached the end of the road where they lived. There, standing in the darkness beneath a broken street lamp, enfolded in shadows, Dave firmly pulled her towards him. But her surprise was outweighed by a tidal wave that left her reeling with relief. With damp palms and a dry throat, Jude could hear the blood in her veins charge like stallions. Feeling more alive than she'd ever done, she raised her face to his and saw he was smiling.

'Kiss me,' he coaxed. 'You know you want to.'

Jude hesitated, unsure what to do for a moment until instinct kicked in. 'Don't patronise me,' she snapped, hastily pulling away. 'I'm not a child.'

'Of course not,' he soothed, tugging her back towards him. 'Any fool can see that. From the way you hold yourself—' he hesitated, and as the arm that was still wrapped around her waist shifted position she could feel his hand working its way up her back beneath her shirt. As his fingers softly stroked the skin just below the clasp of her bra her back arched '—to the way your body moves beneath your clothes.' Burying his nose in her hair, he sniffed theatrically. 'The way you smell.'

Blindly, Jude moved her face towards his in search of his mouth. With lips parted, she brushed the stubble of his roughly shaven face. She inhaled deeply, intoxicated by the tang of sweat and beer. They stood like this in semi-darkness, clenched like covert statues, unmoving apart from hungry mouths and desperate tongues. She wanted him more than anything she had wanted ever before, and didn't care who might see. But then, as quickly as it had been forged, the physical connection was broken.

Dave looked down at her, eyes bright. 'Another time,' he murmured, linking arms once more to lead her into the umbra of the next street light and on towards their front gate. 'Another place.' And in that split second her decision was made. She would have him, and break her mother's heart.

It began the morning after, when Siobhan had gone out to the shops. Dave was still asleep in bed when Jude went into the bathroom and ran herself a bath. Afterwards, she towelled herself down then gently rubbed in handfuls of body lotion before putting on the silk, knee length dressing gown her mum had given her for Christmas. With a racing heart, she lay back down on her bed to wait until an hour later she heard him go into the bathroom and turn on the shower. As the water surged, Jude opened her bedroom door and padded softly towards her mum's room. Once inside she turned off the main overhead light, straightened the dishevelled bed covers, then carefully positioned herself on the freshly puffed pillows and closed her eyes.

'I think you're in the wrong room, Jude.' He was standing in the doorway, a damp towel knotted around his waist. A few beads of water trickled down his body like sweat.

'I don't think so,' she murmured, shifting position slightly which made the silk fabric slide upwards to reveal another inch or two of thigh.

Dave walked across the room to the bed to stand over her, looking down. 'Is that right?' he said, reaching towards the belt of her dressing gown.

As soon as the bow was untied, the fabric slid apart like red silk curtains to expose her nakedness. He took his time, scanning her creamy breasts and taut belly which tapered down to the dark triangle of closely cropped pubic hair. Then he reached out a hand to gently run his forefinger around the darker skin now puckered at the base of the hard button of each nipple. Her back arched as she felt her body tense with anticipation. He smiled as he loosened the towel around his waist.

'You know, you really are a very, very naughty girl,' he said, slipping his hand between her legs then leaning forward to take her in his mouth.

'Ssh,' Jude whispered, holding a finger to her lips. 'Don't tell Mum.'

Chapter 22

West Sussex, July 2013

An alternating pattern of red brick, whitewashed and pebble dash Fifties semis line either side of Hill Rise as it gently climbs the low hill behind the coaching inn. At its highest point, where it turns sharply to the right, on a tiny patch of green is a single swing and a wooden bench. It is a windswept vantage point for viewing on a clear morning the distant line where air meets land and sea. Though today the peak is busy with children kicking footballs or pedalling bikes.

As Katy drives along Hill Rise she wonders what she's looking for. Why it even matters what the house looks like. Somehow, she thinks, knowing where Jude used to live will help her understand.

Outside house after house, men tinker with cars or dab paint at flaking window frames while women in sun tops tend flowerbeds or direct their lobster skin towards the open sky. Then, spotting a stooped figure walking along the road towards her, she pulls to one side and winds down the window. The elderly woman is carrying two string bags filled with shopping, the weight from which is pulling her shoulders down. As she walks towards her, slowly, her head is bowed, her gaze fixed on the ground.

'Excuse me,' Katy calls. 'I wonder if you can help. I'm looking for the Davies' house, where Siobhan Davies used to live?' Drawing level, the woman stops and stares. Her expression seems wary. 'I'm a friend of her daughter, Jude,' Katy adds casually. 'We were at school together. Before she moved away.'

'Well in that case...' she replies, her face softened by the fine detail of Katy's enquiry '...you need number forty-two. Can't miss it, it's an utter mess. There's a broken down Mini in the driveway, has been for years. I don't know how many times he's been asked to move it, but he couldn't care less. If you ask me he was the death of his nan.'

'Thanks,' Katy calls, but the woman has already turned away.

She stops outside number forty-eight where she leaves the car before casually walking on a few houses further. Number forty-two is located at what to a casual observer might pass as the run down end of the street, though it is a close run thing. One of the upstairs windows is boarded up, broken at some point but never mended. Stained curtains hang lank at salt-smeared windows. A white splash from a passing seagull has striped the smoked glass front door.

Katy hesitates. Behind the washed up carcass of a Mini Cooper now mouldering in the driveway looms the dark interior of a wooden, lean-to garage with its doors thrown wide. Siobhan may be dead, but she still has relations living in the house. Perhaps she can still return home with some fragment of information which can help. Her right fist tightens around the car keys which, instinctively, she has kept hold of rather than put away into her bag.

The touch of metal against her palm is comforting, strengthening her nerve as she steps onto the drive and draws level with the Mini.

'Hello?' she calls into the darkness beyond.

Silence.

Even the movement she glimpsed in her peripheral vision a moment before has gone. Like time has stopped, she thinks. Though the dog howl of the seagulls now circling overhead prove this is no freeze frame. Nervously, she glances around her then calls out again. A little louder, this time. Shading her eyes from the sun's glare, as she squints into the blackness.

'What?' a male voice bounces back. Abrupt. Hostile.

Before she can reply, a figure steps into the sunlight. Katy hesitates, derailed from her mission by the raw physicality of his presence and an angry expression made more intense by the brutal line of his buzz cut hair. The army-green boiler suit he is wearing is unbuttoned to the waist revealing a toned chest streaked with oil. With a scowl, the man takes another step forward. Now close enough to register the finer detail of his face, she finds the pale wetness of his eye is unnerving.

'What are you doing here?'

The stranger's emphasis on the 'you' takes Katy by surprise as she searches his face for any indication that she might be able to defuse the situation with gentle reasoning. It's almost as if he knows her. 'I'm so sorry,' she says lightly, trying not to acknowledge the gathering thought that she's seen him some-where before. 'I must have got the wrong address.'

'A mistake, you say. But you're looking for the Davies' house, yes?' he says, tugging a rag from his pocket which he uses to wipe his greasy hands. The dirty piece of cloth is part of the front panel of a T-shirt on which a pyramid-shaped logo comprising three capital letter As and a drawing of interlocked hands is visible. Distracted for a moment by her inability to place just where she has seen this moniker before, all she can do is nod. 'Well in that case, Kat,' he continues with a fleeting smile, reaching out as if to take her by the arm. 'You'd better step inside.'

But before he can get a firm hold Katy stumbles backwards. She spins around on her heels then lunges forwards – every fibre in her being attuned to achieving the single goal of getting back to her car.

Waving the fob of the key as she gets close enough in a desperate attempt to release the central locking. Wrenching open the driver's door and throwing herself inside. Tumbling into her seat then fumbling with the key she misses the ignition on her first try and scratches the base of the dashboard. On her second attempt, comes the engine's reassuring purr.

Blind to the fact that he's not moved from the driveway, Katy locks herself in then kicks down onto the accelerator jerking the car forwards.

The roar of the engine makes people tending their front gardens look her way, but from their expressions they are clearly used to such goings at number forty-two. Only as she passes the driveway does she look back towards him and as their eyes meet time seems to slow. He is standing on the pavement, hand on hips, watching. Then, like an old movie played out at half speed, he raises his right arm towards her and starts to wave and appears still to be waving as she looks one last time before the rounds a corner and the house disappears from view.

Katy drives on for a few miles with no clear idea of where to go until she reaches a roundabout and sees a sign for London and, in the opposite direction, the sea.

Without pausing to think, she takes the latter and quickly finds herself on a B road lined with tatty warehouses and dusty yards crammed with agricultural and marine equipment. After a mile or so more the buildings become more widely spaced, punctuated on one side by sporadic outbreaks of grey salt marsh. On the other, parallel to the tarmac are railway tracks which once served the coastal branch line east of Portsmouth but are now covered in nettles and bramble. A short distance further, a huddle of signs announce a caravan park on the outskirts of a village that feels like the end of the line.

The seaweed tang of the salt air makes her nostrils flare as she climbs from the car in the visitor's car park. Spotting a sign behind a cluster of recycling bins in the far corner, she follows the arrow pointing towards the sea front.

A few minutes later she is standing by a concrete wall staring at a slab of glistening blue which might have passed for Mediterranean if it wasn't for the uneven wall of giant concrete slabs stretching as far as the eye can see in either direction. And the beach itself which is a steep slope of mottled pebbles, clumps of weed and gobbets of tar which levels to a thin strip of grey where sand meets sea. A barren landscape, but one that's temporarily lifted by a colourful patchwork of beach towels, wind breaks and sun tents secured with boulders arranged in Stone Age piles.

Barefoot children with pink faces stumble up banks of stones that bear their weight as reliably as quicksand. Adults are littered like broken soldiers across the uneven terrain.

Hoisting herself up onto the waist-high wall, Katy clambers over then drops down onto the beach. Slowly, she makes her way towards the remains of a wooden breakwater then clambers up to sit on top and stare out to sea. Her eyes feel scooped out and raw, like she's been crying. Her lungs ache, as if exhausted in defeat. Closing her eyes, she focuses on her breathing – inhaling deeply, then exhaling long and hard. In a few minutes her head starts to clear.

Who is he and what does he want, she wonders, baffled by the thought that the man she's just fled from is the same man who abused her on her doorstep back in London a few days earlier. And what's he got to do with Siobhan? She thinks of Jude, cursing her for crashing back into her life, and the trouble she's still able to cause. Following her. Intimidating her mum. Poisoning the past.

Though that's not right, is it? For the past has never been pure, just tainted. Shadowed by the cruelty of her so-called friend and her own inaction. What was it Jude had said? *I'm not the one who ran away.*

But that's not right, either. She did run, yes, but she tried to help, too. Showed remarkable courage, in fact, or so the doctors at the hospital said – the ones she'd seen over the months after for recurrent bouts of nausea and vomiting, eczema and panic attacks. Everyone tried to reassure her that her anxiety about what happened would fade, with time. But they didn't know, did they? Not really. They weren't there, so how could they? Because the truth was buried so deep she could barely remember and dared not to try.

Once more, Katy tries to recall the precise chronology of events and apportioning of actions, screwing up her eyes with the effort of it. Once more she fails. What did I do, she wonders, miserably, exhaling slowly as she opens her eyes. Because I know, just like I know I jumped into the canal that day, no matter what anyone else told me. I know, like I've always known, that it wasn't me. I'm not the one who ran away.

''scuse me, love – you got the time?'

Katy has to shade her eyes with her hand as she turns to answer a woman around her own age wearing an ankle length wet suit. It's almost midday and as she tells her so she realises she can't got back to Spike's for lunch, not now. The thought of making small talk, the pretence that everything's OK, is far worse than what Michael will say.

Pulling free her mobile, she gazes at the screen. She should call him, of course, to let him know but cannot face it. Instead, she will compose a text. Still holding the mobile, she stares at the waterline where the wetsuited woman is now standing, ankle deep. Tell him something's come up, she thinks. But a new message from Andrew, by text this time, kills the idea before the lie can take shape. The hospital is discharging Diane early, he tells her curtly. He can't get hold of Joyce, so Katy must be at Parkview by teatime for her return.

Too soon, she thinks. Just four hours then her mum will be alone. Not enough time for her to track them down, though she senses once Diane is discharged it won't be long before Jude finds her. Not enough time for her to think of what to tell Michael, either. Without pausing to consider the implications of either decision more closely, she charges back to the car to retrace her route back home.

Chapter 23

The girls were drinking double espressos, sticky and black. *A bitter taste that's worth it for the buzz*, Jude always joked. As she did again that day, sitting side by side at a window table in Deb's Kitchen overlooking the new shopping precinct, though the content of her cup was untouched.

Kat reached towards a white ramekin that sat at the table's centre beside a matching vase containing a single, candy-pink gerbera. Dipping her fingers inside she selected a rock-like crystal of brown sugar, popped it into her mouth to temper the coffee's acrid kick, then began to crunch. Her left hand was cradled in her lap. With the teaspoon now held in her right hand, she drew shapes in the soft pile of the tablecloth.

An idle gesture, meaningless and without malice, and yet despite that it made Jude want to scream. Or maybe that was more to do with the fact that it was the last week of term. Almost the Easter holidays. And over a month since she had last seen Andrew.

What with his refusal to respond to the messages she'd left for him at college and Kat's whinging – about Andrew's growing aloofness, her parents' marriage, the forthcoming exams – she couldn't think of anyone she'd less like to be sitting with in a cafe not drinking coffee. Yet, in a curious way, being with Kat made her feel closer to him. Andrew. Jude sighed. Could the hollow ache inside her, this desperate sense of neediness, be love?

Through the window opposite, she could see the red brick façade of the new shopping centre. Though unfinished inside, the precinct's exterior was complete. Featureless and pristine, its dull functionality depressed her. The building was due for completion the following autumn. Where would she be then, she wondered? Pray to God, no longer living with Siobhan.

'What plans, then, for the Easter holidays?' she asked eventually. Dully. Just to kill time.

Kat grimaced. 'Revision, mostly. Though now Dad's back he's trying to persuade Mum we should all go on a family break – a long weekend somewhere – our last chance before Andrew starts his exams. Did I tell you he's bought a round-the-world ticket and says he'll set off the day after his last A level?'

He'd mentioned it, of course, but then he'd said a lot of things. Moving to London with the band as soon as his A levels were over. Studying sociology, not accountancy as Charles had hoped. Getting a flat where she could crash whenever she liked.

'No, you didn't,' Jude answered, tightly. 'How nice.'

'I know – he's planning to start in Sydney then work his way back via Thailand, Hong Kong, India…'

'I meant the family break.' Jude felt queasy. Perhaps she should have had some breakfast.

'Oh. Yes. Well it won't be anything exotic,' Kat backtracked awkwardly, as words tumbled from her lips way too fast. 'Dad's been talking about north Wales or south Devon – where we used to go on summer holidays as kids. Just for a few days. He doesn't want to distract us too much from our revision. Andrew's start the week before ours, you see—'

'Ironic, isn't it, how he's now so desperate to recreate something that only exists in his own head,' Jude cut in. The inside of her mouth was bitter with resentment. How dare Charles choose to rekindle interest in his family just as she had found out about his dirty little secret. How pathetic of them to fall for it.

'What do you mean?' retorted Kat. For once she seemed angry, Jude noted, ready to challenge instead of accept the latest in a growing line of digs and jibes that she'd been tossing her way like small incendiary devices in the weeks since half-term.

'You know exactly what I mean,' Jude pressed on. 'He's always been a shit husband and a shit dad and nothing's going to change that now.'

Kat sprang to her feet. 'Who are you to pass judgement on me and my family?' she cried. 'Oh sorry, I forgot, the only daughter of a single mum with the world's worst taste in men. Which makes you amply qualified, of course. I do apologise.'

'I'll tell you who I...' Jude's voice was low and unexpectedly threatening as she too rose to her feet. Stepped towards Kat. Reached out to grasp the arm of her friend. But she didn't get the chance to finish.

'That's £1.60, girls,' trilled the waitress, a middle-aged woman in a black dress and white apron whose wiry hair was pulled back into two grey plaits she'd pinned onto the top of her head German-style. She'd crept up on them unnoticed and now stood staring, expectantly, her lashless pale grey eyes half-raised.

Handing over their money in silence, the pair made their way towards the exit in silent single file where, once outside, Jude paused to gulp fresh air. Rubbing her eyes with the heel of her palms, her head started to clear and she began to feel better.

Opening her eyes, Jude saw Kat was already striding towards the traffic lights, back towards school. She smiled. No, it would have been wrong to tell her about her mum and Charles like this. Today. She would pick her time. Plan something more lingering than a mere tiff as the backdrop to her revelation. Something more considered that would wipe away the smug innocence of her so-called best friend once and for all. To kick her bastard of a father in a place where it would really hurt.

Jude took her time walking up the high street back to St Mary's. Outside the Civic Hall, on the narrow strip of grass opposite the box office, stood an empty bench on which she sat for a few minutes. With her face tickled by the watery spring sunshine, her mind drifted until a distant church bell struck a quarter to. She sprang to her feet.

With just five minutes to get back before the start of afternoon lessons, she'd need to cover the last part of the hill at double speed. And would have done so, too, if she'd not drawn level with an artfully dishevelled figure carrying a guitar who'd been walking a short distance ahead. They stopped at the junction with Rossingdale Road together, and only as she turned to check for traffic did she realise who it was.

'Hello, stranger!'

Spinning round on his heels, Andrew didn't look pleased to see her. In fact if anything, he seemed annoyed. 'Hi.'

'Anyone would think you'd been avoiding me,' Jude pressed on with a cool smile that belied the surge of excitement she felt inside.

His face knotted into a frown. 'Well they'd be right.'

'Hey, don't be like that—'

'I can be however I like,' he said, stepping off the pavement.

'Andrew? What is it?' Jude hurried forwards once more to catch him up. He stopped, as did she, in the middle of the road.

'Haven't you got the message?' he snapped. 'I don't want to see you anymore.'

Jude's stomach lurched and her legs felt like they might buckle. 'What?'

'You heard me.'

'Why?'

Andrew's expression darkened. There was something about the way he was looking at her that made her falter. What was wrong, she wondered, taking a defensive step backwards just as a car behind her turned into the street, braked sharply, then honked. Quickly stepping out of its way, she turned back towards Andrew and saw him now stepping up on the pavement the far side of the road. Taking a deep breath, she tried to call out but no words came.

Andrew hesitated, then turned back towards her. 'I was really starting to think we might have something going there, Jude, you know?' he shouted. 'But then you had to go and spoil it. I don't like people who play games.'

'Sorry?' she gasped, drawing to a halt by his side.

'Come on, don't play dumb. I mean, it's not like I thought we'd get serious, or anything. But when your mates start talking behind your back—'

'Who? Which mates? What did they say?' Jude cried, cursing the telltale flush she could now feel scorching her cheeks.

Dave? No one could know about Dave, could they? Unless maybe he'd said something. Boasted down the pub to some friends, maybe. But if he had, then wouldn't it have got back to Siobhan and if that had happened she'd have known as there would have been hell to pay. No, not Dave. In which case it was lies. Vindictive lies spun by someone who had it in for her.

'You've been seen, Jude, and I don't want to know who he is or hear some lame explanation that actually you're just good friends, you've been seen. Everyone's talking about it, even friends of my parents.'

Dave. It had to be.

Panic clenched her stomach. What would her mum...? Unless, of course, it was something else. Some kind of fabrication conceived by Andrew's parents to keep them apart, she wouldn't put it past them. Especially Diane. If true it was a hand played well. A malicious embroidering of what her son already knew about Jude's restless character and colourful reputation. Nothing too extreme, but just enough to poison him against her.

How could he? She hated Andrew for his readiness to believe their lies, yet her heart and body still yearned for him. How could she stop him slipping away? What could she do to make him see the truth about her? But then she said it. Words that lashed out wildly, like a severed hawser, forged in the heat of anger then fired at the peak of the emotional storm.

'Mummy's boy,' she spat too loudly to take back, too firmly to ignore.

Andrew stared at her, coolly. 'You're getting a bit of a reputation around college – did you know that, Jude?' he said in a low monotone. 'You should really learn to cover your tracks a bit better next time.' Now, however, she said nothing. Felt nothing. Just shock at his harshness; his readiness to believe what others might say. Finding himself vindicated by her silence, Andrew bent down to pick up his guitar. 'Look, forget it, OK?'

'But Andrew, I don't—' Jude began. Having finally discovered her voice, she was desperate not to let this moment – her chance with Andrew – just trickle away without a fight. But he was already walking away.

'I said, forget it,' he shouted over his shoulder, without turning round.

Too proud to beg, Jude stood and watched Andrew walk towards the next junction, take a left, then disappear from view. She would have cried but her eyes felt dusty and bruised. Anger and humiliation had scorched away her tears.

Chapter 24

Richmond, July 2013

Katy arrives at Parkview just before three to find a number of visitors' parking spaces empty. She picks the one closest to the communal front door then checks herself in the rear-view mirror before climbing from the car. Her eyes are skirted by dark shadows, her lips tightly pursed. Pale but determined. With a flick of her wrist, she waves her fob to lock the door.

The bay opposite, the one Joyce usually uses, is empty. Glancing up, Katy shades her eyes with a hand to scan the apartment block's meticulous façade. She scrutinises the corner of the building on the fourth floor where her mum's flat is located for an open window or any other indication of life within, but there is none.

Hurrying through the main doors into the communal hallway, she finds the lift lodged stubbornly on the sixth floor so takes the stairs. Halfway up, Joyce rings to confirm she is with Diane waiting for her to be officially released by the on-call doctor who's running late.

'We shouldn't be much longer, though,' the woman reassures. 'I've told your mother if the young man doesn't make an appearance in another fifteen minutes we're leaving anyway and damn the consequences, just like Thelma and Louise!'

Slipping the mobile back into her pocket Katy can't help but smile, tickled for a moment by the image Joyce's words have conjured. Distracted, briefly, from the tightness in her chest that's been building all day. Her mouth is dust-dry and tastes like metal. Eager for a sip of water, she fumbles in her bag for the spare set of mum's keys as she crosses the landing. Only once she's found this does she notice the cardboard box sitting on the floor outside the front door.

It's the size of a large shoebox – the kind in which a pair of mid-calf boots might fit. But it carries no branding or logo. Instead, the outside is a uniform buff colour with just one thing handwritten on it, in careful capitals: her mother's name. Curious, she picks it up and wonders who might have left it. Not a delivery service – wouldn't it have some kind of printed label? A barcode, certainly. One of her neighbours, probably.

Katy picks up the box and as she reaches up to unlock the door it tilts in her arms towards her chest making the contents inside shift position. Whatever it is seems solid, leaden, and has a curious smell half-past full-blown.

Unable to turn the key while holding onto the package, Katy puts down the box and sees the flaps at its top are inter-folded, not stuck down. Leaving the keys in the door, she drops to her knees and parts the folds to peek inside then swiftly recoils, glad it's no longer in her arms or it would otherwise have crashed onto the floor spewing its sorry contents.

Choking back a gasp of revulsion, Katy stares down at the lifeless body of her mum's treasured cat, Monty. Who would have left this? she wonders, bleakly. Why?

He was a lovely cat, she'd helped Mum choose him as a kitten. Perhaps someone had found him in the street after being hit by a car and thought it best to bring him home… But as she peers once more at the lumpen form she can see no evidence of blood or any external wound. Just the curious angle of his head. Like his neck is broken. She stares for a moment at the silver disc attached to his collar – space too small to carry details of where her mother lives, just a phone number.

How could they have known where to bring him? No one who knows her mum would have left him here, like this, for her to find.

Dropping to her knees, Katy fumbles for a moment with the flaps of the box as she battles to obscure the contents from further view. But then, when it is done, as she starts to straighten up she a feels a gentle yet determined prod inside her belly. Bracing one arm against the door jamb to keep her balance she strokes her stomach with the other, tracing with her fingertips the outline of her bump.

'Easy now, little man,' she murmurs, eager to soothe him with a gentle voice. 'Everything's OK. Because we're all right, you and me. All of this – everything – is going to be OK.' She waits for a minute or two for any further sign of movement and then, when there is none, cautiously pulls herself back upright.

Katy checks her watch. If Joyce is true to her word, she and mum will be back soon but they cannot – must not – see this. No point taking it inside, she decides. Perhaps she can find somewhere discreet towards the building's rear. Inside one of the communal refuse bins. A poor send off, but she can't think what else to do.

Bursting back out into the sunlight, Katy pauses only long enough to see Joyce's spot in the car park is still empty before turning sharply left and hurrying around the corner to the building's rear. Hastily, she selects the closest general waste bin, lifts the lid then pauses as her eyes unexpectedly film with tears. Maybe she should stow him elsewhere, out of view but easier to retrieve. She and Joyce could come back later and bury him in the bushes. Only it seems so awful to dispose of him like a piece of old junk.

The sound of a car bumping over the security ramp and into the car park by the front of the building forces her to make a decision. Quickly, she places the box on the ground then nudges it with her foot between the first bin and its neighbour, partially obscuring it from view. Then, rubbing the sweat from her eyes with the back of her hand, she darts back towards the building's front entrance to see Joyce helping her mum from the car.

Forcing her face into what she hopes resembles a welcoming smile, she hurries towards them.

'Hey, Mum,' she calls out, brightly. 'Let me take your bag.'

—

Joyce pours Katy a second cup of tea. They are standing in the kitchen by the oak-topped island. 'Sorry about earlier,' she says in a low voice calculated not to be overheard by Diane, who's in the sitting room next door. 'But I thought you should know… you know, about the envelope.'

Katy takes a sip from her cup. And Joyce should know about the cat, too, but not now, she decides, for fear of creating a scene. 'How do you think she's doing?' she asks, softly.

'Your mum? Why, perkier by the hour!' Joyce declares, as much for Diane's benefit as her daughter's.

'I just wanted to pop in to check all's well.' Katy backs out of the kitchen to hover in the sitting room doorway, waving her free hand towards the sofa where her mum now sits cross-legged, flicking through a magazine. Dressed in a white linen shirt and baggy, charcoal-coloured trousers, she looks pale but, when she smiles, is almost back to her old self. 'Feeling better, Mum?'

'Not bad, considering.' Diane pats the empty seat beside her. 'And all the better for seeing you. Come on, sit down and tell me all about your day.'

Joyce, who's followed Katy into the sitting room, flits back into the kitchen to busy herself with washing up and wiping down.

'In a minute,' Katy smiles, patting her mum's knee. 'But first, how are you, really? Go on, tell me the truth.'

Diane's face clouds. 'Really? Sore.' She drops her voice. 'Embarrassed. And angry — that this could happen to me on a busy shopping street at four o'clock in the afternoon.' She frowns. 'It's not just the money. The bag was nothing special. But I hate the idea that someone got away with my keys. It just makes you feel so, well, powerless.'

'With new locks on the door you really mustn't worry about that,' Katy briskly lies.

She can't bear for the woman who looked out for her for so long to be vulnerable. Exposed. Yet she doesn't know what else to do. She can hardly mention the break-in: what good will that do? Besides, the police know all about it, and the doors and windows are now secure. On the mantelpiece before her stands the old Polaroid she put in the frame to replace the one that was defaced. Of course the mugging and the break-in must be related, but something else is bothering her.

Can it really be a coincidence that the hospital called just as Jude was on hand to offer her a lift?

'It was your purse he was after, I'm sure,' Katy adds with more confidence than she feels. 'I bet whatever else you had in there was dumped somewhere soon after so if he was caught he'd have nothing on him to incriminate himself...' As her voice trails away there's a lull in the conversation during which both listen for a moment to the sound of Joyce in the kitchen. Then somewhere outside, a dog begins to bark.

Diane moves her hand onto Katy's and gives it a squeeze. 'Don't worry about me,' she whispers. 'I'll get over it.' But before Katy can reply the phone begins to ring. 'Be a love and see who it is, I'm still a bit slow getting up.'

Katy crosses the room, picks up the phone and says her mother's number. 'How was the seaside?' the caller gruffly demands.

Chapter 25

I was gutted when your darling brother dumped me, Kat. I knew it was wrong, but by the time I found out it was too late. You know what really hurt, though? The way he looked at me that last time we met. Like he deserved better. And in that instant I understood how Siobhan must have felt... To think for a while there I thought we had something, that he was different. Like someone who cared. It wasn't fair, but what in life is? I didn't deserve any of it, just like I never asked to be born. Then I got trapped — by circumstances beyond my control.

Chapter 26

Guildford, June 1989

'You're back early,' said Dave, glancing up from his copy of the *Daily Mirror*. He was drinking a mug of tea. A half-eaten cheese and pickle sandwich sat on a plate by its side. Wiping his mouth on the back of his hand, he then rubbed his hand on the thigh of his trousers. 'I thought you had lacrosse practice on a Wednesday.'

Jude scowled. 'Shouldn't you be at work?' All she wanted was to be upstairs, in her own room with the door closed, alone.

Dave folded the newspaper then leaned back in his chair. He was wearing a pair of dark jeans and a black T-shirt which accentuated an unseasonal tan – the by-product of a motorbike obsession which saw him out riding, racing or simply watching biking events around the country in all weathers whatever the season.

'I had to see a man about a dog in town and finished early so thought I'd give myself the afternoon off. How about you?' Though he patted the chair next to him, Jude stubbornly refused to take the bait choosing instead to stay where she was, poised in the kitchen doorway. 'Come on,' he added, softly, rising to his feet. 'Talk to me. Tell uncle Dave all about it.'

'Fuck off,' snapped Jude, walking back into the hall. But before she'd reached the stairs he was at her side.

'Hey, don't be like that. I was only joking.' As a conciliatory hand reached out to clasp her arm the touch of his skin on hers made Jude hesitate. She turned toward him, her anger momentarily cauterised, although she said nothing. 'Jude, have you been crying?'

'No.' With a sniff she looked away.

'Yes,' Dave corrected.

Reaching out with his free hand his fingers skimmed the side of her cheek and before she could think she found herself rubbing her face cat-like against his hand. Despite herself, deep down inside, something stirred.

'Forget it, it's nothing,' she said, willing herself to believe that that was true. That Andrew's words had meant nothing. That later with Dave, upstairs in the double bed before her mum got home from work, would be enough. 'I've just been feeling a bit under the weather, that's all, so I came home early, OK?' She smiled and realised she meant it. 'I'll be fine when I've had a bath.'

Dave left his hand on her arm a moment or two longer than necessary before stepping back to let her go. 'Catch you later, then,' he said.

She smiled. 'Not unless I catch you first.'

Once inside the bathroom Jude closed the lid of the toilet and sat down. The storm had passed, now, but so too had the glimmer of sun between the clouds and she was starting to feel sick. Bent double, as if bracing herself for a crash landing, she cradled her head on her knees. It had been coming in waves like this for a few weeks, now; bouts of nausea and occasional vomiting. She'd been more irritable, too, and then there was the soreness.

Inside the bathroom cabinet, she could find nothing for indigestion so she crept into her mother's room. Apart from a man-sized box of tissues and a large tub of Vaseline, the bedside cabinet where Siobhan usually kept headache pills and cough sweets was empty. There was some Anadin and three sachets of Beechams Powders in the drawer below, but no Alka Seltzer or Rennies. What she found in the bottom of the drawer, however, made her forget her nausea.

Beneath a packet of folic acid capsules, already half-consumed, was a brown paper bag containing a folded printed sheet entitled Boosting Your Chances and a slim rectangular box. Jude picked up the leaflet in surprise and turned it over, before registering the writing on the end packet by its side. A pregnancy testing kit.

The thought that she might be pregnant had never entered Jude's mind. Because she'd been taking the pill. And besides, her periods had always been irregular – something to do with not eating enough, Siobhan had once said. But what if something had gone wrong? It did happen. To other people, at least. Unless... In that instant Jude knew exactly what had to be done.

Stuffing the box in her pocket, she briskly shut the drawer then crept back into the bathroom. Locking the door behind her, she took a seat once more on the edge of the toilet. What if she was? Well, she could forget any hope of life in London and a clean break from Siobhan. It would be the end of all that. The end of everything, she thought. As she tried to read the instructions, the words before her slid into a dizzying kaleidoscope of letters. But she forced herself to concentrate. To try again. She had just the one chance so she had better do it right if she was to be sure.

As she waited she sat crossed legged on the floor trying not to look, trying not to think of Andrew. Four and a half minutes from start to finish – not long. But long enough to think of each of the dozen or more times they'd made love. The how, the when, the where. His cruelty made no sense. What had she done to deserve his hatred? What happened with Graeme had ended the night she and Andrew had begun. And they'd always been so careful. The one time she'd missed her pill he'd worn a condom which would have meant they were safe, wouldn't it?

But then, before she could follow this thought through, before she could prepare for the worst, the chemical proof signifying the end of life as she knew it was there to see.

The next morning, on her way to school, Jude took a detour. Rather than turn right outside the gate she took a left and headed down to the narrow cut-through that led to the pedestrian footbridge over the railway line. She stood with her back to the mainline station on the south side of town and stared northwards into a cluster of tattered trees fizzing with green. She could just make out the flat roofline of the low blocks of flats that lay behind where the railway track arced northwards towards London.

With a quick glance around her to make sure she was unobserved, she opened her school bag and took out the rectangular wad of tissue in which she'd wrapped the used predictor kit. In the distance a low rumble signified that for once, British Rail was sticking to its timetable. With no time to lose, she leaned over the railing and dropped the cardboard box and the bitter secret it concealed downwards onto the tracks below.

As the anonymous package rested briefly on the railway line Jude gazed down at it, bitter and resentful in the face of a looming sense of guilt. Then, with a dragon's roar, the 7:15 a.m. Portsmouth Harbour to London commuter train thundered between her legs churning and shredding sticks, leaves, litter and any other detritus it found in its way.

She felt a familiar quiver of delight at the pounding noise and the juddering of the bridge as the train passed by. She wanted to scream but fought the urge, fearful that once she began she might not to stop.

So instead Jude held her breath and, with tightly closed eyes, turned her face to the sky wishing she could click her heels and disappear.

The air was still when the sound and the fury had passed as she looked down to the tracks once more and saw it was gone. The world felt empty. Silent. She would have to tell someone sometime about Andrew's child, of course, but not yet. She needed time to think what to do. How to deal with this. To sit her exams. Then and only then would she decide what to do, she thought. Because there was still plenty of time.

Bending down, Jude picked up her bag. Then she retraced her steps back up the narrow path towards school, oblivious to the creamy daffodils budding knee-high through the rusting railings.

Chapter 27

Richmond, July 2013

'Andrew! I was going to call—'

Katy winces. It has taken just four words to make her regress to childhood. To become again the silly little sister incapable of doing or saying the right thing, the anxious and insecure teenager, the high school drop out who despite his fatherly cajoling once he'd graduated from university and started in the city, never quite found her way.

'It's what mobiles are for, Katy,' he presses on, tightly. 'Emergencies. And staying in touch when you are out and about—'

Catching Diane's eye, Katy mouths her brother's name and gives an apologetic shrug as she retreats onto the balcony then perches on the edge of the nearest chair.

'Stop it,' she interrupts. 'Because before you say anything I want to say I'm sorry. I know I should have called, but there's been so much going on. When the hospital rang there was no time, then I spent the night with her on the ward and the next day getting the flat straight, OK? They told me she'd be in until Monday, which is why I was out of town sorting something else out today. But now I'm back, here, with mum. And she is all right, really.'

'Yes, yes, of course I can see you've been too busy.'

Pulling herself upright, Katy leans against the balcony railing to direct her voice away from her mum's apartment towards the gardens below leading to the edge of the park beyond. Down on the street, four floors below, two small children are playing on the narrow strip of grass by Parkview's front entrance. She tightens her grip on the phone 'Of course I understand you feel bad about not being able to be here with Mum, but please don't take that out on me,' she says and Andrew grunts. 'So how was the flight back? And how are Dee and the kids?'

Her brother sighs, his anger gone. 'Fine. They're all well. In fact they're at the beach today. I had some work to do so they've gone off for a barbecue.' His voice has softened. Slightly.

'That sounds... nice,' she says, thinking of the pictures she'd seen of Dee's parents' beach house. Its interior all white wood floors, nautical paraphernalia and Cath Kidston. Like something from a mail order catalogue.

Andrew lets slip a weary laugh. 'Yeah. Well, I wish I could have gone too.'

There's an awkward pause as Katy registers his regret and yearns to reach out to him to ask him if he is really OK. To share and to confide. But she doesn't, of course, and can't bring herself even to try. For their lives are light years apart and have been for years. But not always, she thinks. Perhaps it is worth a shot. As she casts a glance over her shoulder towards the sofa which is now empty, a burst of laughter comes from the kitchen.

'Listen,' she says in a low voice. 'While you're on, I need to ask you something.'

'Shoot,' he says.

'Someone from school has got back in touch and started talking about stuff—'

'What kind of stuff?'

Closing her eyes, Katy slowly counts to five before answering in as neutral a voice as she can manufacture. 'Stuff about us, the family. Mum and Dad. And you.'

'Me?'

'Yes, you. And... Jude.' She wonders if it is her imagination that she can detect a subtle shift in the rhythm of her brother's breathing.

'And the name of this old school friend who has just got back in touch is...?'

Katy hesitates. It's now or never, she thinks. And with the conviction that it was Jude's son, James, who followed her in the park, mugged Diane, confronted her on Hill Rise and, most likely, instigated the attack on the flat and trashed her car there really is no choice if she was to put a stop to all this. Though fearful of how Andrew will react, she needs his response.

'Jude.'

'It would have to be, wouldn't it!' he exclaims with a humourless chuckle. 'That's sweet, real sweet. So surprise me, what else did she say?'

'She told me Dad had an affair with her mum, Siobhan. She told me Siobhan had a baby as a result, and that that baby was her. She told me you and she... that you and she went out together. Is this true?' Katy bites her lip, willing what Jude said to be a lie. The thought of her brother and her best friend, together, behind her back. Her face burns with a sudden flush of jealousy, though of whom she's not quite sure.

Now it's Andrew's turn to hesitate. 'From what I was able to piece together, yes,' he replies after a moment. 'I remember Mum and Dad having a massive argument soon after Jude started at St Mary's. It was around the time you and she started hanging out together. Dad didn't want the two of you to be friends, but he didn't tell Mum why – not at first. Though as you know, Mum never liked Jude...'

'Why? Did she ever say?' Katy wills herself not to react to his judgement on their friendship, and the bitter truth buried within. But her pulse races at being so close to the truth.

'Because she had such a hold over you, I guess. That was before Dad woke up and realised who she was. He saw Siobhan waiting in the car outside our house for her one night, you see. Though Siobhan must have always known – did you never think to wonder why she never came in when she came to collect Jude after tea?'

'Well no, actually, it didn't—'

'Though you didn't hold back when it came to tell Dad about Jude and me—'

'Well actually that was a lie. I mean, I made it up. I didn't know, I only wanted to—'

'Get even, right? With her and with me?'

'I guess,' Katy admits, miserably, tears welling in her eyes. 'I'm so sorry—'

'Forget it. It was a close call, that's all. She and I got together for a while. It was after she chatted me up one Friday night in a pub down town. She was a laugh. It was just a bit of fun. We met up a few times at the weekend, too. Then the next thing I knew Dad took me to one side and told me to break it off, not that it was ever that serious. Still, I couldn't believe he'd have the nerve so of course I said no. Then he told me she'd been putting it about – playing the field, was the phrase he used. And when I said so what, he told me he'd once had an affair with Siobhan... Well that was enough for me. I dropped her. Felt I had to, really. She was quite cut up about it I think.'

'So Dad told you he was Jude's... father?' The words stick in her mouth like stale dough.

'No, no. To be honest, I guessed.'

'How?' she whispers, not entirely sure she really wants to know for sure. How does he know all this? How is it that she does not?

'The weekend after the incident on the heath, while Mum was with you in the hospital a woman phoned dad at home. He answered the call downstairs but then asked me to transfer it to his office. I did, but there was something about his expression... so I listened in on the downstairs extension. She was asking for money, a lot of money, to go away and never bother him again. She told him something about having a baby and he lost his temper, accused her of making it up. Then he started to cry.'

'But it might not have had anything to do with Siobhan. Or Jude. How can you be so sure?'

'Oh I'm sure.' Andrew says in a low voice. 'Because when I went up to bed he was still sitting at his desk. It looked like he hadn't moved an inch. I said goodnight to him and he spun round and ordered me into the room. He accused me of still going out with Jude, of sleeping with her, of making her pregnant. I couldn't believe it. It was rubbish, of course. We'd always been careful—' he interrupts himself with a bitter laugh '—though given how much help Dee and I needed to have the twins there was never any risk. So I denied it, and I think he believed me. But then he buried his head in his hands and told me either way, whatever the truth, it was all too late.'

Closing her eyes, Katy swallows hard as a bell rings somewhere in the background. 'What did he mean?' she whispers, tightening her grip on the phone.

'Damned if I know.' Andrew has snapped back into business mode. 'Listen, that's my other line: I've got to go. Look, I'm not sure there's any good to come from raking over all of this now, you know. Knowing Jude, whatever she's up to it will be no good so I'd steer well clear, if I was you. Move on – it's ancient history. And for god's sake ring me if anything – and I mean anything – is going on with Mum, right?'

'Of course.'

'Tell her I've got to take a call but will buzz her right back.'

Katy returns the phone to its cradle and picks up the Polaroid of her younger self that stands on the mantelpiece. So it was true. Andrew did have a fling with Jude. The truth is incredible. Especially as Jude by then must have known Charles was her dad. Then there was the business about the baby and Jude's lie about Andrew.

Excited shrieks from the children still playing on the grass below merge with the sound of Joyce and Diane's voices as Katy ponders all this. And wonders, too, just how much her mum had really known. I look so small, she thinks, gazing down at the picture in her hand. So innocent of what would come. Remembering the message her father wrote, Katy slips the image from its frame. She turns it over to read once more and notices the browned square of folded newspaper stuck to its back.

Unfortunate incident on heath, the local paper's headline reads. An understatement that makes her heart double beat.

'Will you be staying for dinner, Katy?' Diane is standing in the sitting room doorway staring at her, intently.

'No, thanks,' Katy mumbles, slipping the photo back into its frame then placing the frame back on the mantelpiece. How much did Mum hear, she wonders.

'You were talking to Andrew just now,' her mum continues, dully.

'I was.'

'About Jude. And your father and Siobhan.'

Katy drops her gaze. 'I was,' she mumbles, awkwardly.

'About who knew what, and when.'

'Yes.'

Diane lets slip a sad smile. 'It was a very long time ago, you know,' she sighs. 'And I'm not sure Siobhan meant to do it, not at first.'

'What do you mean?' Katy sinks down onto the edge of the sofa.

'Well as far as I can remember, she moved back from the coast with Jude without knowing for sure your father was still there. And she enrolled Jude at St Mary's because she wanted the best for her. But then, when you and Jude became friends, the penny dropped. For her, at least – it took your father, bless him, considerably longer. Then when he confronted her, told her to leave, she asked him for money to keep silent. I noticed a number of monthly withdrawals from our joint account, but didn't work out what they were for until later. Then—'

Diane steps forward and takes up position on the sofa beside her daughter before pressing on.

'—when Jude fell pregnant, Siobhan threatened to tell me everything if he didn't give her more cash. Which is when he admitted to me the whole story.' She shakes her head, lost in thought for a moment. 'I was deeply hurt and so very, very angry. But I wanted to protect the rest of my family, you see.

Which is why I did it – I gave her a lump sum to move away. So you mustn't blame yourself for any of this. Because none of this is anything to do with you, you see?'

Katy stares at her mum, unsure quite what to say. Because there's something not right. A missing piece to this story. Something to do with her, though she can't pinpoint precisely what it is. Not yet.

'Listen, Mum, it's all right. Really. But it's getting late and I should be going.' Pocketing the slip of newsprint, she gives Diane a hug. 'And Mum? Andrew said he'll call you right back, only he had a take an urgent call.'

'Not to worry.' Diane quickly squeezes her daughter's thigh. 'He's rung me twice today already. Such an attentive son.' She smiles. 'And so very, very much unlike his dear, departed father.'

A few minutes later, as Katy leans back into the driver's seat with folded arms, the shadow stirs once more. The problem with all this is not what Jude and James are up to, she thinks, staring at the steering wheel. It's to do with her. Not what she didn't do, but something she did. Out on the heath that day. An action, rather than inaction, that set all this in motion.

It's not your fault.

That's what mum had said when she admitted how guilty she'd felt for all these years about what happened to Jude. About not being able to help her. But now she has a curious feeling that the key to this is something else entirely. That the truth is close by, but still just beyond her grasp.

She rubs her eyes, willing herself to think. Cursing ragged gaps in memory and the lost hours following the last time she saw her friend that day.

Remembering the newspaper article, she slips it from her pocket. It's a news story about the fire on the heath that happened later that afternoon and includes an interview with one of their classmates, Ruth Creighton, who had been walking alone on the heath that day with a drawing pad and box of watercolours.

On reaching the copse, Ruth had found a place to paint then been distracted when the wind turned bringing with it the acrid smell of something burning, the report reads. Hastily, she gathered up her things then, as she made her way back through the copse and out onto the footpath she noticed a bag discarded in the dust and recognised it as belonging to another girl in her class who she'd seen the day before in the same spot secretly meeting her boyfriend. Unable to see her classmate now and fearing her in danger, Ruth ran – back towards camp to raise the alarm.

Jude. It had to be Jude, Katy thinks. But she can't make any sense of reference to a boyfriend. Not Andrew of course, not by then. Noticing for the first time the grainy picture that accompanies the story, she sees the caption: Heroine of the hour. The picture is of Ruth Creighton – and just as she remembered, her, too, complete with thick plaits and mouth brace. A doctor now, Mum had said.

You should be careful, Kat Parker, of the friends you choose, Ruth told her once. *Jude's saying all sorts of things about you behind your back, you know. And stuff about your mum and dad.*

Once more Katy pulls out her phone, activates the web browser and keys in Ruth's name. In only a couple of seconds, she has found her: a senior partner in a medical practice in Brentford. The irony of how close she is to where Ruth must now live makes Katy's breath come quick. There it is, the surgery's address, but what about Ruth's? A couple of clicks later she finds Ruth's name once more on the latest edition of a newsletter for the Sandycombe Residents Association near Kew Gardens above what must be her phone number and address.

Siobhan may be gone but perhaps there is someone else who can help her understand what Jude was referring to, Katy thinks. But the prospect of seeing her former classmate once again makes her inside clench. And whether this is caused by anticipation, guilt or fear, she cannot tell.

Chapter 28

Guildford, July 1989

Jude retied the belt of the kimono around her waist then tried again.

Stretching her arm upwards into the open cupboard before her, reaching her hand forwards to find the last clean mug tucked behind assorted cracked plates and chipped dishes to the cabinet's rear. Standing on her toes, her fingers strained towards the handle and this time she managed to move it forwards, just a millimetre or two. But before she could grasp it securely a sudden arm looped tentacle-like around her waist and in her surprise the mug fell forwards, narrowly missing her head before crashing onto the floor.

'Wouldn't it be easier just to wash one up?' Nuzzling his face into the back of her neck, Dave sniffed her hair.

'Stop it, Mum's upstairs,' she whispered, crossly pushing his arm away then squatting down to gather up the chunks of broken china.

Dave stood back and watched in silence as she briskly dropped the debris into the bin then noticed her right hand where blood had started to well from a tiny porcelain cut. 'Hey,' he said, following her gaze then taking a step towards her. He reached for the injured hand and brought it to his lips then, taking her finger in his mouth, he sucked it gently. Powerless to resist, Jude said nothing but as his warm tongue licked her skin she felt the anger subside. Instinctively, she shot a glance over his shoulder towards the kitchen door and the empty hallway beyond but there was no sign of movement from Siobhan; no sound from upstairs.

Still holding her hand, Dave pulled away then smiled. 'Don't worry, she's taking a bath – I think she'll be a while.'

Jude loosened his grip and stepped just out of reach to lean against the kitchen worktop by the sink, noticing for the first time his skin was damp and his hair wet. He must have showered already. 'You're up early,' she said.

He lifted the kettle and filled it with fresh water. 'So are you.'

'I've got things to pack. I'm leaving for camp today, in case you'd forgotten.'

'I'd not forgotten,' he smiled, rinsing out two used mugs under the hot tap. 'I wanted to see you off.'

'Oh.' Jude turned towards the open window through which she could now hear the distant clink of bottles from the milk van parked on the street a few houses down.

The trip to Gallows Hill had been her idea. Though organised by the school, the trip wasn't compulsory but when the confirmation slip arrived Jude knew she had to get away, just for a few days. To have some time to herself – away from Kat, away from Siobhan – to clear her head. Decide what to do. But now, although her exams were over and she was free to embrace the summer that lay ahead, she was having second thoughts.

For one thing, Kat was now going. Initially, she'd dismissed the opportunity as her dad was supposed to be taking them all away on the family break that had never quite happened at Easter. But then his plans had changed again of course and, despite her initial qualms, Diane had unexpectedly agreed to let her daughter go. Jude had teased Kat about not signing up for the trip at first, taunting her for lacking any spirit of adventure. But then when she'd discovered the real reason, that Charles was taking them all away, she'd felt bloated with envy and resentment.

Now the girl would indeed be there Jude's mood grew even darker. Because she didn't care about Kat. The only person she now wanted to see was Andrew. Andrew, who she'd not managed to speak to since that awful afternoon a few weeks earlier, would be leaving on his round-the-world trip soon after their return. There was so little time left to try and see him one last time, to try to explain.

Then there was the tiny life beginning to stir inside her. She'd still not confided in anyone, choosing to immerse herself instead in last minute exam preparation. Although she knew this would change soon enough, once she began to show.

'Jude?'

Stepping towards her, Dave reached out and loosened her hair from the rough ponytail she'd scooped it into and let it settle, loose, around her face. Sliding his free hand down to her waist, he grasped the satin bow she'd just retied and tugged her towards him.

Jude wanted to tell him to stop, but as his hand untangled her hair all she wanted was for her body mould into his. Then, as he leaned against her, pushing her back against the worktop with the force of his body, securing her firmly, she was thrown off guard momentarily by a familiar aroma she couldn't quite place. A floral smell, light and zesty, with a hint of pine. 'She'll be a while,' he said.

Dave kissed her again, harder this time, forcing her head back against the cupboard door, filling her mouth with his tongue as she tried to blot out the voice now nagging from somewhere deep inside her head that asked her whether it might be possible, just a few minutes earlier, that he'd been upstairs with Siobhan sharing that bath. And then she knew what she could smell on him. Her mother's special Bronnley soap which she'd used for years and guarded so preciously.

Any doubts, though, were quickly overwhelmed by desire as Jude blindly pulled him towards her. Oblivious of the silk now slipping to the floor. Excited by Siobhan's close proximity. Eager for Dave to be inside her. For the discoveries of recent weeks had made her reckless, and the strain of keeping her secrets had left her craving sensation and risk. Not knowing she'd been living a lie. Now she knew, though, she realised that for the first time in as long as she could remember she felt truly alive.

Their bodies parted at the telltale surge of the bath water draining away through the pipes from the bathroom above. As he darted into the utilities room to wipe himself down, Jude hastily rearranged her kimono and retied her hair. She glanced up at the clock on the wall above the kitchen window. If she didn't get a move on, Siobhan, who'd found a temporary job at the local Co-op, would be late. She rinsed out another mug and made three teas as Dave walked back into the kitchen dressed in an unironed T-shirt and old pair of tracksuit bottoms he now used only for DIY.

The pair took a seat at the kitchen table where the contents of an information pack for the outward bounds centre at Gallows Hill were spread out. Dave picked up the photocopied map. 'We could meet, you know—' he began, stabbing the paper with his forefinger. 'Here, at... Coulter's Copse.' Casting a glance at the printed itinerary on the table he rubbed his hands together. 'It looks like you'll have plenty of free time to slip away.'

The thought of secretly meeting Dave during her stay at Gallows Hill stirred Jude's spirits. 'What will you tell Mum?'

'Not your problem,' he grinned. 'Anyway, I've been planning a bit of a surprise.'

Jude frowned.

'Don't worry. Trust me.' As he tapped a finger against the side of his nose he started to laugh. 'Just meet me there on the first afternoon at four, OK?'

'What's so funny?' asked Siobhan, hurrying into the kitchen to make a cup of tea. She was wearing her staff uniform, a navy long-sleeved dress and matching waistcoat both made of the same rough fabric, and had her hair scraped back into an unfashionable bun.

'Oh, just the idea of Jude in hiking boots and a rucksack, orienteering,' Dave replied without missing a beat. He pointed to the grinning figures on the outward bounds centre brochure cover. 'Anyway. I'd better be off if I'm going to make it to Birmingham in time.' He rose from the table and picked up his motorcycle helmet and a small rucksack. With his free hand he reached round Siobhan's waist to tug her towards him for a goodbye kiss, then gave her bottom a swift pinch as he pushed her away, dismissed. 'See you later, girls!'

As the door had closed firmly behind him, the smile swiftly faded from Siobhan's face. 'Do you think he's going off me?' she asked, pushing the mug and its tepid contents away from her, then slumping back in the kitchen chair.

'Why do you say that, Mum?' Jude stared intently at the map as she spoke, eager to conceal both her surprise and sense of satisfaction sparked by the frankness of her mum's admission.

'Oh, you can always tell,' Siobhan replied, vaguely. Reaching deep into the pocket of her waistcoat she extracted a ball of tissue which she quickly used to dab her eyes. 'I've a lifetime's experience in that department. Besides, he's not as... affectionate... as he used to be.'

'Mum,' Jude grimaced. 'Do I really need to know?'

'Don't come all Little Miss Goody Two Shoes with me. I know what you get up to when I'm not looking,' Siobhan snapped. Without looking up, Jude bit her lip as she scanned the brochure for a moment then snapped it shut, straightening the loose papers inside with a single, brisk tap to the table top. 'Yes. You've been seen,' Siobhan pressed on, clearly warming to her theme. 'In various pubs down by the river on the far side of town. And with a number of different boys. So don't play the innocent with me. Staying over at Kat's, indeed. I've a good mind to ring her parents.'

'But you won't, though, will you?' Jude retorted, narrowing her eyes to glare in silence at her mum, challenging her to say more until, eventually, the older woman looked away.

Preoccupied now with folding and refolding her tissue into a neat and tidy parcel, Siobhan stared at her busy fingers in silence as, at last, their work completed, then slipped the wadded paper back into her pocket. Picking up her mug, she went to the sink where she tipped away the undrunk contents then made her way into the hall. Only once she'd pulled on her coat, slung her bag over her shoulder and had her hand on the front door catch did she pause.

'Don't make the same mistakes I made, Jude,' she said, turning back to look at Jude who was still sitting in her dressing gown at the kitchen table, pretending to read the local paper. 'You deserve better than that.'

Chapter 29

Kew, July 2013

The Ruth Creighton who opens the door is not what Katy expects but tall and slim with none of the dumpy awkwardness of her teenage years. Her hair is blonde, too, not a dull, washed-out brown and when she opens her mouth to speak the full extent of her transformation is most apparent. Once too self-conscious to talk without a protective hand hovering to shelf the metal framework encasing the inside of her mouth, her smile now is immaculate and uninhibited.

'Can I help you?' she says, snapping a pair of Marigolds off her hands. 'Sorry, just scrubbing the barbecue,' she adds in explanation. 'We've got people coming round.'

Katy feels her cheeks flush. 'Actually…' she mumbles, falteringly. 'I wonder if you can… I'm looking for—'

'Directions! I've an A to Z if that's of any—'

'No, I'm not lost, Ruth,' Katy interrupts with a nervous laugh as the woman standing in the open doorway before her stops smiling. 'I'm—'

'Kat?' The word hangs in the air like a bad smell between them as Ruth's mouth tightens. For her, at least, there is nothing more to say.

'Yes,' Katy presses on, trying not to think of the times she stood by while others, Jude especially, bullied her mercilessly. 'Look, sorry to drop in unannounced but I was just passing and, well, I wondered… if you might be able to help.'

'Aren't I the popular one now?' Ruth exclaims then, taking a step back to steady herself, her manner becomes more formal.

Clinical. She checks her watch. 'Well, I'm sorry but I'm not working today—'

'No, not like that. I meant as a friend.'

'A friend, now where have I heard that before?' The woman muses, fixing Katy with a grey-eyed stare that makes her conscience squirm. 'That's... rich.'

'Listen,' Katy blurts, noticing how Ruth now grips the side of the front door in anticipation of forcing it shut. 'Just let me say something before you ask me to leave, please?'

Ruth hesitates, momentarily disarmed by her visitor's direct-ness. She checks her watch then, with a sigh, beckons Katy inside. 'All right. Straight on then first on the left for the sitting room. Take a seat while I put the kettle on.'

A reluctant intruder, Katy makes her way into a large, timbered room to perch on the edge of a three seat brown leather sofa facing a stone-clad open hearth. Behind her, at the opposite end of the room, an entire brick wall has been replaced by concertina glass panels beyond which she can see an expanse of garden. The house, though double-fronted, had looked modest in size and predictably Victorian from the front. The rear, however, is stylish and modern and its design is bright and airy. She wonders how Ruth can afford such a lovely home on a local GP's pay. Clearly, her old classmate has done well.

Turning her head towards a large, ornately-framed mirror on the wall to her left she sees a family gallery of framed photographs hung on either side. Twins, a girl and a boy, pictured at a range of ages between birth and eight or nine are a recurring theme. In a number of images, Ruth poses beside a striking, dark-haired man with piercing blue eyes.

Fighting the urge to leave her seat to take a closer look, Katy quickly turns towards the door at the sound of approaching footsteps. 'Your children?' she asks lightly, waving a hand in the direction of the photographs as Ruth enters the room holding a tray.

With a nod, the other woman hands Katy a mug of tea. 'Archie and Ellie. And that's my husband, Geoff.'

There is something in the tone of her voice that makes Katy think some sort of comment or response to this is called for. 'What a good-looking family!' she declares.

'Surprises you, does it?' Ruth sits back in a chair then crosses her legs. 'That someone like me could end up with something like – all of this?' The words sting.

'No.' Katy puts down her mug on the latest edition of *Condé Nast Traveller* that sits on a low table by her side. 'Not at all.'

Taking a deep breath, she looks up to see Ruth observing her embarrassment with a wry smile, calm and in control. 'I'm not proud of how we all treated you at school, you know. We were horrible, especially me and Jude. But kids are like that, aren't they?' She laughs, awkwardly. 'Desperate not to stand out. Eager to go along with the gang. They lack the imagination to put themselves in other people's shoes, I suppose.'

Ruth takes a sip from her mug but says nothing, deepening the void between them that Katy now feels obliged to fill.

'Anyway, I'm not here to say sorry,' Katy presses on. 'We both know the way people behaved was wrong – and that by not standing up for what's right I was just as bad as Jude. But what's done is done. If I could change it I would, but I can't.'

'Well that's honest, I suppose,' Ruth says quietly, her expression softening. 'I think if you'd sat down and said you were sorry I'd have asked you to leave. Back then was a lifetime ago. An experience I stopped dwelling on a long time back. So go on, you've got my attention. Why are you here?'

Though excused, not exonerated. Katy smiles. 'I know I've got a real nerve coming here, but as I said: I need your help. It's about the summer I had the accident – you remember, while we were all staying at Gallow's Hill?' Ruth nods. 'Well I need to ask you something—' Ruth nods again, waiting for her to get to the point. 'It's about Jude.'

Now Ruth's cheeks redden. 'Jude.'

'Well, some of the things she—'

'They called me a liar,' Ruth butts in. 'For what I said I saw there, out on the heath that day. Either I was mistaken or else I was making up lies to get her into trouble, that's what they said. When the local paper interviewed me, though, I mentioned what I saw. But they didn't put it in because by then, as no one else had seen anything, it was all down to me.' She sighs. 'Me and my overactive imagination.'

'I'm sorry—'

'But the real liar, of course, was Jude.'

'Well yes, that's what I was hoping...'

'Hoping what?'

'That you could tell me what you meant that day, just before the exams. When you warned me about Jude saying things behind my back about me, my mum and my dad.'

'Did I?'

'You did, yes.'

Ruth frowns. 'Well Jude said a lot of things, none of them pleasant.'

'I know, but—'

'And then she told everyone I was the liar, even when I know what I saw. Meeting in secret, out on the heath – Jude and her lover.'

'Lover?'

'No question. I saw them, together, earlier that week. I used to go out walking alone, you see.'

A nerve buried in the skin somewhere just above Katy's left cheek bone begins to twitch as her focus on the story unfolding, the woman opposite, the room around her, starts to slip. 'Not really, what do you mean?'

'Then, the afternoon of the fire, before I went to get help, I saw him again – a tall man, with dark hair, dressed in black—'

Katy raises her hand to rub her face. Her fingertips brush the fine white line of scar tissue just beneath her eye where, when Jude slapped her, that last day on the heath, the intricate silver setting of the amber ring she always wore caught the skin just below Katy's left eye. A shadow shifts making her stomach flip. She should leave. Right now. But it is too late. Something is stirring in the darkness, flexing its limbs as it slowly comes back to life.

'—good-looking, too, in a David Essex kind of way—'

Him, it was definitely him, Katy thinks, her throat tightening. The darkness inside her is moving, and for a moment there is a flicker of memory just beyond her reach. Until she experiences the fleeting sensation of cowering within dense foliage. Hiding from something. Someone. So Ruth saw him, too. But why hadn't this part of the story come out? What did Jude know that she'd chosen not to say?

'—only this time he was on the ground—'

Her palms are moist now and she almost drops the mug of tea. Because now she sees him. A man on all fours. Straddling someone. *Stop it!* Thrusting, beast-like. His pelvis pumping. Making her friend scream. *Run, Jude, run!* And then a voice inside her screaming. *No.* She hears a whimper. The sound has comes from her, but Ruth's not yet noticed.

'—injured—'

Smashed and broken.

'—I thought there'd been some kind of accident...'

His head all caved in.

'That something dreadful must have happened to Jude. But by the time the people from camp arrived there was nothing—'

The makeshift weapon dangling from her own hand.

No. This didn't happen, not really. Because it's just fantasy. Something she saw on a movie once. A waking dream. And yet she knows Ruth is telling the truth. That this is the shadow – the thing that made her run and refuse to look back. The thing that's kept her running every single day since it happened. Running so hard as to obscure the truth with the dust kicked up by her heels.

'Katy? Are you OK?'

She is on her feet now, swaying slightly as she tries not to spill the undrunk tea. She puts it back onto the side table then swings her bag over one shoulder. 'I'm so sorry,' she gasps. 'I'm feeling a little… Terrible morning sickness, you see,' she presses on. 'And what with the heat and everything. So sorry, but I think I really should go.'

Stumbling out of the room, Katy retraces her steps to the front door.

'Can I at least call you a cab,' Ruth asks, eyeing her belly anxiously.

'No, no – I could do with some fresh air,' Katy gasps. Thank God she parked round the corner. At least she won't have a debate with the woman whether she is in any fit state to drive. All she needs is distance. Space. To get away from Ruth. To catch her breath and gather her thoughts. To think.

But no she cannot think. Because to think is to look back and see the truth of what she did that day. The very wicked, evil thing that no matter how hard she has tried to outrun it, inter it, obscure it from view, has never gone away. For it is part of her, she thinks, her blood now pounding against the inside of her skull. It's who she is, and why. A very bad, bad person.

'Look after yourself, then,' the other woman smiles. 'If I were you I'd let it lie.' Her mouth curls into a knowing smile. 'There comes a time, you know, when you've got to realise that life's just too short to get hung up on what happened in the past,' she calls, as with a mechanical wave and a forced grin Katy makes her stumbling retreat through the front gate.

'Like I said to Jude when she stopped by here just the other day: just let it go.'

Chapter 30

It was you who made me do it – you and your stupid misunderstanding of what was going on. It was how he was, you know. We both liked it rough, sometimes. I never needed rescuing, just in case I'm not making myself clear.

Chapter 31

'Run, Jude! Run!'

Jude dropped her bag and span around on her heels, every sense in her body straining to locate the direction from which the shout had come. A movement in the bushes at the far end of the clearing opposite where she stood held her attention. But the contrast between light and shade was too stark for her eyes to decode.

Struggling to see, she raised her hand to shade her eyes and saw two figures standing in the shaded end of the clearing. Kat and Dave. Both were facing each other. He behind her, his arm locked around her neck, pulling her backwards. She in front, her body twisted at a broken angle, her hands tearing blindly at the figure behind her as she struggled to get away.

What was happening? Incensed, Jude stumbled forward across the dusty ground, the distance between them closing. How dare he! Then she faltered.

How often had she heard Siobhan complain about his wandering eye? She could still recall the stab of satisfaction she'd feel as he stared just a little too long at the girls in the playground at the end of the school day. Girls in A-line navy skirts they'd taken in by hand so the fabric clung taut across their hips and up, too, so their hem hung well above the knee. Girls in regulation blouses consciously worn a size too small. Girls in pleated PE skirts that barely skimmed their pants.

And it had been OK. Because back then this simply meant he was growing bored of her mum.

But that was before she and Dave got together. Afterwards it was different. Once she was sleeping with him not only did she notice it more, he seemed to do it more often. Those glances towards the Saturday shop girls sharing a ciggie at the bus stop. The furtive smiles slipped across the bar when he ordered drinks from Cherie. And once, when Kat dropped to her knees on the drive to gather up the spilled contents of her schoolbag, how he watched her through the kitchen window. Appreciatively.

The sudden recollection of this made Jude's face knot into a scowl. Because she needed him more than anything now. She hadn't told him yet, of course, but knew she must – and would do, soon. For who else was there? She couldn't tell her mother about the tiny life now unfurling inside her. And Andrew was off limits. Even if he wasn't her brother, he couldn't have made it any more clear he didn't want to know. Which left the man before her her only salvation.

Dave. He had a job, money, and still couldn't keep his hands off her. One way or the other, he'd help her do what she had to do. But what did she want? She wished she knew. She was too young for a baby. What about all the things she wanted to do? Get a place at drama college. Move away, to London. But then again… No. The future was bleak if she ended up like Siobhan. Which wouldn't happen.

Because Dave loved her, she was sure. He'd grown tired of older meat as her mum had grown irascible and grumpy. Why, she'd even started to put on weight.

Jude rubbed her eyes, refocusing on the scene unfolding before her. And then, a beat later, with legs pounding and arms pumping, she was speeding towards them. Rearing across the final metres of dusty ground; screaming as loud as she could. Stretching out her arms before her and bracing her palms. Barging her way between them and throwing both off balance.

'Stop it!' she yelled.

Dave slipped, ricking his ankle, then cursed. Seizing the moment, Kat slid from his grasp. Falling to the ground, she sat there for a moment like a winded foal. Then she was springing upwards onto her feet. She charged towards the bushes where she dived into the greenery, careless of the spring-loaded branches. Without a backward glance, Jude noted, as the rasp of Katy's breath, her sporadic sobs, quickly faded.

Which left just the two of them, standing side by side, staring in silence in the direction she'd just gone.

Until Jude noticed how her own body was shaking, the tumult of resentment and anger now raging inside.

'What the fuck was that about?' she spat, clumsily mis-aiming a slap towards his face which he had more than enough time to deflect.

'Easy, now,' he soothed, clamping a firm hand around her wrist.

'Let go of me!' she snarled, twisting her arm left then right in a vain attempt to force him to release his grip. She tried to kick him, too, but he was too quick.

He laughed. 'No, not until you promise not to hurt me.'

'You shit.'

'Jude—' he began, softening his tone.

She smelled something on his breath. Whisky. 'Stop it'.

'No, you stop it. It was just a bit of fun.'

'A laugh? Just a bit of a joke. Come with me – my stuff's over there. Come and sit down.'

Though unconvinced, she made no further objection as, still holding her wrist but gently now, he led her to the far side of the clearing. Through a gap in the bushes there was a moss-covered patch of open ground beneath a tree where a tarpaulin was spread. To one side of this stood a small hiker's sack. Its mouth gaped open revealing an assortment of paraphernalia inside.

'Come on,' he repeated, releasing her arm. He took a seat beside the bag and patted the space beside him. 'Sit.' He pulled free a half-drunk bottle of scotch from the bag, uncapped it then held the bottle out towards her. 'Oh Jude,' he sighed. 'Don't be cross.'

She stepped onto the tarpaulin then sat cross-legged facing him, just out of reach. Leaning forward, she took the bottle. She swallowed. The liquid burned the back of her throat but quickly calmed her. Maybe he was right. Perhaps she had got the wrong end of the stick. He patted the space beside him again. Slowly, she slipped towards him.

'Cigarette?' She nodded. He lit one and passed it to her. 'Hey,' he said, reaching an arm around her waist to tug her more closely to him. 'I'm sorry, OK?'

'Me too,' she nodded once more, taking a drag.

Lying back onto the ground, Jude slid her free arm beneath her head and stared up at the flickering fragments of sky. Tiny explosions of light burst every now and then through the canopy of leaves above her head. The wrong end of the stick! What did he take her for? But no, she must not get angry.

Stretching out his legs, he lay back on the tarpaulin then rolled onto his side to face her. He watched as she exhaled, slowly. Then he reached out his hand to rest it softly on her stomach. He let slip a quick laugh as he began to stroke the gradual dome of it. 'Better watch it, Jude,' he murmured. 'What you eat – you're starting to get a bit of a belly.'

Angrily, she grabbed his wrist to halt his hand then pulled herself upright.

'Hey, Jude—'

'Fuck you,' she snapped, hugging her knees towards her. Tears welled in her eyes which she tried in vain to blink away.

Dave sat up, too, and took another drink from the bottle. 'I didn't mean that you were getting—'

'Fat?' Jude interjected. 'No, of course not. And for your information I'm not. Only it's... it's just... I'm...' But the words wouldn't come as, instead, she started to cry. Huge, deep sobs that made her body judder. Like a nerve once pressed that would never stop.

He slid towards her, reaching an arm around her shoulders and holding her to him. 'Christ, Jude,' he soothed. 'Whatever it is, it can't be that bad. I mean, exam results aren't everything—'

'What?' she demanded, pulling away. 'One minute you tell me I'm fat, the next I'm stupid? For fuck's sake I'm pregnant, Dave. And yes, before you ask, it is yours.'

He blew a low whistle as he exhaled, slowly; shook his head from side to side as he played for time. With a sideways glance, she tried to gauge his expression. But she didn't have enough confidence to look at him directly.

'Pregnant.'

'Yes.' Stay calm, she told herself. Don't blow it. But as she closed her eyes she saw herself standing on a wooden jetty watching the only boat for miles drifting away, the end of the rope tied to it floating in the water just out of reach.

'Christ.'

Just one word, but the way he said it was enough. It stung, like a slap to the face. Her eyes snapped open. 'What, haven't you ever fancied a kid?'

'One, perhaps. But I couldn't eat two.' Then his face closed in on itself. He laughed – a humourless sound, rubbed his face, then sighed. 'Like mother, like daughter.'

'What?' she demanded, unsure what he meant.

'You heard me.'

'But what did you mean?'

'Should we, shouldn't we? As if there was ever any choice. Of course we couldn't, so I drove her down to the clinic myself. Gave her the money for it, too. Which I suppose is what you want me to do?'

'Clinic?' said Jude, fumbling for the meaning of his words. Trying not to decode the true implication of the capsules of folic acid she'd seen in her mum's bedside drawer. The conception leaflet. The pregnancy testing kit.

'The week before Easter. When she told you she was going to stay with your Nan. Oh, sorry luv,' he added, noticing her surprise. 'Did you think we were having an exclusive relationship?'

'Of course not,' she insisted. 'Only...' Of course she had. Why wouldn't she? Because of course she'd never imagined they'd still be doing it, given the breakdown of her own relationship with her mum. Given the blind naivety of her faith in her own youth. The supreme arrogance of it. She bit her lip and tasted blood.

'Hey,' he said suddenly, looping an arm once more around her shoulders and gently tugging her towards him. 'Don't. There's no point thinking about the what ifs. Come on, Jude. It can be sorted, OK?' With his free hand he passed her the whisky.

'Sorted?' she echoed, raising the bottle to her lips and kissing the glass. The strap of her sundress had slid down off one shoulder. Never mind, she thought as she swallowed and a wave of heat ignited her chest, she'd adjust it in a minute.

'Sorted.'

He touched her bottom lip with his forefinger then softly traced the contours – of her chin, the soft skin beneath, her throat, her collarbone – to rest his hand on the silky spot just above the beginning of the dip between her breasts. 'Together, you and me, all of this can be sorted. Really, there's no need to cry.'

With a sniff, she nodded.

'That's it. Good girl,' he murmured, putting an arm around her waist then tilting her onto all fours. With one hand he pulled her upwards towards him and as his other rubbed her breasts through the thin cotton of her dress, she realised for the first time in weeks they no longer felt like they were about to explode. But the relief was only fleeting because by then he was thrusting her dress up above her thighs and tearing her pants sideways. She tried to wriggle free but his grip was too tight.

'Wait—' she began as, with his free hand, he unbuckled his belt and undid his flies.

As something hard poked the small of her back. As he pushed her legs apart with his knee then entered her firmly from behind. This wasn't how it had been before. Back at home he'd been playful when they'd done it on her mother's bed. Insistent, certainly, and definitely the one in control – but never cruel. 'No, Dave, please – you know I don't like it this way.'

Crouched on all fours, Jude arched her back against him as he bore down on her. But his determination, the sheer weight of him, was more than she could resist. So with head bowed and jaws clenched, all she could do was brace as the pumping inside her began to build. 'Really, I mean it,' she gasped. Pleaded. 'You're hurting me, please.'

'Oh Jude,' he groaned. 'You're such a little prick tease.'

As tears filled her eyes, the gathering swell of him felt fit to burst. But then, without warning, it stopped abruptly as something else happened. Her face hit the ground. There was dirt and grit in her mouth. And as she was flattened by the dead weight of him, her rib cage crushed as her lungs flailed for breath, she felt the spent force of him trickle wetly between her legs.

Jude knew she must try to move, to push the heavy thing from on top of her, to wriggle her body free. So with immense effort, she drew her knees towards her belly, ignoring the pain as the ground grated the fronts of her legs. Then, after a few more seconds struggling, she was on her side. Sobbing with relief, she hugged herself back to life. Waited for the strength to come.

Gradually, as the tearing pulse inside her began to subside and when, at last, her breathing was even she opened her eyes, she saw him. Dave. Lying on his front beside her with his face flat into the ground spread-eagled. His trousers half mast. A different place a different time it might have been comical, but not now.

Jude scanned his body, struggling to make sense of it, until her gaze settled on his head. His face was into the ground, his nose crushed, his mouth slightly open – as hers had been just a few seconds before – but it wasn't this that held her attention, but his head. The back of it. Clotted with bloodied bits of bark and shreds of skin. His matted hair.

Confused, she rubbed her eyes with the heel of her palms. But no, when she refocused he was still there. And then she heard it – part sob, part gasp of pain. The sound came from close by.

Springing into a runner's starting position, on her knees once more but this time ready for flight, Jude turned her head. Someone was standing behind them a few paces out into the clearing. A slight figure, pinioned by the sun's accusing glare. With shoulders slumped and head bowed. Her body trembled as her left hand balled into a fist, unclenched, then balled into a fist again.

'Kat?'

As Jude spoke, the stout shaft of a broken branch the figure before her clutched in her right hand, clattered onto the ground. Both girls stared at the makeshift cudgel for a moment as if deciphering what it could possibly mean. Then Jude was charging towards the other girl, fuelled by shock. Resentment. Fury.

'What the fuck have you done?' As Jude drew level she grasped Kat firmly by the arm. Leaned her face into hers. Shook her, hard. 'What were you thinking?' she began, then laughed. 'Oh, but of course! You were jealous, weren't you? Not of me, mind, but him, right? How dare you, you frigid lezzer. Because I've seen how you look at me, you dysfunctional bitch. No, don't turn away. Look at it – look at him…'

Unperturbed by a sudden sob that erupts like a hiccup, Jude pressed on.

'Do you know what you've done – do you? Taken away the one person who—' Her body shook, and for a moment she feared she was about to be sick, but then it passed and she was raising her arm upwards. Flattening her palm. Swinging with all her force towards Kat's face. Slapping it – hard enough to draw blood, she noticed with a stab of satisfaction as she pulled her hand away.

'—the one person who was going to take me away from all this.'

Whether it was the verbal or physical hurt that did it, Jude couldn't tell. But at that moment the broken figure before her raised her head, met her gaze and held it briefly. Then, without any warning, Kat span around. She twisted her body away from Jude's to face back across the open clearing. Setting her sights on something uncertain in the middle distance, she once more broke into a run and darted swiftly across the dusty clearing before, with a quick sidestep, disappearing behind a ragged rhododendron.

Too stunned to react, Jude stared at the ground a few paces ahead where the branch Kat had been holding still lay. It was snub nosed and shoulder shaped – an ideal makeshift weapon, she noted, grimly. Then without knowing quite why, she stepped forwards, crouched down and picked it up. After weighing it in her hand for a few moments, she tossed it into the bushes.

A few feet from where she now stood was a crumpled packet of Marlboros. Jude picked it up and looked inside. There were two left and a half-used book of matches. Quickly, she lit up then slid the pack into the front pocket of her dress. The taste of the tobacco soothed her. Her pulse began to calm. Only then did she turn back to look at Dave.

Tentatively, she took a step towards him. Nudged his leg with the toe of her plimsoll. But his lack of any response, the undeniable, irrevocable dull weight of him, made the blood inside her head once more pound.

What should she do?

It was too late to help him, she should leave. But if she did that, left him here like this, someone would find him and then what might happen? It would all come out, wouldn't it? That they'd been together. How he'd chosen her over her mum. How hurt and humiliated the woman would feel. How bitterly she'd feel her daughter had let her down. Would Siobhan stick by her after that? Jude wasn't sure.

What she did know was that she couldn't deal with the baby growing inside her alone. That only her mum would know what to do. That they could get through this, together. She let slip a weak smile because of how long she'd yearned for just that. The two of them united against the rest of the world! But she must hide her true feelings to make this work.

The time had passed to want it to be Andrew's, or to convince herself it was Dave's. She'd need a new story. To bury the truth deep as best she can.

He would be too heavy to move, of course. Besides, the thought of touching him was awful. So she grabbed her bag which lay in the dust a short distance from where she now stood and darted away from him, across the clearing to where the bushes resumed on its far side, then hesitated. Partially covered by shade, she straddled lightness and dark. Decided yet uncertain, she stared ahead into the shaded foliage, her mind still wrestling with what best to do.

No, she couldn't leave him. Shouldn't. This was all so very wrong, damn it. What she had done with Dave. What they had both done to Siobhan. At the thought of her mum, the only one who could understand the predicament she was now in, tears poked Jude's eyes and she rubbed her face on the back of her hand.

Her heart lurches at the thought of how the woman had taken it when she admitted she was pregnant. She'd expected anger and I-told-you-so recrimination but, Siobhan had been strong and practical instead. Resolute in her pledge to back her daughter in whatever course of action she chose. Determined, too, in her decision to approach Andrew's parents for more money. For though Jude had refused to divulge to her mum the identity of the baby's father, Siobhan had insisted whatever the truth they pretend it was his. That way Charles and Diane would be persuaded to give them what was needed to move away and start again.

Damn Kat, of course, over and above everything – for killing her mum's hopes by killing Dave.

Glancing towards a gap in the bushes ahead Jude could see the tinderbox heath across which she would soon have to return. Parched and livid beneath the sun's glare, its face looked brutally exposed. And on it, now clearly visible between the trees, was something moving. A figure. Too far away to make out very clearly, but someone was coming, making their way along the pitted path between the gorse and brambles towards the shaded refuge in which she now stood. Almost there, but not quite. Five minutes away – maybe a little more, probably a bit less.

Her first thought was that it must be Kat. But as she stared once more she could make out that the figure wore a sun hat, broad-rimmed and conical, Chinese coolie-style, and carried a small rectangular box. Not Kat, someone else.

Jude shot an anxious glance back towards the spot where Dave lay. She must hide it, she thought: any evidence that they'd been here, anything that might link them together. Darting back, she snatched the whisky bottle from the ground then deftly lobbed it into the bushes. Then she noticed the bag. It was still leaning against the trunk of a tree a short distance away. She dived towards it, almost tripping, and grabbed it. But the thing slipped from her grasp and upended, scattering its contents across the ground.

Dropping onto the dusty earth, Jude quickly gathered up an Ordnance Survey map of the local area, a dog-eared copy of *The Dice Man*, an unopened packet of plain digestives. There was a ten-pound note which she slipped into the front pouch of her own bag, and also a small yellow can with conical nozzle lying on its side on the tarpaulin by Dave's leg. This made her pause.

Scanning the ground, Jude quickly spotted the Zippo lying on its side on the straw-like grass a few paces away. Her stomach clenched. Andrews's Zippo. She'd kept it after their last night together. But Dave had found it when it fell from her jacket pocket and taken a fancy to it – even claimed it as his own. Andrew would be in Sydney soon. The thought of this made her almost cry. How different it could have been if everything

286

hadn't gone wrong. If they hadn't argued. If Diane hadn't turned him against her. If her mum and his dad hadn't...

What the hell was she going to do?

Bending down, Jude picked up the lighter and flicked its lid. Intoxicated by the smell of it, she held the flame ignited before her and stared transfixed by how the world around her now shimmered and danced in the halo of fumes. Light-headed now, she knew of course that she must leave. Whoever it was out there on the heath was surely coming her way. If she hid herself to one side of the bushes by the path she could wait unseen for them to pass before making her own way back across the heath. Yes, that's what she would do.

But then, before she could stop it, the hot metal was scorching her fingers. Her hand was burning. And the Zippo was in the air.

She watched it soar upwards, charted its glittering trajectory towards the tarpaulin, plotted its likely point of impact. Realised, too late, that it would fall short onto – no, not a shadow, but a dark patch of something wet on the ground sheet. Spilled lighter fluid from the yellow can beside Dave's body. Then, as the fire caught, she heard him groan. And though they remained shut, his eyes flickered as he tried to move.

Powerless to move, Jude was conscious only of how the air now smelled like ash. How tiny fragments of dust had begun to dance around Dave's leg. How the barely perceptible gasp of a breeze softly fanned the budding flame. If she moved quickly she could kick it out; smother the smoking fabric with its flickering flame. Quell the building heat. But instead she looked away, her attention snagged by the frenzy of ants now zigzagging away from the inert bulk of him in all directions like cartoon lightning bolts. Then she remembered those words.

Did you think we were having an exclusive relationship?

Because he'd been fucking her and her mum, hadn't he? Both at the same time. A thought which makes her think of that Patti Smith track she loved so much. The one that kept her

287

sane, almost. It went: *I don't fuck much with the past but I fuck plenty with the future.* Well she'd fuck with all their futures now, wouldn't she? And he'd deserve it, too, she thinks, tightening the straps on her bag. Turning her back on the figure lying at her feet.

Moving away from the path along which the walker she'd spotted approaching across the heath would soon come. Throwing herself into the bushes. Her single thought: to run away. To lose herself in darkness.

Chapter 32

Kew, July 2013

With hands clamped to the steering wheel of Michael's car Katy sits, rigid and shaking. Uncertain how long she's been here on this street a few minutes walk from Ruth's house, willing herself to once more forget; to re-bury the dreadful memory. Wishing it wasn't true. But it is done. The lock is broken. And she can no longer deny the truth of what she did. That she killed a man. An admission of guilt that makes her eyes dart anxiously up and down the empty street, fearful of exposure.

Of course it had been a decision made the instant she saw her friend being hurt, a voice inside her offers in her defence. In a way, hadn't what she'd done been brave?

But there was more, wasn't there? More to why she did what she did than courage, that's for sure. Because at that very moment she'd been overwhelmed by a very different kind of emotion, hadn't she? Her total and utter hatred of Jude. How she'd treated her. The way she'd made her feel. All those nasty things she'd said about her parents. Even fucking Andrew. Though of course she'd not known that back then.

Katy slumps forward, slamming her forehead onto the steering wheel. Cursing herself for being so stupid. So self-deluded. Because of course she'd known, hadn't she? It was why she'd told on Andrew to her dad. To split them up. Because of how much her parents disapproved of Jude. To punish, certainly. But also, in a way, to have control for once. To make Jude hers.

Not true, the voice inside her cries as she bangs her forehead on the wheel once more. And then, again. *It's just not true. You're not the one to blame. The bad one. You're just, as Jude said the other day, the girl who ran away.* But then, in that instant, Katy sees herself back on that canal-side years ago, staring down at the leather strawberries on her sandals. Green and red, she thinks, slamming back down her head. The colours of freedom and deceit.

'Why did I say that, Daddy?' she mumbles, her body still now as tears of self-loathing cascade down each cheek. 'If only I could tell you now how sorry I am for that lie.'

At the sudden and unexpected sound of a sharp rap-rap on the passenger window, Katy's eyes snap open and she finds herself face to face with the anxious face of a stooped man wearing a Day-glo tabard. One hand grips the handlebar of a racing bike while with the other he flaps his palm up and down in indication she should open the window.

'Are you OK?' the stranger mouths.

No, she wants to scream. *I most certainly am not OK.* As her hand hovers for a moment over the window release button on the inside panel of the driver's door, she thinks. *I am about to lose everything. I am in hell.* And then it is gone. The voice inside her. Her panic. The fear. To be replaced, instead, by a curious sensation that she is floating. Upwards, at last; free, now, of the leaden weight that has kept her cowed and bound to the past for so many years. Because it was not her fault, not really.

The stranger was attacking Jude. How was she to know they were together? For Christ's sake, he was hurting her. It was rape.

Frigid lezzer, Jude called her. And jealous, too. Of her and of him. *The one person who could take me away from all this.* And perhaps she was right – back then, at least. Which is surely why Jude's come back into her life after all these years: to get even. How far will she go to spoil things for me, she wonders with a shudder. Mum. Michael… the baby?

But Jude is wrong, Katy can now see, her hand now turning the ignition. Because she does not deserve this, none of them do. Though she lied to mum about her father down by the canal, it didn't change anything. Not really. The problem between them was their problem, not hers. As for Jude, well, the woman is being totally unreasonable – unbalanced, even – and so is her son.

The car jumps forward making the man with the bike hastily back away.

'Sorry,' she mouths, not bothering to wind down the window.

For all she can think of now is Michael and the sudden craving she feels to be by his side. The way being with him makes her feel protected and secure. How now's not the time to push him away but to explain and do so, fast. How if she is to get through this – if they are all to, unhurt – she must confront Jude, first.

–

It's almost nine when Katy finally turns back into Linden Gardens. The evening is close and a distant thud of music fills the air. As she slips through the front gate she notices he's thrown open every upstairs window. But the realisation that Michael is in serves only to rekindle her fear. She's neither called nor texted since abandoning him at Spike's without any explanation. Hardly a positive place from which to try to make her feelings and intentions clear.

Standing on the doorstep, Katy fumbles in her bag for her house keys but cannot find them. Which is ridiculous, she thinks, because she's sure she had them earlier. Though maybe when they left for Spike's it was Michael who'd locked up. Which meant she must have left them upstairs. Though she cannot recall seeing them since she went into Phil's place to help Kevin with the French windows. When was that – only yesterday? Reluctantly, she rings the buzzer. Without a word she is let in. A beat later she is hovering on the landing.

Watching him through the open kitchen doorway she is transfixed by the fluid movement of his hand as he chops an onion chef-style with rapid wrists and fingers clawed. Dressed only in a pair of shorts, Michael's body gently rocks in time to a Red Hot Chili Peppers track. Carefully positioned on the top of the microwave to his side is an electric fan on full pulse and set to rotate to counteract the room's shimmering heat. To his right, on the centre ring of the five hob steel cooker, a cast iron pan lightly dressed with extra virgin is just starting to spit.

With a brisk sideways movement, Michael slides the onion into the oil then sets about gathering up his other ingredients. Only when he glances up to check the clock above the fridge does he register her presence with a tiny flicker of his eye. Carefully, he puts down the knife then wipes his face on the back of his hand. Only then does he turn towards her. Only then does she notice the jagged cut above his left eye.

'Michael, what happened—'

'Katy!' he interrupts. 'So tell me, where the hell have you been?'

'Sorry,' she smiles, weakly. 'The car... I mean, the traffic coming back in... it was awful.'

'What, from the wine and flowers run to the supermarket?' Though his voice is measured and his tone even, his eyes narrow.

'I'm sorry,' Katy mumbles, her face burning. 'I should have rung—'

He nods but says nothing, waiting for her to fill the void.

'—it was an emergency. The hospital... they decided to discharge mum early but there was no one else available to meet her.' Damn it, she thinks, silently cursing her reflex response to lie. Why is concealment her default position? 'I know I could have left a message – should have – but somehow there just wasn't the time. And besides, the battery on my phone went flat. It must have been both worrying and embarrassing,' she adds, contritely. Miserably. 'And I can only apologise.'

'OK,' Michael replies, coolly. 'Apology accepted. So, how is she?'

'Mum?' Katy mumbles, uncertain how she's just managed to get off so lightly. 'A lot better – and all the more so, now, for being back home.'

'Well that's all right then,' he murmurs. Turning his attention back to the sizzling pan for a moment he gives it a stir then holds out his free hand towards Katy. 'Plug it in here, then.'

'Sorry?'

'Your mobile – you said it was flat.'

Reluctantly, she hands over the phone, holding her breath for a beat as he checks the screen then exhaling slowly as he finds it dead and connects it to the kitchen charger. 'That smells good,' she offers, tentatively.

'Onions and garlic – they always do.'

'Enough for two?'

'If you're hungry.'

'I am, though first I could really do with a bath.'

'Be my guest. Oh, and you'd better take these.' Michael extracts her house keys from his jeans back pocket.

'Oh,' Katy exclaims. 'I thought I'd lost them. Where did you—'

'You left them at Kevin's,' he answers tightly. 'He dropped them off earlier.'

'That's good,' she offers.

He frowns. 'What?'

Her smile fades. 'Only, I thought I might have locked him out.'

'He said the same, you know.' As Michael runs a hand through his hair he winces, briefly, as his fingers brush the cut above his eye. 'Then we had a little... chat. He's moved on, so you know. Kevin. Gone to north London to stay with some friends.'

'That's funny, I thought he said he worked not far from here...'

But Michael is no longer listening, his attention focused back on the saucepan. 'You go and sort yourself out Kat,' he murmurs. 'This will be another twenty minutes, at best.'

In the bathroom Katy adjusts the taps then places a freshly laundered towel over the radiator before rinsing her face in the sink. How can he be so calm, she wonders, patting her cheeks dry. It's not the time to question, though, but to be grateful. Because she needs him now more than ever. But before he can help she needs to come clean.

Sliding into the bath, Katy thinks of the many times since she found out she was pregnant he has talked about them being a team. She has to give him a chance to prove he really means it. Yet does she really dare test his love by revealing her true self? How typically Parker, she smiles, grimly. For she has never been at ease sharing confidences that really matter. Previous relationships eventually ran aground on her inability to provide the emotional intimacy expected, the longer each affair went on. But maybe it's not too late to change.

Maybe Michael is the one, the right man in the right place at the right time. She must at least try: he is her only hope.

Hope stirs and with it comes the realisation of how hungry she is. When did she last eat? She can't recall as she slips into the kitchen a short time later to find him seated at the kitchen counter with his back to the door. As she steps towards him Katy does not notice at first what he holds in his hand. Only as she enters his peripheral vision and his body tenses does she register her mobile phone in his hand. How he excavates its contents. Scanning contacts. Searching diary details, emails, texts.

Private things.

'Maybe I can help you find what you are looking for,' she says, only just managing to control her anger at this betrayal.

Michael's laugh as his body snaps towards hers is almost as lame as the excuse that follows. 'Sorry. I thought it rang and picked it up... but what with the noise of the fan... it must have been a phone ringing outside.'

Taking another step towards him, Katy holds out her hand. Reluctant to meet her gaze, he passes her the mobile then scoops up her bag, through which he's also been sifting, and jams the contents back inside.

'And there's this new app I thought you'd be interested in,' he continues, rising from his seat to take up his position once more at the stove. 'Just trying to be helpful, OK?'

Katy stares at the hunch of his back, fumbling for words to say. What's he been searching for? Doesn't he trust her? Is it any wonder? But anger stops her from voicing any of this.

'Space,' she snaps, briskly making her way towards the door. Desperate now to be away from him. She needs time now to work out how best to play this. To get her head straight. 'All I need's a little space, Michael. Why can't you just understand and let me be? You're always trying to butt in – upgrading this, downloading that. But you know what? You can't always fix everything and sometimes you've just got to accept that. Sometimes it's best just to hold me, to tell me you love me and that everything will be OK.'

Michael's face hardens. The tension in his body, all too evident from the angular set of his shoulders and the clenching and unclenching of his hands, tells her all she needs to know about his hurt and anger. Slowly, he shakes his head. And when at last he speaks his voice is low.

'Listen to yourself, Katy,' he begins, reaching across the kitchen counter for his wallet and keys. 'Then imagine, just for a moment, how it feels to be me. Held at arm's length. Locked out. Pushed away. And all because deep down inside you don't really trust me. Well I don't trust you very much any more, either, Katy. And it's tearing me apart. You've never been so distant and if you want to know the truth I feel sorry for our baby—'

'Michael—' Katy starts to object.

'We need to be a team, you and me, but it feels like we're living on two different islands,' he presses on, moving towards the door where he hesitates, briefly. 'Get a grip on yourself, Katy. Sort yourself out. It's time to grow up. Because there's only room for one child in this house – and I'm not talking about floor space.' Turning away from Katy, Michael steps out onto the landing then makes his way downstairs.

'Don't wait up, by the way,' he calls from the front door. 'I might be some time.'

Chapter 33

Let me tell you about my baby. A bit of a handful — as you'd expect — but not a bad boy. Though that's not what his teachers said. Disruptive, they called him. We had to keep changing schools, you know, until he walked out at the age of sixteen fit for nothing better than signing on. It was Siobhan's idea he join the army. And it could have been the making of him, too, if there hadn't been a fight one Saturday night in town. It was self-defence. Even so, he got a conviction for aggravated assault — more than enough for the army to throw him out. Failed by everyone but, as Siobhan always said: especially me. Which was rich coming from the one who'd spoiled him rotten.

Chapter 34

Hand over hand, like a diver battling buoyancy, Katy tugs herself towards oblivion; wills herself to sleep. Though she can only stay down so long and after just an hour or two she is wide awake, her mind fizzing with thoughts of Michael's betrayal. Lying on her side, her back towards him, she wonders what time he turned in. Whether he too is conscious in the half-light, restless and troubled. But the room is silent, the mattress still.

If she is gentle, maybe she can shift position without waking him. So cautiously repositioning her left leg to adjust her weight, she tilts her body then lowers her spine down onto the sheet before turning her head. But the far side of the bed is empty and, judging by the plumpness of the pillow, unused.

Katy glances at the bedside clock. It's half past four and though the sun is yet to rise the air is thick and soupy. Where did he sleep last night, she wonders, pulling herself upright.

The glass on the bedside table at her side is empty. Suddenly thirsty, she climbs out of bed, slips out onto the landing and towards the stairs. Down one flight and she finds the door of the study is open and the room inside is empty. Down another and she can see the kitchen is pristine. All the debris from last night's cooking has been neatly washed, dried then put away. Gently pushing open the sitting room door, she peers inside and sees a folded sheet and pillow resting on one arm of the sofa. Other than this, there's no sign that Michael's been there.

Turning around, Katy notices the door of the landing cupboard is ajar and pulls the handle. The shelf where he keeps his running stuff is empty and his trainers and Camelbak are also gone. But it's still so early – can he really have gone out for a run? It seems unlikely, but as she peers down through the half-light towards the front door she can see he has left it unchained.

Powered by a sudden fear of being found undressed when he returns, she hurries back upstairs to the bedroom and tugs on some clothes. Only as she starts to retrace her steps back towards the kitchen in search of iced water does she notice the door to Michael's store room, the one he uses for his cameras and usually keeps locked, is open. It is a small box room, barely large enough for a single bed, with a tiny window which when covered makes it ideal for developing photographs using his dad's old Leica.

Leaning against the wooden door panel, careful not to move it, Katy listens for any evidence of movement from within but there is none. Willing herself to ignore the drumming in her chest, she reaches out, gives the door a light push and peeps inside. Airless and stuffy, sealed from the outside world by a blackout blind drawn tightly across the window, the room is empty.

Curious, Katy steps inside and turns on the light. Against one wall is a narrow trestle table beneath which a selection of rigid metal boxes containing camera equipment are stowed. But it is what is on the table's top that catches her attention. Michael's laptop, open, beside a pile of papers. As she approaches, she brushes the table with her thigh making the sleeping screen flicker into life. At the sight of the St Olave's Hospice home page Katy's stomach clenches.

Why would he have this open on his screen, she wonders, as the previous evening's anger starts to stir. How dare he!

Reaching out towards the touchpad she hesitates for a moment. For isn't what she is about to do the same as what she last night condemned him for? But this is different. A response to his provocation. So she quickly opens his recent search history. As her eyes scroll from the bottom of the screen up, she sees a postcode she does not recognise and a Google Map she does – it's of the area where she went yesterday. Then there is a street map detailing Hill Rise, another mystery postcode and finally the hospice's details.

Has he been following her?

She notices the corner of her mobile just visible beneath the pile of paper. Tugging it free, she sees she has a text from Sally-Anne: 'Something big's come up – we need to speak ahead of Monday. Call me as soon as you get this.' Sent just an hour or two earlier. Christ, does the woman never sleep? As Katy exits the message, however, she notices something else – an icon on the phone's screen depicting two stick people; an app she's not noticed before. Curious, she taps it with her finger and sees a small icon moving across a local map and, beneath it, Michael's name.

Baffled, Katy turns to the computer and taps into Google the name of the app. The first result is a five star review of how it allows users to follow people by tracking the location of their mobile phone. Glancing back towards the map on her mobile she sees Michael, for the pulsing dot is surely him, moving along beside the river on the south side near Kew Bridge. He is on the return leg of his usual Thames-side running circuit, she realises. Fifteen maybe twenty minutes away.

Stunned, Katy's mind races as she tries to decide what to do. She could pretend she's seen none of this, of course – go back to bed like it didn't happen. But though she needs his help she must be able to trust him, too. Not that he can trust her, of course. For isn't that what all this is about? Trust or rather, lack of it. And it's all her fault. If she had opened up to him sometime sooner. The thought she might have left it too late makes her eyes well with tears.

As she wipes her face on her T-shirt, she reads for the first time the top sheet of the pile of papers. Notices the photo accompanying the estate agent details describing their home. How could he do this without telling me, she thinks, staring at the sheet now clutched in her hand. There is business card attached to a letter beneath bearing the same logo – from a company called Estelle Property Services.

Angrily, her eyes scan the letter of appointment. The standard terms and conditions. The sender's details. An Estelle Davies, Managing Director. Her throat tightens. Davies with an i-e-s, of course. But how...?

Tears come now, hot and fast. Because he's doing it, selling their home without telling her. Appointing Jude to manage it all, too. Which is some kind of scam on her part, of course. Another trick to get at them. But if that's all it is, why's she handwritten a personal message on the back of the business card? 'Always at your service,' it reads, above what must be Jude's mobile number beside which she's added, in brackets: 'Any time, day or night. x.'

Katy rams the card into her pocket and backs out of the room. She is outraged by his behaviour but fearful, too. With a barely suppressed sob, she thinks of Michael's lame excuse for searching her bag. How long has he been spying on her?

Spurred into action by the sudden thought that in just a few minutes he will return, Katy darts back towards their bedroom. She will stay at Mum's for a few days, she decides. For as long as it takes to get things straight. There's a twenty-four-hour mini cab office just ten minutes away but in the opposite direction to Michael's running route. That's where she will wait, unobserved, for a driver to take her to Richmond where she will find somewhere to wait, buy a coffee perhaps, for it to be late enough to wake her mum.

Katy scans the bedroom, fingers drumming on the chest of drawers as she tries to think. After what feels like minutes, she spots an old sports bag on the shelf above the cupboard. She has to clamber up onto a chair to tug it down then, as soon as it falls onto the floor, she is on her knees stuffing inside whatever's closest to hand. A change of clothes. Some underwear. A pair of plimsolls. From the bathroom, toiletries and make-up.

She hesitates, uncertain what else she should take, until she spots the bedside phone charger and crams it into her shoulder bag. Then she has an idea. Pulling free her mobile, she briskly keys in the number from Estelle Davies' card.

Enough's enough, she decides as she hurtles down the stairs two at a time. The words of the text she will send once she is safely belted inside the minicab start to assemble. *This has to end. Meet me this morning, alone. Text to confirm where.*

Chapter 35

He followed me to London. And do you want to know why I didn't stop him from getting involved? Stalking you. Hospitalising Diane. Pretending to be your downstairs neighbour. Because of those last weeks in the hospice. Those hours he spent by Siobhan's side soaking up her bile. And she almost won. Nearly turned him against me with her talk of his dad being the elder brother of a rich school friend. She was only guessing, of course. Because I said nothing — what right did she, of all people, have to know? He pinned me against the wall the night she died, you know. With his hand around my throat, taunting me to deny I was a dirty, lying slag when the only reason I said nothing was I didn't know. But it was all worth it, later, when he said sorry. Anything, I'll do anything, he cried, to make things right. What else could I do, Kat? At last, with Siobhan finally gone, I'd got James back.

Chapter 36

London, July 2013

The interior of The Rainbow Cafe smells of cheap margarine and fried fat. Inside a glass-fronted counter is an array of ice cream tubs filled with an assortment of sandwich fillings — shreds of iceberg; slivers of dry-edged cheese; a tuna concoction bearing a passing resemblance to cat food. To one side, a selection of rolls and bread slices are stacked in anticipation; to the other, days-old doughnuts make a stale pyramid. But all Katy orders is a drink.

Choosing a seat at the window, she perches on a stool then puts her cup onto the Formica ledge running the entire length of the window. Scattered strategically along the counter are plastic salt and pepper shakers like the ones she remembers from school. She doesn't need her fingers to brush the wipe-down surface to know it is sticky to the touch. On the street beyond the window, the early Sunday morning traffic is starting to build on Brompton Road.

Katy checks her watch. Nine o'clock outside the main entrance to the cemetery, she'd told Jude. A strange place to meet, perhaps, but one she knew well as Dad's buried here; a place she's chosen because it is familiar; somewhere she feels safe. Her lips curl into a half smile. Will Jude guess, she wonders? But her mood is dark.

Jude had tried to take control, of course. Suggested meeting somewhere else at a different time. But Katy was determined to remain strong. For both of them, she thinks, glancing down at her belly. Now it's just us two.

Her body braces as something hot and wet scalds her thigh. Coffee from the cup she's barely noticed she's still holding. What's wrong with you? the voice inside her demands as, with a fistful of paper serviettes from a nearby dispenser, she dabs herself dry. Inside her bag Katy finds a compact mirror which she now uses to inspect her face. Exhaling, slowly, she works every fibre of her being to regain control.

Yes, they are in this together, the two of them, as Jude said. Just like they always have been. Complicit. But in spite of her own fumbled attempts at self-denial, Katy now knows what she has done. But what will it take to make Jude go away?

From her vantage point beside the window Katy can monitor the approach of any passers-by from either direction. The pavement the near side of the busy thoroughfare is almost deserted. Across the road, though, pedestrian traffic is busier and a flower seller is doing brisk trade from his mobile stall beside the cemetery's wrought iron gates. Glancing down she checks the screen of her mobile phone which rests on her lap, juggling for a beat in the hope that Michael has sent some message by way of an apology. But there's no evidence he's even tried to get in contact.

A phone rings behind the cafe's counter. The man who's just served her, a middle-aged Pole with grey hair who's teased his dark moustache into a tight curl either side of his nose, answers the call.

Staring at the only other customer, an old woman sitting alone in the corner nursing an empty tea cup, Katy listens idly to the man's guttural response as he grunts into the receiver. The distraction is a welcome one. The call ends and then, like a novelty town crier, he clears his throat to broadcast his announcement.

'Is there a Catparker here?' The voice is heavily accented and his smile encouraging as his gaze darts between the two women until one of them, Katy, nods.

'Yes, that's me.'

'Message for you,' he continues. 'Mrs Jody says she has change of plan. You will meet her inside. Go to the bench by the war memorial halfway down Central Avenue.'

How dare she? Though this is text book Jude, of course. Even if it is odd she didn't bother calling Katy direct on her mobile. Because both network coverage and battery level are fine, she notes, glancing down at the screen. Noticing the time, she wonders if, with five minutes still to go, Jude's inside already waiting. Slipping off the stool, she approaches the counter to pay, then with a nod turns to leave.

'Only a short walk,' the man smiles. 'But use main entrance, not West Gate. Just three or four minutes at most.'

–

Inside the cemetery, Katy hurries along the Central Avenue towards the main gate. It has taken her longer than she hoped to reach the Brompton Road exit from the Fulham end at the far side of the domed chapel, not far from Dad's grave. And all she wants now is to reach the meeting point in good time.

Checking her watch once more, Katy finds herself hungry for their meeting – unlike last time. For things have gone far enough. People – Mum, for God's sake – are getting hurt. Which is why all this has got to stop, she thinks, touching the barely perceptible lump of scar tissue on her upper hand for a moment; grateful for the reminder of it. How even now, the injustice it embodies keeps her strong.

She may only be starting to get used to the idea that Jude's real father was her own; that the anger and resentment Jude clearly still feels towards her is for this as much as it is for what she did on the heath that long, hot summer's day. Yet she is in no doubt the time has come to stop running; to challenge and defend herself from the campaign of retribution waged by Jude and her son. Her phone rings. Expecting it to be Jude she answers it without checking the screen then stumbles to a halt at the sound of Sally-Anne's voice.

'Is there something you want to tell me?' her boss demands.

'Sorry?' Katy mumbles, blindsided by both the woman's meaning and tone.

'When you offer someone a leg up professionally speaking you expect some kind of acknowledgement, at least – unless they're playing you off against a better offer from somebody else. So what's the story. Are you thinking of leaving?'

'Leaving? What, me? Really, no. It's just that now, well, it's not really a good—'

'It's Sunday morning, I know. And we're meeting tomorrow morning, of course. But I need to talk to you ahead of that. Today. Because there's—'

'No,' Katy interrupts, firmly. 'I'm sorry, Sally-Anne but... I'm flattered, and definitely interested... and more than happy to speak to you later today if you need to. But I really... can't do this... not right now.'

Sally-Anne laughs. 'You're out running,' she exclaims. 'Why didn't you say?'

'I did try—'

'Keep at it, and call me back when you get back home.'

Thrusting her phone back into her pocket, Katy tries to get her bearings. Just ahead, an imposing wall of arches line the avenue on either side sheltering the grey battalions of silent figures, marble tombs and stone crosses that face the footpath like hungry crowds. A few paces on, the avenue cuts through open ground that's rough and grassy.

Here, the cemetery is mathematically dissected by smaller footpaths leading away from the high rent, city centre domain of the rich and influential to memorials of humbler scale scattered randomly beneath bushes and trees. So she runs on until, at last, in the distance but fast approaching, she sees the main gates. Their bleak ironwork is thrown open wide to embrace all comers – legitimate mourners, the curious or simply exhausted refugees from the hectic Brompton Road.

Almost there, she thinks, darting left along the gravelled footpath that she knows will lead her to West Gate and, beyond,

The Rainbow Cafe. But before she can reach it she sees a familiar figure crossing the avenue ahead. A figure which she recognises immediately.

'Jude,' Katy shouts. 'Stop. You're going the wrong way.'

With a diesel roar, the nearby traffic suddenly snaps back to life and the sound of it swiftly carries her words away. Which explains why the figure ahead shows no sign of having heard her. So Katy presses on, quickening her pace to narrow the gulf between them; tugging free her mobile from her pocket at the sudden sound of a text alert.

Change of plan, it reads. *Meet me by the war memorial halfway down Central Avenue.*

Just keep on running, she thinks with grim determination as the path spins away beneath her; as the knuckled ground bruises her pounding feet. Bridge the gap, override the stitch now ripping into her side. How the hastily-packed bag on her shoulder makes the skin beneath her armpit chafe.

'Jude,' she roars. 'Wait!'

But the distant figure turns off the central path then disappears from view down one of its tributaries.

Anxiously, Katy scans the point at which she last saw Jude for any memorable landmark. On the side of the avenue opposite where she'd just been standing looms a tall statue of an angel, its broad wings bone-white against a bleached sky. At its feet she can just make out from this distance a seated figure dressed in red. She hurries on, stopping only when she reaches the junction to pause, briefly, bending double to pinch away the stitch which is now tearing into her side.

On the bench before her sits a whale of a woman with waist-length hair wearing an expansive green T-shirt bearing the unseasonal plea: *Unwrap Me for Christmas*. Gazing blankly into the middle distance, her only movement comes from dough-like hands as she strips from a loaf on her lap hunks of bread to toss at a ragged scattering of pigeons on the ground at her feet.

'Sorry, but… did you see…' Katy pants, forcing a smile as the woman refocuses her gaze in her direction. '…A tall, slim woman… with dark hair… come along here… a few minutes ago?' Without a word, the woman raises her free hand and points. Straightening up, Katy spots the side path to her left that Jude must have taken and hurries on.

Unlike the main avenue the path she now finds herself on is rocky and uneven. Its surface is cracked by the sun's heat and clumped by the subterranean Spaghetti Junction of ancient roots beneath. Her ankles jar with every pace. Just one misplaced foot will launch her, tumbling, towards the ground.

Yet on she runs, no longer fuelled just by the need to reach Jude but a preternatural urge triggered by memory of that dreadful day. A memory that's no longer an immovable fact buried away from view deep inside. Because it has become a sudden flare, fast-rising upwards like a rocket, that promises to light the pathway she must take to confront then overcome the horror of the past.

At last, Katy arrives at a sunbleached bench marked by pale patches of lichen. It sits in the centre of a gravel clearing bordered on three sides by rhododendron bushes. To its right is an imposing slab of marble streaked with green: a memorial to an earlier battle. On the shingle at its foot lies the remnants of a dusty wreath of last year's Remembrance poppies.

'Hey,' calls Jude, suddenly appearing a short distance behind. Hot and dishevelled, her face is flushed. As she draws level she lets her shoulder bag slip to the ground with a dull thud. Bending double, she rubs her side vigorously before turning her head towards the bench. 'Didn't… you hear me? I've… been trying… to catch you up… since the… gate.'

'Better late than never,' Katy declares, coolly. Though as she rises to her feet she finds she is genuinely relieved to see her, and alone. 'I was beginning to think this was some kind of a wild goose chase.'

'What… do you mean?'

'Your messages – changing where to meet?'

Jude frowns. 'Your message, you mean. What was wrong with the caff – coffee there not up to your standards?'

'The man behind the counter gave me your message, remember?' Katy retorts.

But Jude, bored by the exchange, waves her hand dismissively. 'So what's so urgent?' she demands. 'As if I didn't know. Because you want to know if I've said anything, don't you? To Michael and to Diane. And, if not, whether I will. Because I'm the only one apart from you who knows what you did. And before you ask, whether I will say something, some time, comes down to you.'

'To me?' Katy echoes, determined to stand her ground; battling to resist the age-old urge to run.

'I said, it's your choice.' Jude seems taller, somehow, as she takes a step forward. 'Or to put it in the words of your dearly departed father: you scratch my back, and I'll scratch yours. Convince your mum and Andrew to do their duty by us and I can make sure all of it goes away like you want it to. What all of you did to me and my mum – no one will ever know. But it will cost you. Oh, and I'd like to hear you say sorry.'

'Sorry?'

'Not good enough,' Jude snaps. 'Try harder.'

'I mean, I don't understand,' Katy answers, coolly. Her voice, though low, is calm and measured which elicits a barely perceptible change in Jude's expression; a flicker of doubt. 'Of course I remember what happened out on the heath that day. And you will never know how sorry I am for what I did. But he was… you were… it was awful. And a very long time ago. And trust me, every day since I've had to deal with the memory of it. To try not to think of what happened. To hope that after everything, you were OK. Which was all I wanted, Jude – to help you—'

'Crap,' Jude interjects. 'Because you were jealous of me – hated me, too. It was easy to read, just like it was easy to see you fancied me. Which probably explains why you were so moody the whole time, because you couldn't have me. Believe me, Kat, you always were the world's worst actress.'

Livid, Katy lurches forwards. 'If I hated you it was because of how you treated me,' she spits. 'You were a bully – still are, by what I can see. A bitch to me and to everyone else you come into contact with – no wonder Andrew didn't want you.'

'Don't you dare—' Jude's hands are clenched, her eyes are slits.

'Not so in control now, are you? Because it's true, isn't it: Andrew saw right through you and dumped you, and you never quite got over it.'

'You don't know anything,' Jude jeers. 'Never did.'

'Don't I? Really? I know you screwed your own half-brother and Siobhan tried to blackmail my dad—'

'No more than they deserved,' Jude snaps. 'He was a great shag, by the way,' she spits, though tears now glisten in her eyes. 'Even if I'd known I wouldn't have cared.'

'You stalked my mum and had something to do with the mugging,' Katy presses on. Buoyed by the realisation that her words are hitting home, she steels herself against being deflected. 'And you've been stalking me, too – trying to spoil things for me. I know you met with Michael pretending to be an estate agent. I know enough to really drop you in it when I go to the police—'

'I stalked you? But you put the wedding announcement in the paper – Siobhan showed it to me. Honestly, Kat, you weren't that hard to find.' Then Jude lets slip an unexpected burst of laugher.

'As for the police, well, you won't do that, will you?' she presses on. 'Because you'd have to come clean and you've too much to lose. We're more alike than you think, Kat. The two of us: such accomplished liars! Though hats off to you, girl, I think maybe you have the edge on that count. I mean just think about what you all did – your mum and dad, especially... Because the lies we tell are nothing compared to the lies we tell ourselves.'

Incensed by the smug expression on her opponent's face, Katy's fists clench. 'Go on, surprise me,' she challenges. 'What have my mum and dad got to do within any of this?'

But then, a beat later, her attention is elsewhere. A barely perceptible shift in the sound and shade of the undergrowth behind them has made Katy aware that they are alone in this distant, far-flung corner of the cemetery. Vulnerable and exposed. As, with a snap of a twig, the undergrowth close by parts like a curtain through which steps a wiry, clench-fisted missile of a man.

Fearfully, Katy registers the snapback baseball hat worn back to front this time to reveal the embroidered message on the back: No Lie. The toned body beneath the sleeveless Everlast hoodie and low-slung combat trousers. The tattoo like a band of thorns which encircles his upper arm. His pockmarked face, almost handsome, now pinched into a look of eager expectation as he slips his wire-framed sunglasses into his back pocket. The swollen, purple ring around his right eye.

'What are you doing—' Jude begins. She seems genuinely surprised, Katy can see. At the look of him, perhaps. For without the lank ponytail, he looks quite different. Like Robert de Niro in that film about an American army vet.

'I might just ask the same of you,' he glares, waving a hand accusingly at Jude. 'Didn't I warn you not to try and cut me out? But I'm not as stupid as I look, you know. I mean, why else do you think I brought the two of you here? Like the new hair cut, by the way? Not to worry, I didn't do it for you.'

Then he turns to Katy, lunges towards her and laughs at her flinch. 'Catching up on the good old days, or just being nosey? You should be more careful,' he sneers. 'Don't you know what curiosity did to the cat?'

Katy tries to swallow but her mouth is dry as she stares at him in horror. It is the youth from the park. The charity fundraiser who came to her front door. The mechanic from the garage at Siobhan's place. The stranger from the flat downstairs. Though desperate to run, Katy finds herself struggling to remember how.

'Stop it,' Jude says, firmly. 'It's over. Let it go.'

'Too late. And you've only got yourself to blame.' As he turns back towards Katy his lips twitch. 'By the way – nice to see you again, Auntie Kat.'

Katy stares at him, confused.

'Enough,' cries Jude, springing to her feet. 'James? I mean it. Things have gone far enough. No, James, wait—'

In less than a second he has hold of her right arm and is twisting it upwards, sharply, at an awkward angle behind her back. 'I don't think so,' he mutters, darkly. 'Because, Mother dearest, this is only the beginning. You may not have the balls to follow through, but I certainly do. And I am not going to let this go. So, come on girls—' As James releases Jude abruptly, making her stumble, he shoots Katy a broad smile that marks the widening of his address. 'Sit down, why don't you,' he offers, gesturing toward the bench his mother has just vacated. 'Get comfortable. Let's have ourselves a nice little family parlay.'

Glancing towards Jude, who's begun to back towards the bench, Katy's unsure which is worse – the fear, like rising flood water, now pushing against her feeble defences or her friend's meek compliance. What sort of trick are they trying to pull off? A sudden anger burns in her as she sees an image of her mum from a few days earlier, when she first saw her in hospital. Well she's not about to play.

Anxiously, she calculates the quickest route back to the gate: a zigzag dash between overgrown paths. She remembers this part of the cemetery from previous visits with Michael and recognises the war memorial as one they'd returned to a number of times after finding an inscription to commemorate a First World War soldier who had the same name as his. This time, she thinks, it won't take long to get help.

'You've been following me.' A statement of fact not a question, spoken simply by Jude as if to a child. 'Last night?' James grins. 'And this morning, probably. Then here. You rang the cafe, too, then messaged me.' He nods. 'OK, well now we've got that straight let's get this sorted. This ends right here, right now.'

Distracted by thoughts of her escape, Katy is looking the wrong way when James pounces.

Yet it is neither surprise nor brute strength that incapacitates her as surely as a bullet to the knee, but the knife in his hand. The sort you find in a tool box, with an easy-grip handle. Though its tip looks small, she can see from its angle that the blade is sharp. So she hesitates, just for a moment, and in that instant he has looped his left arm around her neck and pressed his right hand, and the blade it holds, against her side.

Still, just keep still, Katy tells herself over and over, trying not to think how close the sliver of metal is to the just perceptible bulge of her belly. So close to him now she hears the rasping of his breath; inhales the pungent smell of his sweat. Unable to turn her head, her eyes dart towards Jude, silently pleading. But as Katy registers the look of fear on her face she knows the situation has quickly spiralled beyond her control.

It's hard to breathe now, impossible to talk. Then she hears another voice.

'Enough,' Jude says calmly. 'Put the knife down.'

James lets slip a feral snarl.

'I said, that's enough.'

Jude is closer this time, moving towards him like a trainer attempting to pacify a crazed animal. The arm around Katy's neck retightens its grip making the cemetery slip in and out of focus. Dizzy, she tries to focus on something. Anything. The memorial. The gathering breeze which has begun to stir the bushes. The familiar voice now pleading on her behalf. Desperate to save her.

'Talk to me. Tell me what you want.'

'I want what's mine,' he snaps. 'And I'm tired of waiting.'

'And you'll get it, too,' Jude soothes. 'Just as long as you don't do anything stupid.'

The hand holding the knife presses harder against Katy's side making her cry out in fear. What is he talking about, she wonders, wildly. What can she or Diane possibly have that belonged to him?

314

'James, give me the knife,' the other woman repeats, taking another step towards them. 'Stop this now.'

James looks down at Katy. 'What's it to be, Auntie Kat?' he whispers, softly. 'Junior? You? Or should I pay another visit to Granny?'

'James—' Jude warns.

'It's a bit late to go all soft on me, Mother dearest, don't you think?' her son retorts. 'You made me, after all. You and all you lies. We asked you – begged you – didn't we, Nan and I? Not to do to me what she did to you. But you couldn't bring yourself to tell me the simple truth about my dad.'

Teetering on the edge of consciousness, Katy's eyes dart between Jude and James as she struggles to keep pace with this switchback of a conversation. She fears she has started to hallucinate; convinces herself she is about to die. He's clearly mad, and as she has no idea what he's talking about, anything she does risks provoking him further. And yet despite this – against all rational thought – she finds herself struggling to speak.

It's as if she is fuelled by a gathering momentum as, some-where at the back of her mind, the shadow once more starts to stir. 'But I'm not your aunt,' she rasps. 'My mum's not your nan. Because there's no way that my brother is or could ever have been your dad. Because he can't have kids.'

James glares at Katy with burning eyes but says nothing, as if preoccupied with an internal battle to extract order from his chaos of conflicting thoughts. Shooting a desperate look towards Jude, Katy sees the leaching colour in the other woman's face as she opens her mouth, hesitates, tries to speak, fails, then tries again in a faltering voice.

'What do you mean?' cries Jude.

'Can't… He and Dee tried… every doctor.'

'But he had twins.'

'Dee had twins—' Katy corrects, gaining in confidence now at a perceptible loosening of James's grip around her neck though it's still not enough for her to wriggle free '—using donor sperm.'

'No, no, that can't be right, I know, all right? It was him, because...' Unable to identify a reason, Jude falters.

'An immaculate conception?' James challenges. Statue-like Jude stands in silence, her eyes fixed to the ground. Passive now, it's as if she's resigned herself to something inevitable. 'Because there was no one else, right?' he goads, angered by her silence.

'No,' Jude whispers. Her face is ashen. She swallows hard then pushes a loose strand of hair behind her ear with a trembling hand.

As son stares at mother his face twists into a knot of hatred and resentment. 'Who?' he demands, abruptly dragging Katy forwards with such unexpected force she stumbles.

'Oh Mum,' Jude murmurs, shaking her head. 'I never meant to... didn't know.'

Regaining her balance Katy stares, waiting for her to elaborate.

'Who?' James demands impatiently.

'A long time ago... he lived with us for a while...'

'What, your mum's boyfriend?' Katy blurts.

As soon as it's out she knows from Jude's expression it must be true. How often he came early to collect Jude from hockey practice, she recalls. How he'd lean nonchalantly against the bonnet of his car, arms crossed, as he waited for the girls to finish their game. How Jude had grinned as she described the casual confidence of him as he stalked the house shower-fresh dressed only in a knotted towel. How he'd rarely been there on any of the times she'd stopped at Jude's house. Had all of that been coincidence?

Like playing with a loaded gun, Jude once confided, was how her mum described him. An analogy lost on Katy at the time, but not now.

It was him, she thinks, as the air starts to thin and the world around her dance like beaten metal. The man in black. The man who... It was her. She hurt him, to save Jude. Because he was... just to make him stop. So she'd hit him, hard. With a blunt branch across the back of his head. Stopped him, too. Left him lying there. Still and unmoving.

Katy lets slip a single sob.

'Un-fucking-believable,' James snorts. 'Because it's lie after lie after lie with you, isn't it, you slut. So go on, thrill me. Where is he now?'

Dead, Katy knows as, desperate to hold the word back, she covers her mouth with her hand.

The same hand she used all those years ago to grab the branch and swing it high, feeling the weight of it gather momentum as she crashed it downwards with all her force. How heavily he fell onto Jude, crushing her momentarily until she scrambled free. The look on her face. The venom with which she spoke. The shame of the uncontrollable passions that had driven her.

Anger and fear and something else. Jealousy.

But as hard as she tries, Katy cannot stop the truth from tumbling out even as her mouth dries, her throat tightens and tears start to come. 'I—' she begins, then falters. Fumbling for the right words, she dominates the heavy silence as the spotlight of their attention turns to her. 'Dave – he's dead.'

It takes time for the word to be absorbed, slowly, like water on parched ground. But then, in a beat, James has released his grip and Katy's foot is slipping. Her legs buckle and she is crashing to the ground, howling in fear and pain as she twists her body in a desperate attempt not to fall on her bump. Then she is down on the path sprawled on her front, scraping her knees across shards of stone as she slides onto her side into a foetal position.

Hugging herself tight, she wills the tiny life inside to be OK. Gulping for air, she pulls herself on all fours, desperately trying to gather her strength. Ignoring how her hip throbs with pain, she stares at the scabbed earth before her which is boiling with slick-winged ants readying for flight.

'No,' Jude declares. 'She's wrong.'

Unable to decipher the meaning of Jude's words Katy watches, dumbly, as James strides towards his mum and pushes her backwards with the heel of his palm. Clambering back onto her feet, Jude takes a faltering step to regain her balance before he pushes her again, harder this time, then raises his fist.

'What did you say?' he cries.

'You heard me,' Jude gasps, struggling to right herself. 'Dave. He's alive. Because there was another girl on the heath that day who saw the fire and fetched help. And before she did she saw him, but when help came he'd gone. Not burned, thank God. I never should have—' Suddenly, she lets slip a clipped laugh. 'Just gone. I always wondered… There was a break-in not long after we left and they only took his stuff which Mum had stacked in the garage, you see. Then when I saw Ruth recently she confirmed it.'

Jude stares her son straight in the eye as if daring him to strike her, which, a moment later, he does. Spinning to her left, she falls backwards onto the ground where she lies, barely moving, her body crumpled against the base of a tall headstone worn smooth by time into the anonymous shape of a human thigh. Crimson fingers of blood reach down one cheek from a gash just above her left eye. Her face is waxen and her breath is coming in shallow gulps.

'Stop it,' Katy cries, stumbling to her feet.

But all of a sudden her body feels light. As if the boulder that's pinned her to that moment all these years has rolled away. She braces her arms then lunges with all her strength at James as he stands gazing at Jude, whose battered face tilts to one side revealing blood smeared on the plinth against which she is lying. The papers spewing from her opening bag. Estate agents' details depicting Michael's flat.

Katy's unexpected broadside takes him by surprise and he loses his balance. Gauging the distance she'll need to cover to get back to the gate, Katy knows she'll not outrun him. So she steps out of his reach then turns to face him down.

'Maybe you could track him down,' she challenges, every fibre of her being now braced for his response.

'Maybe I could,' he retorts. 'If I had some money. And your family has money, right? I mean, think about it. First your dad, then your mum paid off Siobhan to get her to leave town, and now he's dead she still has enough to live in a penthouse apartment that must cost a pretty penny or two? I'm sure that between you, you could see me right. Sorry about the cat, by the way.'

Swiftly lunging forwards, James swings out his arm and catches Katy low and hard in the solar plexus. Then he laughs. 'It was a spur of a moment kind of thing.'

Poor old Monty, is all Katy can think as she crumples downwards. But as her head hits the stony ground she is aware only of something else. A familiar somersaulting sensation in her stomach that stops, abruptly, as a shaft of pain sears her lower abdomen. Its epicentre is just at the point where the baby now sits.

'Not nice, is it—' Jude's voice is cracked and breathy. 'Someone else taking control of your life?'

As she clutches her belly Katy hears a low, guttural moan. Though it's come from nearby the sound seems barely human. *No*, shrieks the voice inside her. Don't let this happen. Keep with me. Be strong. Clenching her thighs, she wills the child inside to still be OK. Thinks for a beat, too, that the moan comes from her. Until she opens her eyes and sees, as if in slow motion, James's legs buckle and fold. The next moment he is on his side on the ground. Groaning like a wounded animal. His body fishtailing in the dust.

Only then does she notice the feet of someone standing over him; male by the size of them, she sluggishly reasons as it takes her a moment or two to recognise the ankle before her bearing a familiar tattoo. Slowly, Katy raises her eyes to meet Michael's. In one hand he is holding a heavy branch, in the other he clutches James's knife.

319

'All I could find at short notice.' He frowns at the figure on the ground. 'And you, whoever you are, had better stay down there if you know what's good for you, OK?'

As the world around her starts to fold in on itself, darkening from the edges, inwards, Katy hears from someone close by – maybe her – emit a low, guttural groan.

Tossing away his makeshift club, Michael steps towards her then stops, abruptly. There is a sharp intake of breath. 'Oh Christ, Katy. Lie still, OK?' he begins reaching into his pocket for his mobile phone. 'Breath slowly to stay calm,' he murmurs, once the ambulance is on its way. Barely able to nod she is too stunned to speak as he squats by her side and softly strokes her head. 'Don't try to get up – the operator said it will just make the bleeding worse.'

Only as she becomes aware of the wetness between her legs; she understands the words he's just fired into his phone. 'My fiancée's just been attacked and it looks like she's having a miscarriage,' he said. 'Send someone, quickly.' And then, a single sob, 'As soon as you can, please.'

Chapter 37

West Hampstead, September 2013

Rain drums the pane of the open window with a sound like children's heels, the force of it forming small puddles along the wooden sill. In the world outside, the parched city slowly lifts its head; opening itself up to embrace the deluge while tall buildings kiss the sky.

Katy raises the sash further. Oblivious to the downpour now clumping her hair, she leans outside. Her gaze ranges across the rooftops of north London towards the distant patch of green marking the start of the heath. Her bare arms shine slick with wet, but she doesn't care. For change is coming and the summer has broken. It's five to eleven. Almost five weeks to the hour since the confrontation in the cemetery. Thirty-five days since Jude and James's arrest. The day she and Michael have agreed for him to come to the new flat with the last of her stuff.

There were phone calls. Maybe a nurse had lent Jude a phone during her stay in hospital. Pleading her innocence, of course. Urging Katy to meet one more time.

But instead, Katy told the police about Jude's calls. How, due to their frequency they felt little short of malicious. This and her behaviour while in custody led to Jude's application for bail being turned down. She will stand trial soon for blackmail, fraud and encouraging and assisting James who, facing charges for possession of stolen goods, burglary and assault, is also now being held on remand thanks to a past conviction for grievous bodily harm.

At last, the fear is gone.

Whether Katy sees Jude again or not, she no longer cares. Certainties provide little consolation; uncertainties even less. Neither change the way she now feels. Numb, at last, to Jude's influence. Distanced but also, in her pity for her, reconciled. Which is how, staring at the envelope of the letter she received in the post earlier that morning from HM Prison East Sutton Park, she finds the strength not to wonder at Jude's message within but, instead, to tear it into halves, then quarters, then eighths before tossing it into the bin.

Katy turns back to face the interior of the flat where she's been staying since moving out from Michael's. It belongs to Spike, though he's in little need of it these days, as he rarely – if ever – comes to London during the summer months. Staying here was Michael's suggestion. Just like spending some time apart was his idea, too, though she supposes she'd have suggested it if he hadn't.

The anxious hours they spent in hospital, the awkward explanation to Diane then its replay via a lousy Skype link to Andrew had drawn so heavily on her emotional reserves she'd little strength left to focus clearly on what should happen next between her and Michael. Which is how, as days passed, the situation had drifted.

Temporarily, she'd moved into Diane's spare bedroom. Then, when Michael had suggested that maybe some time apart would be good for both of them, rather than get to grips with how she felt and what she really wanted, she'd dully acquiesced. Convinced there'd be no post New York-style reconciliation this time around. Maybe he was right, she'd concluded miserably. Because what he really seemed to be suggesting was that their relationship had run its course.

Now Katy stares at the cardboard boxes of her belongings that line the far side of the sitting room wall. There seems little point in unpacking them all, given how few of her clothes still fit her these days. Spike says she can stay here as long as she needs to, which she hopes won't be long. For now, though, it's a welcome base from which to gather herself and start moving forward – which she must do, for both their sakes.

She looks at her work suit hanging from the door frame still wrapped in its plastic, adjusted and dry-cleaned. She's due back on Monday following a combination of sick days and holiday leave. Sally-Anne has found someone else to replace Miriam, of course. But luckily for Katy, the role will be filled just for eighteen months by a woman from Janssens' New York office who wants to be in London only for the duration of her husband's temporary reassignment from a US city bank to its UK headquarters near St Pauls. If all goes well, the promotion could still be Katy's next time.

A distant church bell chimes the hour. He's late. But as she glances at her watch to confirm it she hears a tentative knock on the inside front door. He has a key, she knows, but will not use it unless invited. So she steps onto the landing. Shoots a quick look through the peephole, just to be sure. Then she opens the door.

'Hi.' With a tentative smile, Michael puts down the boxes he has carried up four flights of stairs then shakes himself free of the holdall slung over one shoulder.

'You're soaking,' Katy exclaims, padding into the bathroom to find a towel.

'Sorry,' he replies, stepping back onto the door mat where he slips off his jacket and trainers and towels the excess from his face and hair.

'Go straight in,' she calls from the kitchen where she fills a kettle to make tea. How horribly formal, she thinks with a grimace as she pops a builder's tea bag into a mug for him and a herbal sachet into her own. A sad marker of how far things have come. 'Make yourself comfortable.' At this, she winces. 'I'll be right in.'

He is leaning out of the window, just as she had done earlier, when she enters the room with the drinks a few minutes later.

Only the rain has stopped now and the low cloud looks as if it might soon stir. She hands him his tea then takes a seat on the sofa, cradling hers in cupped hands. He stares at her directly for the first time, appraises her for a moment, then almost smiles.

'You're looking good,' he offers. 'Both of you, I mean.'

Looking down across the swollen shape of her, the thickening ankles she can now only see when her legs are raised at a certain angle, she frowns. 'You are joking.' She blows out her cheeks to emphasise her point. 'About me, at least. I'm becoming a human whale. Sprog though, well, you're right...' She casts a quick glance towards the printout from the twenty-week scan that sits on the shelf above the fireplace. 'He is perfect.'

But Michael frowns. 'Seriously, I mean it – you're glowing.'

Katy's face burns. 'Today is nine years since my dad died, you know,' she blurts suddenly, regretting it as soon as the words are out. But it is too late. Michael looks crestfallen and the air between them has cooled.

'Really, I didn't know that,' he murmurs, taking an awkward sip from his mug.

Conscious now of the set of house keys in her pocket – Michael's house keys which she will shortly be returning to him for the final time – Katy's throat tightens.

What am I doing, she wonders. How did I let things get to this? It is the anniversary of her dad's death, and she has been thinking of this a lot this morning. How long ago all of that business now seems. How time passes and the world moves on. And the anniversary is simply that. A calendar date that marks the further passing of time.

A day, today, which in future will also be the day she and Michael split.

The poke inside her belly, just below her rib, is as forceful as it is unexpected. So sudden, too, that it makes her almost gasp. He'll be a handful, this one, she thinks. And he'll certainly keep them – her – on their toes.

Michael leans forward, eager and alive with expectation. 'Is it the baby kicking?'

'It was,' she sighs, her face softening as she pats the seat beside her. 'Come see.'

They sit together, side by side, her hand on his as she directs him to the point where she guesses the foot will next strike. For it is the baby's foot, she's sure of it, and the kicks almost always come in twos and threes. They sit quietly for nearly a minute, almost unmoving, breathing as one. And then it happens – less powerful this time, but unmistakable – and when they look at each other next she wonders whether it's her imagination or are his eyes a little shinier than usual?

'How have you been?' she asks him, softly. The question makes his shoulders dip.

'I've a new job starting soon,' he answers. 'You remember that headhunter I told you about? Well, you're looking at the soon-to-be senior creative partner at Octagon.'

'Well done you,' she exclaims. Noticing a fleck of something trapped in his hair, she reaches out without thinking to remove it.

Intercepting her hand with his own, Michael reaches up to pat the front of his head then, locating his target, tugs it free. 'Paint,' he smiles, ruefully. 'I've been redecorating the office back home. I cleared everything out and got rid of loads.'

She nods her approval. 'White?'

'A blank canvas. Until... I... decide what to do.'

Katy swallows hard. Her mouth feels dry and the keys in her pocket seem hot against her thigh. Can he really want this? she wonders. Does she?

Shutting her eyes, she sees her dad's face. Her mum the age she was when Katy was at school. A younger Jude. It's her own fault – all of this. If only she had been honest sooner. Trusted him to be on her side. Learned her lesson from the time he spent those months in New York. Why hadn't she followed through with her plan to confide everything once he'd returned?

Because back then, she wasn't being honest with herself. Buried memories. A repressed truth. Whatever the official name for it, there was no way she could open up to Michael if she was lying to herself. And now? At last, now that she's at peace, she knows for sure that she wants him and to be with him, forever, more than anything she has ever wanted before. Opening her eyes, she fears she might cry.

What was it Jude said about the worst lies we tell being the lies we tell ourselves? If she doesn't stop now she's going to lose him, for good.

'I should have talked to you, I know,' she says, reaching into her pocket and closing her fingers around the keys. Awkwardly, she dips her gaze. *Like peeling the layers of an onion*, he'd once said. 'About everything. Far sooner. But I didn't, and you don't know how sorry I now feel for that.' Michael opens his mouth as if to speak but she holds up a hand to make him wait. 'Which makes it all the more clear to me now that what I'm about to say must be said and can't wait.' Putting down her mug, Katy raises her gaze to meet his. Scans it briefly, eager for any sign of encouragement. Though for the moment his expression is blank. 'Michael,' she says, holding up his house keys. 'Can I keep these?'

But now he looks confused. 'Sorry?'

'The keys to... our place.' Michael frowns. She tries again. 'Because what we had was good and could be great if both of us want to make it work. And I do, Michael – I really do. Now there's nothing left to tell.' At last, he nods. 'Michael?'

'Keep them,' he says, his lips softening into a slow smile. 'You can come back any time, but sooner would be best. For good. If you really mean it and really want to.'

Leaning towards him, Katy plants a firm kiss on his cheek. 'How about today?'

Taking her hand, Michael gives it a squeeze.

'Today, then,' she nods, firmly.

'No point unpacking anything else then.' Michael casts a glance towards the boxes stacked on the floor the far side of the room.

Katy smiles. 'I guess not.'

'Apart from this.' Michael rises to his feet to retrieve a small carrier bag he left with the other things in the hallway by the front door. Slipping the contents free of the damp plastic, he hands Katy a small parcel loosely-wrapped. 'It's from your mum.'

Diane has folded whatever it is inside brown paper.

It's the shape of a slimline hardback book though as she feels it through the wrapping Katy realises it is something else. Intrigued, she slips off the paper then the inner sleeve of bubble wrap and pops both in the bin on the floor by her side on top of the fragments of Jude's letter, unopened and unread. She stares at the reverse of a chestnut picture frame. Hinged at the centre, it has space for two photos, side by side.

Carefully, Katy turns it over to see in one space a tatty Polaroid, its colours diluted by time to a tea-stained patina. An image of a young child whose fine hair shines white in the sun's glare. If she screws up her eyes just so she can see she is dressed in a simple sundress in a blameless sky blue. On her feet are a pair of strawberry sandals. At the bottom Mum's left a brief handwritten message: *Seize the day!*

Unable to resist a smile, Katy turns the picture back over and refocuses her attention onto her childhood self. Will their baby be like this, she wonders marvelling at the stubborn set of her shoulders. The defiant frown. And looming, shadow-like, somewhere close by but as yet unseen, the life she would lead. Katy turns towards Michael who, judging by his expression, has been wondering something similar. As they stare at one another for a heartbeat, Katy senses something lifting.

The weight of the past perhaps, she thinks, heady with expectation. Then, as their eyes meet, they laugh as one – a joyous sound which scatters memories like mice.

Chapter 38

There's this Patti Smith track that means a lot to me, you know — and I've had plenty of time to listen to it recently. I heard it first when James was in nappies and, if you want to know the truth, Kat: it's always helped keep me together, you know? So there's this line from it I just can't get out of my head. A line that now makes me think about you. 'I don't fuck much with the past,' it goes, 'but I fuck plenty with the future.' Well the way I see it, Kat, I fuck with both, you know? Which is why if there's one thing I could tell you now, face to face, it would be this: you still owe me. It's not over, none of it, until it's over, Kat. And that won't be until I say so.

Judith Davies
HM Prison East Sutton Park
September 2013

Acknowledgements

With thanks to my agent Sallyanne Sweeney and the team at Mulcahy Associates and also to the lovely people at Canelo.

I'd also like to express my gratitude to the many friends who helped inspire, cajole, critique and keep me going along the way – notably Sophie McKenzie, but also Helen Meller and Helen Jones.

Thanks, too, to the critical Zeb-Selina-Lisanne-Alexandra-Lizzy chain reaction and to my fellow Dark Angels from Moniack Mhor – an experience that lit the fuse.

Above all, however, I'd like to thank Martin and Tom, and Fulham FC (without whose distraction I'd never have found the Saturday afternoon head space to start writing, for me).